MUMS
JUST WANNA
HAVE FUN

Lucie Wheeler lives in Essex with her husband and daughter, and her English Bull Terrier, Dame, who loves to sit under Lucie's desk as she writes and keep her feet warm. Never one to sit still, Lucie always has lots going on in her life. Currently, she's writing her novels alongside studying for a degree. She is also one of The Romaniacs.

Lucie loves reading, spending time with friends and eating chocolate – when she gets to do all three, she's a very happy lady!

🐦 @lucie_wheeler
ⓕ www.facebook.com/luciewheelerpage
www.luciewheeler.co.uk

MUMS
JUST WANNA
HAVE FUN

LUCIE WHEELER

A division of HarperCollins*Publishers*
www.harpercollins.co.uk

Harper*Impulse* an imprint of
HarperCollinsPublishers
1 London Bridge Street
London SE1 9GF

www.harpercollins.co.uk

First published in Great Britain in ebook format by
Harper*Impulse* 2018

A catalogue record for this book is
available from the British Library

ISBN: 9780008216566

Set in Birka by Palimpsest Book Production Limited,
Falkirk, Stirlingshire

Printed and bound by CPI Group (UK) Ltd, Croydon, CR0 4YY

MIX
Paper from
responsible sources
FSC
www.fsc.org   FSC™ C007454

To all the mums and dads all over the world.

Whether you are a biological parent, step parent, grandparent, adoptive parent, foster parent, surrogate parent, carer, guardian ... whatever your capacity is, just remember that you are doing an incredible thing.

Keep sharing the love with children all over the world and remember that it is ok to *not* know what you are doing, because to your children, you are doing everything they will ever need just by being there and loving them.

You are not alone – remember that.

Prologue

'**A**re you for real?' Nancy exhaled hard in disbelief as she stared open-eyed at her husband.

'Don't be like that, Nance; try to see it from my point of view.'

He looked tired, unshaven and pretty much like he had given up on life. Nancy couldn't blame him; it had been a hard few years for the pair of them – for all of them actually. But she didn't have the option of giving up, and neither should he.

'Your point of view? Are you actually saying these words? Can you *hear* yourself, Pete?'

He slammed down his glass of wine and stomped into the kitchen, leaning his hands on the butler sink edge and dropping his head in shame. Nancy followed closely behind him, not trusting him to finish what he'd started. They were supposed to be having a nice romantic meal tonight. Jack was upstairs in bed (although not asleep because he didn't really *do* sleep), the dining table in the living room was set out with a bottle of red wine and candles and Pete had chosen the break between their lentil soup starter and the chicken and chorizo tray bake that was in the oven to tell her he was leaving her.

'I ... I ... I don't understand.'

He stayed facing the sink, not giving her the eye contact she so desperately wanted. 'It's too hard.'

'What is?'

'Him!' Pete shouted, as he turned round and gestured his finger to the ceiling, indicating their six-year-old son upstairs.

Nancy felt her stomach turn as she listened to Pete talk about Jack with such frustration. A mix of anger and pain churning round together. She took a deep breath. 'He's our son,' she said, the words barely coming out as a whisper.

Pete threw his hands to his head and covered his eyes, groaning in frustration. Nancy wasn't sure if it was with her, Jack or himself. Either way, she was heartbroken. 'I know! I just ... I can't keep doing this. I can't handle his funny little quirks and his demands and his ... you know ... his ... stupid little *things!*'

'Stupid?' she gasped. 'Pete, he can't help it!'

'There must be a way to make him better.'

'He's not ill!' She was starting to get annoyed now.

'Well, he's not right though, is he!' he challenged, staring her straight in the eyes for the first time since he'd announced his departure from their family.

'What is wrong with you?' She creased her face in disbelief. 'He is your son – how can you be so disrespectful to him?'

'Nance, listen to me.' He moved forward and tried to take her hands but she snatched them away. She couldn't have him touching her. She felt disgusted by the thought of his hands on her right now, and he realised this as she backed away and exhaled, dropping his hands by his side. 'I just need some space. To get my head around it all.'

Nancy shook her head and walked back into the living room, picking up the bottle of red in the middle of the table and topping up her glass. She gulped a mouthful of the red, fruity liquid. *Full Bodied*, the label said. It could have said anything, she wasn't a wine connoisseur. Pete always chose the wine when they bought it as he seemed to know what he was talking about. Before they'd had Jack, they'd gone on a wine tasting retreat in France and learned all about the different types of wine and which grapes created which flavour. Nancy had been more interested in drinking all the tasters, but Pete had taken a real interest in the history of it all and ever since had applied his newfound knowledge to the wines they purchased on a weekly basis, sneakily added into their online basket when they did their shop. Jack didn't like supermarkets – or anywhere where there were a lot of people close enough to brush past him – so they'd chosen online shopping over the last few years. She let the warm liquid slip down her throat, coating it and making her feel slightly calmer. It was never a good sign to turn to a glass of wine for comfort but right now, she didn't care. She needed something to give her time to take in what was happening.

She kept having hot flushes as surges of anxiety bolted through her body, and she pulled her long, freshly curled brunette hair up into a messy bun and secured it with a hairband. She'd spent ages earlier getting ready for their little date night. Actually styling her hair rather than leaving it in the messy mum bun that it normally resided in, choosing Pete's favourite LBD which was maybe a little too dressy for dinner at home but Nancy wanted tonight to be special – a night to remember. Well, she was going to remember it, that was for sure.

Ten minutes later, Pete walked in to join her, holding a second bottle of red. It was only then that she realised she had already finished the bottle on the table. He placed the bottle in front of her, not saying a word, and put the cork screw in, twisting it. Nancy listened to the squeak as he twisted and then pulled the cork free. She watched him smell the cork and gave way to a little smile. It was something he always did. *To see if the wine was corked*, he would tell her.

'Here,' he said, passing her a fresh glass with the new wine in. She took it from him and sipped it straight away. 'Nancy, I'm sorry,' he said softly.

She shrugged, not trusting herself to say any words that weren't *fuck you* right now. It was as though he could sense her resentment. 'Please don't hate me.'

She looked at him. His short dark hair needed a cut and there was stubble on his cheeks. She felt sorry for him. She had been so wrapped up in her own dealings with Jack and his challenges that she'd missed how badly Pete was coping. That's what tonight was about: time for the two of them, because everything over the last few months had been totally focused on Jack and fighting his corner. Getting the school to understand, filling in forms, speaking to professionals, crying because the professionals didn't say what they wanted to hear. Listening to Jack cry over seemingly trivial things, apologising on his behalf for pretty much everything, arguing with each other because they had become so frustrated. The only way to get through it was to release everything and unfortunately the ones who had to deal with the worst of those releases were normally those who were closest to you. It was all coming into perspective now. The last few months, probably even years, had been a roller-coaster of one stressful event after another and Nancy had used all her energy to make sure she kept fighting and that Jack was OK. She hadn't once stopped to think how Pete was coping.

Which was probably why he was leaving her now.

'It's not you,' he said, as if he was reading her mind. 'It's me.'

She laughed. 'That is the lamest break up line you could have used. Could you not be more original?' The laugh faded on her lips as quickly as it had arrived. She dropped her gaze again, unable to keep the eye contact. She felt betrayed, destroyed. After all these years, how could he be leaving her?

'It's true though, Nance. It really isn't you. I love you—'

'Love me?' she said, before she realised what was coming out of her mouth. 'Don't insult me by telling me you love me. Love is supporting someone when times are tough, being there for them no matter what and making sure that as long as you have each other, nothing else matters.' The emotion caught unexpectedly in her throat and she hiccupped. She swallowed it down, taking a deep breath. 'I stuck by you when you were made redundant all those years ago and spiralled into depression. You were just a shell. You didn't talk, you didn't work, you just shut off into yourself and pushed me and Jack out.' He noticeably flinched as she recalled the memory. 'But did I leave you then? No! I stuck by you and supported you. That,' she jabbed her finger towards him, 'is love. You can't love me if you're willing to walk out on us.'

'I do! Look you don't have to believe me but it's true. I just need time. I can't handle everything right now, it's just constant. There's no break.'

'And you expect me to cope with the constant by myself? You're actually going to swan off and leave me to deal with the meltdowns and the tears and the kicking and screaming by myself?' She was hoping that by highlighting all this he would realise what he was doing and come to his senses. That he would say *Shit, yeah, you're right. I can't leave you, I'm sorry, I'll stay.*

But he didn't.

'I'm sorry.'

She watched him finish his glass and then stand, pushing his chair slowly back underneath the table. 'I'll be at my mum's. I'll come and get my stuff tomorrow when Jack's at school.'

'You're not even going to speak to him? Pete, he can't just have this massive change in his life, he won't cope, you know he won't!' The panic was starting to seep in now. He was actually going.

'He'll be fine.'

'No, he won't!' she shouted, slamming her hand on the table, the tears forming rapidly in her eyes, threatening to spill over and flood her cheeks.

'Don't shout, Nance,' Pete said, his brow knitted together with concern.

'Don't go then,' she whimpered, her eyes betraying her wishes for the tears to stay put.

'I'm sorry,' he said yet again and she was sure she heard a

quiver in his voice. He had the decency to look ashamed as he picked up his phone and walked to the front door.

Nancy jumped up and followed him, reaching out for his arm and gripping it tight. 'Please, don't do this.'

He paused and turned to her, gazing into her eyes. She instantly felt the familiar warmth that was the love they had. It had been suppressed recently because of everything going on but this surge right now was enough to make her realise that she really didn't want him to go. She loved him so much. 'Please,' she squeaked.

He took her cheek in his hand and rubbed his thumb down it, wiping the moisture. 'I have to do this,' he whispered, and before she had a chance to reply, he turned and walked out the door, closing it behind him.

Nancy turned and leaned against the wooden frame, sliding down until her bottom reached the floor. It was only then that she let the tears flow without any restrictions.

He was gone – and she truly believed that he would never come back.

Chapter 1

Twelve months later...

'Grab your passport, we're going on holiday!'

Nancy watched Harriet stroll into her house, and waltz straight into the kitchen, flicking the kettle on. She closed the door, a confused frown creeping across her face, and followed her friend.

'I'm sorry, what?' she said, sitting down on the breakfast bar stool and allowing her friend free rein to make the coffee as she always did. Harriet classed Nancy's house as her own and seemed to feel completely at ease whenever she was there. They had been friends for so long, they were more like sisters.

'You and Jack, me, Isla and Tommy – we're going on holiday.' Harriet rubbed her hands together and set about searching for some more coffee as the pot was empty. Her shoulder-length light brown hair was always immaculate, styled straight with subtle blonde streaks throughout and hardly ever up in the mum bun that Nancy regularly sported.

'In the top left,' Nancy pointed, guiding Harriet to the correct cupboard. 'I'm sorry but I just don't understand. Where are we going? How long for? When?' Nancy laughed as the situation started to settle in her mind.

Harriet plonked the coffee granules jar on the side and walked over to where Nancy was sitting. Leaning on her forearms, she exhaled. 'I know this sounds a bit crazy and last minute and totally not like me...'

'You can say that again.'

'...but you need a holiday and I could do with a break and I've found this lovely hotel in Ibiza which is perfect for us and they have a kids' club and loads of restaurants and cocktail bars...' Harriet nudged Nancy at the mention of cocktails as if that would sway her, but actually, it was the mention of the kids' club that turned her stomach. Jack would never go to a kids' club, not in a million years.

'I don't know...'

'Wait, I've not even told you the best bit. You don't have to pay for a penny.' Nancy looked confused. 'It's on me. All of it. Just please say you'll come?'

'So let me get this straight.' Harriet stood back to listen to Nancy. 'You – Mrs Work-a-holic – have decided to take us all on an impromptu holiday to Ibiza. You are paying for the whole thing and all I have to do is pack our bags and leave?'

'Got it in one, babe.' Harriet winked and resumed her stance back at the worktop to make the coffees, her long legs straddling the washing basket positioned in front of the machine where it pretty much stayed constantly.

'What about work?' Nancy felt uneasy – this was totally out of character for her friend.

'They can cope without me.' Harriet brushed off the

comment but then paused and turned to look at Nancy as she placed down the coffee, raising her eyebrows. 'What?'

'*They can cope without me,*' she mimicked. 'Come on, Hari, I have known you for about twenty-two years and that crappy line is not going to cut it with me.' She raised her eyebrows and crossed her arms.

'Babe, I don't care if you believe me or not, fact is, I'm offering you a holiday – do you want it or not?'

'I don't know. It's a bit short notice and I can't just uproot Jack like that. He needs warnings and notice and...' she noticed Harriet's raised eyebrow. 'What?'

'You're making excuses.'

'I'm not! You know what Jack is like.'

'Nance, you *need* this.'

'Why? I'm fine.' Harriet made a *pfft* noise. 'What?'

'You are not fine. Don't think I don't know what today is.' Nancy didn't think she'd remember. Why would she? After all, it was Nancy's husband that had walked out on her exactly a year ago, not Harriet's. That was a whole other story.

'I *am* fine,' she insisted, blowing her coffee after she had tried sipping it and burnt her top lip. She licked away the smarting on her lip and placed the cup back down.

'Well, that may be the case, but I think you deserve a holiday after the year you've had, and Jack will be fine. We will get through this and he will have a great time. I promise.'

'You can't make that promise, Hari.'

'I can and I will.' She poked her tongue out, slid the biscuit jar across the counter and spun the lid off, fingering her way to the bottom to reach the bourbon.

'Hari, be serious for a second though. Think about it, you know Jack; he's not the easiest child to spring surprises on. I don't know how he will cope with this – it's not just a small change in routine.'

'Babe, I get that. But you need to start thinking of yourself too. You need some down time. This last year has been—' she paused, to think of the right word '—challenging for you – in more ways than one. I have spent the last twelve months watching my best friend slowly lose the plot—'

'Thanks,' Nancy laughed, although the comment did sting a bit.

'Am I wrong?'

'I thought I was doing a pretty good job of holding it together to be honest.'

'Hon, you have done a great job. Don't take it the wrong way. What I mean is that you've had a lot on your plate and it has been a bloody hard year. I just wanted to mark this one-year milestone with something positive and exciting.' She smiled. 'I want this date to have positive connotations, that's all.'

Nancy felt her chest constrict with emotion. Harriet did remember, and that small token of friendship and kindness was exactly why Nancy had been drawn to Harriet all those years ago when they'd been ten years old and Nancy had just moved to the area. Her first day at a new school had been so incredibly daunting, and then Harriet had walked up to Nancy and said: '*Come and sit next to me, I need a partner for science week and if you are mine then I won't get put with Jenny. I only have one rule; you have to work hard because I'm not sacrificing my mark again this year...*' And they had stayed best friends ever since.

Harriet's work ethic had only increased the older she'd got – thankfully Nancy didn't have to work with her on a regular basis, otherwise their friendship might have been tested.

'I won't take no for an answer,' Harriet pressed. 'If you're thinking of turning this offer down and spending the next year wallowing then I'm sorry but we can no longer be friends.' She shrugged and cupped both hands around her mug again.

Nancy laughed. One of the things that made her love Harriet was her directness. She always knew where she stood with her. 'OK, I'm not buying the stories that are coming out of your mouth but equally, I agree a holiday will be good for us all, so why not? How long have I got?'

'We leave the day after tomorrow.'

Nancy choked on her mouthful of coffee and placed the cup back down. 'Are you serious?'

'100 per cent, why hang around when there's sun, sea and cocktails to be had?'

'You realise we have children, this isn't a piss up holiday.'

'I know that – but I have chosen a hotel in a really family friendly part. And there is the kids' club so we just pop them in there and get cocktail time too! Best of both worlds.'

'Sounding like mother of the year over there, Hari.' Harriet poked out her tongue and sipped her coffee. 'But I will pay my share – you can't pay for everything.'

'Babe, with all due respect, can you afford this holiday?'

'Well, I can shift some things around and ... um...'

Harriet held up her hand and stopped Nancy. 'That wasn't

a dig, but honey, you are a single parent who works minimal hours and I know you don't have expendable money to just swan off on holiday at the drop of a hat. Which is why I've sorted it. And before you say anything, I don't want any money for it – call it an early birthday present, or maybe your Christmas present for the next ten years.' She laughed and pulled her phone out of her bag as it pinged an incoming email.

'I can pay you back in instalments. Hari, I can't just have you pay for a holiday – you're not my mum.' The feeling of her doing that didn't sit right for Nancy.

'No, but I am your friend and I can afford this. Let me do this for you.'

Nancy exhaled. 'How can you afford it though? I know you have a good job, but this isn't just a weekend in a caravan.'

'You know that contract I was working on since like forever? Well, it came through so I gave myself a little bonus. Figured I would take this moment to take a little break away because I have a new tender going through and if we get this, I am going to be flat out at work for the next eighteen months. So, it's now or never.'

Nancy couldn't argue with that. 'Fine, but I'm paying for the taxi to the airport and any drinks or food we have at the airport.'

'Deal. Mine's a prosecco and a sushi meal.'

Nancy laughed. 'I don't know how you run your own business with *two* kids. I feel like half the time I can't even get the washing and housework done on time, let alone put together contracts and marketing portfolios and all the other zillion things you do.'

'You could totally do it, stop putting yourself down.' Harriet dipped into the jar for another biscuit.

'I actually don't think I could. I don't have the business-woman persona that you have. I would crumble under the pressure.'

'Oh shush! Although I would get more done if I didn't have a child who was as stubborn as hell.'

'I wonder where she gets that from,' Nancy said under her breath with a smile.

'What's that?' Harriet questioned, clearly having heard exactly what Nancy had said.

'I said, are the kids OK?' She poked out her tongue.

'Yeah I'm sure you did. They're fine. How's Jack doing?'

Nancy's stomach dropped a little. 'He's doing alright, could be better.'

'School?'

Nancy nodded. 'He's just not fitting in. I can't help but worry that this school isn't right for him. It breaks my heart every morning when I take him in and he cries because he doesn't want to be there. I walked past at playtime the other day and he was playing by himself.'

'Did you ask him about it?'

'Yeah, he said he likes to be by himself.'

'Well there you go – as long as he's not sad about it.'

Nancy exhaled. 'That's the thing though; he doesn't really get the emotions so I'm worried that he doesn't understand *how* he's feeling.'

'But if he doesn't feel sad, and he's OK, surely that's all you want?'

Nancy nodded. 'I guess so. He's apparently not the same in the classroom though, seems to be constantly agitated and emotional, the teacher tells me. I'm going to go in again after the holidays and ask for an update meeting – they need to reassess his plan and see what needs changing. It can't stay like this.'

'Chin up, things will be OK. And now you have a holiday to look forward to.'

The doorbell rang and as Nancy stood, she said, 'I won't have the chance to look forward to it; it's the day after tomorrow!'

'Look, we have to go now because the kids only get two weeks off for Easter so we need to make the most of it.'

Nancy walked to the front door laughing. A holiday seemed like just what she needed right now. Maybe it would be the perfect antidote for her stress? At least she was eating properly again and sleeping a little better. She opened the door half expecting the postman to be there, but instead got the shock of her life.

'Hi Nance, can we talk?'

Chapter 2

Nancy stared back at Pete, frozen to the spot half in surprise and half in frustration that he had chosen this moment to turn up on her doorstep when she'd been trying to get him to come and see Jack for the past year.

'What do you want, Pete?'

'Aren't you going to invite me in?' He brushed his hand through his dark brown hair, which had grown longer over the past year than she had ever seen it, and leaned on the doorframe, seemingly trying to look more relaxed than he was feeling.

'Can't say that I particularly want to,' she said, but then caught sight of her neighbour in her front garden pretending to be doing some weeding when really she was ear wigging. 'You've got ten minutes.'

The atmosphere between the two of them was tense and things only worsened when Pete walked into the kitchen and was faced with Harriet.

'What in God's name are *you* doing here?' she scowled, putting her hands onto her hips and frowning at him.

'Nice to see you too, Harriet.' Pete forced a strained smile across his face.

'I didn't say it was nice to see you. In fact, I feel quite the opposite.'

'Hari, it's fine.' Nancy manoeuvred around her friend and placed a brief hand onto her shoulder and gave it a gentle squeeze as she grabbed her cup off the side.

'It's bloody well not fine. He thinks he can just walk out on you and Jack and disappear for months on end, ignoring your calls and then swan up on your doorstep like nothing's happened? I don't bloody think so.' She glared at him.

'Last time I checked, this wasn't your house *or* your business, Harriet!'

Harriet marched towards Pete at speed and Nancy quickly put her mug down and stepped into Harriet's path just as she reached him. 'And last time *I* checked, *Pete*,' she spat his name viciously, 'you don't just abandon your wife and your child the second shit gets hard in life.'

'OK, OK, enough you two.' Nancy placed her hand onto Harriet's shoulder. 'Let me talk to him and see what the deal is. I'll call you later and we can talk about the holiday, OK?'

'Nance, don't let him wheedle his way—'

'Hari, I'm fine ... honestly.'

Harriet glared at Pete before grabbing her bag and walking out of the kitchen towards the front door.

'And as for you,' Nancy pointed at Pete, her expression dropping into a serious tone, 'don't you dare think for one second that it is OK to walk into my house and be rude to my friends.'

'Nancy, this was *our* house.'

'Exactly, Pete, this *was* our house – and then you left.'

They both stood for a second staring at each other and then as her words sank in, Pete admitted defeat and nodded.

Ten minutes later, Nancy had made Pete a coffee and refreshed her own mug and the pair were seated at the table clasping their mugs, neither one making moves to speak. Eventually, Nancy said, 'So are you going to tell me why you've suddenly turned up here after a year of silence or am I supposed to just ignore that part?' Her anxious heartbeat had still not recovered from the moment she'd opened the door to him.

He exhaled but didn't shift his glance from the mug of brown liquid in front of him. 'It's complicated.'

'Too damn right, it's complicated, Pete, because I'm struggling to understand why you would leave us. I tried my best to make everything work, even when things got really tough with Jack but clearly it wasn't good enough – maybe I wasn't good enough.' She looked down at her hands as she spoke, saying the words that she had been thinking for months now.

This time he looked up, sadness etched on his face. 'Nancy, no! It wasn't you – you were the best wife.'

'I can't have been that good otherwise you wouldn't have left. No matter how hard life gets, when you have someone you love by your side, you get through it. But you just left. I obviously didn't do a very good job at being a supportive wife.'

This time he didn't respond, instead choosing to drop his gaze back down into the mug. Nancy didn't probe any further because she didn't want to hear that she was right – even though she knew she was. After a minute, he spoke again. It was barely audible but was still loud enough for Nancy to hear perfectly. 'It was too hard.'

'Life *is* hard.' She felt her exterior harden slightly. The '*it's hard*' line wasn't going to wash with her. She was too far into protection mode now, especially as she'd had to deal with the last year on her own.

'It's easy for you.'

'How is it easy for me? He's my son too, I feel how hard it is too, you know!'

'Yes but you know how to deal with him – with it.'

'You're talking about him like he has a disease – he's not sick, he's autistic!' Rage was beginning to boil in her chest. She was sick to death of people treating Jack like there was something wrong with him, like he didn't belong on this planet and should be hidden away.

Pete flinched noticeably when Nancy said *autistic* and this made her even angrier.

'What is it you're even here for Pete? Because it clearly isn't to apologise.'

'I *am* sorry, of course I am. Do you really think that I wanted to leave? That under normal circumstances I would have chosen to leave my wife and son?'

'So, why did you? What was so bad that you felt the only way to deal with this was to leave? That you didn't have any other option in this whole world other than to walk out and leave your son without his daddy and your wife without her husband?'

His head was facing the table in shame but his feeling sorry for himself stance only fuelled her anger. 'I had to deal with months and months of him asking me where his daddy was. Do you know what that was like? Do you even have the capacity to understand how heartbreakingly painful it was to watch him have meltdown after meltdown because Mummy couldn't tell him where Daddy was?' He was still looking at the table. 'I have had to not only be Mummy, but Daddy too. I am trying to work to support us because you weren't answering my calls. But then when Jack has a bad day at school and I have to go and pick him up, I can't work. But do I have that choice? No! And when Jack has a bad night and won't sleep – because he still doesn't sleep, you know, in case you're wondering – I still have to work having had an hour's sleep and having been punched and slapped and kicked all over because he is anxious but can't tell me why.'

Pete shook his head in despair.

'Or when I have to have a cereal bar for dinner because there's only enough pasta for Jack but a trip to the shop is out of the question because I haven't pre-warned him and the sudden change in routine would warrant another meltdown. Do you know how hard it is to be a single parent, let alone a single parent to a child who is struggling like Jack?' She waited, watching his pathetic response as he shrugged. 'DO YOU?' His head snapped up in surprise.

'Sweetheart, come on, don't shout.'

'What did you expect, Pete? That I would open the door and see your face and be happy to see you? That I would welcome you back with open arms and tell you how much I've missed you and how happy I am that you're back in our lives – not to worry about the last year? Is that what you thought would happen?' she pressed.

'Well no, but...' he trailed off, obviously seeing his error in judgement.

'Pete, you walked out on your family when times got tough. I needed you and you weren't there.' Her voice was gentler but the tone still firm.

'You don't know what it was like for me. You completely understood everything the doctor was saying and seemed to know what you were doing.'

'Are you kidding me?' she exhaled in disbelief. 'I didn't have a clue what was going on! I don't think anybody ever does when they get an autistic diagnosis. I had the same thoughts and questions going round in my mind as you did.'

'But you were nodding and smiling and sounded like you knew exactly what the doctor was saying to you – you were asking questions about what to do around the house and how we could make life easier for him and—'

'So because I opened my mouth and asked the questions that were inside my head instead of shutting off and refusing to acknowledge that our son needed help, I'm now a pro at it all?'

'Well no, but it sounded like you were fine with it.'

'We had no choice but to be fine with it – he's our son no matter what. You should've felt the same.' Her voice trailed off as unexpected emotion caught the back of her throat.

'I'm sorry,' he said, shaking his head. 'It was just too hard.'

'So, you're just giving up on him?' She asked the question but wasn't sure she was ready for the answer.

'I'm here, aren't I?'

'So this is you trying, is it?'

He nodded and then sipped his coffee.

'Well, I suppose late is better than never.' He seemed to perk up. 'But don't think you can just swan back in here like nothing happened. It took Jack a long time to change his routine; he's used to you not being here now. I'm not even sure he will be OK with seeing you.'

'What do you mean, "OK with seeing me" – I'm his dad!'

'His dad who left him!'

'Fine,' he conceded, realising he didn't have a leg to stand on.

'We'll have to come to an arrangement, sort out a plan as to how we're going to reintroduce you into his everyday life.' As much as she hated him for leaving, Nancy couldn't ignore the fact that this was potentially the moment that Jack got his dad back. No matter how much she might be angry at Pete, she wouldn't be the one to stop Jack seeing his dad.

'OK,' he grunted, acting like a teenager who had just been told they could have twenty quid if they washed the car first.

'But we can't do anything right now; we can sort it out once we get back from our holiday.'

'Holiday? Since when are you going away on holiday?'

'Since my shitty husband walked out on me, and my son and I have had to tear myself into twenty-five gazillion pieces just to make ends meet – I think we have earned a little break away in the sun, don't you?' She glared at him, daring him to argue. 'Exactly.' She stood and cleared away the mugs, taking his before he had a chance to finish the last mouthful. 'So, if you don't mind, I have some packing to do.' She indicated towards the front door with her head.

Pete stood up and marched towards the door. 'Oh, and this time,' Nancy began, and Pete turned around looking hopeful. 'When I call you – answer the bloody phone!'

She watched him exhale in frustration as he exited their family home, the home he'd decided to abandon. Pushing the door shut behind him, she returned to the kitchen and began loading the dishwasher. It felt strange seeing Pete after all that time. Her reaction had not been what she'd expected – emotionally or physically. She'd spent the last year believing that when – *if* – he walked back through that door, she would be overjoyed to see him. She would wrap her arms around him and thank him for returning to them, for making their family complete again. Instead, she felt an overwhelming feeling of anger and betrayal. Instead of begging him to come back, she had been blunt, stern and regimented in her responses to him. All the memories of the struggles over the last year had catapulted into the forefront of her mind. She wasn't falling apart emotionally without him and after seeing him today, she actually felt that little bit stronger knowing that she had coped. He hadn't been there and she had managed. A small part of her felt sad for the loss of respect for her husband, but she needed to suppress that and focus on making the right changes, for Jack. If Pete wanted to be in their lives, that was fine. But there was no way she was letting him back into her head. The consequences of letting that happen were too difficult to think about.

Chapter 3

Harriet made her way upstairs to see how far Isla had got with her packing. This really went against the grain with her as she was quite the control freak when it came to packing bags and getting organised – it was the businesswoman in her. However, when she had told Isla they were going on holiday, her little girl had insisted on packing her own bag. How hard could it be, Harriet thought to herself.

As she walked into Isla's bedroom she was faced with piles and piles of clothes strewn about the room with just a small pile on top of the suitcase she had placed on Isla's bed. Yet her daughter was nowhere to be seen.

'Isla?' Harriet called out, scanning the room in a bit of a panic.

'Yeah?' came the reply.

'Where are you?' Harriet slowly edged further into the room.

'I'm here!' Isla shouted, suddenly appearing from a pile of clothes in the corner of the room.

Harriet jumped, unable to control the small shriek that spilt out of her mouth as she threw her hand up to her chest, feeling her heartbeat race. Now that Harriet looked closer, she could see that Isla had built some sort of house with her clothes and duvet.

'What *are* you doing?'

'I built a den! Look, here's the door, here's the window and here are the flowers in the garden.' She jumped around the mound of materials as she gave Harriet the grand tour. 'Come inside!' she squeaked.

Harriet was already shaking her head. 'No, not right now. Mummy's busy. I thought you were packing?' Her phone beeped and Harriet took it out of her pocket, reading the email from work as Isla began to whine about wanting her to come inside the den. She exhaled in frustration as she read the email, asking her to a meeting in Ireland next month. Another hassle to organise childcare and have her mum tell her what a failure she was as a mother because she worked instead of staying at home with her two children. She flagged the email so that she could reply once Isla was in bed and she could concentrate better. She looked back at her five-year-old who was expectantly waiting for an answer to whatever question she had just asked her mum.

'Sorry Isla, what were you saying?'

'Urgh! Always have to say it again,' she said, each word spoken with each step she took towards the den. 'I said, can we have five minutes in the den and then you can work?'

Harriet looked at her watch. She should really be getting the packing finished so that she could reply to her emails tonight before they set off tomorrow first thing. And as much as she wanted to spend time with Isla, these things were not going to get done by themselves. The joys of single parenting. She began to say no but then thought against it. All the parenting books and sites talked about making time for your children even if you were busy – although how practical these things were, Harriet didn't know. She nodded and walked towards the den just as her phone began to ring. Isla groaned and threw her hands up into the air as Harriet took the phone back out of her pocket.

'Hello, is that Mrs Fisher, Tommy's mum?'

'Oh no!' Harriet replied and instantly felt her heart sink. 'I'm so sorry, I'm on my way.'

'Thank you,' the nursery assistant replied abruptly and ended the call.

'Isla, we need to go and pick up your brother.'

Isla found this incredibly unfair and sat on the bed, crossing her arms and huffing.

'What are you doing? Come on!' Harriet turned to walk out of the bedroom, so angry at herself for forgetting to pick up Tommy again. She always had so much to do that she seemed to run out of time before she realised. She looked over her shoulder as she reached the top of the stairs only to see Isla sitting back on her floor, getting a puzzle out of its box. She turned on her feet and stormed back into the room. 'Isla! It's time to go, come on.'

'No! I don't want to – Tommy is stinky and he always cries.'

'Oh for goodness' sake, stop being silly and come on.' She put her hands on her hips to show she meant business but Isla was very much her mini me and had every ounce of Harriet's stubbornness. She stayed sitting on the carpet, staring back defiantly.

'Isla...' Harriet warned and did her best mum look.

'I don't want to though,' Isla groaned, standing up slowly.

'It won't take long.' She turned and walked back to the stairs and again, looked over her shoulder. Isla had stood up but was now just standing still in the middle of her room staring at Harriet. 'What now?' she said impatiently, feeling sorry for Tommy sitting and waiting at nursery for her.

'Can I have a biscuit?'

That girl knew her far too well. 'Fine! Get a biscuit on the way out – now come on, let's go!' Harriet rushed down the stairs and could hear Isla skipping behind her saying, *biscuit biscuit biscuit...*

As a single parent Harriet knew to pick her battles – and this wasn't one of them.

Chapter 4

'OK spill, what did he say?' Harriet placed the coffees onto the table in front of Nancy and sat down opposite her, expectantly. Nancy shuffled in her seat, very aware that Jack didn't look too comfortable at the airport. She had sent Harriet a text yesterday and said she would explain all about Pete's visit today; she knew Harriet wouldn't just be content with a condensed version.

'He apologised and said that he wants to be a part of Jack's life.'

Harriet guffawed and sipped her coffee. 'You aren't seriously falling for that tosh, are you?'

Nancy laughed. 'Tosh? Did you actually say tosh? Who says that?'

'Oh, be quiet, just tell me that you're not falling for it?'

Nancy shrugged and sipped her coffee.

'Nance!' Harriet picked up her napkin and threw it at her. 'Come on girl, sort it out.'

'Hari, it's not that simple. He's Jack's dad – I can hardly tell him to piss off, can I? What about Jack?' She looked over to her blonde-haired boy and felt the weight of anxiety drop

29

into the pit of her stomach. 'It's not his fault his dad is an idiot but if Pete is going to try and make things right, surely Jack deserves to have his dad around?'

'Babe I get that, honestly I do, but he's hardly shown the best intentions over the last year, has he? It wasn't like he was dad of the year even before he walked out.'

Nancy stayed quiet, not wanting to delve into the mess that was her marriage. But it seemed Harriet had other ideas.

'What about the time that he left you waiting at that restaurant because he decided to go to the game with his mates and not tell you? Or the time he cancelled your weekend away because tickets came up for the F1? Or the time you slaved over a romantic dinner for him on your anniversary and he rolled in from the pub at 11 p.m. with a kebab?'

'Alright, Hari, jeez!' Nancy sipped her coffee again. 'What is this, *let's highlight how shit Pete has been as a husband over the last few years*? Don't you think I know all this?' It was a sore subject and Harriet knew that. But she was also the kind of friend who was completely honest with Nancy. However, hearing her list these things raised the question in Nancy's mind of whether had been going wrong in her marriage even before Jack's diagnosis.

'Look, I'm sorry; I didn't mean to bring the mood down. I just don't want to see you and Jack get messed around and quite frankly, you have been so much happier over the last few months since things started getting back on track, I don't want you to spiral back down into the person you were when he was making your life a misery.'

'My life wasn't a misery,' Nancy replied defensively, but then took in the no-bullshit look on Harriet's face. 'OK, well I was unhappy towards the end but my whole life wasn't a misery.'

'Mummy? Can I get a magazine?' Isla was pulling on Harriet's cardigan.

'In a minute darling, let Mummy just finish her coffee.'

'And a chocolate bar?'

'In a minute.'

'And a teddy bear?'

Nancy laughed. 'You can tell Isla's in holiday mode already.' She turned to Jack. 'Would you like a magazine, Jack?'

He shook his head but didn't look up from the iPad.

'How about a chocolate treat?'

'It's not after dinner time,' he mumbled, still not looking up.

'That's OK, we're going on holiday mate; you can have a treat.' Harriet stood up and fished for her purse in her bag. Jack didn't answer.

'Jack?' Nancy pressed but he just frantically shook his head. 'OK, it's fine. You don't have to.' Nancy looked to Harriet and shook her head.

'Shall I get him something else?'

'No, its fine. He's brought stuff with him; he probably just doesn't want any change in what he prepared for. But thanks.'

Harriet smiled and walked off over to the shop to purchase the products for Isla who was skipping along behind her excitedly. Tommy was still asleep in his pram, so Nancy focused her attention back onto her son who was still glued to his iPad.

'Are you excited about the holiday, Jack?'

He shrugged.

'There'll be a pool.'

'I don't like water.'

'I know you don't sweetheart, but it doesn't have to go over your head, you can just paddle in it or do some swimming.'

'I don't want to.'

'OK that's fine; you don't have to go in if you don't want to. There's a beach there too – we can build some sandcastles and you can go in the sea.'

'I don't like sea.'

Nancy started to wonder whether she had made the right choice in agreeing to this holiday. Jack hadn't jumped up and down and squealed excitedly when she'd told him like most seven-year-olds would at the prospect of a week away in the sun. Instead, he had asked her a million questions and not slept much all night because of the anticipation of today. She'd spent two hours just going through all the different scenarios she could think of and how she would overcome them should she need to. Jack was obviously feeling anxious today because he was more quiet than usual and had closed off with his iPad and headphones all morning. He didn't want any photos taken – she couldn't feed her Instagram habit today – and he wasn't interested in engaging in any conversations with anyone.

Nancy exhaled and picked up her coffee. It was going to be a long week.

Chapter 5

'Oh my God, will you just look at this place!' Harriet strolled into the foyer and stopped still in the centre of the room, glancing around 360 degrees. 'It looks so much better than in the pictures, Nance!' She looked at her friend who was standing open-mouthed, looking around like a kid who had just walked into Willy Wonka's Chocolate Factory for the first time. The gentle cream softness of the décor made the room instantly inviting. A warm glow from the designer lightshades that hung above them lit the room just enough to feel cosy but was totally unnecessary as it was still daytime and the blistering heat was beaming beautifully outside. The foyer was spacious with huge marble pillars dotted around creating a sense of grandeur. As Harriet approached the reception desk she was greeted with cheery smiles and gentle voices.

'Good afternoon, how may I help you?'

'I have a booking under Harriet Fisher.' She glanced over her shoulder to see Nancy still looking around in awe and the children looking bored and grumpy. Tommy was strapped into his chair and was moaning about the fact that he couldn't get out, bucking his body as though he was in a bucking bronco tournament. Isla was wandering around one of the marble pillars, one hand placed onto the cold surface singing a song to herself and going round and round and round ... and Jack was sitting cross-legged on the floor, his head stuck in his iPad still.

'Yes, here we go. You have adjoining rooms 235 and 236, with 236 occupying a balcony. Here are your key cards and the lifts are to your right. Just sign here please.' Harriet did as she was asked. 'Is there anything I can get for you?'

Harriet took the envelopes and shook her head. 'No thanks, I think we're all good.' She practically skipped back to Nancy and the children.

'Harriet this place is incredible – when you said you were taking us on holiday, I didn't envisage such a ... well, such indulgence!'

'Only the best for my girl.' Harriet winked and blew a kiss and then picked up her bags. 'Come on, let's get unpacked so we can eat, I'm starving!'

***

As Nancy walked into her adjoining room leaving the others still exploring Harriet's room, she couldn't help but feel the emotion catch in her throat a little. This place was truly magical and definitely something that she needed in her life right now after the horrendous year she had had. But equally, she felt sad because being here as a single parent just reminded her where she was currently at in her life right now. After years of building up her family unit, it had all been taken away from her – against her will – and now she felt more confused than ever. This holiday was definitely going to be the break she needed to refocus and decide what she was going to do. Hopefully, being away from Pete and home would help to put everything into perspective.

Nancy walked over to the balcony and slid the door open, stepping out onto the concrete and taking in the view around her. It was truly stunning. The pool below them was heaving with families; children laughing and screaming as they played their imaginary games and splashed around in the pool – which was in the shape of a dolphin. There was the faint tune of local music playing within the complex and if you looked beyond the horizon, you could see the picturesque view of the sea, deep blue and glistening.

Before she came out here she kept telling herself that she needed to do it, needed to listen to her body – and her friend – and take some time out. But she just couldn't shake off the anxiety of bringing Jack here. She and Pete hadn't taken Jack away very much because of an early bad experience when Jack was a toddler. He was struggling with what they now knew was a fear of his ears being touched, and he'd had a huge meltdown which resulted in Nancy and Pete having a blazing row. The rest of the holiday was tainted with the harsh comments both of them had made in the heat of the moment. Since then, they had shied away from holidaying anywhere where there were people or potential triggers. This had been a cause of pressure in their marriage because it had been Nancy's choice to reduce the holidaying and subsequently, they spent their down time locked away in barns and cabins in the middle of nowhere. Pete missed the holidays they took before Jack was born and Nancy resented the fact that Pete didn't understand that she was the one who always had to deescalate the meltdowns when Jack had them, so *normal* holidays were just a stress for her.

But being here was the right thing to do – she knew that. She just needed to ignore the impending feeling of dread that constantly sat somewhere between her stomach and her chest. Jack would be fine. She let a small smile play over her lips as she watched the children below bouncing around in the water and jumping on each other's backs for piggyback races. But the smile wasn't because she was happy; it dressed her face and pretended that she was fine but inside all she felt was deflation. Because she knew that Jack wouldn't be laughing and joking with friends like these children were. He wouldn't be playing race games and splashing other children as he dunked his head under the water. And as much as she hated herself for feeling disappointed about this, she couldn't lie to herself. Other people, sure. But not to herself.

A holiday in the sun where she could try to hide from all the feelings of guilt and anxiety? Yes, this was exactly what Nancy needed right now.

Chapter 6

Nancy glanced around the restaurant as she waited for Harriet to return to the table. The one they had chosen to eat in tonight was the least plush of the three available options. The children had had a long day travelling and Nancy was tired too, so choosing the least fancy one suited her just fine. If Jack was to have an episode – which was always a possibility as they were in a new place – then she would feel more comfortable here, with fewer people to look down their noses at her. She wasn't the type of person to judge others, especially when she knew how horrible it was when people judged her parenting and her son. But she had found that in places where a particular etiquette was expected – like high-brow restaurants – the consequences of a meltdown were not appreciated in the slightest. Children were expected to behave in a certain way and whilst that was understandable, it wasn't always practical. She had been made to feel an outsider last year when out with Hari and the children at a posh restaurant in town. Hari had been given the table reservation as part of a contract and had chosen to take Nancy and Jack along with her as a treat. A waitress had dropped a tray of food, the noise was too loud for Jack and he became anxious and jittery. The waitress then came over to apologise and ruffled Jack's hair but this was enough to tip him over the edge and it all fell apart from there. The looks on the faces of the other diners and the staff had been branded onto Nancy's brain and regularly fuelled mild panic attacks. When she thought about that evening, she could still hear the voices saying things like '*she should learn to control her child*' and '*what's wrong with him*'.

Nowadays she much preferred restaurants with a more relaxed atmosphere towards children.

The tables were set up like picnic benches, but they were pimped up with padding on the seats and the tables were dressed as though they were eating at Buckingham palace; material napkins, beautiful cutlery and the most amazing flower arrangements encased within an ivory birdcage.

'Do you think every part of this resort is like this or will I be able to pick up a burger and chips from somewhere?' Nancy asked, perusing the menu.

'Just embrace the luxury, Nance,' Harriet replied.

'It's alright for you; you're used to eating in places like this with work. You travel here, there, and everywhere, and have your meetings in posh restaurants all the time. I get by on toast, sandwiches and Jack's leftovers.' Her heart sank a little as the reality of how dismal her life had become since Pete had left hit her a little more. She was starting to wonder whether she would ever get the hang of this single parenting malarkey.

'Have things really been that tight since Dickhead went?'

Nancy shrugged, realising her faux pas of bringing up the

money subject. She never brought up money with anyone, all it did was either make people feel uncomfortable or pity her – neither of which she wanted from her best friend. Harriet knew things were tough, but Nancy had never really spoken about just how hard it was getting through each day financially. Their focus tended to be more the emotional effects of Pete leaving.

'You know I'm always here to help. I can lend you some money if you need some?'

'Don't be silly, I'm fine. Things are fine. I'm not struggling.' She was, but now she felt awkward.

'Honestly babe, I can give you some money if it'll help lighten the stress of things and—'

'Hari, honestly, I'm fine.' She cut her short. This wasn't the conversation she wanted to have. Not with Harriet, not with anyone. She wasn't about to start taking charity. She wasn't there – yet. Harriet obviously heard the tone of Nancy's voice and didn't push anymore, instead turning her attention to helping Isla find something on the menu.

Nancy glanced back at her menu and then over to Jack who had his earphones on and his eyes glued to his iPad. She placed her hand onto his forearm and waited for him to remove the headphones – a sequence they had devised that told Jack that she wanted his attention, so he had time to adjust. She'd learnt the hard way that if she removed his headphones without warning him first, it would trigger a disaster because he didn't like anyone touching his ears.

When he had taken them off and placed them on the table, he looked at her with his big blue eyes and instantly Nancy found herself smiling. No matter how tough she was finding things at home, one look at Jack with his cute little inquisitive face and all her worries melted away. Although lately, she did sometimes get a twinge of sadness because the older he got, the more he took on Pete's facial features. They both had this little crease at the top of their nose that appeared whenever they scrunched up their face or yawned. And they both had big, beautiful eyes that you could lose yourself in. It was a feature Nancy had fallen for when she'd first met Pete.

'What would you like to eat, sweetheart? You can have chips, spaghetti bolognese or chicken?' She tried to tempt him with meals she thought he would eat but she knew before he had spoken what his answer would be.

'Pasta.'

She smiled. 'Why don't you try something new?' Again, she knew the response.

'Pasta,' he said, his chin beginning to wobble. Now wasn't the time or place to try to get him to branch out. He had eaten strawberry yoghurt and grapes for breakfast, peanut butter sandwiches (cut into triangles NOT squares) for lunch, and pasta with grated cheese on top for dinner every single day for the last ten months. He wasn't about to change that here.

It frustrated her though, if she was honest. To others it might seem trivial and not something worth getting worked up over, but it was the fact that Nancy didn't have the answers. She didn't know why he had suddenly limited his eating habits or what triggered this. He ate normally when Pete first left but after a couple of months it was like he just decided that this was all he was going to eat. And when Jack had something in his head, that was it. This was something that Nancy had been researching lately though and she was determined to widen his food choices. And actually, this holiday might be the perfect time to try out some of the techniques she had found. It could be her little holiday mission – aside from getting Jack through the holiday itself. She thought for a minute – maybe right now wasn't the best time to push this seeing as they had not long been here so Jack was bound to be feeling anxious about his new surroundings.

'OK sweetheart,' she said and he smiled at her, replacing his headphones. Nancy didn't push for more; she would let him settle in first, then she would tackle the issue of food.

***

Later that evening, Harriet looked at her children sleeping, the moonlight from the window gently falling onto their faces making them look like sleeping angels. She glanced at the clock: 02.53. Exhaling she opened her laptop and checked her emails.

Hello, Harriet@creativeimpressions.com, you have 87 new emails

She felt a lead weight drop into her stomach. She couldn't even be away from work for a day without falling behind. She opened the first email.

Harriet, sorry to bother you on holiday but Colemans are saying that we haven't provided the correct information regarding the Beech Project. I've forwarded you their email – what do you want me to do??

She groaned and began typing. As much as she knew she and her family needed this holiday, her workload was still heavy, and this week would be a juggling act. And she knew Nancy needed this break more. She had watched her friend deteriorate over the last year as she'd struggled to look after Jack single-handedly and Harriet knew that Nancy desperately needed to take some time out. Unfortunately, Harriet's staff didn't understand her decision to be a good friend and leave the business just before a big contract came in, and because of the way Harriet managed her company, they seemed to lack drive and competence when she wasn't there. This wasn't something Harriet wanted to admit to anyone, but she was finding it hard to delegate jobs, instead choosing to take charge of everything which resulted in very little time to do anything un-work related like spending time with her friends and family. This bothered Harriet hugely, yet she wasn't in any position to implement changes to stop this from happening. Hopefully this was about to change though. Whilst this holiday was presented as a getaway for her friend, she secretly hoped that some downtime without the pressures of her everyday routine would mean that she would be able to consider her options and find a way forward. Everyone who knew her – or thought they knew her – would say that Harriet was the type of person who thrived on being busy. Someone who loved a challenge and hated the mundane tasks of everyday parenting. Whilst that had an element of truthfulness in it, the part of her that nobody really knew much about was the part that was screaming out for help. But she was too frightened to acknowledge it and she spent all day, every day, squashing it deep down so that she didn't have to accept the fact that her family life was a mess. Her children spent more time being pulled from pillar to post and having Harriet shout and stress at them than actually enjoying the company of their mum.

When Harriet was forced to become a single parent and watch her husband walk out on them, she decided that she could go one of two ways – she could wallow, feel sorry for herself and fall into a cycle of depression and self-destruction, *or*, she could pick herself up and do what needed to be done to make ends meet. Which, being the type of person she was, was what she'd done. However, along the way Harriet seemed to have lost her focus and instead of plunging into the *Supermum* role she'd envisaged, she'd become a crazed work-a-holic who hardly spent any time with her children and found herself snowed under at work with no one to turn to.

This holiday would be a real test for her. She wanted to use the time away from work to refocus and find answers. Unfortunately, work didn't seem to have got that memo! Harriet didn't need sleep anyway – it was totally overrated.

Chapter 7

'Mummy ... Mummy ... Mummy ... Mummy...?'
Harriet groaned as she turned to face Isla who was tapping her on the arm for the millionth time. 'Yes darling?'

'Can we go for some breakfast, I'm hungry? And Tommy's done a poo – he stinks!'

Harriet looked at the clock: 05:55.

'Isla, it's too early for breakfast – they don't start serving until 7 a.m.' Isla moaned. 'I'm sorry, sweetheart.'

'But I'm starving! I haven't had anything to eat for ageeees!'

'Slight exaggeration Isla, you had dinner and pudding last night.' Harriet tried to keep her eyes open against the brightness of the sunshine streaming through their window.

'But that was forever ago. I'm hungry.' Isla dropped her bottom lip into a sulk.

'Darling, Mummy can't magic food out of nowhere, you'll just have to wait.'

'But I'm starving!'

'You are *not* starving, Isla, you ate last night. All those poor children in the world who are starving and you're moaning because you haven't eaten for a few hours – be realistic!' Isla recoiled at Harriet's raised voice and she instantly felt guilty for her reaction. The children didn't realise she had only been asleep a couple of hours, and why should they? It was times like this that Harriet wanted to grab and shake herself and scream *what are you doing?* She hated the person she was becoming. She was so proud of her career and she knew just how much she had achieved but it had come at a price. She just couldn't understand how people managed family and work side by side successfully, and yet there were millions of people out there doing it. Why couldn't she? She could see everything that was wrong with what she was doing but she just didn't have a clue how to fix it. And it needed fixing. Isla's little face, awash with shock at her mother's outburst was enough to pick apart more of the thread of parenting self-doubt that was slowly but surely unravelling. It shouldn't be this hard to be a mum. It was supposed to come naturally. *'You'll just know what to do when you're a mum,'* people would say to her. *'It's one of the most natural things in the world.'*

Yeah right, she thought. Maybe she was broken then, because it sure as hell wasn't coming naturally to her. She looked at Isla's little face and was brought back to the moment with a guilty bang. 'Sorry darling – Mummy's just tired.'

Isla sloped off the bed and climbed back onto hers, taking her colouring book out of the bag and beginning to colour, clearly in a mood with Harriet.

It was now that Harriet realised that Isla wasn't joking about Tommy – she could smell him from where she lay on the other side of the bedroom. She rolled out of bed and walked over to the cot where he was still sleeping. She was tempted to leave him until he woke up, so she could grab a few more minutes sleep but the smell was so pungent she couldn't ignore it. She gently placed her hand onto his tummy and rubbed. 'Morning little man.' She picked him up – trying not to gag – and instantly took him to the bed to change him.

She needed more coffee for this.

Minutes later a gentle tap sounded on the interior adjoining door of her room and Nancy's head poked round. 'I heard voices – figured you must be part of the Early Morning Club too?' She smiled sympathetically.

'You can only come in if you have coffee.' Harriet pointed to her sideboard where once stood several sachets of coffee but now stood an empty pot.

Nancy walked in. 'Jeez, you drunk all your coffee on the first day?'

Harriet shook her head. 'No, I drank some of my coffee and Tommy decided to put the rest down the toilet.' Harriet could see the laugh growing on Nancy's lips. 'I swear, if you laugh, I may have to kill you.'

'I'll make you some from my room – give me a minute.'

True to her word, a moment later Nancy returned with two mugs of coffee and Jack following closely behind, his head-phones on and iPad in hand.

'Oh, you are a lifesaver.' Harriet sipped the steaming drink and instantly relaxed a little. It wasn't up to the standard of her coffee machine at work, which she was practically attached to intravenously, but it was caffeine and it would have to do.

'So, what's the reason for the early get up? Although by the smell of your room I think I might be able to guess.' Nancy wrinkled her nose and opened the window.

'Yeah, Tommy woke Isla up with the smell and so she woke me up.'

'Morning Isla,' Nancy said, glancing over to Harriet's eldest who was still sulking on the bed. 'What's up?' Nancy asked, nodding her head over to her.

'She's hungry and wants breakfast but they don't start serving until 7.'

'I've got some cereal bars, yoghurt and fruit in my room if she wants some?'

Harriet looked at her friend, confused. 'Why have you got cereal bars, yogurt and fruit?'

'Because I know Jack gets hungry first thing and I have to make sure I have stuff as a backup if there are places where they don't do food that he likes.'

Harriet felt a mix of elation – that she could offer Isla some food now – and sadness – because this only highlighted how bad at parenting she was. Why didn't she think of packing stuff like that? 'Isla, Nancy has some cereal bars in her room if you want one?'

Isla immediately jumped up. 'Yes, yes, yes! I'll get it – where are they?' But she had already disappeared into the next room before hearing a reply.

'I'll go,' Nancy laughed, following.

When she returned, Harriet asked, 'does it come naturally to you?'

Nancy frowned, confused. 'Eh?'

'Being a mum – do you just know what to do?'

Nancy laughed. 'Yeah I'm a total pro – the ideas just come to me in a flash of inspiration and I feel well-equipped for every situation life can throw at me.' She stopped giggling when she saw Harriet wasn't laughing. 'What's up?'

Harriet felt vulnerable. She didn't normally like to talk about feelings; she was methodical, regimented, she got jobs done. She didn't have time to sit and ponder on things. But recently, since Isla was getting older and more demanding, she was starting to question her role in things a lot more. 'I just don't get how you can just know all this stuff. Where does it come from?'

'What stuff?'

She pointed to Nancy's room. 'The breakfast stuff.'

Nancy tilted her head like a confused dog. 'Hari, you're not making any sense.'

She exhaled. 'You brought breakfast stuff, for Jack, in case he needed it.' Nancy nodded. 'How did you know to do that?' Harriet laughed as she heard herself. 'OK, that sounds really weird. I know what I want to say but I just can't get the right words.' She groaned, putting her head into her hands.

Nancy moved towards Harriet and placed a hand on her shoulder. 'Are you OK?'

She flung her hands back down into her lap and looked at her best friend. 'I just don't understand how something as little as thinking ahead about breakfast when you have little ones comes so easily to some people, yet I don't ever seem to think about it. I can chair a corporate meeting, I can collate all the necessary information relating to a project and I can analyse and interpret various work-related deals. Why can't I think of something as simple as packing snacks for my children?'

Nancy laughed. 'Come on, you're being too hard on yourself. Look, I think about stuff like that because I have to. Jack is different from your children; if I don't plan and think ahead, it could mean the difference between him feeling comfortable and him having a meltdown. I don't have a choice. It didn't come naturally to me; I had to learn the hard way. Your children are not the same. If you told Isla to wait an hour for breakfast, yes, she would kick up a fuss and she might feel like it was the end of the world, but ultimately, she would cope. Jack wouldn't.' She squeezed Harriet's hand. 'That's the difference.'

'I guess.'

'Hari, I don't get it right all the time – you know that!'

'I just don't get the whole "it comes naturally" thing people say with parenting.'

'That's because it doesn't come naturally to everyone. I love being a parent, but parenting an autistic child is a completely different story and I certainly do not feel like that comes naturally to me. Everyone is different. It's really shit but we have to learn things the hard way, by experiencing the ups and the downs and working out what went wrong so that it doesn't happen again. And that's why I know to have breakfast stuff – it isn't because I'm Supermum.'

Harriet smiled at Nancy, thankful to have such an understanding friend to travel this rollercoaster of feelings with. 'I just need to balance my life better, I think.'

'What do you mean?'

'Just, you know, work and stuff.'

'I agree, you work far too much.'

Harriet made a noise which was half an exhale and half a laugh. 'It's not as simple as that Nance, I have to work.'

'Yeah I know that, but do you really have to work as much as you do? You have a team of people around you – use them!'

Harriet nodded. There was no point in having this conversation. As much as she loved Nancy, she just didn't understand what she went through with work. She didn't have the same stresses as Harriet. If Harriet didn't work and make it a success, she would lose her business. And not just that, she would lose her house, her only source of income and her dignity. Regardless of how much she wanted to spend more time with the children, the fact of the matter was, work had to take priority. She had no choice. And until she found a solution that would allow her to embrace both aspects of her life, she would have to continue juggling.

She looked over to Jack who was now seated on the chair by the window, glued to his iPad. She then looked over to Tommy who was playing in his cot with some toys. Finally, she looked over to her laptop which was still open but had gone to sleep. She could almost feel the emails dropping into her inbox.

It would be another late one tonight – she needed more coffee for this.

Chapter 8

'Shall we go exploring today – see what the resort has to offer and find out where the best cocktails are?' Harriet winked at Nancy.

'Sounds like a plan.' Nancy cleared her plate of the omelette she had chosen for breakfast from the buffet – trying to forget about the cereal and croissants she'd had before that. This was a stark contrast to how things were at home, where Nancy ate mostly leftovers. She was really thankful to Harriet for giving her this chance to re-evaluate things.

'I found out where the kids' club is, and they open in an hour so shall we drop the kids there and then set off? Apparently, they're doing party games, painting and a mini disco today. Sounds great fun, hey Isla?'

Isla nodded excitedly. 'I'm going to wear my pink dress today so I'm ready for the party and I'm going to paint Nanny a picture of a goat.'

Nancy looked at Harriet questioningly. Harriet shook her head. 'I have no idea.'

'Sounds great. Are you putting Tommy in too?'

'Yeah, they do a babies' club as well and take them from

a year old – bonus.' Harriet paused. 'Are you putting Jack in?'

Nancy pulled a face and looked over to her son. 'I don't know that he'll go to be honest.' She didn't want to come across as negative, but she was already pre-empting how Jack might be feeling. Part of her was willing him to give it a try, to see what would happen, but the more dominant part of her was realistic and felt concerned about letting him go in the first place.

'Do you want to try?'

'I guess so – it's worth a try, isn't it?' It was more of a question. She didn't feel comfortable about it at all and she could already predict how it was going to go. It wasn't like she had spent all her parenting years never challenging Jack. She did get him to try new things, quite regularly. It didn't have a very high success rate though and this was causing her uneasiness now. She knew he would feel worried and anxious. She knew he wouldn't like the new surroundings and if it was noisy inside then she knew he wouldn't cope well. Nevertheless, she was reluctant to be seen to not be trying in front of her friend. Harriet was a strong- willed person and a lot of the time being around her brought out a more confident and risk-taking side to Nancy. Sometimes this paid off and Nancy achieved things she wouldn't normally – like when Jack didn't like brushing his teeth and it was Nancy's confidence and Harriet's idea of finding a teeth-brushing song that ultimately ended with him now loving to do it. Sometimes being brave paid off. Sometimes it came back and punched her in the face. She thought for a minute and finally said, 'It's a new place and he's never been before so I don't fancy the odds, but maybe I'll give him the option and see if he surprises me.'

'That's the spirit.'

An hour later they were all lined up at the hotel kids' club reception, ready to sign the children in, and Nancy was feeling more anxious than she had done since they'd got on the plane to come here. It wasn't just that Jack didn't like things like this, but over the last year everything had been that little bit more difficult and his behaviour had become more unpredictable. She felt like everything she knew about her son had been turned on its head. She wasn't sure if it was because she was more anxious about it all being on her own or whether Jack was reacting to the changes happening at home, but either way, she was on edge constantly, swimming against the tide.

'Good morning!' said a cheery voice from the desk. 'And who do we have here?' she looked at Isla who was performing her best ballet routine for the lady.

'My name is Isla and I do ballet!'

'I can see that, it's beautiful. And will you be joining us today?'

'Yep! I'm going to draw a goat!'

The woman at the desk smiled and looked to Harriet.

'I don't know the relevance of the goat.'

The lady laughed. 'That's fine, we can draw some goats and maybe some other animals too. Can you fill in this form for Isla? And will little man be joining our baby club?'

Harriet nodded. 'Yes please, he's just had his breakfast so will probably go for a nap soon.'

'No problem, when you go into the baby room just tell the ladies in there, so they know.' The woman's attention now moved to Nancy and she instantly felt her panic levels rise. 'And will this handsome young man be joining the party too?'

Nancy looked at Jack who was still kitted out in his head-phones, but he was now noticeably hiding behind her legs pretending to be looking at his iPad. 'He's a little unsure,' she said, placing her arm around him which he promptly shrugged off – he didn't like to be touched.

'That's OK, some children are a little nervous. Why don't you take him in with your friend and her little ones and he can have a look around and if he wants to stay, you can just come back and grab a form – how does that sound?' The woman's smile was so comforting, Nancy instantly relaxed a little. Childcare professionals seemed to have this natural talent of being a walking smile on legs.

'Thank you,' Nancy said and followed Harriet into the club entrance. She chose to ignore the voice in her head that was screaming at her to prepare for disappointment. Maybe today would be different...

Chapter 9

Nancy followed the others into the club, taking in the colourful surroundings as she did. It was very bright and busy, and she didn't have to look at Jack to know that his little heart would be racing. Toys were strewn about all over the floor and the volume levels were loud. Nancy had no idea how these women worked in it every day. She could almost feel the clock ticking, waiting for a reaction from Jack. She had that awful sick feeling in her stomach, the feeling when you just know something is coming and the anticipation of waiting for it makes you feel queasy. She had the urge to turn around and march out of there with Jack, but her head was screaming at her to just *try*. How was Jack ever going to move forward if she kept stifling him and wrapping him in cotton wool? How was he ever going to learn to cope if she always managed situations for him? She needed to let him at least try these things, but she really struggled with the knowledge that she felt like she knew it would end badly anyway. She didn't know what the answer was, what the right thing to do was. She tried to not let the angst show on her face and turned to Jack, plastering on a smile.

'Isn't this lovely, look at all the toys to play with!' His little face looked terrified and pale, and she could see the little white marks on his knuckles as he clutched the iPad to his chest, headphones still on but she knew there was no sound – it was just the comfort of the pressure on his ears.

Harriet came over to where Nancy and Jack were standing, a huge smile spread across her face as she adjusted her sunglasses on her head. 'Right, Tommy's in the baby room and Isla has run off already to draw her goat – you ready?'

Nancy looked back to Jack and then to her friend. 'I'm not sure Jack is going to stay.' She couldn't shake off the unease but equally, Harriet was the one paying for her holiday and she felt pressured to make sure Harriet had a good time – and her ideal day didn't involve having Jack tag along with them.

'What?' Harriet knelt down to Jack's level. 'What's up, little man? Don't you want to play with all these amazing toys?'

Jack shook his head.

'You'll make some friends and have such a good time.'

Nancy knew how wrong this statement was. The reality was, Jack wouldn't be playing with these children. He would, most probably, be sitting with his iPad, stressed, counting the minutes until Nancy returned. He would hate the other children screaming and shouting, he would feel out of place and he would struggle with communicating with the staff, too. The more she thought about it, the more ludicrous this seemed, and Nancy was surprised that she had even enter-tained the idea of kids' club for Jack. Jack was different, she knew that, and it was times like this that she found herself overwhelmed with feelings of helplessness and sadness. As his mother, she so desperately wanted to make it all better and take away the sad feelings for him, but she couldn't. As a parent, that felt devastating. If she truly thought about it, she knew deep down that Jack wouldn't cope here. Now she just needed to work out a way of telling Hari without letting her down.

'You can do some painting or play some games and Mummy and I will be back in a few hours.'

Jack noticeably tensed up and grabbed onto Nancy's skirt, gripping it hard enough that his knuckles returned to their white colour. Nancy crouched down as Harriet stood.

'Do you not want to try, sweetheart?' The words had no conviction; she had already known they were leaving. She said the words to show Hari she was trying, to lessen the blow of potentially ruining her idea of a perfect afternoon without the children.

'It's too noisy – I don't like it.'

He looked like he was going to cry and Nancy's heart broke. Whilst she was getting used to the fact that he now had an autism diagnosis, sometimes it was still really hard to accept that he was different to other children. Harriet's children had strolled straight in without a care in the world – she had it so easy. Nancy had to second guess *everything*. She could never just leave anything to chance, she always needed a plan B (and often a plan C and D too). When Jack was born she'd prided herself on taking to motherhood really well but then as the years went on, her parenting technique suffered, and she went into survival mode. Some weeks were better than others and now that Jack was seven, there were certain elements that they had under control and Nancy was proud of herself for getting to that stage with these parts of his personality – but they still had a long way to go. Pete leaving was the spanner in the works that she just didn't need. She was determined to show him that she was doing fine without him, but it was hard, and she struggled, a lot. Every day was a new learning curve for her and Jack and she quite often went from feeling like an amazing mother who managed to gain little victories with Jack, to feeling inadequate, unprepared and a failure.

She stood up. 'Looks like we have company today then.' She didn't miss the flicker of disappointment on her friend's face and it was like a punch to the stomach. What was she supposed to do? Jack was always going to come first in anything Nancy did but she really resented this when it affected those around her. And this happened more often than people thought. She had lost friends in the past because she wasn't able to stick to play dates or when she did go, it ended in disaster. It started by those around her giving her space when Jack was uneasy and ended with her just not being invited out at all anymore. She still occasionally spoke to these mums, but they weren't her friends and they never included her in their get-togethers. Now here she was again, potentially messing up another friendship. She had known Harriet so long, she didn't think she was so fickle as to let this affect their friendship, but the disappointed flicker in her friend's eyes was enough to make Nancy feel really shit. Her life was led by Jack and his behaviour and even though she knew he couldn't help it, it was a tough pill to swallow.

Harriet quickly covered her disappointment and replied, 'No worries. Let's go.'

The girls made their way back to the entrance and as they exited through the doors, the smiling lady caught them.

'Oh, are you not staying with us, little man?'

Jack hid further into Nancy's skirt. 'He's not feeling very confident today, so I think we'll try again another day.' She smiled and tried to continue walking but the woman crouched down to his level.

'We have lots of games and toys to play with and all the ladies are very lovely – you'll have a great time.'

Jack's hands becoming increasingly whiter as he gripped Nancy's skirt. He had started to rock slightly too. It wasn't noticeable enough for anyone else to spot it, but Nancy knew he was incredibly anxious right now. She needed to get him away from this situation to a place where he could relax. She reached into her bags to retrieve his Calm Cards. A while back Nancy and Jack had spent an afternoon finding pictures of all Jack's favourite things and they'd printed them off and laminated them, so that whenever he was feeling anxious, he could take some time out to look at his cards and get into a better head-space. So far, they had been a hit. He had pictures of him and Nancy, pictures of buildings he had visited and landmarks from all over the world. Jack loved architecture so looking at structural pictures was calming for him. She rummaged around in her bag and after a moment felt the disappointment settle as she realised she must've left them up in the room. She cursed herself – she never usually went anywhere without them. The tension was building and she could feel her temples pulsating.

'I think it's probably best if we try another day.'

But the woman just wasn't giving up.

'I know, why don't you give it a try for just an hour and then if you don't like it, we can call Mummy? How's that sound?' And then she did the one thing she shouldn't have done.

She took his headphones off.

Chapter 10

The next few minutes felt like a lifetime for Nancy, and yet everything seemed to happen so quickly.

The first thing was the rapid movement of Jack's arm swinging at the lady, catching her square on the chin as he flung both arms up when he felt his headphones being removed. Nancy couldn't move quickly enough to stop the connection of his fist hitting the lady's face. The woman recoiled in surprise and screeched which caused Jack to let out an almighty wail as he struggled to take in the sudden commotion around him.

'Jack, no! It's OK!' Nancy called to him, reaching out her hands to try and stop the swinging of his arms as he became more panicked and unsettled. But in moments like this, Jack had an unbelievable strength that would challenge the world's strongest man.

Nancy frantically tried to calm him, making shushing noises and reassuring him that everything was OK, but he was already in the meltdown zone. His anxiety had been building the whole time they had been at the kids' club and the woman removing the comfort blanket of his headphones had tipped him over the edge. Nancy knew he was too far gone now to be pulled back easily. His face contorted with distress, bright red with a look of fear spread across it. He was holding his ears as though someone had hurt them, and it broke Nancy's heart. She was so angry at herself. If she had said no at the start, then none of this would be happening. Instead, her little boy was frightened and distressed and it was her fault. She felt sick with frustration.

'Nancy, what do you want me to do?' Harriet called to her, but she barely heard her, her focus was now purely on trying to calm Jack down.

'Here, Jack, have your headphones back.' She held them out to him, but he batted them away with his hands, dropping to the floor and squirming around as his cry became a wail.

The woman who had started all this was standing open-mouthed, staring at him as she held the area on her face where he had whacked her. She looked from Jack, to Nancy, then back to Jack, unsure of what exactly was unfolding in front of her. She didn't understand, nobody understood. It was an incredibly lonely place to be when you were parenting an autistic child.

'I need to let him get it out of his system,' Nancy said to Harriet, pleading with her eyes for her friend to not judge and just be there. Harriet had never judged her, but the scars from those who had were still raw. Harriet, true to form, just nodded and smiled, showing her unwavering support and this meant more to Nancy than anything she could have said. Words were nice, but it was the comradery of support shown in Harriet's actions that spoke the loudest. She had her friend by her side and she was going to get through this. She hoped.

'What an earth is going on out here!' Another member of staff had joined them from inside the kids' club and her gaze instantly went to Jack on the floor writhing about in distress. 'Oh dear, does somebody not want to come in today? He'll be fine once he's in, Mum, go on, off you go and we'll take little man in with us.' The woman began to kneel down to Jack who instantly kicked out and just missed making contact with her face. She jumped back in surprise and made a comment about being unruly under her breath. This made Nancy's blood boil because it was the conclusion that so many people came to without knowing anything about the situation. So many children were branded as misbehaving without anyone looking into *why* they were behaving in that way. Not only did she have to deal with the pressure of watching her son clearly distressed and inconsolable, but she also had to listen to people who thought they were child behaviour experts pass judgement on them.

'He's not naughty!' Nancy found herself throwing the words back at the woman although she wasn't sure why she bothered. People like that were never going to understand.

'Oh no, I didn't say that ma'am.' The look on her face said different.

'Come on, Jack, let's go.' Nancy said, trying to be more authoritative when inside she was feeling totally helpless. She just knew she needed to get both Jack and herself away from this situation. But as she moved towards him he lashed out at her too, grasping tighter at his ears, practically ripping them from his head. He was pulling at them so much they had turned a deep shade of crimson and looked so sore. 'Jack, stop it! Stop pulling your ears and put these on!' She shoved the headphones at him, but he couldn't seem to concentrate on anything except stopping the feeling that was making him so uncomfortable. His wails became sobs and he curled up into a ball, rocking.

'Hari...' Nancy sobbed, looking to her friend. Generally over the years, Nancy had built up a good coping strategy for dealing with Jack when he was like this. However, being in a new environment, she found herself panicking and becoming stressed a lot quicker than she would do in the comfort of her own home. Seeing Jack in a state was proving too much for her. She was so grateful to Hari, who instantly went into leader mode and took control of the situation.

'OK, what needs to happen right now ladies,' she addressed the two kids' club staff members, 'is that we need you both to step back and give Jack some space. I'm sure we don't need both of you out here so if you wouldn't mind...' She nodded towards the second woman who had joined them and indicated that she return to the crèche. The woman didn't appreciate being told what to do but the receptionist surprisingly backed Harriet up and said, 'Perhaps you should go back inside, I'm fine out here.'

'Right, Nance, put the headphones next to him on the floor so they are there when he calms down.'

Nancy did as she was told, sniffing back the tears that were now falling down her face.

'And just FYI,' Harriet addressed the receptionist, 'Jack has autism, so this isn't just a child having a tantrum, and we would appreciate some support as opposed to the judgemental looks.'

The woman looked away, half embarrassed and half fuming at being addressed in this way but Nancy didn't care right now, she just needed Jack to calm down. She was annoyed at herself for failing to cope in Jack's moment of need. It was day one of their holiday and already she had crumbled. She couldn't help but wonder if she was more wound up about this holiday than she realised. She knew Jack would struggle but she had coping mechanisms in place at home and she thought she'd be able to cope with anything he threw at her. But for some reason, she'd struggled today. It could be tiredness from the travel or worry about what might happen. Either way, she needed to get a grip on things if she was going to make it through this holiday with her sanity. She needed to refocus ... and then she needed a drink.

***

'Here, I think you need this, hey?' Harriet passed Nancy a glass of sangria and watched as she gulped down half the contents in one swift movement. 'Are you OK?'

Nancy exhaled, her gaze fixed on her glass. 'Not really.'

Harriet felt incredibly sorry for her best friend. This last year had been so hard for Nancy, and she'd watched her friend slowly but surely lose her identity and a little bit of her sanity since Jack's diagnosis and her marriage break up. Harriet tried to be there for her but there was only so much she could do and with work getting increasingly busy she knew she hadn't been there for Nancy as much as she perhaps could have, which made her feel guilty. She'd wanted this holiday to be a positive break for them all, but she hadn't envisaged Jack struggling with it. She hadn't even thought about Jack if she was honest, which pretty much summed her up as a parent – useless.

'It wasn't your fault – she shouldn't have taken Jack's headphones.'

'Yeah, but how was she supposed to know? How is anyone supposed to know? It's so fucking hard, Hari.'

'I know it is, but you can't beat yourself up about it. This is going to happen, you just need to learn ways to get past it and help Jack to get past it, that's all.' She sipped at her own sangria.

'But what if he doesn't, Hari? What if he never improves and I spend my whole life one step behind him apologising for what he does and the chaos he creates when people do things he doesn't like. I can't constantly be there for him.'

'You won't have to be—'

'How do you know? Does your child have bloody autism?' Harriet froze at Nancy's sudden outburst. 'Shit, I'm sorry. I didn't mean that.' Nancy exhaled and put her head in her hands. 'I'm just fed up with getting it wrong – I don't know what I'm doing, why is this so hard!'

'You're doing great! You're doing a hell of a lot better than I would. Jeez, Nance, I can't even look after my own children without getting it wrong and they're a piece of cake in comparison.' She held up her hand in apology. 'Not saying Jack is difficult ... I just meant—'

'It's fine,' Nancy smiled. 'I know what you mean.' They sat there quietly for a minute before Nancy added, 'And you're doing a fine job with your children, stop putting yourself down.'

'I don't know, Nance, I know it's nothing in comparison to what you have to deal with daily but I feel like I'm wading against the tide all the time. The children expect so much from me and I don't have a clue. Put me in a boardroom with seventeen directors from multimillion-pound companies from around the world and I'm a pro, stick me in a play centre with my two children and it's like they speak a different language to me!' Hari laughed to lighten the comment. Whilst she was trying to make Nancy feel better about what had happened, there was more truth in what she was saying than she liked to admit.

'You're too hard on yourself.'

'Nancy, the other week the nursery had to call me because I was over an hour late to pick up Tommy. I was too busy replying to emails. And then I did it again the day before we left.' She lifted an eyebrow. 'My own child, Nance, and I forgot!'

'You're under a lot of pressure with your job and everyone drops the ball every now and then, that's just parenting. It's shit.' She clinked her glass with Harriet's. 'Welcome to the Shit Mums' Club.'

'Welcome? Are you kidding? I think I qualify for the presidency role at that club!'

'Oh shush!' Nancy waved the comment away. 'It does make me think, though, Hari.'

'What's that then? Share your pearls of wisdom with me, oh wise one.'

'Well, we can't be the only parents in the world feeling like this. Maybe this is just what parenting is: a rollercoaster of emotions ranging from the very high to the very low on a daily basis with the constant need to self-criticise every single action you take – or don't take.'

Harriet nodded. 'Sounds pretty accurate to me.' She sipped her drink again.

'I just wish more people spoke about it and owned up to struggling instead of putting on a filter and pretending. It makes it so much harder for those of us who are genuinely pulling our hair out because we feel like the only ones. But, we can't be.'

'Well, I am totally on your side, Mrs, I certainly can't say I'm acing parenthood. Screaming, crying, tantrums, poo on the floor, broccoli in the DVD player ... it all happens at my house.' Harriet's confidence began to wane as she listed all the things her children did, the more she spoke, the more vulnerable she felt. Maybe the sangria had loosened her tongue a little too much. But Nancy was her friend, so if she couldn't talk openly with her, then who could she talk to?

'See, this is why mums need to stick together, this is why we should talk about these things because once you realise that every single parent is feeling this shit, it doesn't feel so bad!' Nancy slapped her knee as though she had had a revelation.

'Another one for the road?' Harriet asked, not waiting for an answer and making her way over to the bar. Laughter aside,

Nancy had a point. Surely they couldn't be the only parents out there struggling in some way? So why did she feel so alone?

***

Nancy watched Harriet leave and moved her attention to Jack who was sitting with his feet dangling in the pool, headphones firmly back on. It broke her heart to see him so isolated from everyone else. All she wanted was – dare she say it – a *normal* child. Whatever that was. She loved him with all her heart but being his mum was so incredibly difficult, she wasn't sure she was cut out for it. When Pete had left her, it had broken her heart, but if she was completely honest, she'd been a little jealous of him too. Jealous that he had escaped the daily turmoil of meltdowns and the unknown. It wasn't just the physical stresses of it all that she was finding difficult, it was the emotional side too. Parenting was hard, regardless of whether you had one child or ten, hyperactive or shy, disabled or not. The actual act of parenting itself was gruelling both physically and mentally and she really missed having another person to bounce off when times were tough. She was jealous of the fact that Pete didn't have to watch his son when he was feeling sad or frightened and as a result, endure hours of horrendous guilt and shame that you couldn't make it better. Pete didn't have to deal with numerous wakings in the night and he didn't have to go through the turmoil when you forgot to take Jack's Calm Cards out. She couldn't ever imagine being without Jack but equally she longed to share the worry with someone who understood.

She glanced down at her leg where a bruise was beginning to form where she had tried to restrain Jack earlier. The way the staff member had looked at Nancy, like her son was a monster, made her feel devastated. She was failing as a parent right now and it felt horrendous.

She was snapped out of her thoughts rapidly when she saw a young boy approach Jack from behind, pause and then sit down next to him, dangling his feet into the pool just like Jack. Nancy froze with an overwhelming fear that the little boy would touch Jack's headphones. She moved to stand up to warn the child but then paused as she watched Jack take off his own headphones and look at the young boy. She sat back in her chair, anxiously waiting to see what happened next. Time stood still as she watched the two of them staring at each other, not moving. Jack had never done this before. He didn't usually take his headphones off to interact with another person – it was only when Nancy asked him to or when he was ready. Nancy wasn't sure how she felt about this. She wanted to be happy – this was progress, surely? But a small part of her brain was nervously asking questions like *why?* and *what will he do?* She wanted to intervene, to make sure this encounter went smoothly and positively, but she knew in her heart that he was never going to make the progress he needed to socially if she was always one step behind doing it for him. She waited patiently, her breathing shallow and fast.

Then the little boy with the mousy brown hair said, 'Whatcha watching?'

Jack didn't respond, and Nancy could see him clasping the iPad tight against his chest, his knuckles their usual shade of white. Nancy's heart was racing, willing him to reply to the boy who was staring at him, waiting for an answer, the sweetest little smile on his face ... She fixed her eyes on her son, praying for him to say something – anything – but still he stared back, unwavering.

'Is it YouTube? I like that; I watch stuff on it all the time – what's your favourite?'

Still nothing. Oh God, this was torture. That poor little boy wanted to make friends and have a chat and Jack was just sitting there, frozen.

Then, Jack stood up and walked back to Nancy, leaving the boy sitting in the pool by himself, watching as his new friend just walked off without so much as a goodbye. Nancy's heart broke for him and if she was honest with herself, she was a little frustrated at Jack too. When these social challenges arose, Nancy always wished for the same outcome: for Jack to engage. And every single time she had to accept that this wasn't going to happen overnight. But it was difficult to not let the frustration seep in. She suppressed the feeling, as Jack sat down at the base of her chair and resumed his watching. Nancy walked over to the little boy. Sitting next to him she took Jack's place and put her legs into the pool as he had done.

'I'm sorry about that,' she said. 'Jack struggles a little bit with talking to new people.' She smiled at the boy who smiled back, his whole face lighting up and Nancy couldn't help but warm to his friendly nature.

He shrugged. 'That's OK,' he chirped. 'I just saw him sitting on his own so didn't want him to be lonely.'

Her heart melted. 'How old are you?'

'Seven.'

'Seven? Wow, you are very grown up for seven.'

'That's what my dad says; he says I'm like an old man sometimes.' He giggled, and the sound was fresh, carefree and just how little boys should sound.

'Well, I think it's lovely that you wanted to make friends. Jack just finds it hard sometimes.'

'Does he have friends at home?' The little boy swished the water with his feet.

'Not really.' She shook her head. He had children he played with – or should she say, alongside – but that was because Nancy was friends with their parents. And at school he just kept himself to himself.

'It's OK; some people just like to be on their own.'

Nancy looked at the boy, lost for words. How did this seven-year-old have such a mature outlook on life? She moved her gaze back to her feet in the pool, her brightly painted pink toenails making shapes beneath the water.

'Is this a private party or can anyone join?'

Nancy jumped slightly at the male voice behind her and glanced over her shoulder. She stared for a second at the tall man peering down at them and then realised she was staring at his chest which had some kind of tattoo on it. She coughed to regain herself as she diverted her eyes towards his face. He had a nice face with a cheeky smile, made slightly sexier by the small amount of stubble around his mouth – standard holiday stubble. He had the most gorgeous full head of blonde hair which was long enough for her to run her hands through. She batted away the thought the instant it fell into her head. Embarrassed, as though he could read her mind, she averted her gaze nervously.

'Daddy! I was talking to this lady's boy as he was sitting on his own, but he didn't want to talk so the lady is talking to me now.' He swished his feet again.

Nancy panicked; she didn't want this man to think Jack was rude. She stuttered a little. 'Sorry, um, he's just not very good at talking to new people,' she added hastily.

The man laughed and sat down on the other side of his son. 'It's not a problem, honestly.' He smiled, and Nancy felt a twinge of attraction as he did. He had the most beautiful deep blue eyes. She was definitely an 'eyes' person, she was starting to realise. It was always something she noticed on people.

'I take it you're staying at this complex?' He swished his feet in the water like his son and Nancy found herself smiling. 'What?' he asked, the smile spreading across his face.

'You and your son do exactly the same thing in the water with your feet – the exact same movement.' She realised she must sound like a right weirdo for noticing this fact, so she self-consciously added, 'It was funny. And yes, we are staying here. Me, my son and my friend and her two little ones.' She pointed over her shoulder and saw Harriet was back and sitting on the sun lounger next to Jack who still had his nose in the iPad. The guy's face creased in confusion as he looked at them and Nancy added, 'Her two are in the kids' club. Jack, um, wasn't too keen to go today.'

The guy smiled. 'I don't blame him; I think I would rather be out in the sunshine too.' He gave Nancy another friendly smile and she couldn't help but smile back. 'I'm Cameron, by the way.' He pointed at his son. 'This guy is useless at introducing me to people. Call yourself my right-hand man!' He nudged him and the boy giggled again.

Nancy found herself giggling. 'I'm Nancy,' she said as she shook Cameron's outstretched hand. 'My son is Jack and that's Harriet, who is clearly listening to every single word.' She pointed to her friend who looked up from her phone and waved, at which Nancy giggled again.

Harriet always managed to look stunning. Even now, her black swimsuit was styled in such a way that she looked like she was about to step onto the London catwalk and her hair was poker-straight, with not a strand out of place. Her designer sunglasses and a chunky necklace nicely finished the look. Nancy – on the other hand – had on her trusty swimsuit of the last two years, a deep shade of emerald, hair pulled up into her usual mum bun and zero jewellery on. She wasn't really an accessories person. Simple and easy was her fashion style, if you could call it a style. Usually Nancy was comfortable in her own skin and was happy being the less glamorous one in their friendship, but she felt a tad self-conscious right now with Harriet looking so presentable next to her own Mrs Plain Jane look, as she was introducing this hot guy. Maybe she should make a conscious effort to dress up a bit more, look after her appearance now that Pete was well and truly off the cards.

'I'm not, I just heard my name.' Harriet poked her tongue out and Cameron laughed.

'Nice to meet you guys. And this is Aiden.' He tapped his son on the leg. 'Right Mr, it's time we made a move. We have a waterpark to go to.'

The little boy jumped up excitedly. 'Yeah! Let's go, bye!' he called over his shoulder as he ran off to where his clothes and towel were.

'It was nice to meet you, Nancy,' Cameron said as he shook her hand again. 'Hopefully I'll bump into you again if you're here for a while?' Another huge smile, revealing a row of perfectly white teeth. He had one of those faces that instantly made a person feel relaxed and at ease.

Nancy nodded. 'We only arrived yesterday.'

'I'll see you around then.' He saluted and smiled before running off to where Aiden was. 'Last one to the room has to pay for dinner!' he called and Nancy could hear Aiden's giggling again.

She pulled her feet out of the water to walk back over to Harriet, and she couldn't help but smile.

'Look at you all smiley. Does someone have a crush on the hot guy?'

'Shut up,' Nancy said as she plonked herself down onto the sun lounger.

'I will not. I want to hear everything.' She put her phone down.

'I'm pretty sure you did – pretending not to hear and then making the rookie mistake of responding when we talked about you.' She laughed and shook her head.

Harriet giggled. 'I know! I could've kicked myself. But I didn't hear everything; I was at the bar remember?' Harriet picked up Nancy's new sangria and passed it to her. 'I think you've earned this.'

She took the glass, 'What? For talking to some guy?'

'Yes, for taking some time for you and enjoying yourself with a hot guy, something you haven't done in I don't know how long. It's about time you forgot about that loser Pete and put yourself out there!' She picked up her phone again and started tapping away.

'Hari, I chatted to some guy, I'm not about to marry him. Or even date him. This isn't an 18-30s holiday where I am looking to hook up and get my leg over. My marriage ended a year ago!'

'Oh come on, you're not exactly going to let Pete back in, are you? So why not explore your options?'

'Hari, I am here for a holiday with my boy and my friend. Nothing else.' She leaned back onto her sun lounger and pulled her sunglasses back down over her eyes. 'And anyway, we're too old for an 18-30s holiday.'

'Hey! We aren't that old! 32 isn't old! 30 is the new 20!'

'Still too old.' She giggled and made herself comfortable. Just because she wasn't going to act on anything with Cameron – didn't mean she couldn't fantasize about him.

She turned her attention to Jack who was still watching videos on his iPad. She hated how much time he spent on there but equally, she knew it was a source of comfort for him so she didn't like to take it away. She shuffled on her lounger to be closer to him, placing her hand on his forearm. He looked up at her touch, his big blue eyes wide with interest. He slid off the head phones after pausing his video and waited for her to speak.

'You ok, little man?' She had really struggled with his meltdown earlier in the kids' club but that must be nothing compared to how he must've felt.

He nodded.

'Are you feeling a bit better now?' She knew he didn't really like to talk about it afterwards, but she tried anyway. He might change his mind one day, so she always kept trying. He shrugged. 'What's up? You feeling sad?' Another shrug. 'Didn't you want to talk to that boy? He was just trying to be your friend.'

'I don't like it.'

'What?' she frowned. 'The boy?' No reply. 'He was just being friendly.'

'I don't like it. I don't know ... he's ... I just don't like it.'

She smiled at him. He looked so innocent, and with the sunshine beaming down onto his light blonde hair and making him squint just a little bit, he looked younger than his seven years. She didn't know if it was just because he was her only child and because of the upheaval over the last year, but she felt so much more protective over him. He might be seven now, but he was still her little blue-eyed baby. She missed spending time together when life hadn't always been so stressful. They had some great times together still, but a huge part of his everyday living – especially as he grew older and the social expectation of him – seemed to cause him more angst than happiness. She tried so hard to make his life easy, but she was still learning. It would take time, she knew this, but it was a hard pill to swallow.

She decided to change tactic. 'What are you watching?'

'A video.' He seemed unsure. Nancy didn't normally ask much about his iPad and what he was up to – mostly because she didn't want to intrude on his down time and, if she was being honest with herself, partly because she was too stressed.

'What's it about?'

'Building.'

Jack loved building programmes, and she smiled as she should have guessed that's what he would be watching. She picked up her drink and shuffled closer to him. 'Can I watch it too?' she asked, hoping that he didn't reject her. But instead he just shrugged and put his headphones back on.

She sat quietly with Jack as the video played, wondering how she was going to help him get through his life. Today had exhausted her and she feared that things were only going to get worse for them if she didn't come up with a way to help Jack handle life better. She already felt like she had exhausted every avenue available to them to find solutions, strategies and coping mechanisms, but clearly there was a lot more work to do. Where was she to start? She wasn't sure anymore.

As she rested her hand on his little back, she smiled at the fact that she couldn't hear anything being said on the video, but at least Jack was letting her get close to him. It was a start. And everything has to start from somewhere.

Chapter 11

'For crying out loud!' Harriet slammed her phone on the counter and picked up her laptop.

'What's up?' Nancy asked as she applied her make up.

They were both in Harriet's room getting ready to go for dinner whilst the children were playing in Nancy's room – the adjoining door left open so that they could keep an eye on them. Though *children playing* loosely translated to Harriet's two playing and Jack sitting on the bed with his iPad. Standard practice now. Harriet's two barely noticed Jack anymore.

'Bloody work – as per frickin' usual.' She punched away at the keys as she logged into her laptop.

'Was this holiday not supposed to be a break for you, Hari?' Nancy raised her eyebrows and Harriet tried to not bite, because her stress level was currently at 98 per cent and she wasn't about to take it out on her best friend.

'I would love nothing more than to have a complete break from work but these idiots I employ seem to be incapable of making a decision without running it by me first!'

'You know why that is, don't you?' Nancy replied as Harriet shook her head. 'Because if it goes wrong, it's their fault and you'll fire them. If you take the responsibility of OK-ing something, it's off their shoulders and onto yours.'

'I wouldn't fire them if it went wrong.' Another eyebrow raise from Nancy. 'I wouldn't!'

'Last year – Mr Yao?'

Shit. 'Ok, well he deserved to be fired because his mistake was of epic proportions.'

'And you were on your period,' Nancy said under her breath, but Harriet heard.

She threw a pillow at her friend. 'I was not! I am not that unprofessional!'

'Hari, I know – I'm joking! Jeez!'

'Sorry, I'm just a little stressed, that's all.' She turned her attention back to the screen and loaded up her emails and the spreadsheet for the company.

'You are a good businesswoman – no one ever doubts that. You are the most successful woman I know and you work bloody hard for it. And it's only because I love you that I am willing to overlook the fact that you invited me away for a girls' holiday and have spent 90 per cent of our first two days here on your phone or on your laptop.' Nancy didn't move her eyes away from the mirror as she applied her mascara.

Harriet stopped and looked at her friend, a twinge of guilt settling into the pit of her stomach. 'I know, I'm sorry. I just … need to make this work.'

'It *is* working – your company won Essex Business of The Year last year after just four years of trading and you won businesswoman of the year. You're totally smashing it, Hari; you just need to learn when to give yourself a break.'

'Nance, if I gave myself a break, those awards wouldn't have been mine. It's because I work so hard that we got them.'

'Being businesswoman of the year is great but what good is it if you don't have friends or family around to share it with?' The air between them because instantly tense at Nancy's comment, which Harriet took as a reference to her husband leaving her. Andy walking out had been the biggest kick in the teeth after Harriet had spent years building up her company so she could be a valid, contributing member of the family. She'd done it for them – for all of them – but he'd never been able to see that.

'Low blow, Nance.'

Nancy frowned but then the penny dropped. 'Come on, don't be over-sensitive, I didn't mean it like that.'

'Yes you did,' Harriet said, punching away at her keyboard without looking at her friend for fear of her eyes betraying how much that comment hurt. And it hurt because she knew it was true.

Nancy swivelled round on her seat. 'I didn't, I didn't mean it to come out how it did. I just meant you deserve a break after all your hard work.'

Now it was Harriet's turn to swivel round. 'No, you meant that because I worked so hard my husband left me and our children and I lost a shitload of friends in the process. If I could call them friends – can't have been very good mates if they were willing to drop me the second I couldn't go out every weekend because I was too busy earning a living.' It was a sore subject and Nancy knew it. 'It's a cheap shot, Nance.'

'Hey, my husband left me too! I'm not judging you for it!'

'This isn't a fucking competition, Nance – who has the shittiest husband!' Harriet's heart was racing now as she battled to keep the tears at bay. She didn't do crying – it was a sign of weakness and she wasn't weak. She was a lot of things – shit at being a housewife, a lame mother at times, a rubbish cook and a workaholic – but she wasn't weak.

Nancy stood up and walked back into her room, slamming the door behind her.

Harriet sat for a minute looking at the screen of numbers and Excel spreadsheets trying to blink away the moisture that was filling her eyes. After a moment she slammed the laptop lid closed and walked into the bathroom. If she was going to do this crying lark, she needed to do it in the shower where no one would see her.

She threw the bathroom door shut and leaned onto the sink, looking at her face in the mirror. Her perfect hair was still in place and her outfit today screamed Milan catwalk, but inside she was broken.

She took a tissue and dabbed at the corners of her eyes where tears were threatening to spill over. 'Damn emotions!' she sniffed. 'This is why I like business meetings – no fucking emotion involved. Just get the job done and get out. None of this stupid crying malarkey. I mean what is that about?' She paused and looked at herself in the mirror again. 'And this is why you're single, Hari – you need to stop talking to yourself!'

She sat on the closed toilet seat and shut her eyes, taking a few deep breaths as her racing heartbeat slowed to a steady pulse. It wasn't even that mean a comment from Nancy, Harriet had had worse said to her. The fact that she overreacted to this conversation didn't go unmissed by her. But she was already feeling exposed about the situation and whilst most of the time she pushed all the thoughts and feelings associated with her ex to the back of her mind, occasionally they seeped out and consumed her. It wasn't enough that she felt stressed and inadequate as a mum, she also missed Andy. A lot. She'd been devastated when he'd left but she'd masked her true upset. Now it was too late to reconcile with him as he had moved on and had nothing to do with Harriet or the children. That alone told her he wasn't worth it – it didn't stop her missing him though. Missing the times they'd had. Before the children and prior to Harriet starting up her own company, the two of them had had lots of fun together. They just weren't strong enough to grow into adulthood together. And as for the friends, well, who needed loads of friends anyway? She had Nancy and the people at work, and they all understood. It stung when she stopped getting invited out to things, but she soon learned to get over it and concentrate on what really mattered. It was much easier to throw herself into work than to address why people didn't want to be around her anymore. She didn't like the person she had become – she didn't need others telling her they felt the same too.

She shook her head and straightened up. Hissy fit over, she had some emails to send.

Chapter 12

'Listen, I'm sorry about earlier. I was out of order and I shouldn't have said what I did.' Harriet waved off Nancy's comment. 'I didn't mean it, you know, I just hate seeing you so worked to the bone – I don't want you to burn out, that's all.'

'It's fine, I shouldn't have shouted at you. Just a bit stressed that's all.' The response was clipped, it clearly wasn't OK.

Nancy speared a potato onto her fork ignoring the finality in Harriet's voice. She couldn't have things strained between them whilst they were away. 'But that's what I mean; you've been stressed for the last four years – when do you give yourself a break?'

'A company doesn't get off its feet if the owners want to take a break every five minutes. You get out what you put in.' Harriet didn't take her eyes off her plate, making herself look far too busy with cutting up her food. It was obvious she was doing it as a distraction.

'Yes, true, but when the owner is sending emails from her hospital bed after having just had a baby, there's got to be a line drawn, surely?' Nancy remembered the day she visited

Harriet after she'd had Tommy and was shocked to see her have a complete work desk set up in the hospital. Laptop out, phone next to it and a coffee on the side as Tommy slept in the cot next to her. The nurses must've thought she was crazy, Nancy sure had. 'You were like a woman possessed; tapping away on emails with one hand, your phone going between your ear and your shoulder and I'm pretty sure you had a conference call at one point over the course of that day too. I mean, that's just crazy. You have to learn when to stop and breathe.'

'Are we really going to do this at dinner or can we enjoy it? I'm not working right now, am I? Yet you seem set on talking about work!'

Nancy was taken back by her abruptness. 'I'm not having a go—'

'Could've fooled me.' Hari snapped back.

'Hey! I'm just saying this because I care. Why don't you take a step back for a second? You have employees working on stuff, you said yourself that things are quieter at the moment before your next big contract comes in – I don't understand why you have to be going at 100 miles per hour every second of every day. It makes me tired just watching you.' Nancy laughed to try and lighten the mood.

'Can we just change the subject please?'

Nancy shrugged and continued eating her dinner. She certainly hadn't planned to come away on holiday and row. It was supposed to be fun. Harriet was overreacting but there was no point in trying to talk about work with her whilst she was still in a mood. It was definitely something that Nancy was not going to give up on though. Harriet kept saying how Nancy had had a tough year and needed a break – the truth could be said about her too. She was just too bloody stubborn to admit it. But this was a conversation for another time, maybe after a few cocktails. 'So what's the plan for tomorrow?'

'Waterpark!' Isla shouted and banged on the table.

Tommy saw his sister do it and started repeatedly banging on the table in response. Isla giggled and joined in, chanting *waterpark, waterpark, waterpark.*

Jack clutched at his ears – Nancy had managed to pry his iPad and headphones away from him so he would eat something.

'OK, OK, that's enough you two. Look, you're upsetting Jack.' Harriet pointed to Jack and Isla looked over.

'Sorry Jack,' Isla said, and looked guiltily at Nancy.

'It's OK, sweetheart, he's fine.' Nancy hated it when other children's fun was cut short because it upset Jack. He didn't like loud noises, new people, being touched ... the list of triggers was only growing, and she was becoming more and more aware of how difficult life was for him.

'I'm up for the waterpark if you are Nancy?'

Nancy looked at Jack. He was never going to like it, but why should the others suffer because he didn't want to go? Maybe he would try it – although she didn't hold out much hope. 'Jack?' she said, placing a hand on his forearm gently so he knew she was talking to him. He looked at her with his big blue eyes. 'Shall we go to the waterpark tomorrow? It will have slides and a swimming pool and it will be lots of fun.'

Already he was shaking his head.

'Come on, just give it a try?'

'I don't like water.'

'You don't have to go in – just dangle your feet like you did earlier today in the swimming pool?'

'When the boy came to talk to me.' It was a statement rather than a question and Nancy felt a small bolt of elation as she realised he had probably taken more notice of Aiden when he came over earlier than he let on.

'That's right. That little boy was called Aiden. He wanted to be your friend.'

'I don't like friends.'

'Of course you do – everyone likes to have friends.'

'Not me.' He picked up a piece of plain pasta and put it into his mouth.

'Why not?' Nancy pressed. She always tried to push conversations with him when he was in a talkative mood. She had no idea why he was so chatty tonight but she kept going, afraid that if she stopped, he would too.

He shrugged.

'Because it's OK to speak to new people. That's how we make friends.'

'But I don't know who they are.'

'That's how we make friends, we get to know them. We can ask questions about what they like, and they ask us questions and—'

'I don't like questions.'

Nancy suppressed a groan. She hated it when he disliked everything she said, but she was adamant about keeping her happy face on – if he saw she was frustrated then he would just close off and she needed him to keep opening up or he would never make any progress.

'But Mummy and I ask you questions and you answer us,' Harriet said, decanting some more of her dinner onto Tommy's plate.

'But I know you.'

'So you only like questions from people you know – not people you don't know?' Nancy asked, and Jack nodded. 'I see.' It was a small revelation for Nancy, but it felt like she'd got to know her son that little bit more just now and a spark of happiness sizzled through her body. He may be being difficult about the waterpark, but he was trying his best and that was all she could ask for. She would have to come up with a different idea. 'If you guys want to go to the waterpark, Jack and I could do something else.'

'We're supposed to be doing stuff together though – we don't have to go,' Harriet suggested reassuringly. Isla was not impressed by this and began wailing at her mum. 'Alright, alright, let's see what time it opens and maybe we can go for a little while. What's it called?' Nancy shrugged. 'Do we even know if there is a waterpark around here?' Harriet frowned.

'Yeah, that Cameron said he was going to one.'

'Oh he did, did he?' Harriet swooned. 'Well, maybe we should find him and ask.'

'Trickles Waterpark.' Jack said, not looking up from his iPad.

'What's that darling?' Nancy asked.

'That's what it's called – Trickles Waterpark. It is approximately 63000 square feet and has a zero entry pool, lazy river, lap pool, diving well, slide tower and tipping bucket play structure.'

Nancy stared at him, her mouth gaping.

'It takes 1.2 million gallons to fill initially with a daily top off of 3871 gallons giving it a consumption ratio of 0.32 per cent.' He looked up at Nancy. 'How cool does that sound?' His little face was beaming, he was in his element. Statistics, information and structures – he loved it.

'Wow, Jack, you're like a fountain of information about the waterpark.' Harriet laughed and poured some wine.

'Mum, it says here that the water park is open approximately 100 days per season with an average attendance of 1650 per day – that's a lot of people.'

'It is a lot of people,' she agreed, unsure of how to play this conversation.

'But actually, if it is 63,000 square metres, it might not be very crowded. People might not bump into me.' He was talking to himself more than anyone else. He then gasped. 'Mum, look.' He showed her the tablet and it was a picture of the waterpark as a whole. It looked incredible. Splashes of vibrant colours snaked over the screen as the slides and water chutes intertwined. Some high, some low. Rainbow tunnels, various shaped pools, log flume and a beach scene. It looked like a child's dream. She looked at Jack.

'Wow, sweetie, isn't it great?' she tested.

'Mum, look at the shape that one makes. It's got right angles and obtuse. That one there looks about 110 degrees.' He looked up. 'I want to go.'

'Really?' She almost gasped the word.

'Yeah, but I don't want to go in the water, I just want to see the shapes.'

'That's fine sweetheart.' Nancy looked to Harriet and raised her eyebrows as Jack resumed his research. She was starting to realise that with Jack, it was all about how you approached things.

Chapter 13

The waterpark was a hub of noise, colour and water *every-where*. All the things Jack usually hated. Instantly Nancy regretted bringing him here as he hung off her arm, hands grasping onto her as a safety blanket. But she hadn't forced him; he had told her he wanted to come, she reassured herself. She had tried her best this morning to prepare him for the type of establishment this was. But there was only so much she could say because she didn't want to frighten him unnecessarily or make him feel worried. They had looked through his Calm Cards, at the building ones and he had spoken about what shapes and styles of structure he might see here today – but nothing could prepare him for the real thing.

'Mum, too noisy,' he squeaked. She could see he was trying really hard, but it was a little too much for his ears.

She pulled the headphones out of her bag and placed them over his ears. 'Better?' She gave him a thumbs up as she asked and he nodded.

'Best purchase you've ever made, those, hey?' Harriet asked, nodding at the green headphones.

Last night Harriet had apologised for being snappy with

Nancy and the pair had agreed to let it go over a few pina coladas. Nancy still wanted to approach the work issue with Hari but only when things were relaxed again, she wasn't pushing it. They still had a few more days to get through yet so she didn't want to cause any friction. 'Tell me about it. These ones are great; they're like those ear defenders. I think he likes the feel of the pressure on his ears.'

'Absolute godsend. Bless him. Isla! Careful honey, we aren't ready to go in yet. Let's find somewhere to put our stuff first.'

Nancy scanned the vicinity, looking for somewhere for her and Jack to sit whilst the others explored the waterpark. The sunshine was beating down brightly over the pool and today was incredibly hot. Nancy loved the heat, but she knew Jack wasn't happy when he got too hot so she had to make sure she had lots of ideas in place to keep him cool. Firstly, she needed to find somewhere with some shade so he wasn't in direct sunlight. As she looked, she came across an area which had a group of loungers and a small pool just for paddling. 'Hari look, perfect! Jack can dangle his legs in there.'

'Quick, grab it before someone else does.'

'I'm not running,' Nancy said, but it was too late, Harriet had bounced off, sprinting towards the loungers, her long legs stretching as her bright red kimono flapped around her hips.

A whistle sounded and Nancy glanced at the lifeguard who was staring at Harriet who had also turned round. He didn't look happy and was standing up, pointing at Harriet. 'No running!' he called at her and Nancy burst out laughing.

'Haha, Mummy just got told off by the lifeguard', Nancy

said to Isla who was staring wide-eyed at her. 'It's OK, she's not in trouble,' she added, as she saw the worry in her eyes.

'Sorry!' Harriet shouted as she raised a hand and then casually – but quickly – walked to the spot she was trying to save.

When Nancy reached her friend, she laughed. 'Did someone get their wrists slapped?' She put down her bag and grabbed a lounger, kicking off her flip flops so she could feel the cold tiles beneath her toes.

'Still got the seats though, didn't I?' Harriet retorted, adjusting her floppy cream hat which would look stupid on Nancy, but Harriet totally pulled off.

'Mummy can we go in now, pur-leeeeeease!'

'Isla, let me just get our stuff sorted.'

'But you're taking forever and I reaaally want to go in!' Isla stamped her feet and jutted her bottom lip out, her golden curls bouncing around her ears as she did.

'Honey, I know you do but——'

'Pleeeeeeeease!' she squealed, springing on her toes as though she was about to burst with impatience.

'OK fine!' Harriet said, chucking her bag down and putting her phone into Nancy's bag. 'Look after that for me please and if it rings, come and get me?'

Nancy nodded and watched Harriet get pulled off to the water slide by Isla. She glanced over at Tommy who was still fast asleep in the pushchair and then at Jack who was playing with a stone he had found on the way there.

She touched his arm gently and waited for him to take the headphones off. 'You OK, baby?' she asked.

'Yeah.'

'What do you think of the waterpark?'

'It's loud,' he replied. 'But I like the shapes.'

Nancy smiled. He was so funny with his little ways. How could Pete say that these were stupid? She found it lovely. 'Which one is your favourite?' she asked, enjoying their one on one time.

Jack spent a few minutes looking around him, analysing all that he could see so that he could give her an accurate answer. She watched his cute little face scan the waterpark, taking in each thing that his eyes set upon. To others he might seem closed off and strange, especially when he was feeling anxious and shut off from the world, but Nancy could see past the awkwardness and lack of eye contact. She didn't see the uncooperative, difficult, attention seeking child that everyone seemed to complain about. Yes, he was hard work – sometimes she didn't know how she was going to get through it – but when you got to know him, really know him, he was the most caring, sweet, clever little soul. A part of Nancy felt special that she was one of the only people to know this side of him, like it was their little secret away from the rest of the world. But there was still a small part of her which wanted others to see him how she saw him. Maybe it would come, maybe it wouldn't. Only time would tell.

'I think it would have to be that one,' he said, pointing to the drop slide area.

'And why's that,' she probed, settling back into her lounger and making herself comfortable.

'Well, because it has straight lines. I like straight lines. The curvy ones make me feel funny.'

'Really? Funny in what way?' It was in conversations like this that Nancy learned little nuggets of information about Jack, while he didn't even realise he was talking about his thoughts and feelings.

'Just ... funny.' He still wasn't very good at articulating those feelings though. 'I like the sink.'

Nancy pulled a face. 'The sink?' Jack nodded. 'What sink?'

'The one in the room.'

'Our hotel room?' Another nod. 'Why?'

'Because it is square. It's not like the oval one at home. I like the straight lines.' He turned the stone over in his hand. It was only then that she noticed the stone was a jagged one not a smooth round one. It was sharp, pointed and full of straight edges. She smiled.

'Do you want to dip your feet in the pool, Jack?' She stood up and sat down on the edge of the pool, placing her feet in. 'Come and sit next to me.'

He did as she asked and slowly lowered his feet in. They sat there for a minute in silence and whilst Nancy would normally try to fill the silence with questions and conversation, this time she just sat. Because they didn't need words; sometimes it was enough just to have him sitting next to her.

***

'Well, well, well, look who I found,' Harriet said as she noticed Cameron swim by.

'Oh, hello!' he said, standing up and smoothing out his hair. 'How are you?'

'Good thanks, you?' She could see what Nancy saw in him, he was pretty good-looking. Although he was a little too 'nice' looking for her – Harriet liked the dark, rough and ready type. Cameron was all blonde hair, blue eyes and sweet smile. Like a model for a typical father on Christmas morning, opening presents with his children and then singing carols round the tree. Harriet liked the *I've just got home from the garage and I'm covered in grease and oil where I've been fixing cars all day*... look.

'Yeah great. You here alone?' He looked around and she could see he was clearly looking for Nancy. He might be hot, but subtle he was not.

'No, Nancy, Tommy and Jack are over there.' She pointed to the area where they were siting and could see Nancy and Jack sitting by the little pool with their feet dangling in. Tommy's pram behind them.

'Oh yeah. Her little one didn't want to come in the water?' Harriet shook her head. 'He doesn't really like water.'

Cameron nodded as if he understood and Harriet was glad he didn't press the issue as she wouldn't know what to say. It was up to Nancy who she shared Jack's autism with and Hari would never take that away from her friend. 'Are you enjoying the waterpark?'

'It's AWESOME!' Isla screamed as she splashed around near Harriet's face. 'I like getting Mummy wet on the head because she screams and screws her face up.' She giggled mischievously.

'Yes, Mummy screams because she's wearing contact lenses

and doesn't like getting her head wet,' Harriet said through a strained smile.

'Not one for water, hey?' Cameron seemed to be hiding a smile.

'It's not my favourite thing to do,' she said, tilting her head slightly. 'Nancy is more of a water person. We do a tag team when we go swimming so that one of us is always with Jack and Tommy and the other can get in with Isla. I always take the first shift because Nancy takes forever to come back so I get my turn out the way and then I can sunbathe, and she gets to act like the big kid she really is.'

'She sounds like a lot of fun,' he said looking over to her with a smile and then realising what he'd said, snapped his glance back to Harriet adding, 'not that you don't sound like fun!'

'Yeah thanks for that,' she laughed, splashing him.

'Mummy come on, I wanna go down the slide!' Isla was pulling at Harriet's arm.

'In a minute, darling.'

'Daddy, did you see me? I did a roly poly UNDER the water! My head went UNDER!' Aiden bounced over to where Harriet was standing and shook his head ferociously, spraying water everywhere. Harriet recoiled but tried to stay smiling, to show she wasn't a complete bore. However, she wasn't enjoying this at all.

'You did it, well done you! High five!' Cameron held up his hand and Aiden slapped it really hard, nearly missing it because their hands were wet. 'Woah! You nearly got my face then!' Cameron laughed.

'So, are you a single dad?' Harriet blurted out and instantly realised how random the question was by the look of surprise on Cameron's face.

'Yes,' he smiled. 'Just me and this little guy.'

'Nancy's a single parent too.' She raised an eyebrow, just subtly, but enough to make an impact. They shared a knowing smile between them and Harriet stifled a laugh.

'Are you trying to set us up?' He smiled.

'I'm just giving you all the relevant information.' She smiled and gave him a wink. 'Come on Isla, let's go on the slide.'

She walked off with a little grin on her face.

'Mummy, why are you smiling?'

'I'm just excited to go on the slide, darling. Come on, last one there is a rotten egg!'

She hopped over towards the slide, Isla screeching with pleasure as she skipped alongside her mum. Harriet knew she had probably overstepped the mark here a little bit and she wasn't sure Nancy was going to appreciate it, but she didn't care. Nancy deserved some fun and she sure as hell wasn't going to take the plunge and instigate it herself. All Harriet had done was put the idea in Cameron's head. Hopefully he would take the initiative to pursue this further. Nancy didn't need a man in her life messing things up – but a holiday romance to life her self-confidence and spirits? Who didn't want or need that? It was just a shame she couldn't have the same thing for herself.

Chapter 14

'A little birdy tells me that you like the water?'

Nancy jumped and nearly dropped her book into the pool where she and Jack were dangling their feet. 'Oh God, you scared the life out of me!' She placed her hand onto her chest as her heart pounded. Jack was so quiet next to her that she had fully immersed herself in the story and she hadn't heard him approach.

'Sorry.' Cameron smiled and sat down next to her, putting his feet in too. 'Is it OK to sit here?'

'Of course,' Nancy replied, folding the corner of the page that she was up to and placing the book down. A glance over to Jack to make sure he was OK, and then she turned her attention to the gorgeous man who she had spent the last few hours thinking about. It was weird because she hadn't so much as looked at another man since Pete had walked out, but meeting Cameron yesterday had orchestrated a huge change in her. He wasn't the first good-looking man to approach her, but maybe this was a sign that she had finally put Pete to rest in her mind. For the last year, she had been waiting for him to turn up, wondering how she would feel when he did. And when he had shown up and she'd felt nothing but anger, frustration and loss of respect, it had seemed to almost free up her mind and emotions and she found herself taking more notice of everything around her. And Cameron was one of the things that caught her attention.

'What are you reading?' he nodded his head towards the paperback, which had seen better days and was thumbed to within an inch of its life.

'Oh, it's the latest one from Martina Cole.'

He raised his eyebrows and nodded. 'Hmm, you strike me as a romance novel type of girl.'

'Why's that then? Because I'm a woman?' She tried to hide the smile as she teased him, knowing full well that wasn't what he meant.

'No, no, no, I didn't mean that, I just meant you seem like you enjoy reading about love, that's all.' He shook his head and smiled. 'It was a lame attempt at getting to know you. Sorry, let's start again. Martina Cole, that's great. Do you read a lot?'

Nancy laughed, he was sweet. 'I read when I get the chance. It's hard when you have children to actually find the time to read. I mean, you'll understand that being a parent.' She then looked around them and back to Cameron. 'Speaking of children, where's Aiden?'

'He's in the water with my sister and his cousins. Don't worry, I haven't abandoned him.' There was that cheeky smile again – it made her stomach tingle, a feeling she hadn't felt for quite some time now. She was out of touch with all this flirting business. In the lead up to Jack's diagnosis, her relationship with Pete had been pushed to the limit as the pair of them dealt with unexplained outbursts, irrational tantrums and lashing out for what felt like no good reason. The stress seeped into their daily lives like poison and as a result, all elements of fun, flirting and sex completely vanished, leaving both of them feeling even more distanced and out of sync. Shortly afterwards, Jack had been diagnosed and their marriage slowly but surely fell apart.

'You like it here then?' Nancy asked, and Cameron looked confused. 'Weren't you here yesterday too?'

'Yeah, we were, and the children had so much fun we agreed to come back today. I have a feeling this will be a regular thing for us now – if the kids get their way.'

He swished his feet in the water and Nancy couldn't help but smile. 'How many children are you away with?'

'Three including Aiden. My sister has one on the way too.'

'Wow, another niece or nephew – how exciting.' Nancy couldn't imagine having another baby, not when Jack took up so much of her time and energy. She just wouldn't be able to do it. Not that she ever thought she would be able to trust a man enough again to have children with him. *Thanks for that, Pete!*

'Yeah, she's due in September. Although I hope her hormones settle down because I'm not sure I can take much more of her mood swings – how her husband deals with it on a daily basis, I don't know.' He rolled his eyes and Nancy couldn't help herself, she gave way to the laughter, and noticed she was swishing her feet in the same way Cameron was doing.

He leaned forward to look at Jack. 'How's little man doing?'

Nancy turned back to look at Jack for herself. He was watching his favourite programme and she noticed he had begun to swish his feet too. It was comforting to see. 'Yeah he's doing OK. He's not keen on the heat but we are getting through it.'

'The heat can be tough if you're not used to it. Aiden used to hate it when he was younger. His mum used to—' He stopped suddenly, realising what he had said and decided against continuing. They sat quietly for a moment. Nancy desperately wanted to ask where Aiden's mum was, but it wasn't her business. The two were clearly separated – no big deal there – although looking at Cameron it was hard to understand why anyone would ever leave such a good-looking man!

'Well, I'd better get back to the others – don't want to give my sister any more reason to bite my head off. It was nice seeing you again, Nancy.' He stood up and left abruptly, leaving Nancy wondering if it was something she'd said. Maybe Cameron's break up was fairly new and he was still struggling with it, but he'd been the one to bring up the conversation so he couldn't blame her for that. Maybe she was better off single. Not that dating anyone would be easy with Jack. And Pete was back on the scene now, wasn't he? She didn't want him back, but he wasn't going to make things easy for her. Her life was a bit of a mess.

'It's your turn,' Harriet panted as she plonked herself down onto the lounger and exhaled noisily. 'Oh my word, that is hard work.'

'What is? Playing in the water?' Nancy laughed and shook her feet off as she stood.

'That little one had me going up and down those slide steps fifty million times.'

'You know, if you actually go down the slide, you only have to do the steps one way.'

'I am not going down that death trap – I swear, I would go over the edge. Do you see how fast they go? Not for me, thank you. Did you get drinks?'

'Um, no. I was chatting to Cameron.' She slipped her shorts and top off as she spoke, revealing her royal blue swimsuit which had a hole cut out in the back.

'So, he did come over and speak to you.' Harriet smiled, leaning her head back and closing her eyes.

'I might have known you had something to do with it.'

'I simply said you were sitting over here, that's all.' Nancy rolled her eyes and tied her long brown hair up into a bun. 'Oh, and that you were a single parent.'

Nancy dropped her hands to her sides with a slam against her thighs. 'Are you having a laugh? Please tell me you're joking?'

'What? It's no secret? You're here, with a child, and no fella – it's not rocket science!'

'I could just be on a girls' holiday with my friend and her children. Not everyone goes away with their other halves all the time. What if my partner worked in the army or away at sea – then I would have to holiday without him, wouldn't I?'

Harriet pulled herself up onto her elbows and looked at Nancy. 'Do you know, I didn't even think of that? That's a good point. Which could mean that he might not be a single parent, just because I haven't seen a woman about.'

'Actually, I think he is. He's here with his sister and her husband.'

Harriet sat bolt upright. 'Oooh, so you had a proper chat then. What else did you find out? Where's he from, what's he do, what does he look like with his kit off?'

'Harriet! The children!'

'Sorry bubs,' she said to Isla who was jiggling on the spot, desperate for Nancy to hurry up and take her back into the water.

'We didn't really talk much; he went a bit weird at the end to be honest and rushed off. Anyway, enough of this, I've got some water slides to go down. Isla, are you ready?' She gave her thumbs up and Isla squealed, running off towards the water.

'OK, don't rush back – I've got some tanning to do.'

Chapter 15

'Would you just look at that?' Harriet looked out over the pool that their room overlooked and then further into the distance. The deep navy colour of the sea, as the moonlight shone over the glistening water, was definitely a sight she would never forget. It was 2 a.m. and she and Nancy had been sitting on their balcony for the last four and a half hours since the children had finally drifted off to sleep.

'It's beautiful, isn't it?' Nancy said as she sipped her prosecco and settled back further into her chair. 'Who says you can't be in paradise when you have kids in tow?'

'I agree with you but keep the volume down eh? I don't want to wake the little angels and have to sacrifice my bit of paradise for whinging and fidgets.'

Nancy laughed and pretended to lock her mouth. Harriet smiled at her. 'Thanks for coming away with me – I know things aren't easy with Jack and I admit, I didn't really think about how it would be for you guys. I just saw the chance to take a holiday and grabbed it.'

'It's fine – we are getting through it, aren't we?'

'You sure are. Even after your shaky start with the kids'

club. What a fucking nightmare that was.' Harriet laughed and took a swig of her prosecco.

'Honestly Hari, I was this close to digging myself a hole and climbing in voluntarily. The stuff you have to go through as a parent – it's crazy. In no other job would you put up with this crap. We don't get any holiday pay, sickness pay, days off – nothing.'

'Just an endless stream of screaming, puking and shitting.' Harriet topped up both their glasses. 'They don't tell you that when you sign up to Parenthood for Life.'

'Hey, it's not all bad. There are good times too – we have to just take the crappy times alongside it.'

'Even the puking?' Harriet raised her eyebrow. 'If I could erase one thing from parenting it would be the vomit. Hands down, the worst part.'

Nancy shook her head as she gulped her prosecco. 'No, the worst part is the tantrums.'

'Are you kidding me? You're standing in a supermarket and your child starts having a tantrum. What do you do? You ignore the critter. Straight up ignore the bad behaviour – or whatever it is you're supposed to do according to the imaginary manual that no parent ever gets.'

Nancy giggled.

'But ... you're in a supermarket and your kid vomits. You're screwed. There's no ignoring that – there's puke everywhere and there isn't a hope in hell of walking away from that shit. It's definitely worse!'

Nancy slipped down further in her chair and put her feet up onto the balcony railings, making herself more comfortable. 'OK, fair enough. You win that round.'

'Rounds? I didn't realise we were playing Parenting Mistakes of 2018. I think I am currently the reigning champ of this game having won the title of Shittiest Mum every year from 2014 –when Isla May was born – through to now.'

'Oh shush!' Nancy threw a cushion at Harriet, who ducked just in time to see it go straight over the railings and land directly into the pool below. Both girls jumped up as they gasped, looking down at the floating square of fluff below. 'Crap! Do you think they'll know it's from our room?' Nancy looked at Harriet wide-eyed.

'If they do, the bill is coming your way – that was a shocking throw!'

'Hey! I used to play for the girls' cricket team at college.' Nancy pushed out her chest with pride, although she'd secretly hated it when she was there.

'You have got to be kidding me – with that arm?'

'Yeah, I only lasted three weeks. They kept putting me way out on field and I never got a look in.' Nancy sat back down. 'I do remember one game I played with them, one of the final games I played as part of the team, and there was this guy – Adam – he was the cutest boy in our year and he was the wicket keeper...'

Harriet nodded and picked up a strawberry from the bowl of fruit they were sharing.

'So anyway, this kid from the other team hit the ball so hard and I was running forward to get it and I dropped it. I was so annoyed, especially as I knew this cute guy was watching me. So I grabbed the ball as fast as I could and without even thinking, I just launched it back to him as hard as I could, not even bothering to look if the runner was back or not.'

'What happened – did you get the runner out?'

Nancy shook her head. 'No, I knocked Adam the wicket keeper out instead.'

Harriet choked as a small piece of strawberry slipped down the back of her throat when she gasped at Nancy's story. Nancy passed her some water and she gulped it down, steadying her coughs to a steady growl as she pushed down the rogue fruit piece. 'Are you serious? Is that how you normally get your guys – knock them out and drag them back to your cave!'

'Haha, I wouldn't mind but he was proper out cold. Went to hospital and everything to get checked afterwards. The helmets are supposed to protect you from that kind of thing, but my ball went into his visor – which he should have had closed so I am totally blaming him.'

'Oh!' Harriet threw her hands out wide. 'It's totally not your fault then. The guy should've worn his protective equipment correctly.'

Nancy agreed and clinked Harriet's glass. 'Hear hear!'

The girls resumed their silence as they gazed over the pool area once again.

'It really is beautiful here, isn't it? I could sit here all night and stare at this view. Look, if you lean a little bit my way, Nance, you can see the beach from here. Can you see?' Nancy did as she was asked and nodded. 'Isn't it incredible? Sometimes when I take a second to stop like this, I am amazed at what is around me.'

'That's because you spend your entire life with your nose inside your phone or your laptop – there is a world outside of your little stress bubble, you know.'

'I know,' Harriet replied but didn't pursue the conversation any further. She wasn't ready to have an honest conversation about how much work was encroaching on her life. Not yet. It wasn't like she couldn't see what Nancy was doing, constantly bringing up work. She knew her friend was trying to make Harriet see she worked too much.

'So what made you choose here?'

'Huh?' Harriet questioned.

'Ibiza – what made you book a holiday here? I don't think I ever thought of it as a family holiday resort if I'm honest – just a party island.'

'That's because you watch trashy TV and believe the stereotype. Granted there are elements of this island where you will find the partygoers, but that happens everywhere. A colleague of mine came here last summer with his family and wouldn't stop raving about it. He was showing me his snaps from the holiday and all I kept seeing was the beautiful blue sea, sandy beaches, laughing children, waterpark and lots of families. It sounded perfect for what we needed.'

Nancy nodded with a smile. 'Can't say I disagree.'

'I wanted to take you somewhere special, somewhere you would enjoy but also where Jack and the kids would have stuff to do too. I know how stressed you are with him so I figured if he had a good time, then you would enjoy it even more. But it hasn't quite been the relaxing break we both planned has it...?' Nancy smiled back at her, acknowledging the meaning behind her comment. Harriet hadn't envisaged arguing with Nancy and witnessing Jack's meltdowns as part of the holiday itinerary.

They sat for a while just listening to the music playing from Harriet's phone. The sky was a deep black with the twinkling of stars dotted throughout. They were close enough to hear the sea, which was something Harriet hadn't noticed before. At this time, in the middle of the night when everything was peaceful, the splashing of the waves was clearly audible and incredibly therapeutic.

'Hari?'

'Hmm?'

'Do you think Jack will be OK?'

Harriet frowned, turning to her friend who had gone from looking bright-eyed and laughing at her cricket story, to sombre and on the verge of tears. 'Of course, why wouldn't he?

Nancy shrugged, diverting her eyes back to the sea. 'I'm scared.'

'Why?'

'I don't want him to struggle, like, when he's older.'

Harriet felt a wave of sadness for her friend. As hard as she found parenting, Nancy was playing a whole different ball game. 'With you around him, he will be fine.'

'But, without sounding like I don't care – because I do, I love him to bits,' she nodded at Harriet as if to make sure she knew how much she meant that statement.

'I know you do, hon.'

'But ... I—' She stopped.

Harriet stayed silent as she waited for her friend to continue. She leaned forward and took Nancy's hand in hers. 'Babe, listen to me.' When Nancy didn't respond, she pressed on. 'Look at me, Nance.' Nancy did as she was asked, her hazel eyes full of sorrow. 'Don't ever feel you can't say things to me. You don't have to put on a show for me – I am your friend and I am here to help you, not judge you. Don't ever feel like you have to censor how you are really feeling. Let me in, let me help you.' This was rich coming from Harriet and she knew that Nancy knew that too. Harriet wasn't one for opening up and saying she was struggling. But this wasn't about her, at least not today.

Nancy took a breath. 'I just don't want to have to always be one step behind him apologising for him or taking control of everything he does. I want him to be comfortable and cope with things without me there.'

'And I'm sure he will cope. Try not to worry.' It was a lame response; Harriet wanted to be able to say something to her that would make it all go away, but what exactly was the right thing to say?

'What if he never learns how to cope with what life throws at him? What if he can't ever live on his own, keep himself safe?'

'All these skills come later in life. He will learn them. It doesn't matter if it takes him a bit longer, he will get there.'

Nancy exhaled, her voice giving way to a little wobble, betraying her emotions. 'Hari, what if he spends his life unhappy because he doesn't know how to cope with ... well ... anything? I'm supposed to be teaching him all these things, but I can't even take his headphones off without getting it wrong.' She hesitated. 'I am finding out new stuff about him all the time which is great but, equally, it makes me feel like I don't even know my own son.'

'That is utter rubbish and I refuse to let you wallow in this, Nancy. You're my best friend and I bloody love you to pieces and I will not let you talk yourself into thinking you're a shit mum.' Harriet was waving her finger now, she meant business.

'But Hari, what if—'

'Babe, if we spent our lives saying what if, we would never do anything! You can't run your life on *what if's* and *if only's*.' She lifted her glass. 'You also can't run your life without prosecco – drink up.' She tipped her glass and gulped, watching Nancy do the same.

She was the worst person to come to for advice. She saw things in black and white – there was no grey area and there definitely was no room for emotion in her life. But when it came to Nancy, she couldn't help but be emotionally attached and this was breaking her heart. She didn't have the answers to her friends worries, but what she did have was more prosecco – that would have to do for now.

Chapter 16

'**M**ummy, what does shit mean?'

Nancy pulled her sunglasses off her face and peered at her son, innocently sitting at the end of her sun lounger, his eyes wide in wonderment and clearly unaware of the impact of the word that had just erupted from his mouth. 'Where did you hear that word?'

'On a review,' he countered, still not flinching.

'A review? What kind of review?' The blistering sunshine was beating down onto her lightly pink skin, drying off the beads of water from where she'd recently vacated the pool.

'On YouTube.'

Bloody YouTube, she cursed under her breath. Even with the child filters on, Jack had a way of finding stuff he shouldn't. The kid was a technical wizard.

'Show me,' she said, sitting up and putting her glasses on the table to her left. She took the iPad and clicked play. The video was reviewing a television programme that Jack liked to watch on the discovery channel about ancient structures. The review was presented by teenagers and seemed to be a mock review, rather than a real one. And then, about two minutes in, she heard it.

'If you like watching programmes about shit that was built years ago – then this will be for you.'

Nancy sighed. How was she supposed to filter videos that snuck in things like this – it was impossible. Maybe she should be watching all the videos first before letting Jack? Although, how practical was that in the world of parenting?

'Sweetie, just delete that one, I don't want you watching it. Try to stay to the ones that are done by children. You know the reviews you like to watch that KIDZtV do? Those are fine.'

Nancy handed the iPad back to Jack just as Harriet returned from the bar clutching two cocktails and a bottle of water.

'Ok Mummy, but what does shit actually mean?'

Harriet snorted. 'Jeez, what sort of conversation have I just walked back into? I don't fancy your choice of topic to discuss with your seven-year-old, Nance.' And then Harriet laughed because they both knew that this would be the kind of slip up she would normally make with her children.

'Don't!' Nancy warned and then turned back to Jack. 'Sweetheart, it's a bad word – a swear word. I don't want you to worry about what it means.'

'OK.' He put his head phones on but then took them off again and looked back at her. 'It feels funny though.'

Nancy frowned. 'What does?'

'The word.'

'I don't understand.'

'The word – feels funny on my mouth when I say it. Shh-i-tttt,' he said as he broke the word down.

'Oh my word...' Nancy put her head in her hands as the woman sitting next to them with her husband glanced over to them as Jack continued his vocabulary building.

'Shh-i-tttt, shh-i-tttt, shit!'

'Ok that's enough Jack!' Nancy placed a hand on his arm to bring him out of his daydream and she could hear Harriet cackling next to her. 'I don't want you saying it anymore; it's a naughty word, OK?'

Jack nodded and then resumed his viewing at the end of her sun lounger. Nancy looked over to Harriet who was trying to contain her amusement but doing a terrible job at it. 'Don't you start!'

'Babe, he is hilarious. I love that about him – he has no idea what he's saying.' She quoted him: 'Shh-i-tttt ! He's doing his phonics bless him! I think his teacher would be impressed.'

'Ooh my word, could you imagine:

(Mock teacher voice) *Jack, what did you get up to over your half term?*

(Lowers voice*) I practised my phonics whilst I was on holiday.*

(Teacher voice*) Oh how wonderful, what did you learn?*

(Lowers voice*) Shh – I – ittt – SHIT!'*

Harriet threw her head back onto her lounger as she cackled again. 'I would pay money to see that actually happen.'

'Shut up!' Nancy pulled the cocktail that was hers from Harriet's hand. 'Give me this, I bloody need it.'

Nancy sipped her drink but then noticed the woman next to them still looking over disapprovingly. She could see her looking at Jack, sitting on the end of the lounger, his head in his iPad, and wrapped up in several layers of clothing even though it was 40 degrees and blazing sunshine. She felt the anger begin to bubble up inside, but she suppressed it. It wasn't worth the argument.

'Is there something we could help you with? Maybe you're wondering where my friend's son got his beautiful cap from with the little flap at the back to protect his neck? Did you like the orange colour or was it the polar bear on the front that got you interested?' Harriet challenged.

'Hari, leave it. It's fine.' Nancy knew what her friend was like. Fiercely protective of those around her which was a beautiful trait to have, but highly embarrassing when she didn't know when to let things go. Once she was on one, that was it.

'I wasn't staring at your child,' the woman replied, defiantly.

'Hmm, well I beg to disagree with you. Is there a problem?' Harriet was now sitting up on her lounger and Nancy put her hand on her arm to warn her to chill out. Jack was none the wiser, still fixated on his screen.

'Mummy, did you see my jump? I jumped right in and the water went in my face,' Isla giggled as she ran over from the toddler pool in front of them, her little pink tutu style swimming costume flapping as she ran, mimicking her curls.

'This is *my* child if you wanted to have another object to stare at and my baby is in the crèche – he's only one so does a lot of screaming if you wanted some more noise?'

Nancy gently pulled Isla over to her and sat her on her lap as she looked confused and a little worried at her mum's tone – she could hear she was angry.

'I wasn't staring at your child; I was simply appalled by his choice of language.'

'Oh, shit? You didn't like the word shit?'

'It's no wonder he speaks like that if he's surrounded by people like you. And with his head in his iPad – he should be out playing, not sat with that thing. That's what's wrong with parents of today, letting their offspring spend hours on tablets and computers. In my day we were all outside climbing trees and playing tag.'

'Are you for real, lady?'

'Hari, leave it.'

'No, Nance, this woman thinks she can just sit here and be all bloody judgemental about our children and our parenting when she knows nothing about our situations.' She turned around to fully face the woman. 'For your information, this woman never swears in front of her son, he has heard the word from elsewhere and simply asked what it meant. As a good parent, my friend didn't shout or berate him; she simply explained that it was a bad word and that he didn't need to know what it meant. And because he is a *child*, he commented on how the word felt and was experimenting with his sounds and learning. He wasn't abusive in the way he said it and quite frankly, I don't think he said it too loudly either.' The woman stayed defiant but Nancy could see a flicker of regret over her face as she was clearly now realising she'd picked the wrong parent to judge. 'And yes, he is on an iPad, but did you ever stop to think that there might be a reason for that?'

'What reason could you possibly have to—'

'Oh, I see,' Harriet laughed excessively over the top. 'You're a professional child psychologist, I didn't realise. My mistake!'

'I'm not a professional—'

'Exactly! You're not – so why don't you keep your nose out of our business!'

Nancy leaned forward so the woman could see her face. 'My son has autism. He struggles in social situations and doesn't like loud noises – like the screaming you can hear where the other kids are having fun. And he doesn't like changes in routine – like this holiday. So for him to feel comfortable, he likes to watch videos on his iPad and use his headphones so that the noise isn't too much. The alternative would be a breakdown, and I'm guessing you wouldn't appreciate that either, or for my son to feel anxious and very poorly. And I'm not willing to do that. He's not hurting you by sitting here minding his own business, so I would appreciate you giving him the same respect and leaving him be without feeling the need to stare at him.'

Her heart was racing. There had been numerous times over the years where people had stared and given judgemental looks to Nancy and Jack and she'd never addressed the issue. But today was different, this holiday felt different. She still had her concerns about him and his future, but she felt stronger in her approach to coping with it. Seeing Pete before she'd left had put a finality on the last few years, and now she felt like she was moving forward. Yes, she'd had a hiccup on their first day with Jack's incident with the kids' club lady, but she was starting to realise new things about her son every day. This in itself was making her feel stronger. When she heard Harriet defending Jack, she felt this overwhelming urge to take over and put the record straight. Because she wasn't ashamed of Jack.

She and Harriet clearly had different ways of handling things though.

The woman gathered up her things and began to tell her husband that they were moving away from this revolting family and something about how autism wasn't even a real thing and in her day...

'In your bloody day lady, everyone probably had their heads stuck in their arses and a closed mind. Times have changed – deal with it!'

The woman huffed and put her belongings in her bag, waiting for her husband to get up.

There was a silence between the two groups of people and the tension was high but Nancy glared at Harriet to warn her to stay quiet now – keep the moral high ground after their speech. But Isla didn't seem to get the memo.

'Nancy, what does arse mean?'

Harriet burst out laughing as Nancy put her head in her hands.

Chapter 17

Nancy walked into the reception area that afternoon to book a table for dinner that night. After consulting with the children, which had been challenging, they'd finally all agreed to eat at the buffet restaurant again as they did the pasta that Jack liked, the garlic ciabatta for Isla and Harriet was happy as long at the restaurant had gin. Everyone was a winner.

Nancy scanned the foyer whilst she waited for the woman at reception to complete her booking and was surprised to see Cameron sitting on the cushioned benches by the pool entrance, looking a bit stressed out. She watched him for a minute as he sat with one leg bent underneath him, tapping away at his phone. His face was crumpled with frustration and occasionally he would exhale in what seemed to be annoyance at whatever he was reading. Nancy figured he must be like Harriet and have work stuff that he had to keep doing whilst he was away. Nancy knew he was a single parent, but she also desperately wanted to know his back-story – he looked the type to be harbouring a complicated past.

'That's all done for you, booked for 5 p.m., just give your room number to the maître d'.'

'Thanks.' Nancy smiled as she took her card and began to leave but decided – on impulse – to turn around and say hi to Cameron. If he was busy she would just leave him to it.

She walked over to him and he must've been enthralled in what he was doing because he didn't even notice her approaching until she said, 'Hey!'

He snapped his head up in surprise. 'Oh, hey.' A smile spread across his face in welcome, but it looked strained. He had lines around his eyes – she hadn't noticed those before – and there were noticeable bags under each eye. 'How are you?'

'I'm good. You?'

'Yeah, not bad.' She could see he wasn't great.

'How's Jack doing? Is he enjoying the holiday?' His phone vibrated, and she watched him try to glance at it discreetly, his temples bulging as he read whatever message had come through. He looked back at her and smiled again with the strained smile.

'He's OK, finding it a little stressful with the heat but he's enjoying it, I think.' He was finding it more than a little stressful, but Cameron didn't need to know the ins and outs of her complicated family issues. 'How about Aiden?'

'Yeah, he's good.' He stood up. 'Listen, I'm sorry but I have to rush off. It was really nice seeing you again. Have a good afternoon.' And he didn't even wait for her reply before walking off at speed towards the stairs leading up to the rooms.

Nancy walked back to Harriet and the children, Cameron's

quick exit playing on her mind. It was the second time he'd walked off abruptly now – maybe she needed to start taking the hint. Now she was feeling like a bit of an idiot for thinking he might be interested.

'All booked?' Harriet asked, and then spotted the frown on Nancy's face. 'What's up?'

'I just bumped into Cameron. Well, when I say bumped into, he was in the foyer on his phone so I went up to him and said hi.'

'Ok, so why the frown, did he tell you he wasn't interested?'

'You make it sound like I was pestering him for a date! I'm only being friendly, I don't want anything else.'

'Yeah, likely story.'

'Hari!'

'What? He's hot, he's single, you're single ... I'm struggling to see the problem here.'

'I am not looking to tie myself up in a relationship right now – I've got all the issues at home with Pete and things are going to be more stressful once we get home and we try to get Jack into a new routine with Pete involved, I don't need the added complication.' She was saying what her head was telling her – however, she couldn't help but be a little disappointed that Cameron clearly wasn't thinking about her the way she had started to realise she was thinking about him.

'Holiday romance?' Harriet pressed. Nancy raised her eyebrow. 'Oh come on, I'm not saying you have to marry the guy, just that you deserve to let your hair down a bit. That's all.' She turned over and lay on her stomach, exposing her back for tanning.

'I don't need to let my hair down and have a holiday romance, I'm just trying to be a friend to him. His little boy was so sweet with Jack, it might be nice to try and encourage that relationship, that's all.'

'Uh-huh,' Harriet replied and Nancy could hear the smile on her face even though she had buried it into the sun lounger.

'*Anyway* ... I went over and said hi but he seemed really stressed out and said a few words then made an excuse and left. Quite abruptly I might add!'

'Maybe you've scared him off.'

'Oh, if you're going to be unhelpful then forget it.' Nancy plonked her stuff down and began stripping off, revealing her swimsuit.

Harriet pulled her face up and rested on her elbows. 'I'm not being unhelpful, I don't know what you want me to say? He's obviously having a bad day – just let him get on with it.' Nancy ignored the comment. 'I have exactly—' Harriet looked at her watch which was resting on the floor next to her phone '—32 minutes until I have to make that conference call so I'm going to grab as much sun as possible.'

Chapter 18

'Ihope you're taking a proper break and looking after those children of yours.'

Harriet stared back at her mother on the screen. She didn't know what possessed her to answer the Skype call once she had finished her conference call with work, but her mum's name had flashed up on the computer as calling and she'd clicked answer before she'd even thought about what she was doing.

'I'm taking a break, Mum.'

'So why are you in your room on your computer then?'

Harriet felt her cheeks flush red and contemplated lying. Instead she chose to bend the truth. 'I came up to the room to get Isla's goggles and saw you were calling.' It wasn't strictly a lie. She had said to Isla that she would bring her goggles back down with her once she had finished her conference call.

'Harriet, I am your mother and I can tell when you are lying. If there's one thing I hate more than salespeople knocking on my door whilst I'm trying to watch *Neighbours*, it's when people lie. And you, my darling, are lying.'

Harriet exhaled, feeling like a teenager again having been told off many times by her mum for lying when she got in late from parties after curfew. 'I just needed to make a quick conference call, so I came up to do that and am now on my way back down to the pool. Isla is playing in the water with Nancy; she's having a great time. She doesn't even know I'm gone.' This statement hurt more than Harriet liked to admit. If there was one thing she wished she was better at, it was being a mum. She sucked at it. Massively sucked at it. She had the perfect image in her head when she first fell pregnant, of juggling work and parenthood and achieving everything on both levels. In reality, she struggled to achieve consistently in both, one always had to give. Harriet's natural talent lay in the boardroom. She was incredibly good at her job and always did well in her career – which was why it made sense to start her own company. However, motherhood didn't have the same effect on her and she had to try really hard at it. She didn't like to fail at things. So rather than admit she was failing, she found it easier to pretend that everything was fine and not listen to the fact that she knew her children didn't see her as much as they should. Or that sometimes the time she spent with them was half-hearted because she was afraid to get too far in and realise how rubbish she was at it.

'And Tommy?' Her mother asked.

'What about him?'

'Where is he?'

Harriet knew the lecture that was coming as the words came out of her mouth in a defeated tone. 'He's at the kids' club.'

And here it came.

'Harriet, why on earth are you putting him in kids' club when you're away on holiday? He should be with his family. This isn't a working holiday; it's for you to be seeing those kids of yours because they need to know that Mummy is there for them, and that she doesn't always have her nose stuck in the computer.'

'I *am* there for them! I work bloody hard so that I can be there for them. You don't realise how hard it is to be a single mother who is working full-time and trying to keep a company going whilst keeping a house going too.' As soon as she said it she regretted it. She should know by now, never to answer her mum back. She would never back down. It was where Harriet got her business head from and her spunkiness in the boardroom – no one messed with her. Apart from her mum, of course.

'*I* don't understand?' The emphasis on *I* set the tone for how the rest of this argument went. 'Do you not remember how *I* juggled looking after you and your sister when your father left? And you say *I* don't know what it's like to be a single parent?'

'With all due respect mum, you weren't working though so you could afford to put in the time with us.'

'So now I'm not good enough because I wasn't working – because I was a stay-at-home mum?'

'Oh for goodness' sake mum, that's not what I am saying.' Harriet put her head into her hands and clenched her teeth. Why had she picked up the call? She should know by now, *never* pick up the call unless she had a G&T in her hand.

'I suppose your sister doesn't understand either seeing as she is *just* a stay-at-home mum.'

This was a lost cause. 'I'm not saying that Mum, and you know it. I'm just saying that I'm trying to keep my business afloat so that I can provide for my children because my arsehole of a husband didn't stick around to pay maintenance or anything, did he? He just fu— ... went off.' She curbed her language remembering who she was speaking to.

'You could provide for your children by getting a job during school hours and then being there to pick them up – I was always there for you and Bethany at the end of the day. You were never picked up by anyone else. I always made you nutritious meals – from scratch – and every time you needed a costume for a play I would spend hours hand stitching one for you. When do you ever get time to do any of that with your full-time job, huh?'

Harriet was forced to think of the throw together meals she served her children, last minute dashes to the shop for whatever costume was left the night before World Book Day (mostly superheroes) and all the times she'd spent running into the playground with her phone glued to her ear shouting *Thanks, sorry!* to the teacher who was sitting with her child because she was late – yet again. 'I'm trying my best, Mum.'

'Well, clearly you aren't trying hard enough. It's your holiday, Harriet. Get yourself down to that pool and enjoy spending some time with your children. And promise me you will go and get Tommy out of the crèche right now.'

Harriet nodded, defeated. If anyone could make her feel worse about being a shit mum, it was her own mother!

***

'Well hello there, little guy,' Nancy smiled at Tommy in Harriet's arms and then looked at her. 'Everything OK?'

Harriet was too proud to tell Nancy that her mum had given her a telling off and now she was trying to play at being a better mum for the sake of her children – and her sanity. 'Yeah, just thought he could come and do some swimming with us seeing as he's been in the club all morning.' She sat down and wriggled Tommy out of his top and trousers, ready to put him into his little swimsuit. Her phone beeped from inside her pocket and she knew instantly that it was a work email. She tensed, knowing that she should check it because it was likely to be the office feeding back about the meeting, but she could hear her mother's voice in the back of her head telling her not to dare touch that phone. She also knew it was something Nancy was aware of too, so she felt pressured not to look at the email. It was frustrating because she wanted to look at it. She enjoyed her work; it interested her – that was why she did it. She had always been a career-driven person and she genuinely found her work enjoyable, so it becoming such a big issue was causing her quite a bit of stress. Half of her wanted to engage with the office and find out what was going on because she was interested, but the other half knew that she should be making the most of this holiday and using the time to try to make progress with the children. Her head was a hard place to be at times!

'Do you want me to read it to you?' Nancy asked.

'No, it's fine, I'll check it later.' Even as she said it she knew it sounded weird coming from her mouth. She never just checked things later, Nancy was sure to know something was up.

'Is everything OK?'

'Yes,' she answered a little too abruptly. 'Why wouldn't it be?' She struggled to get Tommy into the swimsuit and he began to wriggle and whinge. 'Sit still, sweetie.'

'Well, you went to do the call and came back with Tommy and you're not checking your emails which is very unlike you.'

'Tommy sit still, I am trying to get your arm in so we can go swimming!' Tommy began to cry, and Harriet stopped what she was doing and let him fling his arm out for the fiftieth time.

After a moment, Nancy added, 'And you seem a little stressed.'

'Nancy, I'm fine!' She took Tommy's arm again and tried to get it into the suit. The heat was probably contributing to Tommy's agitation, and it certainly wasn't helping her own mood. She was normally a sun worshipper – she only had to look at a blue sky to tan. But now the blistering heat was scratching at her skin as she manoeuvred her one-year-old's spring loaded body.

'Look, do you want me to do it?' Nancy began to move towards her.

'No Nancy, I don't! I am perfectly capable of getting my

son into his swimsuit – I'm not completely useless.' She felt the tears well up and immediately blinked them back. There was no way she was shedding tears over this crap. Why was this suit so hard to put on – arms in, legs in, simple! Why couldn't she do it?

'Hari, what in God's name is wrong with you? No one said you're useless. Has something happened – did someone say something to you?' Nancy was now sitting up with concern etched on her face. As nice as it was that Nancy clearly cared about her, Harriet wished she would just drop it.

Hari softened her tone in a bid to appear like she wasn't falling apart and losing grip on everything and said, 'Nance, honestly I'm fine. Just a bit of work stress but I'm taking some time to enjoy swimming with my children and I'll sort it out later.' Nancy didn't move so Harriet added with a forced smile, 'I'm fine, honestly.'

She took a discreet deep breath and tried again with Tommy's arm, but he just wasn't playing ball at all. 'What is the deal with these wetsuits, they're impossible to get on!' Tommy's arm flung out again. 'Why can't I do this?'

'Look, I'll show you a trick.' Nancy leaned over and within a few seconds Tommy was all kitted up and ready to go in the water – he had even stopped crying.

Thanks Tommy, for making it obvious that you like your mummy's friend more than her.

'See? It's quite easy once you know how. I remember Jack being a pain when he was Tommy's age and would have a meltdown because he didn't like the feel of it going on, so I had to work out a way to get it on with minimal effort.'

Harriet smiled and pretended she had seen exactly how easy it was when in reality, it looked like Nancy had done a sweep, flick and point, and it was done. Mummy magic – something Harriet lacked.

'OK, I guess we are all set. Come on, little man, let's go swimming.' The second Harriet took Tommy he started whining and reaching out for Nancy again. Just another stab to the heart. 'Come on, Auntie Nancy is having a rest, you're coming with me.' He squirmed in her arms as she walked to the water's edge and she felt herself welling up again. What the hell was wrong with her – why was everything getting to her so much? She swallowed down the emotion and walked towards Isla who had made friends with some of the other children in the pool and was pretending to be a spider.

Harriet waded in until she was knee deep and then bent down so she was kneeling and then sat back onto her feet. As soon as Tommy's feet touched the water he screamed. Harriet quickly lifted him up in a panic. 'What is it? Did I catch your toe?' She inspected his foot, but it looked fine. She looked at the other foot. Nothing. She tried again and lowered him in, another scream and he clambered up her, digging his little nails into her shoulder.

'Ouch! Tommy, careful!' She peeled his hands off.

'He doesn't like the water, hey?' A woman near her said and smiled warmly.

And then it dawned on her; of course that was it. Why hadn't she figured that out instead of looking for an injury like an idiot? She glanced around her, the pool was heaving with people. Families, couples, parents, children – absolutely packed. She felt like everyone was looking at her. When she was at work, she didn't mind people looking at her – in fact, she got annoyed when people didn't look at her when she was addressing them or presenting something. But she knew what she was doing in that situation. Here, doing this whole parenting thing when your child had decided they would rather spend time with anyone but you, wasn't the time you wanted people looking at you and judging your every move.

She looked away from the woman, unable to make eye contact for fear of seeing the judgemental disappointed glare she was normally met with. 'Guess not,' she replied, nervously laughing. She felt the most inadequate she had ever felt. When she was at home, she had a routine and she knew what she was doing – granted, it was a hectic mess but at least she knew where she stood. But here, it was like everything was magnified; other parents were rubbing in her face how much fun they were having and how incapable Harriet was.

She tried again, gently talking to Tommy and willing him to not scream again as she lowered him towards the water. Another wail accompanied by kicking the legs and scratching her skin off her shoulder. 'OK, fine! We won't go in the water!' she said, feeling highly embarrassed. She turned to leave the pool when she felt a hand on her shoulder. She spun round to see the woman who had spoken to her a moment ago.

'I don't want to step on your toes or anything, but my little boy had a fear of water when he was a baby.' Harriet looked to the woman's little boy who was frolicking around in the pool, splashing his father and dunking his own head under the water. She turned her head back to the mum and raised an eyebrow. 'I know, he's like a totally different person now but believe me, when he was a baby, he would scream blue murder every time we went near the water.' Harriet turned to face the woman who was smiling sympathetically. 'It's tough and can be so upsetting to see them like that so I just wanted to tell you that you're not alone and to not beat yourself up over it.'

Harriet didn't know what to say in response. She wasn't used to this expression of comradery between mothers. This act of kindness between two strangers was … well, strange. It didn't feel natural so the more the woman spoke, the more uncomfortable Harriet became. She supposed, in a way, she was bit like Jack. She didn't feel comfortable with people until she got to know them. It was nice to make that little connection with him.

'I hope I haven't offended you!' Her comment snapped Harriet out of her daze. 'I wasn't trying to make you feel bad. You looked a bit stressed so I just wanted to say you're not alone, that's all.' She looked a bit worried. 'I'm Jayne, by the way.' She smiled, and the smile lit up her whole face. Her auburn, poker-straight hair, pulled over one of her freckly shoulders, was slightly tucked into her mint green costume and, as a result, gave her hair a kick of volume that Harriet could only wish for. Her own hair was about as flat as you could get it.

'Harriet,' she held out her hand formally, the only way she knew how to act when meeting new people. It had taken her years to get to the hugging stage with Nancy and even now, Nancy knew when she wasn't in the mood for touchy feely stuff. It was one of the things her husband had commented on when he'd left.

'You're so closed off – I feel like you're shutting me out all the time. If you're not at work you're planning work at home. You won't let me touch you, not even give you a hug. It's like you're married to your job! I'm supposed to be your husband, for crying out loud!'

The words still stung when she thought about it. But he didn't understand, Harriet felt as though no one did. A woman was expected to be naturally maternal. Any woman who said they didn't want children was seen as a monster in this society. But Harriet *did* want children – she just wanted her career too. And if you wanted to get anywhere in life, you had to make sacrifices. And her marriage had been one of those sacrifices. She didn't have the time – or emotional capacity – to have a husband as well as a demanding job alongside her two children. Something had to give. It was damn hard though and she really missed having that extra person to bounce off or to moan to when things were rough. Not that she would admit that to anyone! She never told anyone, not even Nancy, that some days she regretted not doing more to save her marriage. She wished she'd spent more time nurturing her relationship instead of whittling away hours at the computer. She had never been good at that balance – it was something she desperately wanted to change. She just didn't know how.

'Nice to meet you, Harriet, and who's this handsome little guy?' Jayne put her finger inside his hand and he gripped it, giving her a huge smile. 'Oh, you're adorable and look at that little toothy peg coming out up the top!'

Harriet found herself smiling at her son who was quite the little charmer, she realised. She then felt a pang of guilt as she realised that she had spent so much time juggling everything over the last year since he was born that she felt she didn't really know who he was. She didn't know he didn't like water. She didn't even know he had another tooth coming out at the top. Why had it taken this stranger noticing for Harriet to see how bad things had got? That fact alone was so disheartening. She was a work-a-holic, yes, but she always felt like she had her children's best interests at heart. But she was missing things, big things. She had to try to figure out a way to balance things better when she got home – otherwise, Tommy and Isla were going to grow up resenting her. The idea of that made her feel sick. How could trying so hard to do the right thing for your family be so damaging at the same time? It was draining.

'This is Tommy,' she said, rubbing her finger down his chubby cheek and almost melting when he looked at her and smiled. He hardly ever smiled at her. 'And my little girl is over there with the rainbow swimsuit on.' Just talking about the children made her a little emotional.

'Well, Tommy you are just adorable and I love the rainbow suit your sister has on!' Jayne pointed over her shoulder. 'That's my husband, Richard, with our son Frankie and over by the slide with the purple swimsuit, that's April, our daughter.' She turned back to Harriet. 'Have you been here long?'

'We arrived three days ago. You?'

'We are on day five. Still have a few more days though so no need to start thinking about work yet, hey?' she laughed.

'Oh, you work?' It came out sounding a little patronising. 'I mean, what do you do?' She was back on familiar ground talking jobs.

'I'm a freelance editor. How about you, do you work?'

'Yes, I run my own marketing company.'

'Oh, how exciting – your own business. And you have two children. Hats off to you – you must be like a super mummy! I struggle to get work done and I'm only part-time.' She was beaming, and her eyes lit up every time she flashed a smile. Harriet found herself smiling along reflexively.

It was meant as a compliment, but Harriet felt like a liar, this woman thinking she was totally acing parenthood when really, she was holding on by the skin of her teeth! 'It's not easy but we get by.'

'Well good for you, are you here alone or with family?'

'I'm here with my friend, Nancy, and her little boy.' She pointed over her shoulder back to the loungers where Nancy was fully reclined and holding a paperback above her head, with Jack now back at the loungers, resuming his usual position.

'How lovely, a girls' holiday, hey?' Jayne smiled. 'Well, I'd better get back to the others. I just wanted to say hi – I'm sure we'll see you around the complex. Just don't give up with the water and this little one.' She tickled Tommy's feet and he giggled. 'He'll get over it, you just need to persist and don't worry about what others think when he screams – he's a child, they all scream.' She gave a friendly smile before turning and going back to her family.

Harriet felt a burst of confidence after chatting with Jayne and decided that she wouldn't give up and *would* get Tommy in the water and loving it even if it was the last thing that she did. She bent down again and dipped his feet in – he responded with an almighty wail and threw his arms up, scratching Harriet in the eye and knocking her sunglasses off her head into the pool where she trod on them, snapping them clean in half.

'OK, maybe we'll try another day.' She grabbed the remains of her glasses and stomped back to the safety of the sun loungers.

Chapter 19

Sorry to be a pain – I know you're going to hate me but
I can't do this.

Nancy looked at the text message that had pinged up on her
phone and felt her world crumble a little bit. She checked
that Jack was still lying on the bed, amused, and then replied.

What do you mean?

She knew what he meant but she needed to hear it from him
properly. None of this coded crap, she needed him to say the
words so that she knew exactly what she was dealing with.
Her hands were shaking with anger. She didn't have to wait
long for a reply.

I'm not good at all this sort of stuff and he would be
better off without the disturbance. Without me. I'm sorry

She closed the message and pressed call on Pete's name. It
must've rung about fifteen times before cutting off. She tried

again but this time it went straight to voicemail – he had switched his phone off. She walked into the bathroom so that Jack couldn't hear her and lowered her voice.

'Don't you *dare* do this to our son! He deserves better than to be messed around again.' She hadn't actually told Jack about Pete coming back which was a touch of luck – but Pete didn't have to know that. 'Yes, it's hard, it's damn hard, but he is your son and you don't get the choice to pick and choose whether you fancy being a dad or not and you can't keep changing your mind. He needs you in his life, no matter what kind of lowlife you're turning out to be. If not for anyone else, do it for him. Call me when you get this!'

She hung up and found she was shaking even more. She threw the phone onto the side of the sink and took a deep breath. Why had she thought that he was going to be anything but a let-down? She should've known the moment he'd stepped out of her life that he wasn't worth chasing. But she wasn't doing it for her, she was doing it for Jack and no matter how much she disliked Pete, he was Jack's daddy. She jumped at the sound of her phone as it beeped another message through, moving across the table as it vibrated.

I don't want to talk, stop calling me. It's done – I'm done. Sorry

She groaned and dropped her phone to the floor, sitting down on the toilet lid and putting her head into her hands. Tears began to stream down her face and she gave into the uncontrollable sobs. She felt like she had let Jack down and now it really was just the two of them against the world. She had felt a little ray of hope when Pete had come back, and had almost dared to imagine getting some help, some support with it all. And then he did this again. What a mess.

'Knock knock!' Harriet chirped through the bathroom door. 'Can I come in?' She opened the door before Nancy had a chance to reply or wipe her face. 'Oh no, what's up?'

'Pete,' Nancy squeaked and then blubbed again.

'OK, hang on,' Harriet left the bathroom for a few minutes and then returned with a glass of something clear in both hands. 'Talk to me.' She handed Nancy the glass, sitting on the floor by her feet.

'What's that?' Nancy eyed the liquid suspiciously.

'What do you think?'

'Gin?'

'Exactly. Drink up and tell me what the prick has done now.' Harriet shifted back to lean against the marble-edged bathtub, crossing her legs ready for the gossip.

Twenty minutes later, in between sobs, Nancy had relayed to Harriet what Pete had said, including the details of when he had come to see her before they left for Ibiza.

'Right, what you need is a plan.'

'A plan?'

'Yep, you don't want to have to rely on that lowlife for anything – I know you haven't for the past year anyway but we need to get you strong and independent, so Jack has a stable home life and nothing can break that.'

'Ok … so you mean, like a new job? You know it isn't that

easy for me. Work at the moment is ideal because I can say no to a day's work when Jack has a bad day.'

'Yes, but that doesn't pay the bills Nancy!'

'I can't help that though, can I?' Nancy replied, feeling defensive. 'I am trying my best with what I've got. I can't change jobs just like that, Harriet.'

'It doesn't have to be a full time job. What are your restrictions?' Harriet pulled out a notepad and pen from the bag over her shoulder and began scrawling.

'You're in your element, aren't you?' Nancy laughed, sliding off the toilet and joining her best friend on the floor. 'Taking control and formulating a plan – I'm not one of your projects you know.'

'I know, but you could be. I'll help you, we are going to sort your life out and make Pete regret leaving.'

'And what about you? Shall we sort yours out afterwards?' Nancy grinned because she knew the reply before it came.

'My life doesn't need sorting out.' Harriet dismissed the comment, but Nancy knew that she'd have to address it soon. But now wasn't the time. 'So ... your restrictions?'

Nancy took another sip and finished her gin. 'Needs to be school hours and term time only – I can't use a childminder or anything because it's out of routine for Jack, he needs me.'

'OK, that's fine. What else?'

'Something that I could potentially either do at home all the time or have the option of working from home on difficult days when Jack has a bad day and doesn't go into school.' There were too many of those to count at the moment. He spent more time at home than at that school.

'OK, so that's the job brief. Life-wise, what do you need to get in place for Jack?'

Nancy sighed. 'I need to either sort out the school he is currently at or I need to find a new one where the staff actually want to help him rather than isolate him.' Just thinking about the recent meeting with the school where Nancy had been told that Jack spent a lot of time with his one to one support teacher in the art cupboard because he struggled within the classroom environment just made her feel physically sick. 'I want him to be with other children, not kept out of the way like a crazy child.'

'Understandable. OK, so finally, what about you?'

'What about me?'

'What are your goals – what's missing from your life at the moment and what do you want?' Harriet tapped her lip with her pen.

'I hope you're not referring to a man because quite honestly, after today, I'd consider turning gay and marrying you over getting into another relationship.'

Harriet raised her eyebrows, 'Honey as much as I love you, you couldn't handle me. Plus I haven't got time for a relationship so you'd be shit out of luck with me, I'm afraid.' She winked and tore off the paper. 'OK, here's your initial draft life plan. We are going to sort you out – don't you worry.'

Nancy took the paper and then smiled. 'Thanks Hari, I don't know what I'd do without you.'

'You would be absolutely fine without me, I am just helping you get there faster, that's all.'

Nancy shook her head. 'No, you're not. You have made the

situation so much better. I think just talking about it with you has helped, even if we didn't have your foolproof life plan on paper.' She smiled cheekily. 'Honestly though, I really think it is time I made some big changes in my life. I am fed up with being miserable and letting the days tick by. Ever since Pete left, I feel like I've lost my sparkle; I just plod along, every day is the same.'

'So then do something about it,' Harriet countered.

'It's easier said than done.'

'There you go again, making excuses. Forget about Pete, forget about work and forget about anyone else but you and Jack. What do *you* want to do with your life?'

'I don't know.' She felt scared by the prospect of making big decisions about her life. Having everything plod along had its benefits – it was easy. She knew exactly what was happening. 'Making changes scare me.'

'That's good. If it didn't scare you then I would be worried. Nance, you're still young and you have so much of your life ahead of you. You shouldn't be wasting time stressing over the likes of Pete. You need to think about you. I am not saying you have to find a man, but let your hair down, enjoy life. Think about what you want to do job-wise, this could be your chance to try something new. And just, you know, live! Jack will be OK without Pete – he has coped this last year, hasn't he?'

Nancy nodded as she felt her self-confidence swell. 'You're right.'

'Of course I am right, I'm always right.' She poked her tongue out. 'Now come on soppy, let's get the kids dressed and get down to the entertainment complex – I hear there's some show on and two-for-one cocktails.'

Chapter 20

'Look, over there!' Harriet pointed to a table on the far side over by the front of the stage. 'You go grab the table and I'll get some drinks.' She began to walk off before Nancy even had a chance to respond. Harriet reached the bar area and set about reading the cocktail menu. They needed something fruity and strong – today was shaping up to be quite a stressful day for the pair of them so Harriet was determined for it to end on a high.

'I'd recommend a Singapore Sling, it has quite a kick to it.'

Harriet jumped and looked up startled to see Cameron smiling back at her. 'You scared the life out of me – do you always creep up on women like that?'

'OK, you make me sound like a pervert weirdo.' He frowned, and Harriet laughed.

'Hey, I'm not the one creeping up on women and whispering in their ear.' She shrugged to add weight to her words.

'Let's not continue down this trail of thought.' He grabbed the menu and opened it up. 'But seriously, get the Singapore Sling, it's amazing.'

'Well, I might just do that; I'll tell Nancy it comes as a recommendation from you.'

He nodded, not taking his eyes off the menu. 'And can you tell her I said sorry for being a bit off earlier?'

Harriet leaned on the bar looking at him. 'And why exactly can you not tell her yourself? I'm not your messenger.' Maybe she should become a professional matchmaker – she was having far too much fun with this.

He looked back up at her. 'I know ... I ... um ... can't.'

'You, um, can't what?' She retorted. 'She's sitting just over there.' She pointed to the table where Nancy had set up and was currently bouncing Tommy up and down on her knee. Harriet felt the disappointment settle in her stomach as she realised he must've woken up – she was hoping he was going to be down for the night. She could never fully relax when the children were around her. She always felt like she was fighting a losing battle, trying too hard at something that technically she should be a natural at. She found it so draining, but she had her professional image to uphold, and she couldn't be seen to be struggling. And she really did want to enjoy it – she just wasn't sure she knew how.

'Well, you see, I'm here tonight with my sister and her husband and, well, we're sitting all the way over there and I need to get the drinks back to them. If you could just send my apologies, I'd really appreciate it.' He smiled and then walked off back to his table, no drinks in his hands.

Harriet frowned as she watched him leave. He was acting strange, just like Nancy had said.

Moments later she was back at the table handing Nancy her drink.

'What is it?' Nancy asked, eyeing up the liquid suspiciously and then taking a sip. 'It's strong!'

'Yep and it comes recommended by none other than the very sexy Cameron.' Harriet noticed the change in Nancy's face. 'That's right, he's here tonight and sitting right over there.' She pointed to his table on the far side. He had his back to them, but you could very clearly see it was him. His broad shoulders sporting a tight fitted white T-shirt against the navy chino shorts he was wearing. He was leaning across the table talking to his son who was laughing hysterically at something. The pair looked the perfect father-son picture.

Nancy slapped her hand down. 'Don't point!' she hissed. 'I don't want him thinking we are talking about him.'

'But ... we *are* talking about him.' Harriet sipped the pink liquid – it was surprisingly sweet.

'But we don't want him to know that, do we!'

'He has his back to us, will you chill out. Anyway, as I was saying before you assaulted me – he told me to pass on a message.' Harriet took pleasure in watching Nancy's face instantly show interest as she turned to face her. 'He said to apologise for being stroppy with you this morning.'

'I told you he was being weird!'

'Yes, and I totally agree.' Harriet sat down and leaned in a little. 'He was weird with me too. I invited him over to speak to you himself and he went all funny and said he couldn't and then walked back to his table without even taking his drinks with him.'

'So now *you're* scaring him off,' Nancy laughed.

'Listen, I know the guy is hot, but I'm not sure he's the full ticket. Maybe you should let this one go.'

'For the last time, I am not chasing him! No men in my life right now apart from Jack.' Nancy sipped her drink. 'And Tommy, of course' she added, tickling his toes.

'Yeah, so why is he up? Did he wake up by himself or did Isla poke him?' This had become a regular thing of late. Harriet didn't know if it was a jealousy thing or an attention thing, but Isla quite often woke her brother up so he would start crying.

'No, she didn't this time, he just woke up himself. I wonder if he's teething because his face is all rosy and he is dribbling like a trooper!'

'Yeah, he's got one through at the top – it's only just come in.' She didn't tell Nancy that it was in fact a stranger who had noticed this before his own mother did. And right on cue, he started whinging and rubbing at his face. 'Here, do you want me to take him?' Harriet reached out and took Tommy, and his crying increased. It felt like every time she held him or picked him up, he either started crying or his crying intensified. She couldn't do anything right. It was like he could smell the fear, could sense that she was winging it. She bounced him on her knee and gently shushed him, hoping it would be calming and soothing. But instead, it came out a little erratic and forced.

'Have you got any medicine to give him, take the edge off a bit?'

Harriet shook her head. Did Nancy know her at all? If you

looked inside her bag you would find money, keys, perfume, her diary and a pack of mints. Even her changing bag was a little on the sparse side – always running low on nappies and wipes, all the essentials!

'Here, I've got some of these sachet things – they're great for on the go. You can have one of these.'

Harriet took the sachet from Nancy and tried to open it with one hand whilst holding onto Tommy with the other as he wriggled and moaned. 'I can't bloody do this with one hand, open it for me?' She felt his head. 'Does he feel hot to you?'

Nancy opened the sachet and then touched his forehead. 'Yeah, a little. This will help with his temperature, bless him.'

Harriet squeezed the contents of the sachet into Tommy's mouth as he flipped his head from side to side, refusing to take it.

'Well, we managed about half the sachet, which is good considering Tommy has turned into the girl from *The Exorcist* and practically rotated his head backwards to avoid it!' Harriet wiped her face with the back of her hand. 'How the hell did I get it on my eyebrows?'

'Mummy, I need a wee.'

'OK, hang on a minute, let me just settle Tommy first.'

'No, *now*, I need a wee *nowwww*.'

'Isla, sweetie, you will have to wait a moment.'

'Why don't I take you?' Nancy smiled at Isla but she wasn't having any of it.

'No, Mummy take me.' She pouted.

'You're just being difficult because I have Tommy on my

lap, aren't you?' Harriet turned to Nancy. 'She keeps doing this, I don't know if it's a sibling jealousy thing?'

'Might be, it's fine. You take her, here, give me Tommy.'

Harriet handed over her son to Nancy. Tommy had thankfully stopped crying but was still a bit wriggly and whiny.

'Come on then, you.' She took her daughter's hand and led her to the toilet.

'Mummy?' Isla said, coming to a halt outside the toilet.

'Yes darling?' Harriet replied.

'Bend down here for a minute?' Her rosy cheeks bulged as she smiled up at Harriet.

'I thought you wanted a wee?'

'I want to whisper something in your ear.' She waved her hand, indicating for Harriet to bend down. As Harriet did, Isla moved Harriet's hair away from her ear and leaned in. 'This is the best holiday ever!' she whispered.

Harriet leaned back, shocked at the sweetness from her daughter. 'Aw sweetie, that's lovely. What has been your favourite bit?' They may have been crouched in a hallway in the entertainment complex with the dull hum of the DJ talking from the hall and various staff running around them, but this moment meant more to Harriet than she could even voice.

'My favourite bit is you.'

'Me?' Harriet frowned. 'What do you mean?'

'I get to see you and play in the water with you and eat yummy food.' She leaned in again for a cuddle and this time she squeezed and didn't let go.

Harriet fought back the tears. Isla wasn't jealous of her brother taking Harriet's time, she was jealous of her work.

Things definitely had to change now. She wrapped her arms around Isla and squeezed her back. She would treasure this moment forever.

***

Nancy looked down at Tommy slowly settling in her arms. She could remember when Jack had been this small. His perfect little toes and his perfect little face. What she would give to be back at that time when everything had seemed perfect. Happily married with a beautiful bouncing baby boy. And then everything had changed. Pete had become distant, Jack struggled with everything and Nancy saw her perfect life slowly fall apart, piece by piece.

She wouldn't change Jack for the world and she loved him with every inch of her soul, but things were hard, life was hard. And ever since his diagnosis it had felt as though things were getting worse. Knowing what was wrong with Jack had made everything seem more real and there was no more hiding away from the fact that her son had a condition that meant he found the world incredibly hard to live in. Nancy wanted to take all his anxieties away and let him be the child he deserved to be, but she couldn't, nobody could, and that was what hurt the most. When most children went to their mothers for support and reassurance, Jack went into himself and pushed everyone else away. He didn't like cuddles like Tommy did and he hated being touched. Nancy grieved for the little boy she wanted and for that, she felt incredibly guilty. Mum guilt was a bitch!

After a few moments Tommy drifted off. His forehead was clammy and his little cheeks were rosy red. She cuddled him closer, resting her lips on his forehead as she soothed him.

'Poor little guy, his teeth?'

Nancy jumped and looked over her shoulder at the soft voice behind her. 'Hi,' she said and smiled.

'May I?' Cameron gestured to the chair to Nancy's left and she nodded for him to take it. As he sat down, Nancy watched him look down at Tommy and smile before meeting her eyes. 'I wanted to say I was sorry about this morning, I rushed off and I think I may have appeared a little rude and that wasn't my intention.'

'It's fine, don't worry about it.' Nancy shrugged it off but then decided to be brave and ask, 'I hope everything was OK? You seemed a little stressed.' She didn't feel as vulnerable with Tommy in her arms. He was acting like a barrier between them and it gave her a little extra confidence to ask questions she might not normally ask somebody she didn't really know. Cameron noticeably closed off a little when she asked, and she knew she had pushed it. He wasn't about to open up to her and that was fine; they hadn't known each other long.

'Yeah it's fine, just life, you know? Can get a little stressful at times.'

'You're telling me,' she said, almost under her breath as Tommy wiggled and had a little groan.

'Little guy not feeling well?' He leaned forward, placing his forearms onto his thighs and lessening the gap between them quite considerably. Nancy gazed back into his deep blue eyes and for a moment neither of them spoke. The sexual tension between them was intense. It wasn't like anything Nancy had felt for a very long time and part of her felt guilty for that. She'd had a lot of good times with Pete, but towards the end, life had just got too much for them ... and now, feeling how she did when she was lost in Cameron's eyes, she started to question whether Pete leaving might be a blessing in disguise

Nancy forced herself to avert her gaze, looking back down to Tommy. 'He's just had some medicine so once that kicks in he'll be sound asleep. Nothing like a good night's sleep, eh?'

Cameron guffawed. 'I wouldn't know – what's one of those?' And he laughed, but Nancy sensed there was truth in what he said. Tommy started crying again. 'Have you tried putting him up against your shoulder and patting him on the bum?' Nancy looked at him and pulled a face. 'I know he's not a baby baby but I remember when Aiden was his age he still liked to have that gentle tapping when he was feeling a bit under the weather. Sort of a comfort thing.' He shrugged. 'Just a thought.'

Nancy manoeuvred Tommy round and tried what had been suggested. And amazingly, after a moment, he stopped crying and settled again, nuzzling his face into Nancy's neck.

'Well get you, Mr Genius. Shall we start calling you Father Teresa?'

Cameron held out his hands. 'What can I say, I'm a pro.'

He smiled and Nancy noticed it lit his whole face up. He had a warm, gentle face and it was a stark contrast to the strained smile he had given her this morning. The more she studied his face, the more she realised just how much she liked looking at it.

'So, judging by your wealth of knowledge, I take it you have always been a hands-on type of father?' It was quite a forward question for Nancy. Maybe it was the cocktail, or the baby barrier shield she had with Tommy, but she felt relaxed enough with Cameron to delve a little below the surface with him. After all, she was on holiday. If she messed up then she would never have to see him again. Unless it came to light that he lived round the corner from her – then she really would be in trouble.

'You could say that. From the moment Aiden was in my life I have made it my mission to make sure I'm always right there for him whenever he needs me. I wasn't interested in being the dad that moans about getting up in the night or pretends to be asleep when the baby wakes up crying. Each to their own, but Aiden was my little miracle and I love every moment with him. Although I am a lot less smiley at 3 a.m.' He winked at her.

'Oh, so you decided to come over yourself then?' Nancy heard Harriet's voice as she crossed the dancefloor, even over the music playing. She inwardly cringed at her friend's bluntness and glanced at her, willing her with her eyes to not wind him up. Clearly Harriet didn't get it. 'We were starting to think you were the new Jekyll and Hyde.'

Cameron looked confused at Harriet's reference to the split personality and Nancy shook her head at him to indicate to just ignore her friend.

'Is he asleep now?' Harriet asked, peering over Nancy's shoulder.

'Yeah I think so.' Nancy could feel her neck starting to

sweat as Tommy nuzzled further into her. She pulled her long brown hair to one side to try and cool down and desperately hoped that the bead of sweat she could feel on her top lip wasn't noticeable to Cameron; she casually wiped at it when he wasn't looking. Tommy gave a little cough and wriggled.

'So will you be joining us for a drink, Cameron? Where's your little one?' Harriet picked up her phone and swiped it so it lit up. A casual gesture that would go unnoticed by anyone, but Nancy knew she was discreetly checking her phone for emails. And she could see on the screen that she had an array of notifications already spread out on her home-page.

'No, I won't stay. You girls don't want me sticking around. I just wanted to come and apologise.' He turned to Nancy and looked her right in the eyes. She hadn't had this much eye contact from a guy in she didn't know how long, and she was enjoying the attention. 'It was really nice to see you again,' he said and rested his hand temporarily on her elbow before giving it a gentle squeeze as he stood up. 'Maybe we can grab a coffee or something before you go home?'

'I'd like that,' she found herself saying. And the pair of them stared at each for a second, their gazes interlocked, the sexual chemistry ramping up a notch.

And it was at that moment that Tommy lifted his head and vomited all down Nancy's chest.

Chapter 21

'I am *so* sorry.' Harriet gasped, pulling Tommy off Nancy.
'It's fine, honestly. He can't help it, poor guy.' She passed
Tommy over to Harriet as he began whining and retching for
a second time. 'Here, give mummy a cuddle, little man.' As
she handed him over it was a matter of seconds before
Cameron reappeared beside her holding an armful of tissues
from behind the bar. She hadn't even seen him leave.

'Here, let me help you.' He started passing her the tissues
and then squatted down to wipe the floor.

'You don't have to do that!' Nancy called down to him. 'I'll
do it.'

'It's fine, won't take me a second.'

Nancy continued to wipe down her top, trying her best not
to heave. It became clear that she wasn't going to be able to
save her top so she admitted defeat and took it off. As she
did, she saw Harriet's face whip round to her in shock. 'It's
OK! I've got a top on underneath,' she laughed.

'Thank God for that, here I was thinking you were about
to give Cameron a little show as a thank you.'

Cameron held his hands up. 'Hey, I wouldn't say no.' Harriet laughed but Cameron reacted to Nancy's shocked face. 'I'm joking.'

'I don't think he was,' Harriet piped up.

'Shut up, the pair of you.'

'Listen, I'm going to take this guy back to the room, I'll take the kids with me and you two have a drink. As a kind of thank you and apology.'

'Hari, you don't have to apologise, it's not something you can help – he didn't do it on purpose.' Nancy looked at Tommy who was still crying.

'Well anyway, stay here and have a drink. Cameron, you're not going anywhere are you? You'll keep Nancy company?'

'It's fine, I'll come back to the room with you. You don't want to be sitting up there on your own.' Nancy began to gather up her bag and phone but Harriet walked over and put her hand on top of Nancy's.

'Honestly, it's fine. I need to get some work done anyway so please, just stay here and relax.'

'I know what you're doing!' hissed Nancy. 'Stop trying to set me up.'

'I'm not!' Harriet hissed back. 'I'm not asking you to marry the guy but he just cleared up my son's vomit – at least have a drink with him to say thanks.'

Harriet had a point. 'OK fine, but you don't have to take the children, leave them here with me, they can enjoy the disco and I'll bring them up with me in a bit.'

Harriet nodded. 'OK, if you're sure.'

'Positive.'

'Daddy! There you are!' Aiden came running over holding

a cup with a bright blue mixture in. 'Aunty got me this slushy and look.' He poked his tongue out revealing a bright blue slash of colour.

'Woah!' Cameron replied. 'Can I have a try?' Aiden passed over the cup and Cameron took a sip and scrunched his face up in reaction. He turned to the girls. 'This stuff is like pure sugar – far too sweet for me.'

'Right, I'm off, Cameron thanks again for helping. Enjoy your eve. Nance, I'll see you in a bit.' Harriet turned to Isla who was jumping around on the dance floor. 'Isla, I'm taking Tommy back to the room because he's feeling poorly. Stay here with Nancy, OK?'

'I want to come with you!' Isla wailed and run over to Harriet, grabbing onto her leg.

'You don't want to stay here and do some more dancing?' Isla shook her head and pouted as Tommy began wriggling in Harriet's arms. 'OK that's fine, come with Mummy then.'

Nancy watched Harriet walk off. 'I feel bad,' she said to Cameron as they sat back down at the table.

'Why?'

'Well, because it's Harriet's holiday too and she's going to be sitting in that room with two grumpy children.'

'Didn't she say something about working?'

'Yes, I suppose. No change there.' Nancy said it before she remembered who she was with.

'Works a lot, does she?'

Nancy nodded. 'Yeah but she has to, she's incredible. She like a machine, just works works works – even on holiday.'

'Why isn't she using this time as a break?'

Nancy sipped at her drink. 'She's had a tough few years; she runs her own business so she can't let things slip.'

'Is it just her or does she have employees – surely they can hold the reins whilst she's away?'

'Well, you would think so, but clearly not. I don't think she trusts that they'll do a good enough job. It's like she feels she has a point to prove to everyone, but I don't know why she puts up the pretence for me, we've known each other for years. But as long as she's happy, plus, she's a bit of a perfectionist so I only get my head bitten off if I suggest any different anyway.'

'I can understand that.' Nancy glanced at him. 'I mean, I'm not a perfectionist but I am the same about letting other people do work for me and thinking I can do it better if I do it myself. But sometimes you have to admit that enough is enough and take that break.'

Nancy swivelled on her chair to face Cameron a bit more. 'OK, so come on then, what is it you do?'

He smiled. 'What do you think I do?'

'Oh God, this could go seriously wrong.' Nancy laughed and then took in his appearance. 'OK, so you dress fairly casual – but then again, you are on holiday so I guess you wouldn't be wearing a suit.'

'Correct.'

'Do you wear a suit for work?'

'No.'

'Hmm, do you wear a uniform?' Images of sexy firemen, police officers and army cadets sprung into her mind and she sipped again at her drink to hide the smile spreading across her face.

'Yes I do have a sort of uniform – you can wipe that smirk from your face too. I know what you're thinking.' A cheeky side smile spread over his lips.

Nancy held up her hands. 'What! I didn't say anything.'

'You didn't have to, that glass can't hide the dirty smile that crept across your face as you pictured me in uniform.' Nancy giggled. 'It's not the kind of uniform you would initially think of though,' he said and stood up. 'I'll leave you with that nugget of information and get us some more drinks. Will Jack want a drink?'

Nancy glanced over to the stage steps where Jack was sitting with his iPad and noticed that Aiden was talking to him again. She clammed up, feeling anxious that Jack would ignore him as before. 'He's OK; he has a drink still on here.'

Cameron walked off and Nancy continued to watch her son, fixated on the screen, headphones on. Here was the perfect opportunity to make a friend and he just sat staring at his iPad. Nancy felt a mix of frustration and sadness. She didn't understand why it was so hard for him. She was watching Aiden climbing up onto the steps and then to the stage and then jumping off onto the dance floor, giggling and doing it again. He was so happy. After a moment, Jack lifted his gaze and watched Aiden. He didn't try to talk, or interact in any way, but he watched him. He looked interested and that alone was enough to relax Nancy a bit.

Nancy was in her own little world when Cameron came back to the table holding a jug and two glasses. 'Don't ask me what it is, I asked for something fruity and this is what they gave me.'

Nancy eyed the blue mixture suspiciously. 'Looks a lot like the blue slushy Aiden had.'

Cameron's face changed. 'You're right...' He took a sip and started laughing.

'What?' Nancy found herself smiling.

'I think the barman has had me on – I think it *is* slushy!'

They both burst out laughing. 'Haha, well you did ask for something fruity.'

Cameron put his glass down and walked off again as Nancy poured herself a small glass full and tried it. She recoiled as the sugary liquid hit the back of her throat and practically spat it out into glass.

A few moments later, Cameron returned with an orange-coloured juice inside another jug and a fresh two glasses. 'Let's try this again, shall we?' he said as he sat down. Nancy watched him pour the orange liquid between two glasses.

'Apparently they have a running joke behind the bar to see who will notice that they've been given slushy instead of a cocktail and because I wasn't looking when he made it, I fell for it.'

'You wally! I bet you watched this one though? So what went into this then? '

'Are you testing me?'

'Well, I need to know that I am drinking a legitimate drink and not orange juice with popping candy in.'

Cameron nodded. 'Fair play. OK, so this is called a Sloe Screw.'

Nancy was drinking at the time and spat out the contents of her drink back into the glass as she laughed.

'Nice! That's attractive.' Cameron laughed as he passed her a tissue.

'I'm so sorry!' She tried to hide her face in embarrassment.

'Nice to see what maturity level I am dealing with tonight.' He winked at her.

Nancy laughed and shook her head. 'Honestly, I am a very mature adult and was simply coughing because it went down the wrong way.'

'Yeah yeah, likely story. So anyway, shall I continue or shall we talk about bums, bogies and boobies for a bit?'

Nancy play slapped him on the arm and he smiled cheekily at her. 'Enough! I'm fine, continue.'

'So, Sloe Screw…' He paused dramatically, waiting for her to snigger but she put on a strong face and poked her tongue out. 'This cocktail consists of sloe gin – hence the name – vodka and orange juice.'

'I love sloe gin – we used to go sloe berry picking when I was a kid and Mum would make sloe gin every Christmas.'

'Which you enjoyed … as a kid?'

'No! I would just pick the berries with mum, she drank the gin!' She smiled, she loved how easy and playful this conversation was. Everything in her life recently had been so serious it felt refreshing to relax and be silly for once. She sipped at the drink and felt the warm memories of Christmas wash over her. 'Although as I got older, I did indulge in trying the gin too.'

'There it is! The truth shall out.' He clinked her glass.

She smiled. 'This drink makes me feel festive, I feel like I want to sing carols round the Christmas tree and eat roasted chestnuts.'

'Your Christmases sound like they're straight out of an old black and white movie!'

'Ha, I loved Christmas time – when I was younger it was so traditional with a real tree, carols, no TV, just playing games and spending time with the family.' She smiled as she reminisced.

'My Christmases were more like Home Alone.'

Nancy looked at him confused. 'You spent your Christmases trying to stop burglars from entering your house?'

'Hah! Not quite, I mean my family would go away every year so we never spent Christmas at home.'

'And ... they forgot you one year?'

He shook his head, 'No.'

'So ... you went to New York one year?'

'No, never New York.'

Nancy creased her face. 'So, I'm struggling to work out why your Christmas was like Home Alone...?'

He laughed. 'You have a point there. I just meant that we went away for Christmas, and Home Alone is my favourite holiday film.' Nancy raised her eyebrow. 'Ok, bad analogy. Let's move on.'

'I think it's wise.' She glanced over to Jack who was in the same spot. Aiden had abandoned the idea of trying to talk to him and was now cutting some shapes on the dancefloor with a woman. Jack was still watching him though. This was surely a good thing.

'He gets his moves from me,' Cameron said, following Nancy's gaze.

She turned her head and smiled. 'Maybe you should show me?'

'Oh, no, no, no ... those moves are saved for special occasions – and by that, I mean, when everyone is drunk so they can't see that I have two left feet.'

They sat in silence for a moment as they watched Aiden on the dancefloor. The woman he was with looked up and waved. Nancy turned her head to Cameron who lifted a hand in response. 'That's my sister. My niece and nephew are behind her – the girl with the bright pink dress and the boy holding onto her dress making her have a strop.'

Nancy laughed. 'How old are they?'

'Eight and six.'

'Do you just have the one sister?'

'Yeah, just me and Becca. The guy on the table by the door, with the purple shirt on – that's her husband. We always holiday together – I think they take pity on me and invite me.'

Nancy turned back to Cameron, wanting to ask more about his situation but not feeling confident enough. She thought about asking about Aiden's mum but the words just didn't come out. Instead, she said, 'Do you go away together every year?'

Cameron nodded. 'Yeah, it's nice. Me and Becca get on really well actually, we're close in age and it means the cousins all get to spend their holidays together. Aiden has it tough sometimes so it is nice for him to have this time with everyone. I work long hours back home and he gets pushed from pillar to post – I know you mums say you get *mum guilt*, well I get massive *dad guilt*.' She watched his face change. She could see the sadness behind those beautiful eyes and it made her feel a little sad too.

'I'm sure he's absolutely fine, kids are more resilient than we think.' She wanted to hug him, it would be what she would do if he was a fellow mother and she was having this conversation. But she couldn't just lunge across the table and wrap her arms around him – no matter how much her body ached to do just that.

'Yeah, I know. It's just tough, isn't it? Being a single parent. Not having that other person to take the strain when times get hard.' Nancy felt herself falling for him with every true word that came out of his mouth. He totally got how she was feeling – it was like he saw how much she was struggling and here he was, saying he struggled too. 'It makes me just want to give up work and stay with him all the time, poor little guy hasn't had it easy and I just want to give him the best possible life I can.' He was gazing at Aiden as he spoke and Nancy could see the love pouring out from his heart.

'Has he been poorly?'

Cameron turned suddenly to her, confusion on his face. 'Sorry?'

'You said he hasn't had it easy – I just wondered if he had been poorly or something?' she could almost see Cameron's face start to close down.

'Oh, sorry. I'm rambling. I must've had more to drink than I thought.' He laughed but it seemed a little nervous and forced. 'He's fine. Just having a moment of feeling guilty for working so much – but I guess everyone does, hey.'

'I suppose.' She didn't believe him, there was more to this story and she was left wondering why he had shut it down so quickly. He had just started to open up, she had felt the vulnerability in his voice as he spoke about Aiden and how tough it had been, and then he'd just changed. It made her want to get to know him even more. She decided not to push him as he was looking a little on edge so she tried to lighten the mood again. 'So, I was guessing your job! You say you have a sort of uniform but not what I would expect... 'She trailed off as she scanned her brain for an answer.

'Do you want another clue?' He smiled, clearly glad of the diversion away from the topic of Aiden's past and Nancy nodded. 'My job involves babies.'

Nancy creased her face in confusion. 'Babies?' She wasn't expecting that.

He nodded.

'Are you a midwife?' She pulled a face. 'Mid-husband ... what would you call a male midwife?'

'Ah, I know this answer – the word midwife actually means *with woman*, so the person can be male or female because both work with the woman during pregnancy and labour. So it would still be midwife.' He raised his eyebrows, proud of his concise argument.

'Wow, that's really interesting – so you're a midwife? I got it on the first go?'

He laughed and shook his head. 'No, I'm not a midwife.'

'Newborn photographer?'

Another shake.

'Children's entertainer?'

'Do I look like a clown?'

'Well, you did say you couldn't dance so you might look like a clown on the dance floor.'

He nodded and pushed out his bottom lip. 'That could well be true ... but no, I'm not a clown.'

'OK, I give up.'

He smiled. 'Do you want another clue?'

'No! Just tell me, the anticipation is killing me.'

He stood, lifted the jug and poured more drinks. 'I am a neonatal surgeon.'

Chapter 22

How to be a better mum

Harriet pressed enter on her Google search and watched the links appear on the page.

How to be a better mum in five easy steps

She clicked on the link and checked over her shoulder to make sure Isla was still sound asleep. She could see the top of her head poking out from underneath the bedcovers and one of her toes escaping out the side. Turning back to the page, she scrolled down.

'Read daily to your children, eat a nutritious diet, ensure they get regular exercise...' She read out the points as she came across them. 'So, I'm failing on at least two of those so far,' she said out loud as she thought of the ready meals she often grabbed and the fact that the last time she read to her children was off the takeaway menu.

She closed that link and opened another titled: *Are you being the best parent you can be?*

'OK, let's try this one.'

1/ Spend time with your children – not just when you can, make sure you allocate sufficient time with your children to learn about them and for them to learn about you.

'Yup, definitely failing that one too – this is a good start.' She continued scrolling.

2/ Cook all meals from scratch, ensuring complete nutritional value for the age of your child is being met.

'Oh for fuck's sake – who has time to do that? I do have to work, you know,' she hissed at the computer.

3/ Make sure your children are spending enough time with both parents – even if the parents are not together.

'What if one parent is a complete dick who wants nothing to do with their children? Where's your answer for that, Google, huh!' She angrily closed the tab and opened another. 'OK, last one, come on, please give me something to hold onto before I lose my mind.'

She scrolled down. Time, meals, listening to your children but not letting them dictate. Letting them make decisions. Spending more time with them, spending less time with them, sending them to nursery, not sending them to nursery ... it was all so confusing. Why wasn't there a handbook to follow to make sure you got things right? Some of the articles she read were so incredibly critical, it made Harriet wonder how anyone got it 'right'. No matter how hard she tried, or how well she thought she was doing, there was always somebody one step ahead of her telling her she was doing it wrong.

She angrily closed the browser and opened up her email

inbox. Where she was comfortable. Where she knew what she was doing. If there was one area people couldn't tell her she was doing badly, it was her job. This was her safety blanket, her sanity. If she didn't have this, she wasn't sure she would cope.

***

'A neonatal surgeon?'

Cameron nodded. 'Not what you expected?'

'No, not at all.' She pondered on this for a moment. 'So, you operate on really tiny babies?'

He nodded. 'Newborns, premature babies...'

'Wow,' Nancy found herself gasping. 'That's a pretty impressive job.' She felt like after this revelation, Cameron looked totally different to her. He seemed so much ... hotter! This guy was not only cute, a hands-on loving father and single parent, but he also spent his days working with babies and saving their lives. I mean, if perfect had a human form, she was pretty sure he was it!

He laughed. 'Not quite your fireman or army cadet, but I technically wear scrubs when at work so it's a uniform of such.'

'Definitely, no, I agree. I just ... wow, I would never have guessed that in a million years. I bet it's an emotional job at times?'

'It can be. But I try not to think about those times – you get to a point where you have to cut off emotionally from it

169

all otherwise you just go crazy.' There was sadness and compassion in his face; he had obviously had some tough times with his job.

'Yeah, I can imagine. So I guess your workload is pretty stressful then – you must have full on hours?'

'Some weeks can be full on, but my sister is an amazing support and she has Aiden for me when I'm at work. I couldn't do it without her.' He was back looking at his son, watching him wiggle his bum to *Chocolate*.

Nancy laughed. 'I'm pretty sure every single holiday resort plays this song at some point – I always find myself singing it for weeks afterwards.'

'Chocolate – a choco choco – chocolate – a choco choco!' Cameron sang, bouncing his arms up and down like a chicken, copying the resort staff who all looked like they were high on drugs.

'Are these your moves? Is this why you won't be on the dance floor?' she teased, mimicking his chicken arms and pulling a face.

'Alright Miss Smooth Grooves, let's see what you're made of?' He displayed his hand out to the dance floor, goading her to get up. Luckily, she was saved by Aiden approaching the table.

'Daddy?'

'Yes dude?'

'Aunty Becca is going back to the room now and said for me to come and tell you, so you know where we are.' Aiden hopped up and down on the spot, flashes of blue slushy on his tongue giving away his secrets as he spoke.

Cameron looked over to his sister who waved from the other side of the room to him. Nancy noticed just how alike the two of them were. She had the same smile as Cameron, warm and friendly, and her hair was the same blonde shade, just a lot longer than his. She was sporting a tidy little baby bump underneath a very stylish maxi dress which draped over the bump nicely, making her look blooming. Had Nancy worn that when she was pregnant, she would've looked more like she was carrying a watermelon. She hadn't had the most stylish pregnancy – comfort, ease and necessity had been more her aim. She would maybe try out the stylish look next time ... if there was ever going to be a next time. As she felt right now, she couldn't see it ever happening and she found herself feeling disappointed about that, which surprised her.

He responded to Becca's wave with a salute and Aiden gave him a kiss. 'Goodnight Daddy, night lady!'

'It's Nancy,' Cameron corrected as Aiden ran off. 'Sorry.'

'That's OK, there are worse things he could call me to be fair.' She looked over to Jack who was still in the same place.

'He loves his iPad, huh?' Cameron said, pouring the remains of the Sloe Screw cocktail into Nancy's glass.

'Yeah,' she replied sadly. 'I'm trying to get him to be on it less but ... it's hard.'

'Without stepping out of line, can I ask you something?'

Nancy felt the apprehension drape over her as she looked at him. 'O ... K ...' she said, tentatively.

'Is Jack autistic?' Nancy hadn't been expecting him to say that, and the nature of the question threw her. Instead of playing it cool, she suddenly seemed to freeze, unable to answer. 'Sorry, I don't mean to pry.' Now she could see the panic on his face.

'No, sorry it's not that, you just threw me that's all. I wasn't expecting you to ask that.' She took a deep breath. 'But yes, he is.' Cameron nodded in acknowledgement. 'How did you know? Is it that obvious?' She felt the frustration begin to build. Because if it was that obvious to strangers, why the hell had it taken the doctors so damn long to diagnose him. Was he getting worse as he got older?

'No, not at all. My cousin's son is autistic and he displays some of the same characteristics that Jack does. I spotted it when I first saw you at the poolside and the more I see Jack, the more he reminds me of Archie.' Cameron smiled fondly.

Nancy forced a smile but felt her barriers begin to spring up. It wasn't that she minded Camron talking about it, but she felt incredibly vulnerable and now even more open to judgement. His cousin probably knew what they were doing, managing to raise their autistic son with ease. Whereas Nancy, well, she was struggling, massively.

'I hope I didn't offend you by saying so?' he pushed, after Nancy sat quietly for a few minutes. 'We don't have to talk about it.'

'Its fine, it's just – you know, we haven't had an easy ride with it.'

'I can totally appreciate that. My cousin found the first couple of years after diagnosis the hardest. Having to come to terms with an official statement telling you your child is struggling can't be easy to hear as a parent.'

'It isn't.'

'Do you get a lot of support?'

Nancy shrugged. 'Some, not a lot.' She was waiting for the question – where he asked about Jack's dad. She wasn't ready to discuss him, she was still too mad about Pete leaving. But clearly Cameron had the same thoughts as her when it came to asking about spouses because he skirted around the issue too.

'So what does Jack get anxious about?'

'He doesn't like people.' Nancy laughed. It was strained but it was the only way she knew how to talk about it. Cameron smiled and nodded, gently willing her to continue. 'He's fine if he knows the person, but he doesn't like talking to new people. They're like a blank canvas to him, I suppose, and that frightens him. He also hates his ears being touched – we had a bit of an ... incident at kids' club here the other day.'

'What sort of incident?'

'The woman was talking to him and she tried to take off his headphones without warning him.'

'Oh dear...' Cameron pulled a face and instantly Nancy felt like he understood better than most about her situation with Jack. Their connection was deepening the more they spoke about it. It felt so refreshing to have someone on her side, someone who really knew. Harriet was an amazing support and she was so grateful to her friend, but she didn't understand. Cameron's knowing someone who was going through a similar thing helped, and instantly Nancy felt the relief pour over her. She noticed her chest relax slightly and she didn't feel so strained. She wasn't making excuses for Jack and trying to explain him and his behaviour, she didn't have to say anything and Cameron just knew.

'Yes, big oh dear,' she replied, cringing at the memory.

'What happened?'

'Let's just say a few people were left with bruises and the woman was just as traumatised as Jack was. I don't think they will be inviting us back anytime soon.'

'Did she apologise?'

'I'm sorry?'

'The woman, did she apologise for setting Jack off?'

'Don't be silly, it was of course all Jack's fault,' she said, mockingly. 'No one ever stops to think *why* he's behaving the way he is. They just see the bad behaviour and judge him – judge us.' She looked away, embarrassed.

Cameron put his hand over hers on the table and she felt an almighty surge of feelings that she couldn't describe. 'I totally get what you mean,' he said. 'My cousin had years of the same thing.'

Nancy felt an overwhelming urge to cry. She didn't know why. It felt so surreal for this man to seemingly understand what she felt and after years and years of people blaming her parenting for how Jack behaved, it was strange having someone say to her: *actually, it's not you; you're doing a good job*. She stood up. 'It's my turn for the drinks this time.' She grabbed the jug and left before Cameron could say anything. Talking about Jack's autism was so liberating but, at the same time, the sudden rush of release was a bit overwhelming. Cameron clearly understood and was being the perfect gentleman but the more time she spent with him, the more she liked him. And she knew having Cameron in her life wasn't an option because of Jack. He would not cope well with that kind of change right now. She had to look at her priorities and make sure she was keeping him at the forefront of her mind instead of giving way to these silly feelings like a schoolgirl with a crush.

Chapter 23

'Do you want an omelette?' Harriet asked Nancy as she scanned the breakfast buffet. Nancy shook her head. 'I'm not sure if I fancy one or not. Although the pancakes do seem to be calling me.'

'Now you're talking.'

Harriet made her way up to the breakfast buffet, leaving the kids with Nancy, and glanced along at the selection of food on show. Only on holiday could you get away with such a wide mix of foods for breakfast: cereals, breads, meats, cheeses, yogurts, hot breakfasts, fruit ... Harriet was tempted to get an assortment of everything.

'Quite a selection, huh?'

She looked over her shoulder and saw Jayne, the woman from the pool, next to her with her son on her hip.

'Isn't it? I feel like I'm going to put on a million stone whilst we are here.'

'That's all part of going all-inclusive, isn't it? That's what I keep telling my husband anyway. I'll do some extra Zumba classes when I get home to make up for it.' She laughed. 'Have you had any luck with your little one and the water yet?'

Harriet shook her head. She didn't admit that she hadn't tried him since for fear of failing yet again. This woman would probably be nice to her face but then bitch about her behind her back. She had seen enough playground gatherings to know that was what happened. That was why she never did the school run on time, but instead always left it to the last minute so she didn't have to stop and endure the pointless niceties that would be thrown back in her face as soon as her back was turned. Nope, she wasn't going to feed herself to the lions. Straight out the car, into school and back in the car. Done. Efficient, smart ... safe. It wasn't a *normal* way to work and Harriet wasn't stupid; she knew that her perception on this was slightly warped. But she didn't know any other way to be but firm and regimented. It stemmed from her insecurities as a parent but with no one telling her she was doing OK, encouraging her decision-making, she had no choice but to let those thoughts and fears manifest into self-doubt, prompting her strict playground routine.

'It'll come.' Jayne smiled at her. 'We are going to the beach this afternoon – have you been there yet?'

'No, not yet. Is it nearby?' Harriet picked up several pancakes and piled them onto her plate, drizzling them with honey and putting a few token blueberries on the top.

'Yeah, it's literally five minutes down the road. You should check it out.'

'Oh, what am I talking about, I can see the beach from our balcony.' They used the balcony every night for cocktails before bedtime and she had spent hours gazing at the beach scene behind the buildings.

Jayne laughed. 'Maybe we'll see you down there then?'

Harriet glanced at Jayne who was now picking up yoghurt and a few bananas and handing them to her son to take back to the table. It made her uneasy that she was being so nice because actually, she had to admit that she did quite like her. But she didn't trust her enough to let her guard down. She didn't know her well enough. But she was full of smiles and invitations to meet up and Harriet didn't know how to take it. With Nancy she was comfortable, she knew Nancy would never judge her and so she could relax, enjoy her holiday. If she had mums around her who she didn't know, they could be thinking anything about her and she wouldn't know until it was too late and her guard was down. And that's when it hurt. She should know, it had happened to her before when she was seriously betrayed by a so-called friend who'd decided to laugh at Harriet's expense. There was no way she was going to let someone else do that to her again. No way.

'Well, I hope you have a lovely day whatever you decide to do and if you're heading to the beach, come and say hi.' Jayne smiled and then made her way back to the table.

After piling some more pancakes onto a second plate for Isla and Tommy and adding some cheese and sausages to her own plate, she returned to the table.

'What's with the confused expression?' Nancy asked, turning her mug the right way round ready to fill with coffee.

'There's a lady here who keeps talking to me.' Harriet whispered so there was no risk of Jayne hearing her.

Nancy laughed. 'OK ... why's that so strange?'

Harriet glanced at her friend and frowned. 'Is it not weird?'

'That someone is talking to you?'

'No! That a woman is talking to me ... not just talking to me but being all friendly and giving me mum advice and stuff.' Harriet sat down and took in Nancy's expression. 'Oh, forget it.'

'No wait, come on, what do you mean? Why is that weird to you?'

'Are mums normally like that? Or does she have an agenda?' She slid the plate over to Isla who was already pulling at one of the pancakes before it even reached her. 'Steady girl, let me put it down first.'

'Why would she have an agenda?'

'Well, I don't know. Why would you just start talking to someone as if you've known them for years when you only met them five minutes ago? She's trying to act like my mate and I've known her like two seconds. Its ... well, it's just weird.' Harriet shuffled in her seat. Nancy clearly didn't understand. 'Oh forget it; you'll talk to anyone so I guess you're just as bad.'

Nancy laughed at that comment, spreading butter on a slice of toast and putting some grapes and a yogurt onto a side plate for Jack. 'Hari, the woman is just being nice. Why has it made you feel weird?'

'Well, the only mums I really speak to are the ones at school or nursery and even then, I don't really talk to them I just whizz past and get Tommy and, well, they aren't like that. They're more interested in talking behind my back and sniggering at me because I'm late picking up again.' The twinge of guilt reared its ugly head as she relived her usual frantic routine. 'I guess I'm just not used to women actually being nice to me, that's all.'

'That's not true, women are nice to you – you're just too busy to see it.'

'I am not!' she retorted, defensively.

'Hari, not everyone is like that bitch from the school.' Harriet exhaled as she poured a coffee. She knew Nancy would bring it up. 'You can't let the actions of one woman taint your perception of everyone. Not everyone is a Sandi Thrupton.'

Just the name made Harriet bubble with anger. Sandi Thrupton was a mum at the school whose daughter was in Isla's class. One Friday Harriet had been late and when she'd got to the school, Isla had been waiting in the office, but this time Sandi Thrupton had been there too. She'd taken it upon herself to tell Harriet – and the staff in the office – how sad Isla had been in the classroom today because *Mummy was always late.* Sandi was a parent helper and took pride in thinking she knew all the children better than everyone else because she had the inside info. It eventually came to light, after Harriet had demanded to speak to the class teacher, that Isla had actually been crying because another child had taken her My Little Pony pencil home but Sandi had decided for herself that she must be crying because Harriet was occasionally late to pick her up. Harriet had told her exactly what she thought of her and for weeks after that, she'd had to endure whispering in the playground and comments on the parent page on social media about being on time to pick children up and she knew it had been aimed at her. After a while Harriet had stopped walking through the playground and literally pulled up outside the office and bundled Isla in. She'd also deleted herself off the school's social media page. She was pretty sure all the mums were still talking about her, but at least she didn't hear it anymore.

But it didn't mean that she wasn't still affected by it. Not a single one of them offered to help or asked if she was struggling. They were all far too busy making comments behind her back.

'That woman said she was going to the beach today and that if we were going down there, to say hi to them.'

'Ah that's really nice; you've made a friend there.' Nancy laughed and Harriet felt the need to defend herself.

'I have friends! I just don't have much time to see them, that's all.'

'Hari, I wasn't having a go. Jeez chill out, will you. Look the lady is being nice to you, she clearly likes you, so just stop being weird with it and embrace it. Do you want to go to the beach later? I think the kids would like it and we can't be here for a whole week and not go to the beach.'

'It'll look weird, like I'm stalking her, if I show up there. No, we'll do the beach another day.' She proceeded to cut up Isla's pancakes for her although she did seem to be doing a perfectly good job of ripping them apart with her hands. She could feel Nancy's eyes on her and sure enough, when she looked up, she was staring at her. 'What?'

'Why don't you want to go? It's lovely that this woman wants to make friends with you, you're always saying how you don't have very many mum friends so why not see what she's like?'

'I don't need any mum friends, I have you, don't I?'

'Pfft, one mum friend isn't enough for any parent, Hari; no parent can survive the throes of parenting without friends who are going through the same thing. It keeps us sane being able to talk to other mums and dads.'

'Is that why you like talking to Cameron so much?' Harriet teased and poked her tongue out.

'Exactly!' Nancy countered. 'Cameron is a single dad and he, as much as any mum, needs to have that parenting connection and friendship too.'

'And I bet you're the one giving him that connection, hey?' She winked and Nancy groaned. 'I'm kidding, Nance, chill.'

'I just wish you would embrace having friends a bit more. It might, you know, be nice for you.'

Harriet stood up and picked up her plate to refill even though she still had food on it. 'I don't have time for lots of friends, Nance, that's why you and I are so close. I don't need anyone else, I have you.' And she walked off before Nancy could push it anymore.

***

Nancy felt the warmth of the sun soak into her body as she lay on the sun lounger, listening to the sea. She gently let her arm fall to the side and rest gracefully on the sand below. The small grains of heat felt lovely as she stroked along, feeling totally at ease. 'Oh my goodness, how nice is that sunshine?' This was a million miles away from her life at home and she could feel the stress ebbing away from her body as she listened to the waves crashing onto the sand and the children's laughter as they played. When she was at home, it was easy to get caught up in everyday life and stresses and forget to just stop and breathe. Being here made Nancy realise that there was a chance to make her life a little less stressful, she just needed to learn to stop and listen.

'I can't believe you made me come here,' Harriet snapped back, somewhat ruining the elegance of the moment. Nancy opened her eyes and glanced at her friend who was sat up on the lounger next to her, applying sun cream in a stroppy fashion.

'Why are you so mad at me? We wanted to come to the beach, it's a nice day and the kids are happy. And Jack has put down the iPad voluntarily and is playing with the sand. The sand! Can you believe it? So don't ruin this moment for me. I'm not making you go over to that woman – even though she clearly saw us arrive – so can you stop acting like a baby and enjoy the fact that we are sitting on a beach, in the blazing sunshine, with nothing to do but relax.'

Nancy slumped back down onto the longer and pulled her sunglasses over her face.

'Alright, no need to have a mare over it.'

'Mummy look! I made a sandcastle.' Isla shouted and Nancy heard Harriet stand up. She lifted her head and was surprised to see Harriet sitting on the sand next to Isla, inspecting her work of art.

It wasn't that Harriet wasn't a good mum – she loved her children dearly and would do anything for them – but she wasn't usually a hands-on parent. She sort of flitted around, here, there and everywhere and always seemed a bit absent when her children were talking to her – her job took up her mind space most of the time. It was lovely to see her embracing the holiday for what it was supposed to be – a break! She had noticed on more than one occasion since being away that Harriet seemed to be changing the way she approached her parenting. Little moments like sitting with the children, putting her phone down to talk to them and she had actually heard her telling Isla a bedtime story last night which wasn't something she usually did. Isla's little face was a picture, she loved this time with her mum. It was nice to see Harriet enjoying herself for once and not having the constant stress face she was known to occupy most of the time – or was it resting bitch face?

Nancy spent the next hour soaking up the sunshine and listening to the waves. She could hear children screaming as they played and the odd dog barking. It was like she was listening to one of those mindfulness apps where they played the scenic music to relax you. Here she had the real life mindfulness app. After all the stress over the last year, this was exactly what she needed.

Her phone began to vibrate on the side of the lounger when she had placed it underneath the towel to stop it from overheating. She pushed herself up onto her forearms and pulled it out and clicked on the message.

Are you mad at me?

'Don't you dare reply to that message.'

Nancy jumped at the sound of Harriet's voice and dropped the phone. 'For God's sake don't creep up on me like that.'

'Well, it's lucky I did, otherwise you'd be texting him back right now. Go on, tell me I'm wrong.'

Nancy pushed herself up fully and sat on the end of the lounger. 'You're wrong, I wasn't going to reply.'

'You'd better not, the guy is not worth thinking about, let alone talking to.' Harriet held up her finger. 'Actually, do reply to him.'

'What?' Nancy questioned.

'Reply to him and tell him that yes, you are mad and to do one!'

'Is that how you speak to your clients in the boardroom – "sign this contract and if you don't like it, you can do one!"' Nancy mimicked and even Harriet cracked a smile.

'I wish I could say that to some of the clients I deal with.'

'You're right, I should say that but I just worry all the time. I just want what's best for Jack. I feel bad taking it away from him if there was even just a small chance that he could see him. I don't want him around, but I feel guilty for being the one to make that cut. It was so much easier when Pete said he was done because the decision then wasn't on my shoulders.'

'And have you spoken to Jack? Asked him what he thinks?'

'About Pete?'

Harriet shrugged.

'I don't know that he would understand what's going on.'

'Only one way to find out.' Harriet turned over and left

Nancy wondering if she had a point. Pondering for a second, looking at the message, Nancy decided that it wasn't such a bad idea. However just the thought of having a conversation like that with Jack made her anxious. Where would she even begin?

She got off the lounger and walked over to the area of sand by the slope that Jack was playing in. He liked sand – he liked it better than water which surprised Nancy. Still, after seven years, she was learning things about Jack that she didn't know.

She sat down next to him and he instantly looked up at her. 'Hi Mum. Look.' He showed her his sandcastle and she couldn't stop herself from saying;

'Wow! Jack, did you actually make this?'

He nodded proudly. The sandcastle was an exact replica of the one on the postcard he had bought the first day they'd arrived. It was in the shape of a hexagon and she remembered commenting on how unusual it looked. She looked around for the card. 'Did you copy that from the card?' He nodded. 'Where is it?'

'At the hotel.'

'You haven't got it here?' He shook his head. 'How did you copy it then?'

'From here,' he said, pointing to his head.

'Jack, that is incredible.' She felt the pride wash over her and jumped up. 'Hang on a minute.' She ran back to retrieve her phone and then when she returned, snapped a picture of it. 'Well done Jack, it's amazing.'

He smiled and continued to work on the sculpture so

Nancy sat and watched. He was fascinating to watch. He took in every movement he made, analysing whether it would make the sculpture better or worse, how he was going to achieve what he wanted, standing back and observing before making changes. The detail was intricate and she noticed he had a pile of utensils next to him.

'What are these, Jack?' she asked, pointing to them.

'They're my tools – every workman needs tools. This is what I use to cut bits out—' he showed her a flat stone with a sharp edge '—this is what I use to make lines—' a stick '—and this is how I made that design—' he showed her seaweed.

Nancy was in awe – she had no idea he had these skills. 'Jack, where did you learn to do all this?'

'On my iPad.'

'Your iPad?'

'Yeah, on the game.'

'What game?'

'The building one.'

Then it clicked. Jack liked to play a building platform game that she had found online. It was all about measurements and creating structures – Nancy had thought it was the numbers he liked but clearly it was the infrastructure aspect. 'Well, you're very good at it.'

He nodded, not taking his eyes off the sculpture. 'Jack, can I ask you something?' Another nod. 'You know that Daddy has been away for a little while now and you haven't seen him?' She paused to see his reaction at the mention of Pete. He didn't seem to react at all apart from when his jaw clenched a little. She continued. 'Would you want to see him if he was to come back to see you at the house sometimes?'

She was taking a huge risk. Pete had already said he wasn't interested and his message earlier wasn't exactly saying he had changed his mind. But if she could tell him that Jack had said he wanted to see him, it might change things.

'I don't want to.'

Nancy froze. This wasn't the reply she'd expected to hear. 'What?' she replied.

He looked at her briefly and then resumed his attention to the sandcastle. 'I don't want to.'

'You don't want to see Daddy?' she asked, making sure she was understanding him right. He shook his head. 'Why not?'

'It makes me sad.'

Her stomach turned. 'Why Jack?'

He spoke softly but didn't look at her. 'I don't like the shouting.'

Nancy tried to think when Pete had shouted at Jack but couldn't pinpoint a specific moment. 'But Daddy doesn't shout at you.'

'No, Daddy shouts at you and you shout at Daddy.' Nancy's shoulders drooped as the weight of his comment set down on them. She'd always tried to speak in hushed tones – or hushed shouting – when she and Pete argued but clearly she wasn't as discreet as she imagined she had been. And she'd always assumed that Jack was too enthralled in what he was doing with his headphones on, that he didn't hear them arguing. Now she felt sick with guilt. She never wanted him to feel like that in his own home. She should have been more careful. She was brought back to the here and now by Jack's voice again. 'I like it just us. No one else, just me and you.' He looked at Nancy, pleading with his eyes. 'Just me and you – promise? I don't want anyone else.'

She couldn't speak. She just forced a smile and nodded her head. He smiled back and resumed his workmanship, talking to Nancy as he worked.

'Now I need to make the windows, I'm going to use this and...'

But Nancy wasn't listening. All she could think about was the fact that now it really was, just her and Jack.

Chapter 24

'You've been weird all afternoon, what's up?' Harriet asked as she watched Nancy with her arm around Jack's chair, staring into space. Nancy didn't respond so Harriet leaned forward across the dinner table and clicked her fingers in front of her face. Nancy jumped and looked at her, confused. 'I said, what's up? You've been acting weird all afternoon.'

'Nothing, I'm fine.'

Harriet wasn't convinced. 'Yeah you sound it.' She picked up her phone to check her emails – 35 new emails in the last two hours. She clicked open one of them and saw it was marked as urgent. Exhaling, she opened it up fully and began reading. Within two minutes of reading it became apparent that she would have to call them to sort out this latest mess. She was getting to the end of her patience with this now. This holiday had flagged up the incompetency of the team she surrounded herself with at work. Things were going to have to be shaken up when she got home. She hadn't realised, until she came away, just how much they relied on her. And whilst she couldn't just leave them in the lurch now – it was her business after all – she knew that things were going to have to improve. Staff training, rethinking positions, even dismissals if this continued.

Before she had a chance to stand up and go anywhere, she was interrupted by Jayne's cheery voice. 'Hi, how are you?'

Harriet looked up. 'Hi.'

'Listen I don't know if it's your kind of thing, both of you,' she looked over to Nancy too, 'but there's an event down on the beach tonight, I saw it on the noticeboard earlier today – it's a beach party with a twist, apparently. Only I don't know what the twist is.' She laughed, flicking her hair over her shoulder, displaying the beautiful lace-topped dress she was wearing. 'Anyway, just thought I'd mention it, we're going down there so maybe we'll see you there?'

'Yeah maybe.' Harriet's phone pinged another email. 'Listen, I have to go and make a call. Nance, watch the kids for me, I'll be back in half hour.'

Harriet rushed off towards the corridor, opting to take the stairs instead of the lift.

***

'Alright Nance, I was going to come down in a minute, I was just finishing up here.'

Nancy walked through the door to their room and slammed it shut behind her, ushering Isla and Jack into her adjoining room and turning the TV on before coming back into Harriet's room, gently closing the door behind her and placing Tommy into his cot.

'What's up, why are you being all secretive?' Harriet said, laughing but her face quickly turned when she saw Nancy's expression was far from happy. 'You OK?'

Nancy stood facing her friend of twenty-two years, anger bubbling up. 'No, I'm not OK. *You* told me this was a holiday for us to get away and relax. *You* told me we both needed to get away and that this would be a fun girly holiday with sun, sea and cocktails. Didn't you? Didn't you say that to me?'

'Yes,' Harriet replied, indignantly.

'So why the bloody hell am I constantly hearing you talk about work, reading emails and disappearing off for hours on end for conference calls!'

'I—'

'Look, don't get me wrong.' Nancy held out her hand, palm down. ' I get that you have to work and I get that you're a single parent trying to provide for your children and I get that you are a driven and determined human being who wants to excel with her business ... I get all that! But you need to take a break otherwise you are going to go mad! You will burn yourself out and you will get ill.'

'Nancy—'

'You had the perfect opportunity downstairs to make a really nice friend and you just walked off and practically threw her invitation back in her face. I spoke to Jayne after you left and she's lovely. She kept saying how nice you were and how you reminded her of her friend who really struggled with being a mum but didn't tell anyone and ended up being depressed and making herself really ill. She went out of her

way to come over to you and all you could do was say you
had to make a bloody phone call!'

'If you'll just let me talk—'

'Why? So you can give me your usual spiel of how you
have to work and how the company cannot survive without
you there, blah blah...'

'For fuck's sake Nance, will you shut up a second and let
me bloody talk!'

The girls both stood for a second staring at each other,
both highly wired with frustration and emotion. Nancy felt
her chest rising and falling rapidly, her breathing a reflection
of her heartbeat. Her anger and frustration had built steadily
from when Harriet had walked off; peaking when she got to
their door and she saw Harriet was still working. She had
spent days trying to find the right moment to bring this up
properly and instead, it had just come out in an angry rant.

After a moment of silence where you could cut the tension
in the room with a knife, Nancy prompted her response. 'Well?
Go on, I'm listening.'

But the response that came wasn't what Nancy had expected
because Harriet just dropped down to the bed, put her head
in her hands and simply said, 'I can't do it anymore.'

Chapter 25

'What do you mean you can't do it anymore?'

Harriet let the words wash over her as she sat, head in hands, on the bed. She was exhausted. She just couldn't have this same conversation over and over anymore, she had had enough and Nancy's explosion had just confirmed what she thought in her head. She wasn't coping.

She lifted her head and blinked away the tears that had begun to form in her eyes. 'I can't do *this*.' She gestured to the other room with her hand, indicating the children. 'I'm rubbish at it and I don't know what I'm doing.'

She watched Nancy look over to the room, then back to her. 'I don't understand.' She moved and sat on the bed next to Harriet.

'This is what I mean. You don't understand because you get it, you can do it. You have a lovely relationship with Jack and you don't find it easy, but you still manage to do it – it comes naturally to you.'

'What does?'

'Being a mum!' she shouted, throwing her hands up and slapping them back down onto her knees. 'You just seem to know *what* to do, *when* to do it and *how* you're going to do it. Me? I can't get through a day without failing in some way.'

'Failing? Shut up, you are not failing.' Nancy laughed, obviously trying to be reassuring that Harriet was being silly, but Harriet took it offensively, like she was being laughed at and it made her more frustrated.

'Nancy, I am. I look at all these mums on my Facebook page or at the school gates and they totally have their shit together. And it comes easy to them; they don't even have to think about it. I have to really think about every single thing I do. It's so hard.'

'See, that's where you're going wrong – straightaway,' Nancy replied, and Harriet frowned, confused. 'You're too busy comparing yourself to all the other bloody parents out there.'

'You can bloody talk!' Harriet responded, thinking about how Nancy beat herself up over being a parent to an autistic child and thinking others were coping better than she was.

'Yes exactly, but I am saying do as I say, not as I do.' They both started laughing and Nancy leaned over and gave Harriet a cuddle. 'You're not a crap mum – you're one of the hardest-working mummies I know. You just need to learn when enough is enough.'

'Nance, I feel like I'm going mad.' Her voice was small and childlike.

'Why?'

Harriet paused for a moment, deciding whether to be honest and say what had been playing on her mind for months now or whether to keep covering it up and hoping it would go away, which would be the easier option. But she wasn't sure how much longer her sanity would keep her going. Admitting the truth about how she was feeling would show she was weak, and regardless of how long she had known Nancy, and she knew her friend wouldn't judge her, admitting she was struggling as much as she was meant that she had to admit to herself that she was failing at something. And Harriet didn't fail at anything. If she wanted to be the successful person she so desperately wanted to be and show Andy that he was the one losing out, then she couldn't admit to failing at anything. Not her job and not her parenting.

But the more she thought about it, the more she panicked that maybe this was no longer in her control. Mentally and emotionally, she did not have control at all. Work was controlling her and the feeling frightened her.

Nancy's voice pulled her out of the haze. 'You know you can talk to me. I know you don't like to open up but honestly, if you keep bottling things up inside it will drive you mad.'

Harriet took a deep breath. 'I think there's something wrong with me.' The words barely came out. They felt sticky in her throat and she had to really force them to come up. 'I don't feel ... I mean, I kind of ... um,' she shifted on the bed. 'It's just I ... um...'

Nancy put her hand on Harriet's to steady her. 'It's OK, what is it?'

Harriet looked at her friend and felt an overwhelming urge to burst into tears. 'I haven't told anyone this, just remember that, OK?' Nancy nodded. 'And I'm not proud of myself.'

'O ... K...'

'And please don't hate me...'

'Oh God, Hari, are you in some sort of trouble? Because you know I'll stand by you, but if you've killed someone I'm not helping you bury the body – I don't think I could handle that.'

Harriet slapped her on the arm playfully. 'I haven't killed anyone, you daft cow!'

'Well that's a relief because I was starting to picture us being cellmates and I don't think orange is my colour.'

'I think it's only orange in America – you watch too much TV!'

'Good to know.'

Another pause. 'I don't feel close to Tommy.'

Nancy nodded. 'In what way, because you work all the time?'

Harriet shook her head. 'I feel like we don't have ... like ... a bond.' She looked away, ashamed of herself.

'And how long have you felt like this?'

She shrugged. 'I don't know, I guess I never felt like I connected with him right from the start. He came so quickly and I wasn't prepared at work for him to come and Dickhead wasn't any help and it was hard juggling both a newborn and the workload and I guess I just felt like he was—'she stopped, hanging her head. 'I just felt like everything was fine before he came along.' She hiccupped and let a tear fall. 'I'm such a shit.'

'Hey, no you're not!' Nancy pulled her closer.

'I went to the doctor's.'

'When?'

'When Tommy was about 12 weeks.' She sniffed and wiped her cheek with her hand. 'He said I had postnatal depression.'

'Oh my God, Harriet, why didn't you talk to me!' Her tone was firm but it was laden with love, and with sadness. It just made Harriet feel guilty.

'Because I didn't want anyone to know that I had failed – yet again!'

'You didn't fail, you were depressed.'

'But how can all these other mums do it and enjoy it and here I am, incapable of doing just the normal things any parent does. I just kept crying every time I looked at him and then he would cry and then Isla would cry.'

'And what did the doctor say to you?'

'I had some counselling but the woman just made me feel worse. So I pretended that everything was getting better and I got really good at acting like everything was fine. But Nance...' She paused and looked her in the eye. 'Everything isn't ok. I'm struggling and I don't know what to do.'

'It's OK, we will sort this. The main thing is that you've spoken to me about it and that is the first step, so halle-fucking-lujah for that. I can't help you if you don't talk to me!'

Harriet appreciated Nancy's no-nonsense talk. If she had turned around and been nice to her and soft-spoken, she would probably have broken down and then it would have got messy. Nancy knew Harriet and she knew how she worked, she knew that Harriet would be more receptive to the harsh, regimented approach.

'Nance, Tommy is over a year old now – it can't still be postnatal depression. So what is going on – why am I struggling so much?'

'I don't think there's a set time on postnatal depression,

especially if you never really got proper help for it. The main thing is that you are talking about it. Now that you've spoken to me, you need to speak to a professional.' Harriet was already shaking her head. 'What?'

'No, I can't go back to counselling. The woman made me feel even worse, as though she was looking down her nose at me and smiling with a face like one I wanted to slap.'

'Well, what about your mum?'

Harriet burst out laughing, a little too loudly than was necessary. 'If there was ever a person who makes me feel worse than how I feel about myself, it's my mother.'

'What? I thought she'd been alright recently?'

'No, she's got really bad again. She had a go at me because Tommy was in kids' club and I was working.'

'That's why you got him out of kids' club.'

Harriet looked ashamed. 'I just wanted to try doing the right thing, but it just feels so alien to me. With Isla it was different, I couldn't tell you why. I just felt like with her I got things done and it all happened without any problem but with Tommy, it's like wading through mud just to do the simplest of tasks.'

'Do you think that maybe it's because you had more support when you had Isla at home?'

'But their dad was still around when Tommy was born.'

'Not really though, was he? I mean, in person he was there but emotionally you two were already separated. Do you think that maybe with Isla you were a team but when you had Tommy, essentially you were a single parent before Andy even left?'

Harriet considered this for a moment. 'I guess.'

'But you still feel like it with Tommy now?' she pressed.

'Yeah, I just feel like I don't know him and he's always crying and whinging – it's like he doesn't like me.'

'I think that's probably more a case of he's sensing that you're stressed. Kids are like that, they know when you aren't feeling right so maybe he's sensing your anxiety and that's making him feel anxious too?'

'But I can't help it.'

'I didn't say you could.' Nancy paused. 'Is that why you are being funny with that Jayne? Because you think she's interfering?'

Harriet shook her head. 'No, I just don't want her to see how much I can't do it. I don't want anyone to see that I can't do it. The fewer mum friends I have, the less people can judge and look down their noses at me.'

'Hari, they're not judging you—'

'Some of them are, Nance.'

'Do you know what, they probably are, but isn't that their problem? I feel judged all the time and I agree, it sucks! You're not alone, Hari, I'm right there with you feeling like a rubbish parent. But I guess, we are doing our best and ultimately, we are doing it because we love our children and we want them to be happy. Am I right?' Harriet nodded. 'I am on this journey with you, I'm not against you. Don't shut me out because right now you need support from someone who loves you and guess what ... that someone is me.' She smiled and Harriet wiped away the moisture from her face.

'Why does it have to be so damn hard?'

'Right, step one – stop feeling sorry for yourself. Step two – you need to see a doctor so that they can help you emotionally and step three – you need to make an effort with Jayne. I think she will be good for you. Just try and enjoy her company. See what happens.'

'I guess.'

Nancy took her hand. 'Hari, I am here for you. I won't laugh at you when you get things wrong and I won't judge you. Trust me. Stop trying to take the world on your shoulders. You are always there for me when I struggle with Jack, now it's my turn to repay the gesture. Friends for twenty-two years, Hari, you know I've got your back.'

'Thanks Nance,' Harriet squeaked.

'Right, get in the shower and get ready – we are going to a beach party!'

Chapter 26

'Hey, you made it!' Jayne sauntered over to them holding two drinks, handing them over when she reached them. 'These are called Elderflower Gin Fizz and they are awesome!'

'Sounds good,' Nancy said as she took the glass and gave Harriet a glare.

'Yeah thanks.' Harriet took the glass. 'And, err, sorry for rushing off earlier. It was rude of me.'

'Oh, not at all, its fine. Hey, when you've got to work, you've got to work. Money doesn't grow on trees.' Harriet smiled, and Nancy could see that she felt uncomfortable but she was proud that she was at least trying. 'But listen, make sure you be kind to yourself, yeah? Your health and mind are more important than any job.'

Jayne walked off and Harriet hissed at Nancy, 'Have you said something to her!'

'Of course I haven't,' she replied, sipping her cocktail which turned out to be very nice indeed.

'Then why is she talking about my mind – you must've said something to her.'

Nancy could see the panic in Harriet's face and felt sorry

202

for her friend. As a private person Harriet would be mortified if she thought a stranger knew that stuff about her. But Nancy hadn't said anything. 'Hari, I've been with you ever since we spoke – when would I have had the chance to say anything, huh?'

Harriet was quiet for a minute and then said, 'Hmm, you have a point there.'

'Look she's just being nice, that's what she's like. She was telling me earlier about this mindfulness and holistic therapy stuff she does – she's genuinely just a nice person.'

'Well, you won't see me meditating and doing yoga – but I'll be nice, I promise.'

Nancy rolled her eyes and made her way over to the benched area where Jack and Isla had already set up camp with their electronics and colouring books. The set up for the party was incredible. It was hosted by the hotel and they had a whole area of the beach decorated with fairy lights and bunting and seated areas with draped material creating different spaces – it was really pretty. It was a calm evening weather-wise and there was a slight breeze which was welcome after the blazing hot day they had experienced today. Nancy loved a crisp spring morning , but having the sunshine and heat for a bit whilst they had been away had been lovely.

'Apparently, they do this once a year. It's to celebrate the hotel's opening anniversary.'

'That might explain why it was so damn expensive to come here for this week – I just assumed it was because of the school holidays.'

'That probably doesn't help either!' Nancy took her phone

out and began snapping pictures. She then turned to Jack and Isla. 'Smile kids!' Isla turned and suitably posed as she normally did. Jack did his usual smile where he drew his mouth into a tight line. It wasn't really a smile, but he thought it was so Nancy didn't dispute it. She then spun the camera round and put her arm around Harriet. 'Smile!'

'Here, why don't I take that for you?'

Nancy glanced at Cameron and instantly felt the butterflies in her tummy flutter. He looked gorgeous in his white linen shirt and stone coloured chinos. He smiled, not taking his eyes off Nancy and she felt herself blush. What she wouldn't give to slide her hand into the open top button of his shirt and glide her fingers over his chest. She shook the thought from her mind and broke the eye contact, embarrassed to be thinking of him in that way.

'Cheers Cam!' Harriet took Nancy's phone and passed it over.

'It's Cam now is it?' Nancy whispered as she smiled for the camera.

'What? He's always around, he's practically family now.' She giggled and then demanded to see the photo so she could vet it before it went online.

'My eye looks wonky, can you take it again?'

They posed for a second time and after the fifth time they finally had a picture Harriet was happy with.

'Right, are we happy? This one can go on Facebook, yes?' Nancy waited for Harriet to agree before pressing send; she did it quickly before she could change her mind again. 'It's done, there's no going back now.'

'Right, who is ready for a game of sticky glue?' Cameron said, loud enough for the children around him to hear.

'Me!'

'I am!'

'I want to play!'

'Mummy, can I play?' Isla asked.

'Of course you can.'

'I think the mummies and daddies should play too,' Cameron said, cheekily smiling at Nancy and Nancy found herself smiling back involuntarily. He had one of those faces where you only had to look at him smiling and you found yourself doing it too. Maybe it was because he was a doctor, they always had calming, reassuring faces, didn't they? Especially ones who worked with children. For the second time since she had met him, she was drawn to the tattoo on his chest which was only just visible through the opening at the front where he had left his buttons undone. She still couldn't make out what the design was – maybe she would ask him at some point. Although that would mean admitting that she had been staring at his chest. Maybe not then.

Nancy put her hand up. 'I'll play if the other adults do.'

Cameron looked round to his sister and her husband who nodded. Nancy then looked at Harriet who shrugged and then Jayne and her husband who seemed more excited than the children.

'Great, OK, I'll start because it was my idea and I am brilliant.' Cameron poked his tongue out at Aiden who was pulling faces at him. 'Everyone gather round and hold on.'

They all did as they were told and as Nancy got as close

to Cameron as she could without it being obvious. She reached out and grabbed onto one of his fingers. As her skin touched his, she caught him glancing at her. His eyes looked particularly blue this evening and she felt the connection sizzle as they caught each other's eyes for a second. He then snapped his head back into the game, averting his gaze to the rest of the group. He was so focused and raring to go, his stance was crouched and sturdy.

'Is someone taking this game a little too seriously?' she joked, and he just smiled and winked at her. She tried her hardest not to react to the wink, but every inch of her skin tingled with excitement. That one quick motion had an incredible effect on her insides.

'I went to the shop and I bought some sticky ... sticky ... PANCAKES!'

The children rippled as they went to run but stopped themselves. A giggle erupted around the circle like a Mexican wave.

'Well done, you're all paying attention. OK ... I went to the shop and I bought some sticky ... sticky ... GLADRAGS!'

More squealing and laughter as some of the children began to run at the sound of 'Gl—' ... but then realised and quickly darted back to Cameron's hand.

'Ooh, I very nearly lost some of you then!' And then in super quick speed he quickly shouted – I WENT TO THE SHOP AND BOUGHT SOME STICKY STICKY GLUE!'

Everyone screamed and darted off into different directions and even Nancy found herself screaming as she ran. She nipped in and around the stools and tables which had been laid out on the beach front and as she did, she gripped Jack's hand so that he stayed with her. He wouldn't normally have played, but she'd promised to keep hold of his hand the whole time and he'd agreed reluctantly. It felt amazing just letting go and being free. No thinking about dinner, no thinking about school and the issues there, no worrying about how she was going to make ends meet ... just pure indulgence in being free and enjoying herself. At home she spent all her time worrying. She couldn't remember the last time she had let herself go and laughed like this. As a result, Jack seemed more relaxed too. Maybe if she relaxed more often it would continue to have a positive effect on Jack? She kept telling Harriet that Tommy was feeding off her stress, but she never thought about it with her own son.

'Quick Jack, in here.' She pointed to an opening between two trees and they scuttled inside. From this vantage point, they could see Cameron and the others running around on the sand. Nancy glanced over to Jack and saw him watching the others with interest, his blond hair messily over his eyes where he had been running and his little hands still squeezing hers tight, even though they were standing still. When she looked at his little face, all bright-eyed and taking the world in, she felt a glimmer of hope that things might just work out OK. It was moments like this where she felt the pressures of *normal* life lift, she appreciated that she actually had this amazing little person in her life.

'Are you enjoying yourself, Jack?'

'Uh-huh,' he replied, not taking his eyes off the beach front.

'What about the holiday, do you like the hotel we are in?'

She desperately wanted a more solid conversation with him. She had been spoilt on this holiday with a few special conversations with him. But the more she got, the hungrier she felt. She just wanted to chat with him all the time.

'The hotel is good – I like the balconies.'

'Because they go really high?'

'No, because I like the shapes of them and there are lots so I can count. Did you know there are 418 balconies at this hotel?' His eyes were wide with wonder.

Nancy lifted her eyebrows. 'Really?'

'Uh-huh.'

'That's a really interesting fact, Jack.' She was so proud of him. He might not be the most popular little boy and he might not enjoy swimming or dancing, but he had other talents and was so incredibly special to her. Maybe she needed to do what she'd told Harriet to do and stop comparing her life to others and start actually *seeing* it for what it was. Start practising what she preached to her friend!

'I don't like Mr Winters.'

Nancy had briefly looked back to where Cameron and the others were but when Jack said this she turned her attention round to focus on him. 'Mr Winters from school?' He nodded. 'Why don't you like Mr Winters?'

'He shouts.'

'At you?'

'Sometimes. Sometimes at other people. I don't like the noise. It hurts my ears.'

'Well, we are going to talk to your teachers when we get back from holiday so I will ask them not to shout around you.'

Jack nodded and then pointed. Nancy peered over her shoulder to where he was pointing to and was faced by a smiling Cameron. 'There you two are – we've been looking for you!'

'We are clearly too good for this game,' Nancy said, climbing out of the little cubby area they had shimmied into.

'Well Harriet was the first one caught so now she's in the centre.'

They walked back to the beachfront to start the next round.

After a few rounds of sticky glue, the game began to fizzle out which Nancy was a little relieved at because she was not as fit as she would maybe like to make out. She smiled at Harriet who was making her way towards her with two more cocktails in her hands and Jayne walking by her side. The pair seemed to be chatting and getting along nicely which made Nancy feel warm inside. There was no quick fix for the way her friend was feeling right now but surrounding herself with positive, nice people was definitely a good start.

'We have decided that tonight we want to try at least four different types of cocktail from the menu.' Harriet smiled, and it was the most genuine smile she had given the whole time they were there.

'Four?' Nancy replied. 'Depends what they are – I don't want to be sloshed. Poor Jack will have to carry me back.'

'Well, let's start with this one and see how we go. Jayne said this is one she's had a few times and it always comes out nice. It's called an Americano.'

'I thought that was a type of coffee?'

'Well, there ain't no coffee in this, my love. What did you

say was in this Jayne?' Harriet peered over her shoulder at Jayne who was approaching them; a pink flower perched in her hair matching the dress she was wearing this evening.

'Campari, vermouth and soda water.'

The girls all took a swig at the same time with varying responses. Jayne liked it, Harriet pulled a confused, unsure face and Nancy grimaced. 'No, this one is *not* for me!'

'Nancy? Could I have a word?'

She turned and smiled at Cameron who was holding two drinks and had gained a flower garland which was now placed around his neck, drawing her attention even more so to his unbuttoned top. 'Of course, is everything OK?'

He led her away from the girls and towards a canopied area where he sat down and urged her to do the same. 'Yeah everything's fine; I just wanted to give you something.' He slid the cocktail across the table. 'It isn't this, by the way, I just thought I would get you a drink too.'

She eyed the two tone liquid, the yellowy-orange at the top bleeding into the deep pink at the bottom. It was topped with a glacé cherry and a slice of orange. 'What is it?'

'A tequila sunrise – I have developed a little bit of a soft spot for these since arriving. Best to consume in small quantities.' He laughed, his smile lighting up his whole face.

'I'm not sure tequila is the right way to go for me.' She sniffed the glass.

'Don't sniff it, you wally, just try it.' He laughed again, but his face was full of compassion. She sipped the liquid; it was sweet but actually OK. She nodded as she swallowed it, going in for another sip. 'See? I told you. Never judge a book by its cover.'

'Or a cocktail by its smell?'

He laughed. 'Exactly. And the same goes for people too, hey?'

Nancy tilted her head as she pulled a confused face. 'What do you mean?'

Cameron shuffled in his seat to face her more. 'Well, it's the same with people. We're always quick to judge a person on what we see on the outside. Their disabilities, their hair colour, the clothes they wear, what they do for a job ... but none of these things tell us what that person is going through inside here.' He tapped his brain. 'Too often, people only see what's happening on the outside but we don't realise the struggle people have inside.'

Nancy instantly thought of Jack and then of Harriet. And actually, herself too.

'People are fighting battles that we can't see. So sometimes, we have to look deeper to find out ways to make these people's lives better. Does that make sense?' Nancy nodded, not trusting herself to speak. Cameron had hit the nail on the head and she realised now that actually, this was probably why she had been struggling so much. She had spent so long thinking about what Jack wasn't doing or achieving, why he wasn't fitting in, why he had meltdowns and what people were thinking, she hadn't spent much time trying to get to know the reasons behind all of this. What was going on inside his head? Maybe if she understood him more she would be more successful in achieving some sort of progress with him.

'I have something for you that I think – I hope – will explain what I mean a bit better.'

'O ... K ... sounds interesting.' She smiled nervously.

'There's no need to be worried – I'm not going to give you a human head or anything.' He laughed and pulled out what looked like a booklet.

'What's this?' she asked.

He slid the booklet along the bench and Nancy looked at the front which had a hand-drawn picture of two people – a man and a boy – and said 'Cameron and Aiden' on it. Nancy looked up at him for explanation.

'Aiden has made a booklet for Jack – it's all about us, our favourite colours, what our favourite foods are, how old we are and where we live. It has the things we are scared of and what we want to be when we grow up – or in my case, what my job is.' He smiled.

'Well, this is ... um ... lovely. But I don't understand...'

'You said Jack gets anxious talking to new people because he doesn't know them.' Cameron opened the booklet. 'Maybe he can get to know us a little better – it might help.'

Nancy felt her mouth drop open a little with shock. She couldn't believe that he had done this – it was so thoughtful. She didn't even think he'd remember a little comment like that. They'd just been chatting, and it had been a throwaway comment.

'I ... I don't know what to say.' She smiled. 'It's such a thoughtful thing to do.' And she felt her eyes suddenly fill with tears.

'You don't have to say anything.' He paused. 'Hey, what's wrong? I'm sorry, have I overstepped the mark?' He reached out his hand and placed it onto her shoulder.

Nancy wiped the tears from her cheek and laughed. 'I'm sorry; I'm just feeling a bit emotional.'

'Should I have not done this? I just thought it was a way of making Jack feel a little bit more comfortable with us.' He squeezed her shoulder gently. 'Nancy, I like spending time with you and Jack, but I don't want him to feel stressed or pressured into talking to Aiden. I just thought this way he could have a heads up and it might make the conversation a little easier to try next time.'

Nancy couldn't stop the tears from streaming down her face. She briefly opened up the booklet and scanned the pages. There were drawings scattered about on each of the pages where Aiden had drawn illustrations to support the information given. Pictures of him swimming, his favourite books, spiders and superheroes – Aiden had been so creative. It was such an innovative way to attack the problem of Jack not knowing them and Nancy really started to battle with how she felt. Part of her was so grateful that she had met Cameron and that he was trying to help make Jack's life a little easier. He made her think about how she focused on the outward problems associated with his autism rather than tackling the emotional side. He made her realise that not everyone was out to judge her and how she dealt with Jack's meltdowns. And he made her realise that there were nice guys out there and that not everyone was as selfish as Pete.

But he also made her realise that she was falling for someone she couldn't have. Because regardless of how comfortable Cameron and Aiden made Jack feel, she had promised Jack it would be just the two of them and she wasn't going to go back on her word. She just needed to work out how she was going to manage this newfound friendship with Cameron without it leading to where her mind so desperately wanted it to go. She looked at him and smiled. 'Thank you', she squeaked, sniffing back the tears.

'It might not work – but anything is worth a shot, right?' She nodded. 'Just take it and try it. See what happens. You never know – he might just like it.'

Chapter 27

Harriet glanced around at the people at the beach party. There was a real mix of families, friends, those that had children, those that didn't, and she watched the groups of people as they laughed and joked together. She thought back to how her life was back home – regimented, hectic, manic, frantic ... she was spinning so many plates just managing to keep them up, but she wasn't living. She wasn't enjoying her life.

'Penny for them?'

Harriet turned to face Jayne who had returned with some more cocktails.

'Oh nothing, just enjoying the party.' She took the glass and sipped it. 'Oh, nice. Raspberry?'

Jayne nodded. 'This one is called a Raspberry Ripple and it has raspberry and vanilla vodka in it. The barman reckons it's a good one and I have to say, I agree.'

'Me too,' Harriet replied and clinked her glass with Jayne's. 'These are such a good idea – little taster glasses.'

'I know, they're designed so you can taste lots of different types of cocktails without getting absolutely smashed. I think they created them with parents in mind!' Jayne laughed, sipping her drink and raising her eyebrows. 'We can indulge in cocktails and still be responsible adults.'

They both stood in silence for a few minutes, watching the people dancing and shouting joyfully, when suddenly Jayne said, 'Tell me if I'm overstepping the mark here ... but, you seem a little stressed. Is everything OK?'

Harriet looked at her and hesitated. She wasn't OK, but equally she didn't really know Jayne enough to spill her problems. She settled on smiling and saying, 'I'm fine.'

'Look, I know it probably seems weird that a stranger is saying this to you, but I went through a really tough time in the past – I mean, really tough – and when I came through it I vowed to always be there to help others. And, I don't know, I guess I just see a bit of myself in you and I had a feeling that you needed a friend.' She laughed. 'Again, I'm sounding weird saying that I had a feeling, but I did. I can't explain it, but I just feel like you need a bit of support in your life right now.'

She stopped talking and Harriet stayed quiet. Because actually, Jayne had nailed it on the head, hadn't she? Harriet *was* in need of some support right now and yes, she *was* falling apart, but could she really open up to some stranger she'd met on holiday? The whole idea of it was so completely alien to her it made her feel very uneasy.

Jayne continued. 'I was depressed.'

Harriet turned to face her, giving her the respect of her full attention. The hordes of people around them were still laughing and joking but between them it was like they were in a bubble, a bubble of connection, and it felt strange because Harriet didn't do meaningful talks with girlfriends – and she was equal measures intrigued and uncomfortable.

'And don't get me wrong, I don't mean a little bit sad, I mean I was on the verge of ending things. It had got that bad, I couldn't see the light.'

'Shit,' Harriet whispered under her breath.

Jayne nodded. 'I know. Right now, because I am in such a good place, it's hard for me to remember ever being that low. But I was. And do you know where it came from?'

Harriet shook her head.

'Pregnancy.'

Harriet choked on her drink.

'I really wanted children – like desperately wanted them. We tried for so long and it didn't happen for us. Then, after five years of trying and zillions of tests, it just happened. Just like that. I was over the moon – we both were. I was one of those pregnant ladies who was into everything and I was doing all the classes and reading all the books and searching all the internet columns.' She smiled and shook her head, 'I went a bit nuts about it because we had wanted it for so long.' She sipped her drink and pushed her auburn hair over one shoulder. 'But then one day, everything sort of changed. I was reading these books and I started to panic that actually, maybe I couldn't do this. Being a parent sounded really hard work and what if I wasn't up to the job? What if it was fate telling me I shouldn't have children and that's why I wasn't falling pregnant but I'd just badgered my body into doing it.'

'That's crazy.'

'I know, but that's what I mean, I did go crazy. Everything I read, I started to think I was incapable of doing. Everywhere I went I saw parents with their children and I was thinking to myself, what kind of mother was *I* going to be – because I didn't feel like I fit into any of the normal categories of mum. But, I kept it quiet and just got through the pregnancy – putting it down to nerves.'

'What happened when you had the baby?'

'It got worse – much worse. Now I had this baby that people could actually judge me on. I was in the hospital and the nurses were there to watch over me and make sure I was doing everything right but then they sent me home and suddenly, this little life was down to me and I didn't have the foggiest idea what I was doing.'

Harriet could relate to that feeling. She focused in on Jayne's face as she spoke and she could see the pain in it as she relived this part of her life. She wanted to hug her which was so far away from the person she was back home. This holiday was making her do and say stuff that was totally out of character – she felt a little bit out of control and she wasn't sure she liked it.

'For the first few months I just put it down to feeling overwhelmed and having a newborn baby. Surely everyone feels this way. But then I started going to NCT groups and I felt like everyone else was doing it better than me. Everyone else looked perfectly preened and like they'd had a zillion hours' sleep and here I was, rocking up having been up all night with a screaming baby who couldn't settle at all.'

'Didn't they help you?'

Jayne laughed. 'Don't be silly, of course I didn't tell anyone! I wasn't going to throw myself into the fire pit and open myself up to judgement and ridicule because I didn't know how to look after my own baby. I plastered on a smile and pretended I was fine.' She shook her head. 'But I didn't go back. Going to the classes made me feel inadequate.'

'What did your husband say?'

'I didn't tell him. I kept leaving for the groups every week, but I would go and sit in the park instead. When he asked me how the group was, I would lie and make up little stories about what happened.'

'Really? That's awful that you felt like that.' Harriet wanted to jump up and down and scream *I completely understand – I felt like that too*! Some days she still did. She totally got what Jayne was saying. Hearing another person – and not someone who had to be nice to her – talking about emotions that Harriet felt she was the only person in the world feeling, it was overwhelming. It was as though she was seeing herself from afar. Hearing Jayne speak out loud all the worries that were inside Harriet's head made her feel like she was watching herself from the outside, from another perspective. It was a strange feeling.

Jayne smiled, 'I know. But I was slowly losing my mind. Then I probably made one of the biggest mistakes of it all … I started looking on social media every hour of every day at other mums and their lives. And guess what – it all looked perfect.'

Harriet nodded and pulled a face –she had been there many a time. She still did it now.

'I was seeing every day, every hour, pictures and statuses of these mums who had their little cherubs who were perfect and never cried and slept through the night and here I was with a screaming baby 90 per cent of the time who never slept. They would post pictures of all these amazing days out or pictures of them doing yoga on a white sand beach whilst their bundle of joy slept soundly in the sand and here I was with my mum bun falling out, my boobs still leaking and a purple faced Michelin man baby because she was crying *all the time.*'

Harriet laughed. 'I know exactly what you mean. I would see the same things when I had Tommy except I wasn't at home with the mum bun and screaming baby – I was at work with the leaky boobs, porridge down my suit and snot in my hair.' Harriet instantly felt the release as she began to open up and talk about her own experiences.

Jayne giggled and clinked her glass with Harriet's. 'Proper mummies.'

Harriet grinned, a strange feeling overcoming her. She really liked Jayne. Like, properly liked her.

'But this was where I went wrong because then not only did I think other people were judging me, I was now constantly judging my own parenting and ripping myself apart. Being a parent is bloody hard and we need to be kind to ourselves. So when you get to the point where you are destroying your-self on a daily basis, it's a slippery slope from there. I went downhill very quickly.'

A table came free right next to where they were standing so Harriet darted quickly to grab it and Jayne grabbed the other chair and sat down opposite her. The breeze was gentle around them and because of their location, they were far enough away from the DJ to not have to shout loudly to be heard, but it was nice having the music as a background for their conversation because it was getting personal and Harriet was feeling a little exposed. But she needed this, she felt liberated just listening to Jayne's story.

'What happened?' she pressed. The more she heard about Jayne's story, the more she realised that maybe her own story wasn't far from other people's. Maybe she wasn't as alone as she'd first thought.

'I stopped going out. I stopped talking to my husband so we started arguing. He could see the changes in me but whenever he tried to talk to me about it I would shout blue murder at him.'

'Why?'

'Because I felt like *he* was now judging me and my parenting. He would tell me that I needed help and I would take that as him saying I was incapable of looking after our child. I cut off the friends I had made through the pregnancy and parenting stuff because they could all do it better than me and I didn't want to feel inadequate anymore.' She sighed. 'And then it began to have an adverse effect on my relationship with April and I started to resent her. I didn't want to be around her anymore so I would just sit and cry and then she would cry because babies can feel it you know. They know when you're feeling sad and even if you're not crying, they can sense the stress.'

The words from Harriet's conversation with Nancy rang in her head.

'I wasn't eating properly; I was crying all the time and Richard got so sick of me that he nearly left me and took April with him. I was in a really dark place – I told him to just go and to take her. I didn't care. I didn't want to be a mum anymore because I couldn't do it.' Jayne was a strong woman, Harriet could tell that, but even she was starting to struggle with reliving the dark moments. Harriet was left wondering how Jayne had got through it to be sitting here today talking about it. She felt the emotion begin to creep up and settle at the back of her throat. She tried to swallow it down, but it was lodged there like a ball.

'And then one day, I hit absolute rock bottom. April had been up all night crying and I couldn't do anything to stop her. I had fed her, sang to her, cuddled her, winded her, changed her ... everything you could think of and she still cried. And I just went down to my husband and broke down. I didn't think I could cry any more than I had done over that period but my God, I literally fell apart. My heart actually hurt because I felt like it was broken. I didn't know who I was anymore, I felt like a stranger inside my body. I wanted to just crawl away and die.'

'Bloody hell,' Harriet squeaked. She had felt down – really down – over the last year, but it was nothing in comparison to what Jayne had just described. It put everything into perspective a little bit.

'But Harriet, I got through it. And do you know how?' Harriet very slightly shook her head, fixated by the story so much that she couldn't move. Jayne placed her hand onto Harriet's and normally, she would've recoiled at this very public bodily contact but this time, she really needed it and she was so grateful to Jayne for that instinctive gesture. 'I let people in. I stopped trying to carry the world on my shoulders and pretend that I could do everything. I stopped shutting out those around me because I thought they would judge me. I stopped blaming April for making me feel this way because in reality it wasn't her making me feel shit, it was me. It was the pressure I was putting myself under and it was because I was letting what everyone else thought dictate how I felt and behaved.'

She squeezed her hand gently. 'Don't get me wrong, I'm not saying it was entirely my fault and I should've just sat back and not given a damn what people think – it doesn't work like that. We are human, of course we care what people think of us and it's not as easy as just ignoring them because you can't ignore it and it is totally normal to feel affected by it. But the key is to keep talking about it and let people help you. You don't have to do it all by yourself.'

Harriet took a sip of her drink as the words resonated deeply with her. She needed to sort her life out and fast – before she spiralled down to rock bottom like Jayne.

Chapter 28

Nancy walked away from Cameron clutching the booklet in her hands, in a daze. His gift had come as a complete shock. She hadn't realised how much Cameron had taken in from their conversation that night so for him to have spent time doing this was hard for her to comprehend. She spent so much of her time defending Jack from judgement that it was difficult to adapt to someone's kindness. As she approached the bench where Jack was sitting, she noticed Harriet talking to Jayne. The two of them seemed completely in their own little world, sitting close to one another. Jayne looking stunning in her floral pink dress that was nipped in at the waist showcasing her slim, up and down figure. It was a pale pink colour and had sort a sheer layer over the top of the material, meaning her shoulders were on show but still covered up. She was beautiful and just radiated warmth and happiness, and Nancy was glad Harriet was giving her the time of day now. Harriet, on the other hand, was looking chic and stylish in a pair of black and white stripy shorts and a fitted, white, one-shouldered top with a frill over one shoulder. Her tanned legs went on for miles in the short shorts and tan wedges, showcasing the most perfect of figures.

Nancy looked down at her own legs, which she had hidden away under her lightweight all in one jumpsuit. It wasn't that she didn't like her legs, but she was so slim right now she felt self-conscious that she appeared to be all skin and bones. She had lost a lot of weight since Pete had left and she hated it, her stress showing visibly on her body.

Reaching the bench, she sat down next to her son and gently placed her hand on his arm, gaining his attention from the iPad. He pulled his headphones off and looked at her.

'Alright little man?' He nodded. 'What you watching?'

He turned the screen to show her. 'Grand Designs.'

She smiled. He loved his building programmes. 'Is it a good one?'

'Yeah, they are putting a big balcony on this house right there.' He pointed at the screen. 'And then they are going to open up the roof bit there and put a big window in so they can see the stars!' His voice was full of excitement and wonder.

'That sounds incredible.'

'I wish I lived there – can we live there?'

'What about our house? You like our house.'

'Yeah but there isn't a balcony, or a big window.'

'True, but there is a garden with a cool treehouse.'

Jack's face lit up. 'Yeah, my treehouse!' His face dropped. 'I miss my treehouse, can we go home now?'

Nancy put her arm around him. 'Oh sweetheart, not yet darling. Soon we will be going home. Right now, we are having fun on holiday ... aren't we?'

She watched his little face as he put his headphones back on and shrugged out of her grasp. 'I guess so.'

She put her hand on his forearm again and he looked at her questioningly. 'I have something to show you – I hope you like it.'

'What is it?'

'You remember that boy that keeps coming over to you and talks to you – and I talk to his daddy?'

He shook his head. 'I don't like it, it makes me feel funny.'

'Is it because you don't know who they are – because they're new?' A nod. 'Well, this might be something that can help.' She handed him the booklet and he studied the front cover for a good minute before turning to her and saying;

'What is it?'

'It's a special book for you to read – for us to read together.'

'I like reading.'

'I know you do and do you know why this book is so special?' He shook his head. 'Because it is a friendship book.' He looked at her in confusion. 'This book is about that boy who comes and talks to you and about his daddy who talks to me.' She paused for a moment and watched him turn the booklet over in his hands, analysing the drawing on the front.

'Who is that?' he asked, pointing to the picture.

'That's a picture of the little boy and his dad – the boy drew it for you. Isn't that nice?'

Jack nodded. 'I like his drawing.'

'I like it too.' Nancy's heart swelled with happiness. She tried hard not to get excited but even she had to admit that this was going rather well. 'Do you want to look inside?' He nodded and opened the first page:

<u>All about me: Aiden</u>
My name is: Aiden
I am seven years old
I have brown hair and brown eyes.
I really like … swimming, reading, playing superheroes with
my dad
I don't like … angry voices, Brussel sprouts

Nancy read out all the different sections for Jack and he listened intently. This was ingenious!

'He doesn't like angry voices?' Nancy shook her head. 'I don't like angry voices either.'

'I know. That's something you both have in common – it means you both have something similar. And that's what friends are – they're people who are similar to you and enjoy the same things you do.'

'He says he enjoys swimming, but I don't like water.'

'Yes, but that's OK, because we are all different, that's what makes us special.' She smiled at him as he nodded. She often told him he was special and that it was OK to be different.

'Keep reading, Mummy.'

Nancy turned the page:

<u>My favourites page:</u>
My favourite colour is: Orange
My favourite book is: Horrid Henry
My favourite TV show is: Horrid Henry
My favourite film is: Horrid Henry

Jack gasped. 'My favourite film is Horrid Henry too!'

Nancy took in his shocked face. 'Isn't that wonderful?' A sizzle of excitement was bubbling up inside her. She saw out of the corner of her eye, over Jack's shoulder, that Cameron was watching them from over by the bar. When he saw her looking, he gave her a thumbs up sign. Nancy smiled and nodded in response, to indicate it was going OK. He smiled and winked in return and she pulled her eyes back to the booklet before she started blushing.

She turned the page:

I don't have a mummy but my daddy is like my mummy too. Here is a bit about him too.

All about me: Cameron
My name is: Cameron
I am 38 years old
I have blond hair and blue eyes.
I really like ... going for walks, going to the cinema and reading
I don't like ... getting up early, spiders and when Aiden is sad

'His daddy is older than you are.'

Nancy nodded. 'Yes he is, but only by a few years.'

'Six years.' Nancy nodded. 'Why doesn't he have a mummy?'

'I don't know sweetheart. But it is kind of the same thing with you, you don't see your daddy, and he doesn't see his mummy. That's another thing you have in common – do you see?'

'Oh yes!' He pondered on the thought for a minute. 'Carry on reading, Mummy.'

<u>My favourites page:</u>
My favourite colour is: Green
My favourite book is: Jack Reacher
My favourite TV show is: Countryfile
My favourite film is: Taken

'I don't know what any of those things are except the colour.'

Nancy laughed. 'That's because you are a lot younger than me and Cameron. Those are good choices, I can tell you that.'

'His favourite book has the same name as me.'

'So it does, that's funny.' Jack nodded and turned the page.

My job is to look after babies when they are born and to make them better when they are poorly – my job is called a NEONATAL SURGEON. I am a special doctor for babies.

A smile crept across Nancy's face as she read this part. She found his job fascinating. She felt it showed a lot about his personality and the type of person he was. Any man who chose to work with children instantly found himself bumped up the attraction list, in her opinion.

'Wow, he's a doctor. I see lots of doctors.'

'Yes, you see the doctors at the hospital and the clinic, don't you? They help you with how you're feeling and with school and stuff don't they?' He nodded. This booklet had created a basis for Nancy and Jack to talk. She was getting to know

Aiden and Cameron, but more importantly, she was getting a little insight into Jack too.

'So you see, he has an interesting job, hey? And Aiden seems like lots of fun?' Jack shrugged. 'Do you think maybe one day you would like to talk to Aiden?'

Jack shook his head and Nancy's heart sank. It hadn't worked. 'Why not?'

'I still don't know who he is.'

'But you know a little bit about him now. You know that he likes some of the same things as you and that he doesn't like angry voices so he won't be loud around you.'

She so desperately wanted this to work, but it seemed like a long shot now. As the excitement wore down and reality set in, Nancy realised just how disappointed she was that she wouldn't get to spend more time with Cameron. 'It's OK sweetheart, if you don't want to talk to him, that's fine. But keep the booklet and look at it whenever you like – you might feel differently on another day.'

He took the booklet from her but then placed it down beside him. 'Can I watch the building again?'

Nancy nodded and exhaled as he placed the headphones back on his head. Cameron held out his hand for a verdict and she sadly shook her head. Cameron responded with a sad smile and Nancy turned around on the bench and looked out to sea.

Why was it so hard – all she wanted was a son who was like everyone else. She instantly hated herself for thinking it and shook the thought from her mind. Just her and Jack – it would be fine.

Chapter 29

'You've gone very quiet on me, I hope I haven't overstepped the mark by telling you all this? I don't want to scare you off.' Jayne looked a little worried and Harriet immediately felt bad.

'God no! Not at all. I'm sorry; I didn't mean to go quiet. It's amazing that you felt you were able to open up to me and tell me all of that – you've certainly been through it and I'm so sorry you have.'

'It was a horrible time but in all honesty, it has made me the person I am today. I needed to go through that to be able to come out the other side and change my life.'

'What has changed for you, apart from the obvious feeling better?' Harriet poured some water from the jug for both of them.

'I look after myself a lot more and I care for my body.' Harriet pulled a face. 'I'm not saying you have to turn to yoga and stop eating meat and take herbal supplements, but just being more aware of your body and what stresses you put on it. I exercise a lot more now because exercise is amazing both for your body and for your mental health. I make better choices about the food I eat and little changes like switching to herbal or decaf late afternoon so that I know I get a good night's sleep.'

'I can't remember the last time I slept for a good amount of time.' If it wasn't Tommy up in the night it was Isla, and if it wasn't either of them, it was work emails keeping her up.

'You see, it's not good for you and it all piles up and then you explode. I also started talking about things. I started a blog and I spoke about what I went through. I keep my friends and family in the loop when I'm feeling stressed or low – because it still happens. You don't just switch off depression and never have it again, if you go down once you have the potential to go down again. It's training yourself to notice the signs so that when you start slipping, you stop it in its tracks. I go running when I feel it slipping back in, and I talk to people. Sometimes I'll talk to my husband; sometimes I'll blog about it. But you have to talk.'

'What if you don't have anyone to talk to?' No matter how bad she was feeling, there was no way on this earth she was about to open up to her mum and leave the door wide open for judgement and anxiety. And Nancy had her own stuff to deal with; she didn't need all this unloaded on her like Harriet had earlier. It should never have spilled out like that – that wasn't going to happen again.

'There are many places you can go to talk to someone when you're struggling. It can be the doctor's or a clinic or a group, or if you wanted to stay more anonymous, it could be an online group. You don't have to disclose your identity and you only reveal what you want people to know. But don't bottle it up – it's like poison. It seeps through your body so rapidly and before you know it you can see no way out.' Harriet nodded. 'So what's your situation?' Jayne took her chance and asked the question that had been hanging in the air.

Harriet knew it was coming and there had been times when Jayne was talking that she'd wanted to talk about her own situation, but she couldn't find the words. 'You don't have to talk about it if you don't want to. But just know that I am here and I am impartial.' Jayne smiled. 'And I will never *ever* judge anyone.'

Harriet took a huge gulp of her drink and finished the glass. 'I'm struggling to bond with Tommy.'

Jayne nodded. 'Well done for saying it out loud, I know that's a hard thing to do.'

'I feel like such an awful mother saying that – especially when I have Isla too. But I coped fine with her.' Her heart was racing, pulsing rapidly as she let the words that were haunting her slowly trickle out.

'What's different now?'

She kept her gaze out to sea, not wanting to look at Jayne as she spoke. She said she was impartial, but Harriet was afraid of seeing that judgement behind her eyes. She had seen it so many times before and it hurt. Even if she did try to cover it up. 'Home life, my relationship fell apart, work has increased ... loads.'

'OK, so that's good, you know what some of the triggers are. Identifying them is one of the toughest parts. Is there anything you can change?'

'Well my dickhead husband has fucked off so that's a positive – although it doesn't sound like it. He wasn't very
supportive with my work or the children so him being gone
is a good thing.'

'Do you have support in other ways now that he's gone?'
Jayne was so good at this. Harriet didn't feel harassed for
answers but at the same time, it was forcing her to evaluate
her situation which was what she needed to do to be able to
move forward. And that's what she wanted, to move forward
and go home feeling like things could get better, not stay as
stressed and confusing as they currently were.

Harriet shook her head. 'Not really, I'm doing everything
myself.'

'Do you have to do everything?'

'Who else am I going to ask?'

'What is it you need help with?'

Harriet exhaled. 'I don't know.'

'Can you delegate out some things to others? What are the
most important things in your life that you want to be doing
and not someone else?'

'My job and obviously being with my children. But all I
seem to be doing is cooking – and when I say cooking I mean
bunging a tray of beige food in the oven and hoping they'll
eat it – or giving them a bath or pretending to listen to them
whilst I type emails with one hand.' She took a gulp of drink.
'Bloody hell, contender for mum of the year right here.'

Jayne laughed. 'You'd be surprised just how many people
will understand your situation. It's all about prioritising and
time management. It might be because you are so focused on

work and you don't get that play time with the children that you feel the bond isn't there. Do you think?' she questioned.

'Maybe.'

'So you need to find a way to gain that time with them to get to know them, who they are and what they like – and take out all the unnecessary jobs that you can delegate out to others. You're a businesswoman Harriet so project manage your life. What jobs do you want to keep for yourself and which ones can you delegate out and either get some paid help or ask friends to help.'

Harriet nodded and picked up the empty water jug. 'You're right.' And she was. Harriet spent all her time priding herself on her ability to manage projects at work and hit deadlines and achieve, yet when it came to her home life, all her organisational skills went out the window. Why was that? She wasn't sure she had the answer, but maybe she didn't need all the answers. Maybe just acknowledging that she wasn't doing it was enough. She needed to apply her work self to her home life and make progress there too. It's like Jayne had said – she needed to project manage her life. 'I can totally do that. I have all the skills to make things flow and get the jobs done; I just need to apply these skills at home and with the children. It makes sense – on paper.'

Jayne shook her head. 'Not just on paper, Harriet, you can 100 per cent achieve this. How would you attack a project at work?'

She instantly felt at ease on work ground. 'I would identify all the required needs, allocate the necessary jobs to appropriate delegates, cross plan it with finance to make sure it was achievable and then oversee the project as a whole to ensure the continued smooth transition from concept to delivery.'

'Said like a true pro,' Jayne laughed.

Usually, someone laughing at Harriet would spark annoyance and send her into defence mode. But actually, Jayne was complimenting her and this conversation had shown Harriet that her work talents were transferable to her family. 'Why haven't I thought of this before!' She shook her head in disbelief. 'It sounds obvious now you say it.'

'Sometimes it takes an outsider to help guide you to what's obvious. That's why it is so important to talk. About anything. Talking helps you mentally and emotionally but it also helps to find solutions and focus. You just need to find the people you can talk to, that's all.'

Harriet nodded. She felt about eight feet tall and bursting with confidence. She knew what she had to do – now she just had to put her plan into action. This holiday was giving her more than she bargained for.

Chapter 30

The next morning at breakfast, Nancy noticed that Harriet was surprisingly chirpier than usual. She watched her as she sauntered in to the buffet room, coffee in one hand and pad and pen in the other, and plonked herself down on the table.

'What's got you all happy?'

'I have a plan.' She sat herself down, tucking her black, floor-length, floral maxi dress underneath her bottom. Whilst this was fairly reserved for Harriet, who liked to wear outfits that caught people's eye, the plunging neckline which revealed her bikini top underneath was more in tone with her usual style. She liked to dress to kill and was the only person Nancy knew who had attempted to keep her stilettos on whilst walking in the sand. She didn't last very long. Kudos for trying though.

'Isn't it supposed to be "I have a dream"?' Nancy smiled, mimicking Martin Luther King Jr.

'I have one of those too, but I need a plan to get there.' She sipped her coffee. 'Thanks for bringing the children down to breakfast with you this morning whilst I finished what I was doing.'

'It's no problem at all.' She looked over to Tommy in the highchair. 'Although I hold no responsibility for the fact that Tommy has had five pancakes this morning because Isla keeps going up and getting him more.'

Harriet looked at Isla who giggled. 'He likes them, Mummy.'

'I don't doubt that, Isla, but it doesn't mean he gets to eat them until he looks like one.' Her voice was stern, but she had a twinkle in her eye, Nancy noticed. Something was different with her today. Isla giggled and kept repeating *Tommy is a pancake, Tommy is a pancake.*

'So what's this big plan you have then – is it realistic or are you going to go and live on the moon?' Nancy pressed, desperate to know why her best friend was acting strangely chirpy, especially after all the mini cocktails last night. Yes, they were smaller, but goodness they were still strong.

'Very funny – although I *would* live on the moon if I could actually get away with it. Imagine that, no emails, no constant phone calls...'

'No Netflix or ITV dramas...'

Harriet pointed at Nancy. 'You have a point there; maybe I wouldn't like to live on the moon then. Scrap that.' Harriet drank her coffee and Nancy gave her a look as if to say; *well, come on then.* 'OK, so I was talking to Jayne yesterday for ages and yes, you were right, she is really lovely and she has been through so much and come out the other side. She is amazing.' Nancy smiled at how her friend was talking about the other woman. It was completely out of character for her. Harriet stopped talking and frowned. 'What?'

'Who are you and what have you done with my friend?' Nancy said and laughed.

Isla piped up at that point and said, 'That's my Mummy.'

'I know darling, I was telling a joke – admittedly it wasn't a very funny joke.' She pulled a face at Harriet who giggled.

'You were the one who told me to talk to her!' Harriet laughed.

'And I'm glad, really, I am! This is great. Sorry, I shouldn't be mocking you. Carry on.' Nancy held out her hand to encourage Harriet to continue. Today Nancy had chosen a long skirt – grey pleated – teamed with a plain white vest top which she tucked into the waistband of her skirt. It was simple and comfortable. With all the buffet food and cocktails she had consumed over the last five days, she was glad that her style didn't involve tight-fitting clothes and revealing midriffs. However, she had raided Harriet's wardrobe for a belt and a necklace to add to the outfit – things she didn't really possess in her own wardrobe – and she had plaited her hair so that it came over her shoulder. She wanted it to look effortless and casual. And it had nothing to do with Cameron. Nothing at all.

Harriet pulled a face and opened up her notepad. 'Anyway, as I was saying, I was talking to Jayne and she really spoke some sense. She was saying how I needed to prioritise the things in my life that I want to do and delegate the things that I don't want to do. So I spent this morning – and a huge chunk of last night – going through all my current projects and making a list of tasks I can delegate out to others.' She looked at Nancy with a smile. 'Good huh?'

'Yes, that is good. But what about at home? And there is still the small thing of – you're on holiday yet you are still working.'

'Yes, yes, I know. But if I delegate out work to people then it gives me more time as a result and then I can be with the children more – like properly with them not just in body but not in mind. And listen, I'm sorry about my breakdown yesterday and I'm sorry that you feel like I'm working all the time and you aren't having the girls' holiday I promised you.'

'And I'm sorry too, I shouldn't have shouted at you. I didn't realise you were struggling so much.'

'That's because I didn't tell you – I didn't tell anyone. So you can't be blamed for not knowing. But I promise that for our last two days I will be better and work less.'

'OK, looking forward to it.' Nancy felt a spark of excitement bolt through her at the thought of ending the girls' holiday on a high and actually seeing Hari enjoy herself. Seeing her so happy and bouncy this morning made her feel all warm inside.

'Mummy?' Jack was tugging on Nancy's arm. She turned to face him as she spooned some yoghurt into her mouth. 'Where's that boy?'

'What boy darling?'

'The boy from the book.'

Nancy froze to her chair. Surely not. 'You mean Aiden? The boy who wrote the booklet for you?' Jack nodded. 'I don't know sweetie, he's probably having breakfast. Why?'

'I want to tell him my favourite colour.'

Nancy looked over to Harriet to relay her excitement but

in a cool and causal way so as not to scare Jack off this newfound interest. She glared at Harriet who clearly had no idea what was going on because Nancy hadn't told her about the booklet yet.

'Well, that's lovely sweetheart. We can go and look for him after breakfast if you want? Then you can tell him?' Jack nodded. 'OK, we will do that.'

He carried on eating his breakfast and Harriet hissed to Nancy, 'What's that about?'

'I literally cannot speak right now,' Nancy squeaked. 'It's really exciting!'

'You can't leave me in the dark like that. Let me scooch round to your side, hang on.' Harriet picked up her chair and shimmied round next to Nancy. 'Spill!'

Nancy made sure Jack was back to what he was doing before casually leaning her body so he couldn't see what she was saying. 'I don't want Jack to hear me – he'll think I'm making a big deal out of it and it might curb his enthusiasm.'

'OK, just face me and I'll tell you if he looks over.'

Nancy's smile radiated brightly across her face. 'Last night, Cameron gave me a booklet about him and Aiden.'

'A booklet? Romantic.' Harriet scoffed.

'It kind of is, actually.'

'Wow, Nance, you're easily pleased.'

'No, you don't understand. A few days ago I mentioned how Jack doesn't like talking to new people, to people he doesn't know. I didn't think much of the comment, but then he turns up with this booklet Aiden drew and designed and said they did it because they wanted Jack to feel like he knew

241

them a little bit so it wouldn't be so hard for him to maybe talk to them.'

Realisation dawned on Harriet's face. 'Oh, I see. That's cute!'

'I know! But Jack didn't respond in the way I had hoped and he seemed uninterested in the booklet. Last night I saw it discarded on the sideboard next to our bed so I just wrote it off. But he must've picked it up again to read and, I don't know, something has made him want to talk to them.' She exhaled, trying to calm her erratic voice. 'Hari, I didn't push this with him, he has made this decision by himself. That must mean he *wants* to see Aiden. He has never *wanted* to see another child before. It's incredible.'

'It *is* incredible, I'm so happy for you. Let's eat up so you two can go on your little adventure to find them.'

Nancy nodded and continued with her yoghurt, unable to pull the corners of her mouth down into a neutral position. This smile was staying here for a while and she loved it.

***

After breakfast Nancy and Jack set off to find Cameron and Aiden. It was frustrating because every day since they had been there, they had bumped into them no end of times and Aiden had always tried to talk to Jack and he'd always ignored him. But today, when Jack actually asked for him, they were nowhere to be seen.

'Where is he Mummy?'

'I don't know, maybe he's still in bed.' They weaved around

the complex, looking in the pool areas, the restaurant windows, around the kids' club area ... the complex was particularly busy today. There was lots of noise and running around going on around them and Nancy could feel Jack's grip tighten on her hand. He had been doing so well since they arrived, and this hadn't been the easiest of holidays for him to get used to. Being a family-orientated complex, the place was always very loud with either music or screams of playing children. Nancy was very proud of how well Jack had been coping – regardless of the odd meltdown he'd had. It was all progress. And this was how she knew that she herself was making progress too. Because she was focusing on what positive changes he had made and achieved, as opposed to all the negatives.

'In bed! I never sleep in till this late.'

'No, you're an early riser you, you like to wake Mummy up even when it's still dark outside, don't you, monkey!'

She ruffled his hair and then paused, realising what she had done. But he didn't react. She almost wanted to ask him *why* he didn't react but, of course, that was ludicrous. She knew she shouldn't bring attention to things when he made progress, she didn't want to give him the wrong impression or make him rethink what he was doing. But this was incredible. Sometimes it was easy to overlook these small nuggets of personal growth because they seemed so trivial. A ruffle of the hair – what relevance does that have generally? But for Jack, this was considerable development and Nancy felt warm from head to toe. He giggled and it was so lovely to hear. 'I don't like sleep.'

'I know you don't, sweetie.'

A couple more minutes went by and they were running out of places to look. Nancy stopped walking to think for a minute. The complex was like a maze, and all the different areas looked the same. Each side of the hotel had the same terracotta shade of building with endless balconies lined up along the poolside. There were three main swimming pools and the one that was behind the building where the girls were staying was where the adult only pool was – not that they would ever experience it. The other two pools were family pools with a few slides or water pumps. She glanced over at the bar area next to the main family pool, but she couldn't see any sign of Cameron, Aiden or Cameron's sister and her family.

'Mummy?'

'Yes Jack?'

'Where is he?'

Nancy exhaled discreetly. 'I don't know darling. Let's look down by the beach bit here and if not then we can find them later.' She led him past the pool towards the gates which led out onto the main strip. The beach was just across the road from their resort.

'But I want to tell him my favourite colour. I want him to know that I don't like red, or blue or yellow – my favourite colour is orange.' He followed Nancy, his little legs working fast to keep up with her long strides. She took note and slowed her pace a little for him.

'And do you remember what his favourite colour was?' she asked, trying to distract him from the failed search.

'Orange too.'

'That's right, so you have lots of things in common.'

'Uh-huh ... Mummy?'

'Yes Jack?'

'Where is he?'

'Baby, I don't kn—'

'There!' Jack called and pointed and he was right. Over by the sailing boats on the beach, were Cameron and Aiden, and Aiden's niece and nephew too. 'Mummy?' Jack stopped walking.

'Yes Jack?'

'I don't want to tell him anymore.'

Nancy's heart sunk. 'But why?' she stopped walking and knelt down to be at Jack's level. 'What's wrong?'

'I don't like it.'

'You don't like what?'

'Them.'

'Who?'

'The people, with the boy.' He looked to the ground and kicked the dirt.

Nancy looked over to where Cameron was and it clicked. 'Is it because he has the other boy and girl with him.' Jack nodded. 'But they can be your friends too.'

'I don't know them.'

Nancy smiled. 'Because they aren't in the book?' Jack nodded. 'OK, let's go back to the hotel and we can find Aiden another time when he isn't with the others, how does that sound?' Jack nodded.

So close yet so far. But on the bright side, she really felt like she was starting to learn how her son worked. He wasn't programmed like other children, and she was starting to realise that it wasn't a case of teaching Jack to fit in, it was a case of learning how *he* worked in order to cope with situations. And it was the booklet that had helped to open up this new world of thinking to her. She smiled to herself as they made their way back to the resort. She could totally crack this – she was going to find a way of helping her son to make sense of this world and make it work for him.

Chapter 31

'Did you find him?' Harriet asked as Nancy approached feeling disappointed.

'Yeah but he was busy so we are going back later.' Nancy smiled at Jack who sat down on the floor next to the loungers. She pulled his sketch pad out of her bag and handed it to him along with his pencil case. Drawing was another one of his favourite things to do and it was something Nancy loved herself. As she watched him open up his pad and continue with a drawing he had been working on she decided to join him on the floor and take an interest. 'What are you drawing?' she asked.

'It's a castle.'

She didn't need to ask, she could clearly see what it was. Jack's drawing skills were off the scale for a seven-year-old. One way he differed from the average child artist, was that he drew everything scaled down from the original measurements. So his castle was an accurate representation of one he had found online. But he wasn't copying now; he was doing it from memory. 'I like this part,' Nancy said, pointing to the drawbridge.

'That's my favourite part too.' He smiled at her. 'Can you see, it has a perfect 135-degree angle right there?'

Harriet laughed. 'Jack, you are a mathematical wizard! You should be an architect or something when you grow up.'

Jack nodded as he drew but he didn't seem to respond to the question itself, he was too enthralled in what he was doing and he only really had space in his mind to engage with one person at a time, and that was Nancy right now. Nancy smiled at Harriet for getting involved.

'Jack, can I have some paper so I can do some drawing too?'

He seemed very excited about this and rapidly tore a sheet out of his book and gave it to her. 'Here, you can use my pencils too.'

'Thank you.' She moved to stand up but Jack placed his hand on her arm.

'Mummy, stay here with me.'

Nancy just wanted to grab him and squeeze so hard. He *wanted* to be with her. Of course they had spent time together before but everything just felt different, it felt real. Was it because Nancy herself was relaxing more? Was that why it felt different? She smiled at him and said, 'Of course I will.' Jack resumed his drawing and Nancy rummaged in his pencil case for a pencil. 'So, what have you been up to?' she asked Harriet as she began to sketch.

'Well Isla is in kids' club – she wanted to go, before you say anything.'

Nancy held her hands up. 'I didn't say a word!'

'I know but, well you know, just in case. And Tommy is

asleep in here.' She used her foot to indicate the pram beside the table. 'So I'm using this time to check emails and delegate stuff so that when the children are awake and present, I can do stuff with them.'

'Sounds like you have it all under control – well done. And how are you feeling in yourself?'

'Yeah I'm fine. You know me, just get on and do things.' She smiled. 'So come on, how's your life planning going? Maybe you should speak to Jayne about where you need to focus on and move forward.'

'I spoke to Jack; he said he doesn't want to see Pete.'

'He's a smart lad.' Harriet replied but got a warning look from Nancy.

'So I guess I have to accept everyone's decisions and leave it now. Pete clearly isn't interested and Jack's happy with how things are – so that's it, I guess.'

'Has Pete tried to contact you again?'

'No.'

'And did you reply to the text?'

'I didn't actually. I was going to but when Jack said he didn't want to see him, I thought I'd just leave it. Do you think I did the right thing?'

'Do I! Bloody hell, yes of course I do! Well done girl.' Harriet spotted someone over Nancy's shoulder and waved. Nancy followed her wave, looking behind her and she couldn't help the smile spread across her face the instant she saw him. 'Don't fancy him, my arse!' Harriet hissed.

'Excuse me?' Nancy laughed.

'You practically salivate at the very sight of him and you're telling me that you don't want anything to happen between you two! Bullsh—'

'Alright ladies?'

'Hey, how are you?' Nancy swivelled on her bum to face him and did an up and down check of what Cameron was wearing. She was no style guru but she did notice that Cameron was always dressed well. Today he was wearing a navy long sleeved shirt with the sleeves rolled up and buttoned, with white shorts and beige slip-ons. He had a big chunky watch on his left arm which Nancy knew wasn't a cheap brand and his sunglasses were designer too. The guy knew how to present himself – it was an attractive trait to have.

'I'm good thanks; we've just been down to the beach to look at the boats.' He pulled his hand out of his pocket to point towards the beach and then resumed his stance with both hands casually deposited in his shorts pockets.

'Yeah I know,' Nancy replied and then stumbled over her words. 'I mean, I wasn't stalking you or anything, we were just down there, me and Jack … we saw you.' Why was she rambling? She needed to chill.

'Oh really? Why didn't you come and say hi – we could've shown Jack the boats.'

'Well, that's the thing; Jack was actually asking to see Aiden.'

Cameron raised his eyebrows. 'Really?' Nancy nodded. 'Well, I'll be damned. Shall I go get him and we can maybe go for a bite to eat?'

Nancy looked round to Harriet. 'Oh, so you remember I'm

here,' Harriet joked. 'It's fine, go, have fun.' She waved her friend off with her arm.

'Looks like I'm coming.'

'Great, meet you in half hour at the fish and chip place by the beach?'

Nancy nodded and Cameron walked off, shouting goodbye to Harriet as he went. 'Well, well, well, look who's dumping her mate to go and spend time with the hot guy.'

'Hot doctor,' Nancy corrected, and Harriet sat up.

'Say what now?'

'He's a neonatal surgeon.'

'Shut the front door!' Nancy nodded. 'You are smooching with a hot doctor who works with babies – oh my ovaries!' Harriet groaned and held her stomach.

'Shut up you fool!' Nancy chucked a towel at Harriet who caught it at the last minute and poked her tongue out. 'Are you sure you don't mind?'

'It's not me you should be asking.' She nodded to Jack.

Nancy pulled a face and then turned to her son. 'Jack, Cameron has invited me and you to lunch with him and Aiden.'

'I don't want to.'

Nancy glanced at Harriet and she willed her to continue.

'Why not, I thought you wanted to tell Aiden about your favourite colour?'

'But the people...'

'It will just be me and you and Aiden and his dad, that's all.'

Harriet watched, waiting for Jack's final response. Eventually he said, 'Spose so.'

'Now go,' Harriet said, lying back on the lounger and picking up her phone. 'Go before he changes his mind again!'

***

Nancy felt Jack clasp her hand tighter as they approached the table where Cameron and Aiden were sitting. She paused for a second before they saw them and turned to Jack. 'You OK, sweetie?' She had a last minute stab of guilt as Jack's hand squeezed hers. Had she forced him to come here for her own personal gain? Maybe she shouldn't have pushed it? She wanted him to make friends with Aiden but equally, she had wanted to see Cameron. Now she felt guilty for letting her own selfish reasons take over her actions. Jack nodded that he was OK and it went some way to making her feel a little better 'We'll have fun. And if at any time you want to leave, you just tell me, alright?' Another nod. 'Come on then.' She gave his hand one last squeeze and then strode up to the table, greeting them both with a smile.

Aiden was wearing the cutest little shirt and shorts combo, matching Cameron's style perfectly. They looked sweet together, both perusing the menu as they waited for their guests. Aiden's little face lit up when he saw Nancy and Jack and he instantly waved excitedly.

'Hey you two, really nice to see you here.' Cameron stood and leaned over to kiss Nancy on the cheek. It was the first time he had done that. It felt a little weird, and a tad too formal considering they had spent time together prior to today.

However, Nancy enjoyed the closeness of it. As he leaned in she got a whiff of his aftershave and she found herself getting a little kick from it. She let him brush his lips over her cheek as he softly kissed her and then, as he drew back, he gave her elbow a little gentle squeeze. It was almost like he could read her mind and he knew just how big this moment was for Jack. His attention then drew to Jack and he simply said, 'Hello little man.' Smiling, he returned to his seated position. She was glad he didn't try and shake Jack's hand or ask him any questions, it was hard enough for him just to be here – he needed to take this at his own pace and Cameron seemed to sense this. Nancy took real comfort from Cameron when he was around. He had a way of making her feel completely relaxed about Jack's autism. It was like they were a team. Cameron *got* it. The fact he had experience with his cousin's child and also that he worked with children – he was clearly a very compassionate and caring type of person naturally. So when he was around them, it sort of rubbed off on to Nancy and she instantly felt calmer and more capable of taking on whatever was needed to get through. She had a feeling that if Cameron was around when Jack had a meltdown he would totally be able to handle it and keep her calm at the same time. Like a father should. Or a husband. But he was neither of these to Nancy or Jack. Yet here she was, wanting to spend all her time with him.

Nancy indicated a chair to Jack – the one next to Aiden but Jack hesitated. She then pointed to her one, next to Cameron and Jack nodded and sat down. He was clearly having an attack of nerves, which was fine. He hadn't run away yet or asked to leave so it was still progress. Painfully slow progress, but progress nonetheless.

She smiled at Aiden. 'Hey Aiden, you OK?'

'Yep! I got this from the boats earlier, look.' He held out a piece of rope.

'Wow!' Nancy feigned interest.

'When he says it's from the boat, he means he found it on the floor, near the boat, so of course he had to pick it up and bring it back.' Cameron rolled his eyes and Nancy laughed.

'The amount of things we have come home with after days out. Jack always used to like to bring home stones. All different shapes and sizes, different colours, different textures ... Hundreds of them. Didn't you?' She aimed a question at Jack to gauge how he was feeling. He nodded but stayed focused on the ground.

'Jack do you want to look at this game I've got on my tablet?' Aiden held up his tablet, reiterating his offer. But Jack just shook his head. Nancy tried to hide the disappointment in her face. This wasn't working.

'Jack, we had something we wanted to say to Aiden and Cameron, didn't we? Do you remember what it was?' Jack shrugged and Nancy felt her sadness turn to frustration. He was bloody fine about this before and now they were here, it was like they'd never had that conversation. 'Jack and I wanted to say thank you for making such a fantastic little booklet – we really enjoyed reading all about the things you both liked and disliked. And Jack actually found that he liked some of the things that you do Aiden.'

'Oh yeah? Like what?' Aiden was engaged, cooperative and

interested. Nancy tried really hard not to compare her son to others but when she was faced with a boy of the same age behaving like this, she found it really hard to not grieve for the son she didn't have. And instantly she was also hit by a monumental feeling of guilt for even feeling those things. It was an emotional rollercoaster being Jack's mum.

Nancy looked over to her son. 'Jack? What did you want to tell Aiden about?' Nothing. 'Was it about your favourite colour?' Still nothing. She shuffled in her seat to cover up the irritation that was starting to seep out. She turned to Aiden. 'Jacks favourite colour is also orange – like yours.'

'Ah that's cool. My pencil case at school is orange and my backpack.'

Nancy spotted Jack's head rise slightly at all the talk of orange. She didn't look directly at him in case he went back into himself, but the more Aiden spoke about all the orange things he had, the more Jack seemed to take an interest. Maybe it was because they were talking between themselves, not directly at him. She had noticed a few times recently that sometimes it helped to not directly address him, but to let him come into a conversation when he was ready. So by talking to Aiden in this way Jack's interest had been piqued indirectly. Another thing she had learnt about Jack on this holiday.

Aiden excitedly exclaimed, 'And I like to eat oranges too.'

'I don't like eating them.'

All three of them stopped and looked at Jack. It was the first time he had addressed the others in a conversation and even though he wasn't looking at them, this was huge progress. Nancy wanted to jump up and down and scream with joy, but she composed herself rapidly and tried to see how far she could push it.

'That's right, you don't like oranges. What fruit do you like Jack?'

He still didn't look up but he said, 'Grapes, apples and pineapple.'

'I love pineapple!' Aiden said, and Jack actually looked up at him – although Nancy was pretty sure it was because Aiden's voice went a few decibels louder with the excitement and not actually because he wanted to interact. But it was all progress. This is what she kept telling herself.

'I like pineapple too,' Cameron added and when Nancy looked at him, he smiled.

'You also like Countryfile if I remember correctly,' Nancy mocked and Cameron's face brightened.

'Oh, I see, you're going to mock my answers in the booklet. Listen there's nothing wrong with liking Countryfile, it's an awesome programme. What's yours then? Seeing as I don't have the upper hand right now by having had a booklet to revise on you prior to our meeting.'

'Don't be jealous just because I studied and you didn't.'

'Come on then, I want favourite TV show, colour and food from you.' He crossed his arms but had a smirk drawn across his face.

Aiden was now typing away on his tablet and Nancy could see Jack was looking, but not yet moving. She left him for now – he was better if he could do things in his own time, she told herself. Don't ruin all the hard work by pushing too fast.

'OK, favourite TV show has to be The Great British Bake Off.'

'Oh, do you like to bake then?'

'Nope, can't do it. But I like watching other people bake.'

'Colour?'

'Purple.'

'Food?'

'Ah, well now you see this is a tough one because food is one of my favourite things so it's hard for me to pick just one.' She pretended to put a lot of thought into her answer and she could hear Cameron sniggering. 'What?'

'I've just never known anyone to put so much thought into a food related question before, that's all. You go ahead, think away.'

'Right hang on; are we talking savoury or sweet?'

'Up to you.' He smiled.

'And do you mean like dinner sort of food, or snack food?'

'Oh my goodness, Nancy, just your favourite food,' he laughed. 'What food is your absolute favourite? If you were on a desert island and you could only take one piece of food, or snack, or meal ... what would it be?' He was laughing as he spoke and Nancy couldn't help but laugh along with him.

'I don't see what all the laughing is for; it was a perfectly valid question I was asking.'

'And it's a perfectly simple question I asked; without thinking, right now, favourite food ... GO!' He pointed at her grinning.

'Erm ... err ... a ... um...'

'Don't think about it, what comes to mind right now?'

'I don't know ... um.' She glanced at the table and saw the vinegar. 'Chips.'

'Chips?'

'I don't know, I panicked and saw the vinegar. I can't deal with pressure like that. '

'Nancy, I asked your favourite food not the world's hardest math equation. You are a wally.'

'Wally! That's it!'

He looked at her confused. 'What's it?'

'Wallies? My favourite food.'

'What the hell is a wally?'

'A wally!'

'Repeating it doesn't make me understand,' He held his hands out in confusion and shrugged.

'It's a gherkin.'

'Oh, I love gherkins!'

'Me too!'

'I don't like gherkins,' Jack piped up and both Cameron and Nancy burst out laughing again.

Chapter 32

'Come on Tommy, do it for Mummy.'
Harriet tried to lower him into the water again but still, he just screamed. 'You really don't like this water, do you?' He tried to clamber up her arms. In a way, she did like this part because he pulled right up to her neck and nuzzled in, like he really needed her. She never really got cuddles from him, he wasn't a cuddly baby, so for him to nuzzle right into her neck felt lovely. It was just a shame it took her subjecting him to anxiety to get it.

'What about if Mummy sits in the water and you can sit on my lap?' She began to kneel down but again, he started wailing before he even got near it.

'Oh, you want to put an end to that before it scars him for life.'

Harriet turned around to follow where the voice had come from and was faced by an older woman who was standing with a young girl – clearly her granddaughter.

'Sorry?' Harriet asked, wondering if she was talking to her or not.

'Your boy. You don't want him growing up to be a wuss

– get him in the water, quick dunk and he'll soon get over it.'

Harriet felt the mix of anger and shame gurgle up as she listened to this woman who thought she had all the answers.

'He's a big enough lad, he can handle it. Look at those chunky legs.' The grandma laughed but it sort of came out like a cackle.

'Chunky?' Harriet looked around her to see if anyone else was hearing this.

'Yeah, he's a big lad, isn't he? How old is he, two?'

'Just over a year actually.'

'A year! Cor blimey, no wonder he doesn't want to go in the water, poor guy is probably self-conscious about his rolls.' More cackling.

'I'm sorry, do you think it's funny to be mocking and ridiculing someone else's child?' Harriet glanced over her left shoulder and watched Jayne approach from behind and stand by her side – like her wing woman.

'I'm not mocking; I'm just saying she needs to be harder on him. She's too soft, every time he cries she takes him out. My kids would never have got away with it – straight in I was, dunk, and they were fine.'

'And that's great,' Jayne said, diplomatically. 'But what works for you, might not work for another parent. And what is right for your child may not be right for other children. Do you see what I'm saying?'

The woman pulled a face. 'Who are you, Mother Teresa or summin'? Children need discipline and they need to know where they stand. And where they stand in the pecking order is below their parents. They should respect and listen to the parents, so if you let him dictate when he goes in the water, then he will lose all respect and you'll be setting yourself up for a problem later on in life.'

'So, you're saying that because I don't force my son into the water right now, he's going to be an absolute tearaway when he's a teenager.' She looked at Jayne 'Is this woman for real?'

'As I said, every person parents differently and we should respect that. And, if you don't mind me saying, as an older lady I would like to think that you'd want to be supporting and helping other mums and dads rather than making them feel inadequate.'

'Oh, give over love, I'm helping your friend out by saying this – she'll thank me next year when she can relax whilst her children play in the pool – he won't be scared anymore because Mummy grew a pair and got on with it.'

Harriet gasped. 'Did you actually just say "grew a pair"? Listen here lady!' Harriet walked forward to make her point, but she felt a hand on her forearm as Jayne halted her. Which was probably a good thing or grandma may have got more than just a piece of her mind.

'Let me ask you something,' Jayne started. 'Have you got children?'

'Well, of course I have children,' the woman replied.

'And do you remember what it was like when you had your first, those first few weeks, how scary it was? How you didn't really know what you were doing? How you felt like everyone else knew what they were doing but you didn't?'

'I always knew what I was doing – it's not hard being a parent. You just have to get on with it.'

'Jayne, I don't think you're going to win this one over.'

'I agree,' Jayne replied under her breath. And then louder, to the woman: 'OK, fair enough. That's your opinion. If you wouldn't mind though, we'd appreciate it if you kept your opinions to yourself with regards to our parenting as we clearly have different ideas – which is *normal*.' She put emphasis on the word normal and glared at the woman who tutted and walked off muttering something about kids these days and disrespect.

'You OK?' Jayne asked and Harriet found herself shaking her head.

'What is wrong with people, why stick your nose in just to be horrible.'

'In all fairness, I don't think she thought she was being horrible, I think she's just one of those women who had children yonks ago when times were different and you didn't ever moan about anything or talk to anyone, you did just get on with it. But nowadays, people are a lot more receptive to being open. You won't always win everyone over.' Jayne rubbed her hand on Harriet's arm. 'It's her problem, not yours. Stay positive yeah?' Harriet nodded.

'So what's happening with this little guy?' She bent down so she was face to face with Tommy. 'Are you being a pickle for mummy again?'

He smiled at her. Harriet couldn't blame him. Jayne had one of these faces that just always seemed to be smiling and happy and fresh. You only had to look at her and you wanted to smile. She probably farted rainbows and burps butterflies too.

'Do you want to have a try?' Harriet asked, handing Tommy over but Jayne put her arms up.

'No, if this is going to work, you need to do it. It will be great bonding for you if he overcomes this anxiety with you. Have you tried just putting his feet in?'

'Yep. And I tried to sit down and have him on my lap but he won't even let me sit.'

'I have an idea. Go back to your sun loungers.' Harriet did as she was asked and a few moments later Jayne returned with a bucket filled with water. 'Try letting him put his hands in this – just to get a feel for the water.'

She did that and he was fine, splashing away with it.

'Now try his feet.'

Harriet moved the bucket and put his toes in the water and he gave out an almighty wail. She pulled the bucket away, her eyes wide in surprise at the sudden eruption. 'I just don't get it.'

'So, his hands are fine, but he doesn't like his feet wet. What's he like in the bath?'

'He likes to have a really shallow bath and he hangs his feet in the air because he won't sit up in the bath.'

'Because his feet go in the water?'

'I guess so, I didn't even think about it to be honest. He always just lies straight down when I put him in the bath so I wash him like that.' Harriet gasped as realisation hit her. 'Maybe if we cover his feet up – with shoes or some of those raft shoe thingy's, maybe he won't mind then because his feet will be covered?'

'I guess it's worth a try. Do they even sell raft shoes this small?' Jayne asked.

'Only one way to find out.' Harriet shrugged and packed up their stuff. There were at least three shops on the parade that sold water shoes – surely one of them would have something for Tommy.

***

Nancy ate her food slowly, constantly glancing over to Jack to make sure he was OK. They had been at lunch now for nearly an hour and Jack hadn't asked to leave which was fantastic. Despite Jack's concerned looks, Nancy had changed places with him at the table so that he was closer to Aiden who was playing on his iPad, in the hopes that Jack might take an interest too.

It also meant that she was now right next to Cameron.

'Aren't you going to eat your food Jack?' She eyed up the pasta bowl she had brought with her from the resort, knowing Jack wouldn't eat the fish and chips. Jack looked at his pasta and then at Nancy.

'Can I try yours?'

She frowned, confused. 'Mine? My fish and chips?' He nodded, although he didn't look sure. 'Of course darling, here.' She chopped up a tiny piece of fish and put a couple of chips on a napkin sliding it across to him. He just looked at it, not making any movement to pick it up. 'You don't have to try it if you don't want to.' She wanted to reassure him, to let him know it was alright if he didn't want to but inside, she really wanted him to. She watched him look over to Aiden who was shovelling the chips in and then back at the napkin. Then

Nancy understood. Jack clearly had an interest in Aiden. He'd watched him the other night in the disco hall, he'd asked for him today and he'd taken in the booklet with curiosity. Something about Aiden piqued his inquisitive side and it was having all sorts of positive effects on him. Maybe because he had seen Aiden eating, that was why he wanted to try. He continued to look at the food, not moving. Nancy decided to leave him to his own devices and continue her conversation so he knew he wasn't being watched.

'So come on then, what is it that you do for work?' Cameron asked when she turned back to him.

Nancy took a spoonful from the mushy pea pot in the centre of the table and tapped it onto her plate. 'Maybe I should give you an array of clues like you did for me.'

'Go on then, try me. I like a challenge.'

Nancy thought for a moment to try and think of the most obscure clues so that he would never get it. 'My job involves numbers.'

'Oh, come on, that could mean anything.' He laughed.

'It also involves time management and project management.'

'Maybe something in HR?' he asked, sipping from his can of Coke.

'Nope. Some days I have to liaise with teams of people and plan events and every single day I work with children and food.'

Cameron paused and stared at her. 'Jeez, it sounds like you have your work cut out for you – sort of a jack-of-all-trades. Do you work long hours?'

'Very long hours – pretty much all the time. I don't get sick pay so I have to go into work whether I feel good or not and I don't get holiday pay either.' A smile spread across her face as she watched Cameron's expression delve deeper into confusion.

'What! That's ludicrous. And I thought my hours were bad – are you a sort of carer?' He clearly thought he had guessed it by the raised eyebrow expression he was giving her.

Nancy smiled. 'Yeah you could say that – I do care for people. Well, one person in particular.'

Cameron looked baffled. 'How many people are at your work – do you work with a team of people or is it a solo project kind of thing?'

'I work with just one other person every day and then occasionally I will have meetings with other people.'

Cameron thought for a moment and then exhaled. 'I give up – I actually give up. You've stumped me. It sounds like you are doing absolutely everything for hardly any pay. And, if I'm honest, it sounds like your employer is exploiting you a little bit - maybe you should have a word with them and tell them they can't expect you not to have any holiday. Unless you're under a certain number of hours? But you said it was full-time?' She nodded, a smirk across her face. 'I just ... I don't know. Air hostess?'

Nancy burst out laughing. 'I wish! Then I could get to travel to lots of exotic destinations and get all dressed up for work. Most of the time I am in jeans and a T-shirt of some kind.'

'So you don't have a uniform?'

'No, not like yourself.'

'Still thinking of my uniform, huh?' he winked playfully at her. 'Because I tell you, those green scrubs and hair net are a very attractive addition to any man's wardrobe.'

Nancy laughed and felt her cheeks redden at the flirtatious wink. She changed the subject to save her embarrassment. 'So come on – what is my job?'

He thought for a moment and then finally said. 'I give up! What job could possibly be all those hours, with so many skills involved?'

Nancy smiled. 'I'm a full-time mum.'

Cameron smiled. 'Very sneaky.'

Nancy held her hands out. 'What? It's my job and every aspect of what I said is true.'

'I don't doubt that for a second – you're very clever with this game. Hats off to you.'

'Well, it's not strictly true, I do have another job,' she conceded.

'Oh, I see – thought you would twist the rules of the game.' He dramatically tutted and shook his head at her. 'I'm disappointed in you Nancy, you tried to play me.'

'Woah, woah, woah, hang on a second Mr.' She held her hands up in mock shock. 'All of the skills described in my full time mum role also apply to the job I do occasionally too.'

Cameron dropped his shoulders and frowned. 'What? You just don't make any sense!' She laughed. 'So you do all of that, and then occasionally you do it all again but for someone else?' He thought for a minute. 'Do you have more children?'

This time Nancy burst out laughing and threw her head back. 'No,' she chuckled, 'but this game is hilarious. Just watching your face go from slightly confused to full blown baffled is a picture.'

'Oh, I'm glad I'm providing the entertainment for you today.' She saw a cheeky smile sneak over his lips as he picked up his can for more drink – clearly buying himself some time. 'When you say occasionally, how often do you do this other job?'

'When I'm needed.' She shrugged.

'So they just call you up and say we need you and you go to work?' He frowned as she nodded. 'OK, I give up. You are officially far too mysterious for my brain. Clearly I have switched off into holiday mode and my intelligence is taking a well-earned break.'

'Well-earned? Because you are so super intelligent all the time, you need a rest from it?' She raised an eyebrow and smiled, feeling more and more comfortable in this flirtatious mode they seem to have adopted today.

'Exactly.' He nodded and leaned back into his chair, puffing his chest out in pride. Nancy threw her napkin across the table as she laughed. 'Hey!'

'You're such an idiot,' she said under her breath, loud enough for him to hear but quiet enough so they boys didn't.

'Don't be a hater just because I'm smart,' he said, holding his palms out.

'You're not that smart, you can't guess my job.' She poked her tongue out. She loved this playfulness. It felt liberating to be messing around like this and not spending all her time stressing about absolutely everything. This holiday had been so good for her sanity; she secretly hoped she could sustain this more relaxed nature when they went home. Although when she thought about the school meetings and Pete, she knew that it would probably be harder than she thought.

'Childminder!' he suddenly shouted, leaning forward in anticipation. Nancy left it hanging in the air for a moment before shaking her head, just to build up the tension for him. 'Ah man, I thought I had it then.'

'You're not a million miles away, but you're not right.'

'OK, just tell me then.' He waited, eyes on her. She looked back at him, unable to take her gaze away from his gorgeous blue eyes. They had so much behind them, such depth. He had a story to tell, this one, she just knew it. But what that story was, she didn't know. She just knew that those beautiful eyes were also harbouring sadness, for whatever reason. They drew her in and held her captive. After a minute she coughed to regain her composure and control.

'I am a relief teaching assistant at a school.'

'Oh I really *was* close!'

'You were ... but you still didn't get it.' She laughed as he playfully nudged her shoulder with him.

'Alright smarty pants!' Cameron took a sip of his drink and then leaned in to whisper to Nancy. 'And have you noticed anything?'

'No, what?'

'Your son.' He nodded his head towards Jack, and Nancy looked over to him and was momentarily lost for words. Because whilst she and Cameron had been messing around and chatting, and whilst the attention wasn't on him, Jack had moved his chair a little closer to Aiden and was now leaning slightly towards him, so he could see the screen of his iPad. Aiden was talking him through the game he was playing and Jack was listening. Actually listening.

'Oh my God,' she whispered. 'Cameron, he's interacting with him.'

'I know.'

She couldn't take her eyes off him.

'If you put this bit here and then tie that bit round, then it means it won't fall off and the wall will be stronger,' Aiden was saying, swiping and tapping away at the screen as he spoke.

Nancy turned to face Cameron, her eyes wide with wonder. 'Your booklet idea worked.'

'I guess it did. Who'd have thought it, hey?'

'What made you think of it?' she asked, not taking her eyes off Jack and Aiden. For so long she had wanted Jack to experience the feeling of interacting with a child of his own age and actually wanting to do it. Instantly, this small gesture made Jack look so much older to Nancy. He seemed really grown up, not her little baby boy anymore. The feeling was both thrilling and constricting in equal measures. She was so happy for him but she worried about him becoming overwhelmed and then not wanting to do it again. She wanted to join in, talk with them both and get involved but she knew that if she did, she risked ruining it all and making a big deal out of it, forcing Jack to recede back into his shell. She needed to let him do this on his own. Her stomach tensed as she watched him in awe.

'Do you know, I couldn't tell you? It just came to me. I remember you saying he didn't like people because they were new and he didn't know them so I just thought, why not let him get to know us *before* he meets us. And then Aiden really wanted to draw all the pictures – he's quite the artist.' Cameron rolled his eyes.

'It was a great idea. I really can't thank you enough.' Her hands were clasped under the table as she watched and it was only after a moment that she realised how much her nails were digging into her palms. Her whole body felt tense. She tried to relax a little bit.

'Don't thank me. Just, maybe, agree to have dinner with me one night before you go home?'

The comment shocked her into turning her head to look at him. She blushed. 'Dinner?'

'Yes dinner. You know, the meal that generally comes after lunch and before bedtime.'

She playfully hit his arm. 'I know what dinner is, you wally!'

'Wally? I'll have to watch out in case you try to bite into me.' A cheeky smile. 'Although maybe that wouldn't be such a bad thing,' he added, quietly.

'OK, if you're going to take the piss then I think I'll decline dinner and save the embarrassment.' She turned and crossed her arms, pretending to be annoyed.

'Oh now, come on, I didn't mean it. Forgive me. Let me take you to dinner, to make up for it?' He lifted his arm and placed it onto the back of her chair. It was a smooth move and he technically didn't have his arm around her, just resting on her chair. But it opened up his body language and Nancy was reminded of his tattooed chest as it peeked out from his unbuttoned top.

She tried to change the subject. 'What's your tattoo? What does it mean?'

'Looking at my chest, huh?' He raised an eyebrow.

'Well, no ... I ... it's poking out.'

He laughed, a shocked expression forming fast. 'Oh, is it now!'

She blushed crimson at the realisation of what he'd insinuated and covered her face in embarrassment. 'No! I didn't mean that and you know it! You're just trying to embarrass me.' His chuckling was contagious and she found herself laughing with him. 'You're mean; you knew that would embarrass me.'

'I couldn't help myself, sorry. Listen, let me take you out to dinner and we can discuss my tattoo – and it's poking out – then.' He tried to look innocent – it didn't work.

'You do realise this is an all-inclusive resort – so you won't actually be taking me to dinner as opposed to eating alongside me,' she said, crossing her arms at her smart comment.

'Fair enough, would you like to eat alongside me at dinner time – after lunch and before bed – one evening before you leave to go home ... ma'am?'

Nancy smiled, she liked his playfulness; it was refreshing. He made her laugh. He made her feel like the old Nancy. The Nancy who could have a laugh and a joke and mess around. Not the serious, stressed Nancy she had become of late. 'I guess it could be fun.'

'No, don't do it like that, it'll fall down. Look, let me do it.' Jack took the iPad off Aiden and began swiping and tapping and now it was Aiden's turn to lean over and watch. 'Look, like this.'

Nancy put her hand onto Cameron's forearm. 'Is my son playing with your son – like actually talking and playing a game, together?'

'I believe so.' He replied and placed his hand on top of hers and squeezed gently. 'He's doing great.'

She turned and gave him a smile. 'Thank you, Cameron.'

'Anytime.'

Chapter 33

'Hari ... Hari?'

Nancy couldn't contain her excitement as she walked into the pool area later that afternoon after finishing lunch with Cameron and the boys. She spotted Harriet sitting on their usual loungers, typing away on her phone. As she neared her she hissed again, 'Hari?'

Harriet looked up startled.

'Guess what?' Nancy watched Jack perch on the end of the lounger next to them, his headphones already on from the walk home and he was now plugging into the iPad. But she didn't care, he could have his time on the tablet right now; he had done so well.

'What? What's going on – is everything OK?'

Nancy crouched down next her friend on the side furthest from Jack and whispered. 'It worked!'

'What worked?' she replied, confusion etched on her face.

'The booklet, the lunch, everything.' She took a deep breath and then said, 'Jack spoke to Aiden and he played with him. Not like sitting next to him and playing on his own, he actually *played* on Aiden's tablet and *spoke* to him – showed him what he was doing. It was incredible.'

'Are you serious?' Harriet's face lit up.

Nancy nodded frantically, 'it's a miracle.'

'This is awesome. How long for?' She sat up straight, taking a genuine interest in what Nancy was saying. They had known each other so long, their children meant as much to each other as they did to themselves. They were like a big family so this development was huge to Harriet too and Nancy was so grateful to have someone to share this with, someone who loved Jack like she did.

'Well...' Nancy pulled a face. 'Granted it didn't last very long and after a few moments it was like Jack realised what he was doing and didn't like Aiden leaning so close to him, so he got a bit edgy and we had to swap seats, but Harriet, he's not done that before. This is progress, right?' she pleaded, desperate for Harriet to reassure her and not take away this moment.

'Of course it is babe,' Harriet pulled Nancy in for a hug. 'I'm so happy for you. For both of you.'

'I'm so happy for me too!' She really was. 'I cannot describe the feeling when Cameron pointed it out to me.' She leaned back and sat on her knees. 'I hadn't even noticed, I was too busy talking and he was like '*have you seen your son*' and I was like '*no*' and then I looked and I saw ... I *saw* him!' She clasped her hands together in a bid to steady them.

'I've got to say, I'm loving your voices you're doing in this story. And he said, and I said,' Harriet mimicked. 'It's cute.'

'Shut up.'

'So how did the actual lunch itself go? What's Cameron like once you get to know him a bit more?' Harriet picked up her drink and sipped as she listened.

'Harriet, he's lovely, really nice.' Nancy couldn't hide the smile on her face.

She pushed Nancy playfully. 'Ooh, does someone have a crush?'

Nancy giggled. 'It's not like I'm going to do anything about it, but there's no harm in a little flirting, hey?'

'That's my girl! This calls for a celebratory drink!' Harriet started to get up from her lounger.

'Oh, and Jack asked to try some of my food.'

Harriet sat back down with force as though the statement had pushed her. 'Are you for real? What the hell has happened to that boy here – maybe you need to move to Ibiza!'

Nancy laughed. 'Don't get too excited, he spent ages staring at it and then went back to his pasta. I think the food thing is going to be a hard nut to crack but at least he asked, right? It's a start.'

'It sure is, my love.'

'Mummy, look what I can do!' Isla came running over and did a roly poly next to where they were sitting. 'See!'

'Awesome baby. Well done!' Harriet stood. 'What you drinking?'

'Surprise me.' Nancy stood up. 'Come on Isla, I'm going to show you how to do a roly poly in the water.'

She glanced back at Jack on the chair. Now all she needed to do was get him in the pool and she would be winning at life. Baby steps.

***

'So come on then, tell me your grand plan.'

Harriet laid out her papers on the table in front of her. The girls had put the children to bed and were enjoying a drink out on their balcony. The heat had dropped a little and wasn't so stifling hot as it was during the day. Harriet didn't mind the heat, but the children were getting a bit aggravated around midday so most days they had taken to having a little indoor break over the lunchtime period. Swimming in the pools inside the spa, playing games or watching TV in the room (or napping for Tommy) and then there was the kids' club which Isla absolutely loved. Jack still hadn't been, but he was quite content to read a book or watch his programmes. There was always a sense of ultimate relaxation though when the children went to bed for the night and the girls could enjoy some downtime by themselves.

'So hear me out for the whole thing first and then talk, OK?' She couldn't help but feel a little anxious about this. She wasn't the type who admitted she needed help and so by doing this, she was showing everyone that she couldn't do it alone and that was scary. Scary, but necessary.

'So with work, I have gone through all the projects we currently have on and listed the tasks that need doing. I then allocated specific tasks to specific people. I created teams for jobs and targeted the most prevalent jobs first.' She looked at Nancy who nodded. 'Then I took out all the really difficult and pernickety aspects of the tasks and kept them for myself.'

'Why? You're supposed to be giving yourself an easier life.'

'I said wait until I'm finished!' Harriet barked back and Nancy held her hands up. 'I've done this because these are the jobs that I know I can do the way I want them done. Call me picky, call me a perfectionist, but I want these bits done in a certain way and I'll only end up re-doing what the others do so if I just take them in the first instance then that essentially saves me time. See?'

'I do see – I think you're mad, but I do see.'

'Why am I mad?' She leaned back on her chair and picked up her Seabreeze cocktail.

'Because life isn't perfect and everything can't be perfect. And for you to get any sort of respite from this new plan, you're going to have to learn to let others take the reins. If you want everything a certain way then you will have to do everything yourself – which is essentially what you're doing now and why you're in this stress bubble – so you need to learn what battles are worth fighting and which you just need to let go.'

Harriet nodded. 'Uh-huh, right, I hear you.' She placed the glass down. 'But I'm sticking with the plan. It's only a few bits, I'll be fine.' Nancy rolled her eyes. 'Look, it's a start, OK – just let me do it in my own way. I can't change the person I am, Nance.'

'Alright, alright, chill. Carry on'

'Right, so tasks are delegated and I've kept the bits for me that I need to do. Also, by doing this, it means that I will get more of the bigger stuff done whilst at work during the day and then when I get home, I can concentrate on being with the kids.'

'Sounds good,' Nancy nodded.

'OK, so moving onto the kids.' She took a deep breath. This was where she was on shaky ground, where she felt most vulnerable. With her job it was easy, clear cut. Emotion was eradicated from the situation and she simply approached it all with a regimented work head on. When it came to the children, she faltered. 'I need to sort myself out, Nance. I'm not saying I'm incapable of looking after my two, but I really struggle. Like, *really* struggle.'

Nancy nodded at her but for once stayed quiet, which Harriet appreciated.

'I spent the best part of last night going over and over things in my head trying to find a way to move forward and be happier.' Nancy nodded for her to continue.

'Maybe I can't be one of these earth mothers who cooks meals from scratch and manages to fit in exercise with her little ones and has an immaculate house and the like. That's not me.' This was hard for her to say. She was glad she had her cocktail with her. She picked it up and took another sip.

'It's alright to not be that mum, Hari.'

'I know it is – *now* I know it is,' she corrected. 'But then I started thinking, well what kind of mum am I? And do you know what, I am a career mum and that's OK.'

'It *is* OK!' Nancy said, banging her hand on the table and the pair laughed. 'It has taken you some time to realise but I'm glad you finally got there.'

'Nance, I bloody love my job. As much as it stresses me out and I sometimes feel like jacking it all in – I really love my job. When Andy left, it broke me. Maybe I drove him away but Nancy, for a long time, my job has been the only thing I am good at. My job makes me feel alive, it gives me purpose and when I achieve my goals at the end of the day, I feel proud of myself.'

'And so you should! You haven't exactly had it easy and especially over the last couple of years, now that you've spoken about how you've been feeling and all your problems with Tommy, I actually can't believe you have achieved what you have and still been through all that.'

'Speaking of Tommy...' She took a deep breath. 'I know there's an issue and I'm working on that. But something Jayne said made me think – I really need to get to *know* him. I don't know who he is. I don't know what he likes and because I've been feeling so crap, the more crap I feel, the more I hold him at arm's length and then the cycle continues to get worse.' The guilt dropped into her stomach like a lead weight. All the words that sometimes parents think but never dream of voicing out loud, here she was saying them.

'So what's the plan for that?' Nancy pressed, driving the conversation forward.

The easiest way to do this was to just say it. 'I'm going to get a nanny.' She paused and waited for Nancy's reaction.

After a moment's silence, Nancy said, 'I think that's a great idea.'

And it was like a weight had been lifted off Harriet's shoulders. 'Really?' she breathed. 'You think so? Because I was so worried that you'd think I was shirking my responsibility as a mum.' She felt her whole body relax as she sunk a little deeper into her chair. As much as she was happy with the decision she'd made, she realised she'd needed that back up from someone else. She wasn't normally a person who needed people behind her to do anything, but this was different. Having someone tell her she had made a good decision made this transition so much easier to bear.

'Are you kidding me? Harriet, as much as you *want* to be – you cannot be superwoman and you cannot do everything!'

'My thinking is ... if I get a nanny, she—'

'Or he.' Nancy lifted a finger.

Harriet laughed. 'Fair point, or he, could clean and cook the meals for the children whilst they are at nursery and school and then pick them up. Give them dinner, sort any homework out or whatever and prepare lunches and so on for the next day and then when I get home, my time with the children is purely play and get to know them time, build up the relationships. The bond. I'm essentially taking the chores out and just enjoying my time with my kids. Does that sound selfish?' She pulled a face. It felt unnatural for her to relinquish so much control.

Nancy shook her head. 'It's not selfish. There's nothing wrong with finding your strengths and playing to them and your strength is working and providing for your family. And as long as your children are provided for, they are loved and looked after, who's to say that's wrong? Harriet, you're a single parent just trying to do the best for your children whilst maintaining your own identity doing what you love. Ain't nothing wrong with that, my love.'

Harriet sighed and she could almost feel the tension unravel from her neck. 'You do not realise how stressed I was about telling you this.'

'Why? I'm not a dragon.'

'No, I didn't mean that. I just meant saying it out loud, to anyone. It's scary.'

'I know but trust me; you're doing the right thing.'

'So, with having a nanny, it means I can work slightly longer hours and then I won't have to work at home. So, I'll take the kids to school – so I still see them in the morning – and then go to work and work until 6 o'clock. Then by the time I get home it'll be dinner, playtime, bath and bed.' She paused. 'Shit that doesn't sound like a lot of time with them does it.' She ruffled her papers. 'Maybe I need to think this through again.'

Nancy placed her hand on top of Harriet's to still her scuttling. 'It's fine. You are a working parent and this is what you have to do – stop beating yourself up over it. You'll have the weekends, won't you?'

Harriet nodded. 'Yeah that's a point.'

'And maybe every so often you'll have the chance to finish up work early. But let's just take it one day at a time. Try this, see how it works and go from there.'

Harriet nodded. 'You're right. Thanks Nancy.'

'What for?'

'For not being a judgemental twat like the rest of them.'

'Hey.' She lifted her glass in a toast. 'Here's to not being judgemental twats of society.'

Harriet laughed and clinked her glass. 'To not being judgemental twats!'

Chapter 34

'I seriously could not do that job even if you paid me a million quid.'

Nancy looked over to where the children's entertainer was and laughed at Harriet's facial expression. 'Are you kidding? Jump around a bit and sing some songs and it's like £100 per hour.'

'Shut up, is it really?'

'Well, I looked into booking some magic guy for Jack before I realised that he wouldn't really do well having a party – and the guy wanted nearly £200 for two hours!'

'Daylight robbery!'

'I know, although looking at what these entertainers have to do and thinking about getting up at the crack of dawn, even with coffee, and being so bouncy, I'm not sure I could do it.'

'What about if you're having a shit day and you feel really miserable – if you're hungover – and you have to go and be like *heeey kids!*' She waved her hands like a clown and plastered on a huge fake smile. 'I don't think I could do that even for a million quid.'

'I don't think you'd get booked very often if you showed up smelling of tequila from the night before and asking for a million pounds.'

'That's a good point.' Harriet turned her attention back to scrolling through her emails.

Nancy watched the entertainer prance around by the pool, singing and dancing and then pull out a balloon kit and start making balloon animals for the children. She looked over to Jack who was still sitting with them. Isla and Tommy had moved to sit closer to the balloon guy.

'Jack?' Nancy asked, surprised that he didn't have his headphones on. He turned in response to his name. 'Do you want to go closer?'

He shook his head.

'It might be fun, you could get a balloon?'

Another shake.

'Is it because he's very loud?' A nod. 'Well, I'll tell you what.' She stood up and grabbed his ear defenders and his hand. Leading him over so that they were closer to the guy but still at the back of the group, Nancy sat down and sat Jack on her lap. She then put his ear defenders on and tried to cuddle him to relax him. The tiled floor was very warm from the sunshine and Nancy had to shuffle her bum about a few times to adjust. Jack squirmed and climbed off, choosing to sit behind Nancy instead. He still didn't like being cuddled like that then. Nancy looked over her shoulder. 'Jack, you won't be able to see from there.' She started to move but he put his hand on her back.

'Stay there, Mummy.'

She listened to him. Well, she thought, at least he was sitting here. Even if he was behind her. The things parents had to do.

After twenty minutes of watching the entertainer, Nancy came to the conclusion that she most definitely could not do this job.

'Are you enjoying the show?' Cameron sat down on the ground beside her and crossed his legs. He had just his swim shorts on and no top and Nancy had to use every ounce of self-control to not stare at his chest. He wasn't particularly muscly but he clearly paid attention to his appearance and maintained a healthy physique. His arms had some nice definition to them and as he spoke, she could see a bicep flex slightly, like a twitch. She instantly looked away, so he didn't catch her eyeing him up.

'Well, you know, when you have kids you've got to do what you've got to do.'

Cameron looked around her and laughed. 'So ... which one of these kids is yours then?'

Nancy pulled a face. 'What are you talking about, Jack's behind me.' She shook her head at his silly comment but then noticed he was still smirking. 'What?'

'Look behind you.'

She did and Jack wasn't there.

'Where is he?' she panicked, feeling her heart jump into her throat. Cameron pointed back to Harriet who waved and laughed, Jack perched up next to her. 'Little monkey! How long have I been sitting here on my own?'

'About fifteen minutes.' He chuckled as Nancy laughed and

put her head in her hands. 'So ... my question still stands, are you enjoying the show? Does it make you laugh when the guy pulls the rabbit out of the hat or do you just prefer the balloon animals kind of guy?'

She pushed his arm and stood up. 'You can shut up! I was doing it for Jack.'

'Yeah?' He stood up and walked alongside her. 'Seems like he really enjoyed it.'

Nancy reached the sun loungers and sat down next to Jack. 'Didn't you like it?'

He shook his head. 'It was boring. I wanted to see my iPad.'

Nancy exhaled. 'Sweetheart you can't just sit on your iPad the whole time we're here. It would be nice to explore some bits, hey? So you have stuff to talk about when you go back to school.' She knew that was a long shot because Jack wouldn't exactly be willing to do a show and tell about his holiday in front of the class, but still, she did want him to create some memories from the trip.

Jack just shrugged and put his headphones back on. She was going to have to be more creative about what to do with him. Cameron's voice pulled her attention away from her thoughts and back into the here and now.

'So listen, about that dinner.' Cameron stopped to correct himself. 'Sorry, let me start again, about us eating alongside each other one evening.' Nancy sniggered and Harriet looked confused. 'I was wondering if you were free tonight?'

Nancy smiled. 'I might be, what time are you thinking?'

'About 8ish?'

Nancy looked to Harriet who piped up. 'Oh, I see, you're

wanting to swan off and leave me again, is that right? After saying I work too much?'

Nancy felt bad, she had a point. 'You're right.' She turned back to Cameron. 'Maybe another time.' She then felt a towel hit her on the back of the head and spun round confused. 'What the...'

'Are you having an actual laugh? I'm bloody kidding ... go, drink, be merry or whatever it is that you will be doing.' She held up her hands. 'And no, I don't want details. There are children present.'

Cameron laughed but Nancy was mortified. 'Hari!'

'Oh shush, we all know what you're both thinking when you look at each other. It's natural, part of human nature.' She cackled, knowing full well what she was doing to Nancy.

'I can't believe you sometimes!' Nancy gasped. 'Honestly, its fine. You're right; I've already left you once.'

Harriet stood up and pulled Nancy to one side. 'Stop being so stupid, I was joking. There is a hot guy asking you to dinner, just go will you! I won't take no for an answer!'

'Fine.' Nancy whispered and Harriet poked her tongue out. 'OK, 8ish is perfect. Where?'

'There's a really nice place down by the seafront called Banningtons – shall I book us in?'

Nancy frowned. 'But that's off site.'

'Yeah?'

'That won't be part of our all-inclusive thing though.'

Cameron smiled. 'I know – but rather than just sitting alongside me, I'd like to take you out to dinner. What do you say?'

Nancy felt a flutter in her stomach as he smiled at her. 'Sounds good,' she said quietly.

'Great, I'll see you there.' He winked at her and threw a 'bye' over her shoulder to Harriet before turning and leaving.

Nancy sat down on the sun lounger and laughed.

'What?' Harriet asked, poking Nancy with her toe.

'Looks like I have a date.'

'I think this calls for a selfie.' Harriet said, angling round and pulling Nancy in for a picture. She gave the biggest smile, all the while singing in her head that she was finally moving on emotionally and letting herself have some fun for once. It didn't have to amount to anything; she wouldn't do that to Jack after promising it would just be the two of them. But a bit of holiday fun – nothing wrong with that, surely?

'Big changes are happening with this one,' Harriet said as she typed. 'Hashtag – she's going to get her leg over.'

'Hari!' Nancy gasped.

'I'm kidding. Hashtag – making memories. Better?'

'Better.'

Chapter 35

'Right, Jack is all sorted and chilling in his bed. You shouldn't hear from him now really. So about nine, if you go in and take his iPad – otherwise he'll stay on it all night – then he can go to sleep. I've told him that I'm popping out and he's a bit anxious about it so I said that if he needs me then to tell you and you can ring me. And make sure you do – if he misses me, I'll just come back.'

'You bloody well wont,' Harriet replied, pulling the curtains shut next to Tommy's cot where he was fast asleep.

'Hari, please, I promised him. If he gets upset I'll just come back – Cameron will understand.'

Harriet walked over to Nancy and gave her the perfume she had asked to borrow. 'Cameron will understand, you're right, but you deserve this night. Please, just go and enjoy yourself. You have plenty of time to go back to being a stress mummy when we get home, at least indulge in this fun for now. '

Nancy exhaled. 'I'm really nervous.'

'Why?'

'I haven't had a date for years! And my date nights with

Pete were just full of arguments leading up to when he walked out. I just don't know what to expect or what I'm supposed to do. What if I just talk about Jack all night and he finds me boring?' She wasn't sure who she was anymore. She'd spent so long trying to make sure Jack was ok and that everything was sorted for him that she was worried she had forgotten how to have fun herself.

'Nance, he has children too, he'll probably enjoy talking kiddie stuff with you.' Then as an afterthought she added, 'Just don't talk about poo or willies.'

'Willies?'

Harriet shrugged, 'I don't know, I'm just saying, keep it light.' She paused. 'Unless that's the direction you want this evening to go, and in that case, talk about willies all you want. Throw in some boobs and sex talk too, set the mood.'

'Oh my God, there is just no filter with you, is there?' Nancy laughed at Hari's attempt at lightening the mood. 'Are you sure Isla doesn't want to go through into my room and watch the iPad with Jack?'

Harriet shook her head as she picked up her phone. 'She's fine; she's absolutely knackered so it'll do her good to get an early night. She's been up late every night since we arrived – she's not used to getting less than ten hours' sleep.'

'OK, how do I look?'

Harriet took in her friend's appearance – sleek black dress, sparkly gold sandals and cute little clutch bag with the gold chain handle. 'You look beautiful. Knock him dead!'

Nancy took a deep breath and nodded, turning to leave the room. And as Harriet watched her leave she felt a pang of jealousy

– she hadn't been on a date in so long she had wondered if she ever would again. Not that she had the time for dating. Her marriage hadn't survived alongside her job so a new relationship wasn't going to either. Maybe in years to come when things at work settled down, but until then, work was her relationship. And the children, that was her new focus. There wasn't space for anything – or anyone – else. She kept up the stern exterior if anyone asked but deep inside, she was gutted about this. She wasn't a robot, she had feelings – contrary to what her staff thought – and to think that she would continue to be on her own for the foreseeable future was a little hard to take. It wasn't that she didn't *want* anyone, she just couldn't make it work for her situation. She was better off alone. She waited for about an hour until Isla's breathing had fallen into a steady rate as she slept and then she took out her laptop. Time to find herself a nanny.

***

Nancy followed the waiter to a table out in the courtyard at the front of the restaurant. From here they were facing the beachfront and she could hear the sea as it gently rolled in, frothing over the sand and drawing back out into the ocean again. It was a beautiful vantage point for their date. She had a sneaky suspicion that Cameron had deliberately asked for this table precisely because it was so romantic. She could get used to this being spoiled malarkey.

'Can I get you anything to drink?' The waiter had an accent and it only added to the holiday experience.

'I'll have a glass of your house white please.' She shuffled in her seat and picked up the menu so that she was doing something with her hands. She was so nervous. It was one thing having lunch with Cameron and the children, because if the conversation dried up, you always had that buffer of talking to the kids. But tonight, it would be just the two of them. Would they even have anything to talk about? She tried to compile a list in her head of back up topics to talk about should they struggle for conversation. They had done jobs, so that was out. And she wanted to limit the children talk as they had done a lot of that too. The panic started to fizzle in her stomach – was she that boring? Why couldn't she think of any topics that weren't lame? At this rate she might have to resort to talking about boobs and willies!

The waiter brought back the glass of white and she instantly sipped at it, feeling the ice cold liquid slide down her throat and immediately calm her a little. She glanced around the street to see if there was any sign of him. She supposed it was a bonus sitting out the front because, besides having the beautiful scenery and the sea, she would be able to see Cameron coming before he arrived, so he wouldn't catch her off guard. The streets were still relatively quiet for early evening; she had expected it to be bustling with families and groups, not that she was complaining. Whilst this place was essentially on the high street, it was still sort of tucked away a little so it didn't seem so overpopulated. Cameron certainly scored top points for his choice in restaurant. She loved the cobbled streets and the sound they made when the odd passer-by walked past. There were cute little streetlamps dotted all the way along this strip and she imagined, when it was fully dark, the twinkling lights from them would be quite romantic and really set the scene for a date. When she glanced inside, the restaurant was fairly empty which made her a little uncomfortable. Did this mean the food or service was terrible here? Or simply that they were here a bit early for dinner? Maybe everyone went into town for drinks first. Although now she thought about it, this place was situated literally a stone's thrown from an all-inclusive resort so, she guessed, most people would probably choose to stay on the resort rather than pay for food. It was a sweet gesture of Cameron to bring her here actually.

Ten minutes passed and Cameron had still not arrived so Nancy pulled out her phone and typed a message to Harriet.

How's Jack, is he asking for me yet?

A reply pinged back almost instantly.

For God's sake woman stop texting me and enjoy your time with the hot doctor.

She replied with a sad face and: he's not here yet.

Harriet called her immediately. 'What do you mean he's not there yet? Isn't the man supposed to be there first? I thought it was the women who were fashionably late?'

'Maybe I was too keen by showing up on time. I'm sure everything's fine, he must just be held up with Aiden or something.'

'Can't you message him?'

'I haven't got his number.'

'All the time you have spent with him over the last few days, and you haven't exchanged numbers yet? Have you friended him on Facebook or Instagram or something?'

'Nope.' Nancy shuffled in her chair as she felt something brush against her leg. She glanced down and saw the restaurant cat running circles around her legs, its furry tail tickling the back of Nancy's knee. She moved her leg slightly and encouraged the cat to move away. 'Do you think I've been stood up?'

'I damn well hope not. Not in that dress you were wearing – it's wasted on the waiting staff.'

'And the resident cat, don't forget him.' She laughed but more for something to do. She continued looking around, searching for a silhouette of a man that could be Cameron. 'How long do I wait before I leave?'

'What's the time now?'

She pulled the phone away from her ear to check the time. 'Eight-fifteen.'

'OK, give him until twenty past and then leave.'

'Twenty past?' Nancy really didn't want to have to leave having been stood up. 'I'll wait until half past and if he's not here then I'll leave. OK?'

'OK, keep me informed. Good luck!'

Nancy hung up and clicked onto her Facebook. Maybe she should try and search him. She typed in Cameron but then realised she didn't even know his surname. Damn it. Suddenly she had a lightbulb moment and called Harriet back. 'Hari, in my room in the top drawer of the dresser there is the booklet that Cameron's little boy did for Jack. Can you get it and tell me what Cameron's surname is? I'm going to look him up on Facebook whilst I wait.'

'Ooh good idea – stalking him, I like your style. OK hang on. I'm on charge so I'm going to leave my phone here whilst I go get it.'

Harriet disappeared from the line so Nancy took the time to gulp down another few mouthfuls of wine. The sun was beginning to set and it was making the most beautiful colour shine down onto the glistening sea. Swirls of orange and red striped the horizon, mixing in with the blue from the sky deepening to a navy. This would be an incredibly romantic place for dinner – if her date showed up. She was getting to the point now where her understanding and excuses for him were starting to turn and she was feeling a little frustrated with him for being late.

Just as she was waiting for Harriet to return to their phone call the waiter returned to her table. 'I have a message for you from a Cameron?' the guy said, his strong accent piercing through his words.

'Oh?' she replied.

'He sends his apologies but something has come up and he cannot make your date. He has offered for you to have whatever you want and he will pay the bill by way of apology.' The waiter hovered whilst Nancy took in the information he had relayed to her. She was genuinely upset that he wasn't coming, she had really been looking forward to getting to know him better. But then the more it sunk in, the more the frustration began to brew. After going to all the effort to arrange this, he'd stood her up. She had a bolt of guilt when she realised that maybe something had happened with Aiden and that's why he couldn't come – something *'coming up'* could mean anything.

'Its fine, I'll just make my way home. Thank you. Can I just pay for the wine please?'

The waiter held up his hand. 'No need, it's all sorted. Your date has already left his card details for your meal.'

Nancy smiled, what a gentleman. 'OK, well thank you and I'm sorry to have taken up your table.'

'Have a lovely evening, ma'am.'

Nancy picked up her bag and began the short walk back to the hotel. The view was beautiful along the seafront so instead of walking straight back, seeing as Harriet was looking after Jack, Nancy decided to walk towards the beach with the plan of walking part of the way home in the sand.

'Hari?' she called down the receiver, wondering what was taking her so long to go into her room and grab the leaflet. She was tempted to just hang up and text her to let her know what had happened. She would see it soon enough when she returned to the phone. Knowing Harriet, she'd probably been distracted by an email pinging up on her laptop or something and forgotten Nancy was on the phone. She would give her another minute and then just end the call.

The horizon was a beautiful streak of pink and navy and as Nancy stepped onto the beach, the sand still felt warm between her toes. This holiday had been a real eye-opener for her. She had been seriously let down by Pete and, thinking about how Cameron standing her up made her feel, maybe Jack was right; maybe it was better being just the two of them. Coming on this holiday and getting away from the house that she'd shared with Pete for so many years, she was able to see a bit clearer and she'd realised that she didn't need him – or anyone else for that matter. She was coping fine by herself and Jack was doing really well. He had made such good progress in the short space of time they had been here – and she started to wonder if the life they used to lead back home, the house they lived in and the constant reminder of what they used to have, might be making the transition to life without Pete harder to do.

And then there was Cameron. He was lovely, and Nancy had enjoyed flirting with him and just the fact that she was able to do so meant that she had come a little further in getting over Pete and that made her happy. Cameron might not be *the one* but spending time with him had meant that she had got to know herself a little more. It didn't have to lead anywhere. People come into your life for a reason; maybe Cameron's reason was to make Nancy realise that she was capable of being on her own.

'Nancy!'

'Oh about bloody time – did you go to the moon and back or something?' Nancy laughed, 'Hey listen, Cameron hasn't stood me up...'

'Nancy...'

'I just got a call from him at the restaurant. Well, I didn't get a call, the waiter did. He then came and told me and—'

'For God's sake Nancy, SHUT UP!'

She froze on the spot, her phone glued to her ear and her face creased in confusion. Harriet had never spoken to her like that before but there was a tone of terror in her voice and it unsettled Nancy right to the core. 'What's wrong?'

'It's Jack.'

The words hit her with such force she almost felt winded by them. Her heartrate increased tenfold at the sound of her son's name, a thousand scenarios ran through her mind and the second's pause in Harriet's voice felt like years.

'What?' she croaked.

'Nancy, he's gone.'

Chapter 36

'Gone? What do you mean gone?'

She was glued to the spot, unable to move anything but her chest as she panted. Her heart was racing a thousand beats per minute, the blood pulsating through her veins, the ringing in her ears increasing. Was this what a heart attack felt like? Was she going to collapse? She couldn't control the rush of adrenalin mixed with fear as it burst through her body, destroying every inch of her like an unwanted gate crasher to a party.

'I just went into your room to get the leaflet like you asked and I couldn't see him in the bed.'

Nancy found her feet and started to walk forward, quickening her pace until she was full pelt running back towards the hotel. She had to keep moving forward. She couldn't think straight, everything was blurring around her, but she couldn't stop. She needed to keep moving forward and get back.

'I looked everywhere, under the bed, in the wardrobe, in your bathroom, in my bathroom ... I can't find him anywhere.' The panic in Harriet's voice was making it tremble and it really unnerved Nancy.

'What about the balcony – he wouldn't have gone on there would he?' The balcony led out from Nancy's side of the room so he would have had access to that, but they always kept it locked unless one of them was out there. Had she locked it before she left? Oh, she couldn't remember. The fear was clouding her brain and it was all she could do to concentrate on not vomiting.

'He's not out there, I just looked. It's still locked.' The more she spoke, the higher her voice rose.

'Have you called reception?' Nancy panted, running through the gates of the resort and swinging left immediately to try and cut out the pool area. This way was quicker back to her room, she was sure of it. She stopped, momentarily losing her sense of direction. The panic was starting to take over her brain and it was clouding her judgement. She needed to focus.

'No, I ... I ...' Harriet stuttered.

'CALL THEM!' Nancy felt her temples pulse as she screamed down the phone. 'You need to alert them Harriet – there are swimming pools and roads here, there are so many things he could hurt himself on.' Not to mention the fact that he would be terrified. He didn't cope well with new places and he didn't know his way around here. He could be wandering about anywhere. The thought of Jack being scared made Nancy want to vomit and she had to continuously swallow down the bile that was fast rising in the back of her throat.

'Oh my God, what if he's been taken?' Nancy gasped as she tried to swallow back the tears. She couldn't cry and run at the same time and right now her priority was to get back to the hotel room so she could find her little boy.

'He can't have been taken; I've been here the whole time!'

'Well, he hasn't just vanished into thin air, Hari!' Nancy stumbled as her ankle turned over on the curb side. She swore and picked up her shoe which had snapped, shoving it into her bag and whipping off the other one so she could run properly. 'Call reception, get security looking for him. I'll be there in like two minutes.' She hung up the phone without even waiting for Harriet to answer, she couldn't keep talking and running and hiccupping back the tears all at once. She needed to get back and find him – it was as simple as that. There was no plan B.

The run back to the hotel room was the longest few minutes of her life. How was this even happening to her? She took the stairs two at time and practically fell through the doorway of their room which was open. She ran inside and found herself face to face with hotel security and a sobbing Harriet.

'Have you got him?' she barked at them, not even caring that she was being rude.

'We haven't found him yet, but we have security out looking as we speak. The police are on their way and the swimming pool areas have been checked and closed.' The security man turned back to Harriet. 'So what was he wearing when you last saw him?'

'Um, pyjamas,' Harriet squeaked, terror emblazoned across her face.

Nancy kicked into action, the reality of the situation dawning on her. 'His pyjamas are orange and black – orange top and black bottoms. He has blond hair and blue eyes. He's about this tall,' Nancy put her hand up to her waist. 'And he's autistic.' The seriousness of Jack being alone and vulnerable dawned on her. She let out a little sob. 'Oh God.'

'Is there any place he has particularly liked since your stay here? Anywhere where he might try to return to?' The tall security guard was writing things down on his notepad. Both guys had friendly faces but appeared very professional in the way they executed their questions.

Nancy frantically shook her head. 'No, I don't think so.'

'OK, well I think we have what we need here. We will circulate these details and as soon as the police arrive, we will be sending them up.' The guards made their way to the door to leave.

'What can we do to help?' Nancy shouted, desperate for them to give her a job. Make her feel like she was doing something. 'I'll look round the hotel, the streets ... the beach! What about the beach.'

'I can assure you we are doing everything we can, it would be best if you waited here just in case he comes back.'

Nancy turned to Harriet as the security staff left. 'Hari...' she squeaked.

Harriet stepped forward and pulled Nancy into a hug squeezing her tight and letting her sob into her shoulder. 'I'm so sorry, Nance. I swear I was looking after him, he just disappeared. I just don't know how it happened. I promise you I wouldn't neglect watching him – I was just here!' she pointed to her chair which was where she had been sitting once Nancy left an hour earlier.

'Its fine – I'm not blaming you, I just ... I need to find him.' It was the truth; she didn't blame Harriet, not completely, but right now she was struggling to not break.

'Do you want me to go and look for him – we only need one of us to stay here.'

'I'll go, you stay here.' She picked up her bag and practically threw it over her shoulder. 'If you hear anything, anything at all. Call me.' Harriet nodded. 'I'll be back in a bit.' And she stormed out of the room, frantically throwing her head around trying to take in every inch of her surrounding as she walked along. She didn't want to miss any nook or cranny. She had to find her little boy.

***

Harriet paced the room, her hands on her head. 'Fuck,' she kept whispering over and over again, tears streaming down her face.

'Mummy?' Isla squeaked from her bed. 'What's going on?'

'Oh sweetheart, I'm sorry. This must be really scary for you.' She walked over to her bed and put her arm around her daughter, feeling the tears constantly well up as she did. She couldn't even imagine what Nancy was feeling right now, she didn't know what she would do if Isla or Tommy went missing.

'Why were there all those men in here – they were loud, they woke me up.'

'Sorry sweetheart, everything is fine. We just have some work to do, that's all.' She decided against telling Isla the real reason right now. The last thing she wanted to do was scare her and have her being upset as well. 'Why don't you watch a film – shall I put a film on for you?'

'Is it morning?'

Harriet's heart ached at her innocence. 'No darling it's not morning. But we are on holiday so if you want to watch a film tonight, you can, that's fine.' Isla clearly couldn't believe her luck because she jumped out of bed before Harriet could change her mind and scooped up the DVD pack they bought with them.

'Frozen – no, Chipmunks – no...' She scrolled through the pages of the pack, discarding them one by one.

Harriet stood up from the bed and walked over to the window. It was getting dark out there – really dark. She thought about Jack being somewhere he didn't recognise and she felt the nausea creep up again. Why hadn't she heard or seen anything? It didn't make sense. She caught a glimpse of a shadow outside and noticed immediately that it was Cameron. She gasped and opened the window, calling his name. 'Cameron!'

He wasn't that far from their room and because they were only on the first floor, he spotted Harriet straight away. He gave a sort of salute and carried on walking.

'No I'm not waving to you, you idiot,' she said under her breath. 'Cameron! Quick!' It was all she could think of saying that would get his attention but not concern others around her, namely Isla. He had a look of confusion on his face and stopped in his tracks. 'Can you come up here please? It's urgent.'

'Everything OK?' he asked, still not moving.

'No!' she replied. 'Room 236 – hurry up!' She closed the window and walked back to the bed hoping that he would actually come up. They needed all the help they could get.

A few minutes later, there was a knock on the door. Harriet had just put the DVD in the player – Alice in Wonderland – and ran to the door. Throwing it open she came face to face with him. 'What's going on?' he asked.

'Cameron it's awful,' she said, glancing over her shoulder and lowering her voice. 'It's Jack, he's gone missing.'

'What?' he gasped and then took in her whispering and adopted the same tone. 'When?'

'Just now, about half hour ago.'

'Where's Nancy? Is she still at the restaurant? I'm a bit late – I'll get her and...' He pointed over his shoulder.

Harriet shook her head. 'No she's back, she's out looking for him. I just don't know what to do. Can you go help – go see if you can find him?'

'Of course,' he replied, before immediately running off down the corridor.

At least that was an extra person. Harriet walked back to the bed and sat next to Isla, placing her arms around her and letting her snuggle in for a cuddle. If anything happened to him she would never forgive herself. Not only was she a rubbish mum to her own children, now this had happened.

Maybe her mum was right; maybe she shouldn't have had children.

Chapter 37

Nancy took the corner of the entertainment block at speed, practically sliding round into the hall. All the while her heart was pounding the beat of her pulse throughout her body. The pounding resonated in her temples so hard it made her feel sick. She felt like she was losing her mind, like this was a dream and that she would wake up any minute and laugh about how crazy it was.

She wished so bad that it was a dream. She wanted to wake up – right now.

'Nancy!'

She ignored the voice and kept running, she couldn't stop. She needed to just keep going.

'Nancy!'

Her eyes ached, but she carried on searching as thoroughly as she could. Moving chairs, lifting curtains and bending down by tables. He could be anywhere. Masses of people surrounded her, but no one even stopped to ask her why she was frantically running around in here. She stopped a couple who were walking past her. 'Have you seen this boy?' she flashed her phone at them with her screensaver picture of Jack. They shook their head. She didn't even stick around to say anymore, she took off again, stopping another person and asking. Nothing. Suddenly she felt a hand on her arm and it stilled her in shock. She flicked her head round and came face to face with Cameron who looked equally as concerned. 'Nancy? Any luck?'

She shook her head, trying to keep the emotion locked up. If she cried now that would be it. She had to hold it together, just for now. Just until she found him. Because she would find him, she had to.

'Where have you looked?' His face was pale and shiny where he was sweating. But Nancy just turned and tried to run off. She needed to keep going, she couldn't stop and talk. She had to keep moving.

Cameron reached out to still her again. 'Nancy, wait.'

'I can't wait, Cameron! I can't stop – I need to keep moving. He could be anywhere and if I stop, he'll get further away and I'll lose him forever and I can't do that, I just can't...' she trailed off as her eyes filled.

'Hey, shh, it's OK, I understand. I'm not stopping you. I want to help you.' She shuffled on the spot desperate to keep going but aware that more help meant they would find him quicker. 'Where have you looked? I don't want to waste time going to the places you've been to.'

She took a breath to swallow down the creeping thickness of fear that was slowly but surely clawing its way up her throat. 'The pools, the bar, the buffet restaurant and here.' She shook her head. 'I can't find him.'

'It's OK, it'll be OK.' He placed a hand on her shoulder and gave her a squeeze. 'We will find him.'

'I just – I don't know where else to look.' She scanned the room again looking for inspiration. 'Where can he be?' She looked back to Cameron and said what was frightening her the most. 'Cameron, what if he's been taken?'

He shook his head defiantly. 'No, we are not thinking like that. We don't know what has happened so don't start thinking the worst. The police are here now and the staff are looking for him – it will be OK, we will find him.'

'How do you know that!' she barked. 'How can you be so bloody sure? Huh?' She knew she was overreacting, but she could feel her soul falling apart and it physically hurt.

Cameron took the hit though and didn't even flinch when she shouted at him. 'Come on, let's keep looking. Have you tried the park?'

Nancy whipped her head back to face him after following the sound of commotion outside the door – which just turned out to be some drunken teenagers. 'Park? There's a park?'

'Yes, by the kitchens, round the other side of the complex.'

'Oh my God! I didn't know there was a park!' Slight hope filled her chest. If he came across a park on his travels, he would stop there. 'He likes parks – he likes the shapes! Where is it, take me there please?' She began walking before she even knew which direction she was going in, the burst of adrenalin at a possible lead making her walk without her brain even thinking.

'Come on, this way. Quick!' Cameron started running and Nancy followed behind, praying that this was their lead.

***

Harriet paced the bedroom, every few minutes looking out of the window to follow up a noise she heard. Isla was now asleep again with Alice in Wonderland still playing on the television. The noise from it was just muffled white noise as a zillion negative thoughts ran through her mind. Nancy was never going to forgive her – and rightly so. How could she have let this happen? She didn't know how it could've happened but there must've been something she could have done to stop it. Maybe she had been so into her work that she hadn't heard anything. But he had been next door – the bedroom door had been open for crying out loud. The sheer confusion of it all made her brain ache. She jumped at the sound of her mobile ringing and instantly snapped it up in case it was news – plus she didn't want it to wake the children up.

'Hello?' she whispered down the receiver as she took herself to stand in the doorway of their two rooms. She didn't want to leave the room – she needed to stay with them. If there was someone out there taking children then she'd be damned if she was going to leave them.

'Harriet, its Mum.'

Fuck. The last person she wanted to speak to right now. She should've looked at caller ID. 'Hi Mum. Look right now isn't the best time.'

'Listen Harriet, I know you're a busy woman and you keep telling me how you have lots to do but if you can't just make time for your mother then—'

'It's not that—'

'Don't interrupt me when I am speaking – it's rude.'

309

Pot – kettle, Harriet thought. Maybe talking to her would keep her mind off what was happening right now. It wasn't like she could do anything whilst she was bound to the room. She leaned against the doorframe and laid her head back closing her eyes. It was all such a mess.

'What I am calling for is to ask you what on earth you think you are playing at?'

Her tone was stern and Harriet opened her eyes in confusion, frowning as she racked her brain as to what she had done wrong now. 'I'm sorry?'

'You think getting a nanny is going to solve all your problems, do you?'

Oh, that. She had sent her mum a text explaining her new plan for when she returned from holiday. She'd known it wouldn't go down well.

'Palming off your children to someone else isn't parenting, Harriet. It's lazy and unfair and I am really disappointed in you.'

More disappointment, great. She didn't think her mum could be more disappointed in her but clearly she was wrong. 'Listen Mum, now isn't the best time – we have a lot going on here and—'

'Harriet, you will talk about this nonsense now with me because I am struggling to understand why you don't want to look after your children.'

'I *do* want to look after my children, Mum!' she raised her voice but then instantly dropped it again when Isla shuffled in bed. 'It's not that simple.'

'Of course it's that simple. How hard can it be – you have

children, you look after those children. You don't pop out children to pay someone else to look after them. That isn't parenting.'

Harriet pinched the bridge of her nose with her fingers and exhaled. 'Mum, I *am* looking after them; I just need some help, that's all.' It really pained her to admit she needed help at the best of times, but to have to do it to her mum – this was brutal.

'Oh nonsense. Bethany doesn't have help – I didn't have help.' Here we go, standard comparison to the sister time. Bethany does this and Bethany does that. Bethany is the perfect parent who never struggles and gets everything right. Harriet went to speak but, as usual, he mum was there first. 'I have to say, I am rather disappointed in you, Harriet. I know you like your little career,' Harriet cringed at her mother's disrespect for her company. 'But you really have to look at your priorities again and decide what you want. You have the rest of your life to do your little job, why do your children have to suffer because you're being selfish and choosing to work over spending time with them.'

'I am not choosing work over my children.'

'Looks like it to me. You're going to employ a person to be your children's mother – where is the sense in that. Do you not want to be a mum?'

That one hurt. Harriet could feel the rage building up inside. She was always respectful of her mum – and a little bit scared – so she never really answered back or challenged her. But today she was really testing her willpower. 'Of course I want to be a mum. I just can't do everything.'

311

'But Bethany manages it – I managed it.'

'But I'm not Bethany and I'm not you!' Harriet slid down the door frame and sat on the floor, head in her hands. 'Mum, I need a bit of help, that's all. I will still be looking after my children and I'm not being a terrible mother by asking for some help.' She said the words but she wasn't sure she 100 per cent believed them. It was great when she had Jayne or Nancy behind her to convince her she was doing the right thing, but fighting her corner against her mother, that was always going to be a hard battle to win. And she was flagging.

'Well, I want you to know that I'm not happy about this. If you're adamant on palming off your children, then at least have someone look after them that they know and respect, like me.'

'No Mum, its fine.'

'I can pick them up from school and nursery most days. I normally do the WI on Wednesdays but I suppose I will have to postpone those meetings for now until you feel able to take the children back a bit.'

'Mum, I said I don't need you to do that.' She wasn't listening.

'And then I could take them back to your house and feed them there because, let's face it, they are going to be out of routine as it is with their mother working all the time and palming them off so they will need as much stability as they can get.'

If she said palming off one more time, Harriet was at risk of exploding and saying something she may regret.

'So if you could maybe bring yourself to finish early on a

Friday so my weekend isn't cut short looking after your children then I—'

'Mum! Enough!' Shit. She had committed to this now. Her heart was racing but she just couldn't sit there and let her berate her like this. 'I do not need you looking after my children and I also do not need you saying all this to me right now. There are more important things going on at this moment in time.'

'More important that your children, Harriet?' her mum said sternly.

'That isn't what I meant! Look, Jack has gone missing and we have the whole damn hotel and police out there looking for him so do excuse me if this isn't the right time to be sitting here whilst my mum tells me how much of a failure at parenting I am. Yes, I enjoy my work and yes, I need help. It has taken me a bloody long time to admit it, but I need help – so I would appreciate your support in this instance rather than you reiterating to me that I am not coping.'

'Harriet—'

'No Mum, I can't have this conversation right now so if you'll excuse me, I need to go. I'll talk to you when I get home but I am getting some paid help and the children will be absolutely fine. They aren't neglected, and they are loved. I just need some ... help!'

There was silence on the phone line so Harriet just added. 'I'll talk to you next week Mum, and ... I'm sorry for shouting. Bye.' And she hung up before anything else could be said. Exhaling and putting her head in her hands she swallowed back the tears. Again, if anyone could make her feel like an even shittier mum it was her own mother and her constant comparisons to her perfect sister.

She needed a drink after that.

Chapter 38

'Nancy, what is he wearing?' Cameron called out as they ran along the side of the kitchen area and past some members of staff who were standing outside on their cigarette break, confused looks as they watched the pair of them sprint by.

'His pyjamas. Orange and black pyjamas.' She couldn't breathe. A mixture of being suitably unfit and holding back the emotion meant that her throat felt clogged and restricted as she ran. But it didn't matter, the adrenalin was keeping her going and with every step she took, a surge of energy came with it. They reached the playground area and both stopped outside the gate, scanning round as quickly as they could for an initial check. The moon was bright tonight; it felt like it was trying to help them out, to give them hope. In the evenings it wasn't usually cold, but Nancy could feel a breeze and it made her shiver. She wasn't sure if it was because of the drop in temperature, or because she was panicking, but the hairs on her arms all lifted and stood to attention as she looked at the darkening park area. It had started to get dark really quickly, she thought. When she'd left the restaurant it had still been moderately light but as they had been running around, the sky had deepened in colour as the sun dropped away and the moon rose to take the night shift. It wasn't pitch black, but to a seven-year-old, in a place he didn't know, with his anxious tendencies too – it would be terrifying. The thought of him alone right now made Nancy want to vomit and she had to take a moment to steady herself on the railings that surrounded the playground. The railings felt cold, hard, and metallic under her touch. She looked at her hands, gripping them tight, her knuckles white and she instantly thought of Jack and his white knuckles whenever he grabbed onto her for reassurance. She let out a small whimper as more of her hope ebbed away, through her fingertips and into the nothingness.

There were smaller, streetlamp type lights surrounding the actual park area but these had not been switched on yet. She wondered why they were still off, why they weren't beaming their rays over the playground. It was too dark for children to be playing in here, was that why? The children would all be in bed, which was where Jack should be.

It was a fairly large play area and Nancy couldn't believe they hadn't come across it yet. It may have been in the brochure they had in their room but in all honesty, they hadn't looked at it when they arrived – just vowed to explore the place on foot and find everything as they came across it. Now she wished she had looked at it because the children would love it here. She stood looking into the gloom, the outlines of the apparatus glistening in the moonlight, creating silhouettes of shapes and designs which, under different circumstances, would look pretty amazing. She could see why Jack loved shapes so much; it looked pretty spectacular in this lighting.

Cameron touched her arm to bring her out of her daze. 'If you take the left-hand side, I'll take the right and we'll meet together in the middle, OK?' She nodded in response, puppet like and feeling as though she was experiencing some kind of outer body moment. Was this actually happening? Was she in another country looking for her seven-year-old son who had gone missing? It didn't feel real, yet the harsh reality of it was staring her in the face.

She took off towards the slide and swings, darting around the objects and trying to stay fast but negotiate the obstacles successfully. 'Jack?' she called, bending low underneath the slide and skimming through onto the other side. 'Jack?' She felt the emotion catch in her throat as the sheer scale of the situation was pressing down on her again. She could hear Cameron shouting in the distance, calling for Jack too. Every time she heard his name she felt like a part of her heart fell away. Would she ever see his little face again? Was this punishment? Her comeuppance for saying she was struggling with him? For going out on a date when she should have been with him? She should never have let herself be distracted by a man. Of all things – a man! It was just her and Jack, that's all it ever needed to be. This was what happened when she let unnecessary distractions happen. Annoyed with herself, she climbed over the steps leading into the little hut on the far side of the playground and peered inside the window. Nothing. Not even a discarded flip flop or old juice box. Sheer emptiness. Just like her body – empty, void, nothing without

Jack. She had to find him, but she was fast losing all hope. She pulled her head out of the window and lifted her hands to hold them on top of her head, trying so very desperately to think. Where would he go, what would he do? He couldn't have just disappeared.

'Nancy quick!' Her heart stopped beating for a second as the words washed over her. 'I've found him!'

She stumbled as she ran faster than she had ever run before, the sobs escaping from her mouth uncontrollably as she did. 'Where are you?' she yelled, frantically looking around in her dimming surroundings, unable to make out where Cameron was. 'Cameron!'

'Over here, follow the light.'

Suddenly a small light lit up – obviously the torch on his phone – and Nancy could see Cameron's silhouette. She darted in and out of the different playground equipment, leaping over the see saw like a gazelle, finally reaching the treehouse he was standing in front of.

'Where is he?' she barked, looking around him and then behind herself. 'I can't see him!'

'He's up there.' Cameron pointed to the treehouse. 'He's frightened; he wouldn't come down with me so I told him to wait for you.' He touched the small of her back and ushered her forward to the steps. She took them two at a time and ignored the burning sensation in her glutes as the effects of sudden exercise made her muscles scream out in confusion. Reaching the top, she peered over the edge and instantly saw a huddled shadow in the corner of the room. 'Jack,' she said, more like an exhalation of breath than actual words.

He lifted his head and squeaked, 'Mummy?'

'Oh baby, yes it's me.' She climbed in and crawled over to him, pulling him into her arms and sobbing uncontrollably and he cried too. 'Oh, I was so worried. You poor thing, are you OK?' It was like her body was crumbling. The relief of finding him, the sadness of the situation and the joy that had erupted when she saw his little face looking back at her – it was overwhelming. She could feel her body melt into his as she held him, pain seared in her chest as the release of emotions took hold.

He didn't respond, instead just cried and cried. So she held him. She held him tighter than she had ever held him before. But he just squirmed in her arms, sobbing. She tried to gently calm him but he was inconsolable. He thrashed around, unable to control his emotions and it broke her heart that she couldn't comfort him. He didn't want to be held, he didn't want to move and he didn't want to talk. He just cried and cried and as Nancy watched her son struggling so much with his fear, her world fell apart that little bit more. Touching him made it worse, but he also didn't want her to move away from him. He was battling with his demons and as Nancy watched him, tears streaming down her face, she could see the inner turmoil he was suffering but she couldn't do anything about it. She felt helpless. She was his mum, she should be able to take away all the worry and fear, but she couldn't. Every inch of her skin screamed out to hold him. He howled as he fought with his desire to be reassured but without being touched.

'Jack, it's OK,' Nancy tried, keeping her voice light and comforting, but he couldn't concentrate on his surge of emotion as well as her voice. Nancy sat, just watching. Just being there, being a body. Knowing that at least he was safe. She had to let him get through this first before they could move.

After a few moments, Cameron's head appeared in the doorway of the treehouse and Nancy instantly saw the sadness in his eyes as he took in the scene in front of him; Nancy sat cross-legged in the corner looking distraught and Jack in a ball, crying and writhing around. 'Are you OK?' he asked softly, seemingly not sure what else to say. Nancy just shrugged, her chin beginning to quiver. 'Shall we try and get him back to your room – he might feel better in some familiar surroundings?'

'Jack?' Nancy tentatively tried to get his attention. 'Shall we go back to the room? Harriet will be wondering where you are.'

'I want to go home,' he sobbed. At least he was responding to her voice now.

Nancy looked at Cameron and he smiled sadly at her. She tried a different approach. 'We are going home very soon, but whilst we are on holiday, our home is our room at the hotel. Do you want to go to that home?' Silence. 'Come on baby, it's late and it's nice and cosy in our room. We can get your iPad and you can lie in bed with Grand Designs – how's that sound?'

Still silence, just the occasional sniff and his crying calmed to a soft whimper. Nancy started to move forwards to place her hand on his arm but he squirmed and shouted, 'I want to go home!'

She recoiled in surprise at his sudden outburst and found she was shaking. She looked at Cameron. 'Maybe you could call Harriet and let her know we have him and ask her to let everyone else know – I don't think we will be going back to the room anytime soon.' Cameron nodded and she gave him her phone after selecting Harriet's number.

It was going to be a long night.

Chapter 39

The following morning Harriet woke up to the sound of Isla reading Tommy a book. Actually reading was probably an ambitious word. It was more a case of Isla turning the pages and making up her own little stories which involved a princess who was really mad at a dragon for not being her friend just because she was a girl. So the princess gained some magical powers by eating some sweets and made the dragon change its mind and they became best friends and went on adventures.

Isla clearly had the potential of being a children's entertainer when she was older with that eccentric mind. Either that or a writer – writers were all as crazy as a box of frogs!

Harriet rolled over and checked her phone – 06:45. She groaned. She had finally got to sleep about 4.30 a.m. once Nancy and Jack had returned. It had been a very emotional night and Nancy hadn't said much when she'd got in, she'd just taken Jack into their room and said she would speak in the morning. She really hoped everything was OK. She couldn't tell at that point if Nancy was mad at her or upset with her. Harriet had to prepare herself for that. And rightly so, Harriet couldn't escape the fact that Jack had gone missing whilst in her care. Was their friendship now in question? Would they be able to come back from this? This holiday was supposed to be a positive thing for the pair of them – not a funeral for their twenty-two-year friendship.

'Mummy, is it breakfast time yet?'

Harriet exhaled – all that child did was eat. Even when she was still chewing she was likely to be asking what was next to eat. 'Not yet, Isla, we need to wait until Jack and Nancy are ready.'

'Shall I go wake them?'

'No!' She corrected her tone. 'Let them sleep sweetheart, they are tired.'

'But I'm hungry.'

Harriet groaned and picked up her handbag, rifling around inside for something she could snack on. 'Here.' She handed over a cereal bar that she had shoved in there the other day when she was trying her hand at being a super-organised mum like Nancy. 'Have this for now. Give Tommy a little bit too if he wants it.' Isla skipped off back to where she was sitting with Tommy in his cot and continued her dramatic story which had now taken a twist and involved a fairy as well as a talking cow.

After about twenty minutes of aimlessly messing around on social media on her phone, trying to keep her brain ticking over without letting it drop into the realms of guilt, pity and frustration with herself, she glanced up as Nancy walked into their room. 'Morning,' she said quietly.

Harriet couldn't judge the tone. 'Morning,' she replied. 'Coffee?'

Nancy nodded gratefully, barely lifting a smile. She looked exhausted, although this shouldn't have come as a surprise. Her face was gaunt and drawn and she had dark circles under each eye. Harriet's stomach twisted in sadness for her. She wanted to take away the pain, make it all ok again. But she couldn't.

'Morning Nancy! I'm reading to Tommy!' Isla's voice was a welcome break in the tension. Light, bouncy and full of innocence. Harriet was so glad to hear her speak.

'That's kind of you,' Nancy replied, forcing a smile and Harriet crashed back down to reality.

'Does Jack want to listen to my story?' Isla chirped.

'Maybe in a little while, sweetie.'

'How is he?' Harriet asked as Nancy joined her at the bed. 'Did you both manage to get some sleep?' She tried to keep her face and tone positive, happy ... not the worried, nervous mess she actually was. She stood and made the coffee, just for something to do.

Nancy sat down on the end of the bed and exhaled. 'Sort of. I didn't really sleep, I just lay next to him, thinking. He slept though.' She nodded and a tiny, forced smile played briefly on her lips.

Harriet passed her the coffee and sat down on the chair next to the dresser which faced the end of the bed where Nancy was sat. She needed to say something. She couldn't just ignore the elephant in the room, it had to be acknowledged. 'Nance, I am so sorry. I—'

Nancy held up her hand to stop Harriet talking. 'Please, you don't need to apologise. Really.'

'Yes, I do! You left me in charge of your child and had to come home to all of that. I just don't know how it happened.' She genuinely didn't. But did that make it any better? Or worse? She didn't know. 'Did he speak to you?'

Nancy nodded. 'After we got back and had laid in bed for a bit, he started talking to me. He said that he wanted to see me so came looking for me. But then got lost and scared so stayed inside the treehouse because it was less scary than walking around the hotel and it reminded him of his treehouse at home.'

Harriet put her hand on her chest as it constricted with distress. Thoughts of him just walking out of the room plaguing her mind – how had he just left like that? It didn't add up. 'Oh bless him, poor thing. How the hell did he get past me? I would've seen him come into our room to leave. Your door was locked, wasn't it?'

Nancy nodded. 'He came through when you were in the toilet apparently. I asked him why he didn't just wait and talk to you, but he just kept saying he wanted to see me so he left. Just like that. I don't think he realised the consequences of what he was doing. To him, he wanted to see me so he came looking for me.' She shrugged as she exhaled.

Harriet shook her head in disbelief and sipped her coffee. She thought her life was hard parenting her two children but Nancy was dealing with a whole new level of it. Underneath all the anguish, Harriet had grown a new sense of respect for her friend. 'And how is he now? Is he awake?'

Nancy nodded. 'Yeah he doesn't sleep much anyway and he likes to keep in routine so he's been awake since about six.

He will be knackered later but I can't force him to sleep. I think we'll just take it easy today and see what happens. To be honest, I don't think I could function much more than just chilling today anyway.' She gulped down more coffee.

'Well that's fine; we can just chill by the water or go to the beach?' Harriet desperately wanted to make things better. She tried to keep her voice jolly and upbeat.

Nancy shook her head. 'If it's OK, I might just stay in. I feel a bit anxious about taking him out of the room to be honest, so I might have a day with him in here, playing some games and relaxing.'

'OK,' Harriet replied. 'We can stay with you.'

Nancy shook her head. 'Honestly, it's fine. Don't ruin the last day of the holiday because of it. We are fine on our own.'

'But—'

'Hari, its fine. Your two will want to get out and we can't expect them to stay in all day. Maybe we can meet up a bit later – I just don't want to rush him, that's all. He's still a bit apprehensive this morning.'

Harriet nodded. 'I understand, no problem.' She paused. 'Have you spoken to Cameron this morning?'

Nancy shook her head. 'No, why?'

'No reason, it's just he was really concerned yesterday so thought he would've messaged you or something.' She knew her friend inside out and knew already how this would affect her new friendship with Cameron.

'It's still pretty early though. Plus, he's probably just thinking that maybe he should keep his distance. It was pretty full on last night. I think seeing Jack's meltdown shocked him. Even though he's probably seen similar things a thousand times with his cousin's child, it's different when it's unexpected and with someone new.' She exhaled. 'I'm still not used to them – I don't think I'll ever be *used* to them.'

'Well, everyone has dramas, don't they?' Harriet thought about the phone call with her mum last night and almost laughed to herself. That was nothing in comparison to what Nancy was going through but in her own little bubble, it was pretty horrific to listen to the way in which her mother had perceived the situation and proceeded to tell Harriet what a crap mother she was. She had managed to push it to the back of her mind for a bit but now it came screaming back into her conscious.

'Anyway let's talk about something else. I literally cannot keep going over and over last night – it is driving me insane. If I keep talking about it I am going to continue to pick apart my parenting skills bit by bit until there's nothing left!' She finished the coffee in her mug and placed the cup back onto the side, taking her hands and rubbing them over her face as she took a deep breath.

'Oh, well, you want to feel a little bit better about your parenting?' Harriet asked, still sipping her coffee and laughing. Nancy nodded. 'Apparently I am selfish; I don't care about my children and am a disgrace to my family.'

Nancy's mouth dropped open even wider with each point that Harriet made. 'Oh my God, what?'

'Yep,' she nodded. 'Selfish, a workaholic and a disappointment.'

'Your mother.' Nancy said, more of a statement than a question. 'What happened?'

'Well, I made the mistake of telling her about the whole nanny idea and she completely flipped out. Said I was palming my children off and then ... told me *she* would look after them because they deserved to have some sort of settled life as I was creating so much upheaval!'

'Oh, Hari, please tell me you're not letting this get to you.'

She shrugged and looked away.

'Listen, you're never going to please your mum. You know what she's like – if there is some way of her picking something apart or criticizing, she will. That's just her personality isn't it? Be thankful you're not like her!'

'I guess. It's just, well, she keeps saying how she and Bethany were able to do it and I can't help but wonder why I can't? What is it they have that I don't?' She started using her hands, adding animation to her story the more worked up she got. 'I mean, put me in a boardroom and I'm fine. I can do that – but put me at home with these two and I just feel totally out of my depth.'

'That's just you, it's how you work.' Nancy paused. 'And I guess maybe I need to remember that with Jack.'

Harriet frowned. 'What do you mean?'

She shuffled on the bed. 'Well, I spend so much time thinking about what life would be like if Jack wasn't struggling with his autism and I guess I need to just appreciate that yes he is different but maybe that's OK. If everyone was the same, life would be boring.'

'Our lives are anything but boring, my love.'

'Very true.' Nancy stood up. 'Right, you get yourself sorted and take those kids out and maybe later on you could bring us back some ice cream or something?'

Harriet stood up and nodded. 'Sounds like a plan.' She moved forward and pulled Nancy into a hug. She wasn't a hugging type of person but even she knew that this situation called for it. She had learnt some new things about herself on this break, maybe she should embrace the hugging thing women do too. 'It'll be alright, you know. He's safe now – it's just a hurdle to get over.'

Nancy nodded and smiled. 'I know, thanks Hari. And maybe you should listen to your own advice too, hey.'

Harriet saluted and then tapped Nancy on the bum. 'OK you, off you go – I need a shower.'

Whilst she knew she should practise what she preached, it wasn't as easy as that when your mother was continuously ripping apart every ounce of your self-esteem and flushing it down the toilet.

Chapter 40

'H ey, you OK?'
          Harriet glanced over her phone and was welcomed
by Jayne's beaming smile. 'Hey,' she replied, putting her phone
down.

'You're not working, are you?' Jayne said, teasing her,
because she knew full well that she was working.

'I am but it's only a few emails. Tommy is in the kids' club
because they were doing music and he loves playing instru-
ments,' something she had learned about him whilst away,
'and Isla is playing with her new little friend she has made
in the kids' pool just there.' Harriet pointed her out to prove
that she knew where she was and that she wasn't neglecting
her children in favour of work.

Jayne sat down beside her. 'I'm only messing, I wasn't testing
you on your parenting skills. Is everything OK?'

She nodded. 'Yeah, course. Why wouldn't it be?'

'Well, you just seem a bit edgy, that all.'

'I'm fine, just dealing with the mother from hell, that's all.'
As she said this, her phone began to ring and her sister's name
flashed up. Harriet immediately pressed the end call button

and then looked at Jayne who was staring at her confused. 'I can't be dealing with her right now.'

'Fair enough.' This was the good thing about Jayne; she knew when to push for conversations and when to just leave them. And as much as Harriet liked talking to her, she wasn't in the mood to go through all of her problems again. She was learning to let things go over her head but she wasn't completely immune to it all yet.

Harriet moved the focus from her. 'All OK with you guys? Where are your little ones?'

Jayne pointed over to the other side of the pool. 'Richard's over there with the two of them. We've only just come down but I saw you sitting here alone so I thought I'd come over and say hi. Where's Nancy?'

'She's up in the room.' She knew what was coming.

Jayne looked concerned. 'Everything OK?'

Harriet checked around her to make sure no one was listening. 'Jack went missing temporarily last night.' Jayne gasped. 'Yeah I know, I was looking after him whilst Nancy went for dinner and he wanted to see her but instead of coming to me, he just left.' She was sure Nancy wouldn't mind her telling Jayne. Harriet needed someone to talk to who wasn't so involved in the situation. Nancy liked Jayne – she seemed like the obvious choice.

'Oh my God, is he OK? Is *she* OK?' She noticeably went a little paler, as any parent would on hearing this news.

Harriet nodded. 'Yeah they're fine, just shaken up I think. But they wanted a day in the room, just to spend some time together, I think, it was quite an emotional night.'

'I can imagine, oh poor Nancy. And how are you feeling?'

'Well, you know, he was in my care so I feel awful, but Nancy isn't mad at me so...' She trailed off. Even though no one was mad at her for it, she still felt responsible for not anticipating that he might do that. 'He left when I was in the toilet.' Jayne smiled reassuringly as Harriet cancelled another call from Bethany that flashed up again. 'I feel like my life is hard sometimes, but what Nancy has to deal with is on a completely different level. I just don't know how she does it. And single-handed too. She puts me to shame.' Harriet laughed even though there was truth in what she was saying.

'You're doing a great job too. No one is going to be happy and positive all the time – just make sure you surround yourself with the people who lift you up, not batter you down.'

Harriet thought of her mother. 'I can't shut everyone out of my life though, can I? It's not that simple.'

Jayne had an amazing skill of reading between the lines so she clearly understood what Harriet meant. 'You're right; some people are harder to *not* listen to. But just remember that you do have people around you who are there for you so try and take everyone else with a pinch of salt.' She stood up. 'Hang on a minute.' And she ran off back to where her husband was sitting.

Harriet's phone vibrated again – Bethany. Why did she keep calling her? She cancelled the call again. She probably just wanted to brag about how well she was doing without any help from anyone else. It was clear her mum had been on the phone to her sister, probably bad-mouthing how Harriet had spoken to her and about how she couldn't look after her own kids.

'Mummy, look. That girl gave me some cards.' Harriet inspected the cards in Isla's hands – they were snap cards with animals on. 'Can we play?'

Harriet smiled. 'Of course we can, come and sit here.' She tapped the end of the sun lounger and crossed her legs.

'What do I need to do?' Isla asked, holding the cards out.

'OK, so we shuffle like this.' Isla gasped at Harriet's shuffling skills. 'And then we have to share the cards out equally. One for you, one for me, one for you, one for me...'

'Can I do it? I want to do it? Let me do it?' Isla practically pulled the cards out of Harriet's hands and began sharing them out. 'One for Mummy, one for Isla, one for Mummy, one for Isla ... whoops!' she dropped the pack on the floor.

'Never mind, pick them up and carry on.' Harriet smiled at her daughter. She could do this; she could make this new routine work when they got home. Because this was what she wanted, time like this to play and get to know the children without work screaming down her ear all the time. Jayne was right, she needed to channel out the bad and embrace the good.

Jayne came back over with her phone. 'Ooh, you're playing cards! I love cards.'

'You wanna play?' Isla asked and before waiting for an answer, gathered up all the cards and tried to shuffle them, resulting in more dropped cards on the floor.

'Oh sweetheart I can't right now but maybe another time?' Jayne's face lit up with her smile and as she sat down again, her auburn hair fell over one shoulder and draped down into her lap. Isla nodded and set about picking up the cards.

'I want to give you my number, Harriet. I would really like to stay in touch once we leave, maybe we could meet up sometime.'

Harriet nodded. 'Yeah, that would be nice.' She recited her own number to Jayne and then took hers down too. 'We must only be about an hour away from each other so we could quite easily do a day trip out or something. Nancy would like that too I reckon.' Another change she wanted to implement – make new friends and enjoy being around other mums. Although she wasn't sure the mums at the school were the right mums to be around. Maybe she would take lead from Nancy and Jayne for this one.

'Sounds great. Well listen, we are off later today – I can't believe it's time to go home already, feels like just yesterday that we arrived.'

'Yeah I know what you mean, we leave tomorrow. I'm dreading going back. Don't get me wrong, I'm excited to get back to work and make sure everything is still standing,' she laughed. 'But there will be some big changes put in place when we get back so it's going to be … well … an experience.'

Jayne put her hand on Harriet's shoulder and gently squeezed it. 'You'll be fine. Just remember to keep talking to people – and you've got my number now so no excuses for bottling anything up.'

Harriet smiled and nodded. 'I promise.'

'Mummy?' Isla tugged on her arm and handed her the phone. 'It's Auntie Bethany – she wants to talk to you.'

Harriet exhaled and looked at Jayne who laughed. 'Kids hey?'

'Enjoy!' she replied and walked off giggling.

***

Nancy heard a knock on the door and slowly got up from the bed so she didn't wake Jack. He had finally crashed out about twenty minutes ago so she was hoping that would help him recover a bit from the anxiety of last night's events. She reached the door and opened it to reveal Cameron's face. He was smiling but Nancy could see the concern behind it. He hid it well but she had only too often seen people look at her like this.

'A little birdy tells me you requested some ice cream?' He held out his hands and presented two Mr Whippy style ice creams.

But then he did things like this and Nancy's heart ached to spend time with him. 'Oh, you're sweet,' Nancy laughed. 'But Jack's asleep.'

'How is he?'

She nodded. 'He's OK.'

'And you?' He lowered his head a little to catch her eye contact and she felt the butterflies in her stomach rear up a little.

'I'm ... OK.' Code for – I'm coping but I don't want to talk about it.

'Hmm, not sure I believe you.' He looked at the ice creams. 'Anyway, I'll let you get some rest, here.' He handed both ice creams to her. 'Go wild.'

'What? I can't have them both.'

'Why not? You're on holiday, calories don't count. It's the law.' He winked at her.

She felt bad. He had really helped her out last night; she couldn't just dismiss him like this. They could have a friendship; she just needed to make sure it didn't go too far and that Jack didn't feel pushed out. But he was asleep, so a chat and an ice cream would be OK. 'I'll tell you what; if you don't have anywhere to be right now, why don't you join me and you can have Jack's?'

He smiled and stepped inside. 'Sounds like a plan.'

'We can sit on the balcony and then I'll still be able to see Jack if he wakes up. Is that OK?' She also didn't want Jack to wake up and immediately see a man in his room.

'Of course it is – whatever you need to do. I get an ice cream so I'm happy.'

They sat on the balcony which over looked the pool area and Nancy could see Harriet in the distance playing cards with Isla. It was kind of nice to be on the periphery of all the goings on downstairs. Distant enough from it to not feel suffocated but able to still embrace the joviality of holidaygoers. 'So where's Aiden?'

'Kids' club,' he replied. 'He loves that place. I reckon he would be in there the whole holiday if he had a choice. He does like to make me feel loved, that boy.' He laughed.

'He's such a great little boy. He's a real credit to you.'

Cameron nodded and smiled, but didn't say anything. 'And technically, it was Aiden who introduced us,' she added, continuing to eat her ice cream and not looking at him.

'That is very true. My little wingman. I approve of his choice, too.'

Nancy blushed and kept her eyes looking forward. 'You charmer.'

'Hey, I try. You're not very good at taking compliments are you?' Cameron said with a grin.

'Guess I'm not used to getting them.' That much was true. Pete was never one for giving full-blown compliments. More like observational comments such as *'you don't look as tired today'* or *'I take it Jack got you up early today then?'* when she was able to put together a more comprehensive outfit choice owing to the additional time gained of getting ready some mornings due to Jack's early wake ups.

'Jack's dad wasn't the complimenting type?' he probed.

Nancy shrugged. 'Guess you could say that. He was more the type to get straight to the point and get the job done.' Cameron coughed and Nancy immediately realised what that sounded like. 'Oh my God, I didn't mean that!' she laughed. 'I just meant he wasn't flouncy with his words.'

'Oh so I'm flouncy now am I? Makes me sound pretty.' He pulled a posing face, pouting his lips out and placed his hands around his face to frame it.

'Shut up.' She tutted. 'So come on then, what's your ex like, seeing as we have broken that seal of talking about exes.' It was OK to broach this subject now because she had decided there would be no romance between them. She was going to look at this as a friendship so it was fine to talk about taboo subjects like exes. She wasn't probing for her own gain; she was taking an interest in her new friend.

Cameron noticeably sobered. 'She is ... was ... hard work.'

'Hard work?' She licked round the edge of her ice cream as it dripped down the side of the cone, melting in the heat of the sunshine.

'Yes. I guess she just didn't know what she wanted in life and when we got Aiden she realised she didn't want the family life she signed up for. So ... she left.' His face was sad as he reminisced. Nancy recognised the look behind his eyes. She had seen it before when he spoke about family stuff. She knew there was more than met the eye with him.

Nancy shook her head. 'No disrespect to her, but I don't think I could have a baby and then leave it. But I guess parenting isn't for everyone.' She tried to be tactful in what she was saying. But inside she knew she could never leave Jack and didn't understand how Aiden's mother could.

'No,' he replied, simply. Not elaborating.

Nancy found herself saying, 'But to make that decision to have a baby and go through all the pregnancy and then decide actually it's not what you want and leave, that's got to take some decision-making. I can't imagine the emotional roller-coaster you both must have gone through.'

He exhaled hard, not moving his gaze from looking out at the pool area. 'It's more complicated than that.'

Nancy looked over to him but he wouldn't look at her. 'Oh?' she pressed.

He pursed his lips, looking like he was building up to

something. The silence that followed was immense, but Nancy could almost feel the pressure to stay quiet, to let this play out. He was obviously struggling with something and wanted to talk, so she didn't press it, instead, waiting patiently until he finally spoke. 'We aren't Aiden's biological parents.'

Nancy paused, momentarily confused. It didn't make sense but, after a moment's silence, the penny dropped. 'You mean...'

He nodded. 'Aiden's adopted. We adopted him when he was eighteen months old.'

'Wow,' she breathed. They sat in stillness for a moment whilst the information sank in. Nancy checked over her shoulder to make sure Jack was still asleep on the bed. She could see his little arms poking out from under the thin sheet she had placed over him. She loved him so much. She was so glad to have him back with her, have him safe. She could never be without him. She turned back to Cameron, suddenly thinking of Aiden's role in all this. 'Does he know?'

Cameron shook his head, looking at her for the first time since saying the words aloud. 'No, not yet.'

'Will you tell him?' She kept her eyes on his. Now she knew why he had sadness behind that smile. The poor guy had clearly been through quite an ordeal over the last few years. There was so much depth to him and it really caused a battle of emotions within her. She knew what she had to do – for Jack – but her insides cried out to comfort Cameron. To touch him. To hold him. To kiss him.

'I'll have to at some point. But not yet. The poor little guy was left by his birth parents and then one of his adoptive parents leaves too. I can't put him through that, not at his age.' She could see his broken heart, as if he was wearing it on his shirt for all to see. But not everyone could see his pain, and he had chosen to share this with her. It made him vulnerable and she had the power to take that moment and keep it forever, just between them.

'So, you just raise him by yourself?' Cameron nodded. 'And you work as a surgeon?' Another nod. 'Jeez, hats off to you.'

He shook his head. 'I'm just doing what anyone else would do. I love that little guy so much – it doesn't matter where he came from, he's my son.' He pulled at his shirt. 'So that's what this tattoo is – the top one is his birthday and the second date is the date I officially became his daddy. Both dates just as important to me.'

Nancy's heart swelled with happiness as she listened to how Cameron spoke about Aiden. 'Well, you're clearly doing a very good job because he has turned out to be such an awesome little man. You should be proud.'

'I am.' He looked at Nancy. 'I wish everyone was as nice as you.'

She frowned. 'What do you mean?'

He moved his gaze back out to the pool and focused on the distance. 'I just don't get as much support from everyone as I would like, that's all.'

'Do you want to talk about it?'

He shrugged 'You're very lucky to have Harriet. Friends are so important, aren't they?' She nodded. 'My friends aren't very supportive of my current situation.' He went quiet so Nancy just left him to it, let him have the silence. She just needed to be a pair of ears right now and it was comforting for her to not be talking about her own problems right now.

'When we got Aiden, everyone was really positive and excited. We had a new baby, everyone wanted to come and meet him and the guys were great. But then things fell apart and broke down between me and the ex and when she left, the guys couldn't understand why I kept Aiden.'

Nancy gasped. 'Did they think you would just give him back or something?' The sheer outrageousness of the thought of it made her face contort in disbelief.

He shrugged. 'Who knows? But I became this single father who, when I wasn't working, I was at home with my child and they kept asking me if I was doing the right thing and why didn't I just explain to the adoption agency that my circumstances had changed and give him back.'

'That's awful. If anything, that little guy needed you more than ever.'

He turned and smiled at her, slight humour behind his eyes. 'That's exactly what I said.' She smiled back. 'Your ice cream is dripping.'

Nancy glanced down just as a huge drip landed on her lap. 'Oh damn it.' She wiped it with her hand and then licked round the edges to stop any further spillages. 'So, are they still around, your friends?'

He nodded. 'Yeah, they still talk to me but I never get invited anywhere anymore. I see all their photos of their nights out and parties and I just sit at home.'

'It must be hard seeing all that.'

'It *is* hard – don't get me wrong, I wouldn't change Aiden

for the world. I love that little guy and I will always be there for him, but I do feel like I've been shoved into this little box where no one wants to know me.' He turned to face her with his full body. 'Nancy, I'm sorry for not turning up to our dinner date last night.'

With everything that had happened, she had forgotten about the dinner date – or lack of. She shrugged, it wasn't important anymore, was it? 'It's fine.'

'It's not fine, I should have been there.'

She looked back at him. 'Why weren't you?' She had planned to confront him about it but then after everything that happened, it just didn't feel important anymore. But part of her was intrigued as to why he wasn't there.

'The other day I was in the foyer and I got a message from a friend. They told me that they had something to tell me, but they couldn't do it over text, they needed to speak to me when I got home. But it was bothering me as this guy who texted me wasn't the type to say cryptic stuff like that so I knew it must be serious.'

Nancy recalled the day she saw Cameron in the foyer. 'That's why you were so off when I spoke to you that day.'

He smiled. 'Yeah, sorry about that, it was all kind of happening at once and I couldn't concentrate on anything but what the message had said. I knew I needed to call him so I went up to my room so I could have some privacy.'

'What did your friend say when you called him?'

Cameron's face changed, he looked hurt. 'He had seen one of my work colleagues out the night before. On a date.' Cameron looked up at Nancy. 'He was out with my ex.'

Nancy opened her mouth to talk but didn't know what to say so stayed quiet, instead opting for an understanding nod.

'I know we aren't together, but it hurt.'

'That's understandable.'

'I tried to forget about it, for Aiden's sake, and I tried to continue to enjoy the holiday. But last night, as I was getting ready for our dinner, I got a phone call.' He paused. 'From my ex.'

Nancy used the tissue next to her to wipe her hands now that she had finished her ice cream. 'Oh God, what did she say?' Her eyes widened as the story unfolded.

'She's pregnant,' he said, his body deflating with every breath until he looked every inch a broken man.

'What?' Nancy gasped.

Cameron nodded. 'Yep. Turns out she and my colleague have been seeing each other for a little while now and they decided they wanted to have a baby. She fell pregnant almost instantly.'

'But ... she ... but ... Aiden?' Nancy couldn't communicate what she wanted to say. She wasn't even sure she knew exactly what she did want to say. It didn't make sense.

'I know. That's what I said. She left us because she said she wasn't ready for the family commitment and then she goes off, meets some guy and decides that actually she does want it.' He lifted his hand exasperated. 'Clearly it was just me and Aiden she didn't want.'

'Oh Cameron,' Nancy said, her eyebrows knitting together with sadness for him. What an awful thing for someone to have to go through. Cameron had always come across as a confident, sexy, funny kind of guy but he had so much going on in his life that he just didn't show on the outside. He seemed a gentle soul, someone who worked in an emotional job, someone who loved being a father, so this must've been like a stab to the heart. She really felt sorry for him and the empathy etched itself all over her face. She hadn't met his ex but she found herself disliking her very much for doing this to Cameron. All he wanted was a family and she'd betrayed him – and Aiden – and for what? So she could start a family with someone else. Nancy's thoughts then turned to Aiden. Poor Aiden. He was such a jolly little boy who had no idea what was happening behind the scenes. Cameron had done a good job of making him into the boy he was today. She really hoped he wouldn't be affected when he found out his mum had decided to abandon him and start a family with someone else. She kind of knew in her heart that Cameron would make sure Aiden was OK.

'It shocked me, and I guess I just went into shutdown. I'm sorry, I should've come and told you but I couldn't function and I didn't want you to think I was being an arsehole so I thought the best option was to just cancel. After a while I went for a walk, to clear my head a bit whilst Aiden was with my sister and decided I would come and apologise in person, I thought you might still be there. I felt awful and annoyed at myself for letting that ruin our date when I really wanted to be there. That's when Harriet called me and, well, you know the rest.' Nancy nodded, reliving the thoughts of last night again. 'I'm sorry I let you down.'

'I think you made up for it by helping me find Jack.' She smiled reassuringly. 'Have you joined any parenting groups?' she said suddenly, trying to lighten the mood.

Cameron laughed. 'Give over. There aren't any groups where I live that are for dads.'

'You can go to any parenting groups – they aren't just for mums, they're for parents.'

'Yeah but that's when the children are newborns. Aiden's at school now and I'm working. It just not that easy to make parent friends – especially as a dad.'

'Well, you've made me and Harriet as friends so you can add us to your list.'

Cameron smiled and gazed back at her. They both sat there momentarily, just looking at one another. Cameron then broke the silence. 'You're special, you know that?'

'Am I?' she asked, unable to think of anything else to say. It had been a while since she had received so much attention. But today, with just the pair of them on that balcony, it felt much more intimate. He had shared something so private with her and it had completely messed with her plan to be just friends. She wanted him so much.

But ... Jack...

Camron nodded. 'Very special.' He lifted his hand and moved it across to hers, holding it and gently rubbing his thumb across the top. 'I know things are tough for you right now, but I just wanted to say that I think you're doing a great job. I admire you.'

She laughed nervously and dropped her gaze. She felt completely out of her comfort zone, but she was enjoying it.

His big soft hands resting on hers – she didn't move hers, instead opting to let him hold her. It felt nice.

He turned more on his chair so that he was facing her straight on and took his other hand to cup hers. 'Nancy, I want to ask you something, tell me if I'm overstepping the mark.'

She froze, her heart beating so fast she could hear the ringing in her ears. She looked back at him, his big blue eyes wide and inviting and his hair tousled to the side a little. He was the complete opposite to Pete, but she found that refreshing, energising.

'OK,' she replied, anxiously waiting for his next comment. It felt like everything had been put on mute around them and she zoned out the noise of the pool – children screaming and laughing, music playing, water spraying, she couldn't hear any of it now. Just the sound of her heavy breathing and heartbeat pulsing through her head and...

'Mummy!'

Chapter 41

'Hi Beth, you OK?' Harriet glared at Isla, who didn't even look up from her playing cards, and shuffled on her bum. Aside from her mother, Bethany was the last person she wanted to be chatting to right now. She knew exactly how her mother worked – she would've got off the phone from her and rung Bethany immediately, slagging her off for her decision-making on the nanny front. The two of them would have had a laugh about it and Bethany would have sucked up to their mother by saying how she didn't need anything like that and that she couldn't understand why Harriet did, and how their mother was so right about every-thing ... it had happened so many times before, Harriet would probably be able to relay their exact conversation word for word.

'Hey sis, how's things?'

Harriet wasn't in the mood for frilly talk so she cut straight to the point. 'Mum called you then?'

'Yeah,' Beth replied, not even trying to cover it up. 'How are you doing?'

'I'm fine. More than fine, I'm great. You?'

'Yeah, I'm fine. The kids are at a birthday party so I'm getting the house sorted.'

Harriet nodded and the line went silent. Her sister hardly ever called her, so this phone call was quite painful. After a moment, Harriet got sick of waiting and abruptly said, 'Look is there a point to this phone call?'

'Oh, well, actually there is – although you needn't be so rude.'

'Sorry,' she added, feeling instantly guilty at Bethany's tone.

'I just wanted to tell you something. But, well, it's ... it's not that easy for me.'

Harriet frowned and picked up her drink, sipping the sweet liquid and letting it slowly slide down her throat and relax her sudden anxiety. 'What's up?'

'You know you and Mum had a row over you deciding to get a nanny?'

'Yes – and before you give me the third degree about it as well, I can assure you Mum has covered all angles. I'm a terrible mother, I'm selfish, and I'm palming my children off ... I've heard it all. So I'll save you the trouble of repeating any of it.' As she spoke she could feel the anxiety building again. As much as she was trying to let it wash over her like Jayne had said, it was still a tough pill to swallow when your own flesh and blood said these things to you.

'I wasn't going to repeat any of it. I was going to, um...'

Harriet waited but Bethany just went quiet. 'Beth?' she prompted.

She heard her sister exhale on the end of the phone. 'I have a nanny!'

Harriet tilted her head as the words washed over her, confused at what she had just head. 'What?'

'I have a nanny – she helps me, you know, with stuff.'

Harriet gasped and sat up on the lounger, disbelief rapidly washing over her. 'Are you actually having me on?'

'No, I swear.' Her voice was small.

She spun round so her legs were off the side of her chair, leaning her arms on her knees as she digested this new information. 'But … well … what does Mum say?' It was her first thought.

'She doesn't know.'

Harriet couldn't help but burst out laughing. It was a cross between a nervous laugh and a shocked laugh. This was probably the best news she had heard for ages. She couldn't believe it. 'How in God's name have you kept it from her? I mean, just … tell me *everything*.' She had the biggest smile across her face. This was incredible. She couldn't verbalise how this was making her feel right now.

Bethany laughed and Harriet instantly felt a spark of comradery between them, a sisterly bond that, up until now, their relationship had been lacking. She listened as her sister opened up for the first time in years.

'I was struggling. Massively. Luke works long hours, I was working from home all throughout the school hours and then again when the kids were in bed and things were starting to get too much. I couldn't talk to Mum because – well, you know what she's like.'

Harriet nodded and rolled her eyes. 'Yep.'

'So I looked into getting some outside help. I met this lady and she's just wonderful. She comes to mine first thing and sorts the children. She then takes the older two to school whilst Rueben stays at home with me. Then she comes back and takes him from me whilst I work in the study. I work all day and she cooks, cleans and does the washing. She stays until 6 p.m. when I stop working and then we all have dinner and get to put the kids to bed. She's incredible.'

'But, how does Mum not know?'

'She thinks I'm at home with Rueben. She thinks I get all my work done around looking after him – although I'm not quite sure how she believes I can be so productive with an eighteen-month-old on my hip but the woman is delirious so I guess she doesn't realise. And if she comes over without telling me, I just tell the nanny to wait upstairs until she's gone – she normally does the ironing then.' Bethany laughed.

'And she's OK with that?'

'She understands my situation, she knows I can't tell Mum. Ironing is part of her contract so I'm not asking her to do anything that she hasn't already agreed to do – it's just some-times she has to do it incognito upstairs.'

The words were filtering into Harriet's brain all at once. This revelation was huge, and she couldn't quite believe that it was her sister saying these things to her. 'Why don't you just tell Mum? I thought you two were super close?'

'Why don't I tell Mum? Do you not remember how she reacted to you?'

'Yeah but, she might have been fine with you.'

'Yeah OK, Hari, I'm sure you believe that as much as I do. We both know that the way she reacted with you would be exactly how she would react to anyone. I commend you for being brave and actually saying it to her – I've been a total wuss and chickened out.'

'You should tell her!' Harriet shouted but already Bethany was disagreeing.

'Not a chance in hell.'

'No seriously, you should. We could do it together. If she knew we were both doing it, she might not mind? We need to stick together at this. '

'Hari, like I said, I admire your courage in telling Mum, it's a big move. But there is no way on this earth that I am putting myself into that lion's den ready to be crucified. I'm not as tough as you.'

Harriet felt a strange emotion come over her when her sister said that. The two of them hadn't been particularly close in the past so hearing Bethany being complimentary did not sit naturally with her. 'I always thought you thought I was a hard-faced cow – actually, you have called me that on occasion.'

'I know. And don't get me wrong, sometimes you are a hard-faced cow – but I do admire you. I wish I could be stronger sometimes and I wish I had your drive and determination. You just get things done, no matter what stands in your way. You don't ever stress or fall apart, you just totally ace everything you do – I guess I was a little bit jealous.'

'Beth, I don't ace everything.' Was she really that good at pretending? She got stressed, she failed and she got things wrong. She always tried hard to cover up any mistakes or rectify them, but they still happened.

'You do. I don't think there is anything you've done that you haven't been good at.'

Harriet hesitated for a moment and then looked around her. Isla had got fed up of waiting so had returned to the pool to play with her friends and the sun loungers immediately next to her had been vacated. So she took a very risky move and said, 'I don't get everything right you know ... can I ask you something?'

'Course.'

The two of them had spent years not really communicating or talking and now, through this mutual acknowledgement of needing help, Harriet felt a small element of sisterly bonding happening. A bond over parenting, over the need to ask for help. She decided to take the plunge. 'How did you cope when you had Billy, and Janey came along? Did you find it easy to make that transition between going from one child to two children?'

She didn't know if it was because the two of them couldn't see each other, or because she was learning new things about her sister who she clearly didn't know anything about ... or maybe the cocktails, but she felt able to open up a little and ask these questions. Had this been a month ago, even a week ago, Harriet wouldn't have dared ask anything like this.

'Honestly? I struggled.'

The relief that poured over Harriet was immense, she felt as though she could cry with happiness. 'Really?'

'Yeah. You spend years getting used to your first child, they start eating and sleeping relatively normally, you start to manage things better and get jobs done and then you have another one and it starts all over again. Your routines are messed up, your older child is jealous of the new one and where you once had a child that ate and slept fine, this new one doesn't want to do anything. I couldn't believe how opposite my two were. Billy slept through from about twelve weeks; Janey still doesn't sleep through now, at five. Billy would eat anything and everything, Janey was a little fusspot. Billy had no health problems at all and never really got ill, Janey was always down the doctor's for something or other. The two of them couldn't have been more different and I really struggled with that.'

'I can't believe I never knew this.'

'Well, we never really talked about mum stuff, did we?'

'Yeah because Mum was always there with her opinions and judgements. And I always thought you shared her opinions, you would always seem so on top of things whenever we came over.' She became louder the more excited she got and had to check her volume.

'What can I say, I haven't got a diploma in performing arts for nothing.'

Harriet laughed. 'So why call me now? Why tell me about all this?'

'Because I felt bad. Mum called me and was ranting about how you were getting a nanny and how she told you what she thought of it and I felt sorry for you. You actually had the guts to stand up to her and say something and here I was harbouring this little secret. I guess I just wanted to let you know that I am here if you ever need to talk, even if it's just a sounding board to rant at. I love Mum to bits but I do know how hard it can be with her sometimes and I am lucky because she doesn't rip into me like she does you. So just let her have her moment, but know that I totally understand why you're doing this and I support you.'

This was one of the most surreal moments of Harriet's life. She felt like this was the first time she was really seeing her sister in a different light. She smiled, feeling a weird warm sensation inside.

'But Hari?'

'Yes?'

'Don't you dare tell Mum, OK?'

Harriet laughed. 'OK, deal.'

'I'll give you a call next week and maybe we can chat all stuff nanny.'

Harriet smiled. 'I'd like that.' She hung up the phone and couldn't stop the smile that spread across her face. So this was what it felt like to have a sister. As long as she had gone without having her by her side, it felt nice to experience this new relationship. She caught Jayne waving to her to get her attention from across the pool. Jayne held her thumb up and then down. Harriet laughed and gave a thumbs up to which Jayne smiled in return. Maybe it was going to work out after all.

But there was one thing she knew for certain, she would do everything in her power to make sure that she was not like her mum. Her children were going to be able to talk to her about anything and she was going to be there for them. She had a plan, and now she had the support. She could do this.

Chapter 42

'Mummy!' Nancy bolted from her seat, tripping over the step into the room as she ran to Jack in his bed. He was sitting upright, wide-eyed and clutching his sheet. She sat down on the bed next to him and instantly drew him into her arms, at which he recoiled and looked at her. It was difficult to judge Jack because on occasion he would be fine with the comforting touch, and other times he wouldn't. There didn't seem to be a pattern with it – not one that Nancy had noticed anyway. So she always tried. And it always hurt when he pulled away from her. 'What's up?' she asked.

'I didn't know where you were,' he replied, his chin quivering.

'Baby, I was only on the balcony. I wasn't far, just over there.' She pointed to the balcony to reiterate just how close she was. 'See?'

'That's Cameron,' he said, pointing to Cameron who was standing in the doorway of the balcony looking a little sheepish.

'Hey buddy,' he said, giving Jack a half salute, half wave.

'Where's Aiden?'

It was the first time Jack had used his name. Normally he would call him *that little boy*. Nancy looked at Cameron to see if he noticed this little development. He raised his eyebrows which suggested he did.

'He's at the kids' club,' Nancy answered. 'You remember it there?' She wondered whether it was the right thing to do to mention this to him as she wasn't sure of his emotional stability today, but he seemed OK now that he knew where she was.

'Yeah, I didn't like that lady.'

Nancy laughed as she recalled the headphones incident – it felt like a million years ago that that had happened, not seven days. 'That's right bubs, you didn't like her. But there are other ladies and men there to play with, so Aiden will be OK, I'm sure he is having lots of fun.' She paused and then added, 'Would you like to go and see the kids' club again?'

Jack instantly shook his head and Nancy laughed, looking over to Cameron. 'It was worth a try.'

He nodded, a smile spread across his face.

'I would like to see that boy again. I want to show him my iPad.'

He had reverted back to calling him *that boy*. 'Well, I am sure we can arrange that. What do you say, Cameron?'

Cameron walked into the room but stopped short of the bed so he wasn't getting too close. 'I think that's a great idea. And actually, do you know what?'

'What?' Jack replied.

'There is a competition this evening after dinner in the

disco hall – I think it's a baking competition or something. Aiden said that he wanted to do it, maybe you would like to take a look.' He looked to Nancy to see if it was OK with her too. Jack didn't look too keen, but he didn't say no so it was a start.

'Maybe we will go down and take a look, Jack? And you can decide when you get there if it's something you like the look of. How's that sound?' She was starting to get to grips with how Jack worked in certain situations. How sometimes he needed the chance to see things first before deciding. Or how sometimes he liked to watch things from afar and join in when he was ready, not when it was convenient for everyone else. It was slowly all beginning to make sense now, but that transition between not knowing and learning had been a steep one. He nodded and then picked up his iPad, shuffling down into the bed and resuming his programme from earlier on.

Nancy gave him a kiss on the forehead and stood up, walking over to Cameron who had now walked towards the front door. 'Are you off?' She found herself not wanting him to go.

'Yeah I'd better go. Plus, I think I'm going to go and get Aiden early from kids' club, maybe take him to the boats again. We go home tomorrow so I best make the most of it, hey? Not that he will want to see me. He'll probably be all like "daaaaad I wanna staaaay!"' He laughed but Nancy noticed some sadness in his eyes.

'It's their loss, you know.' He looked at her. 'Your friends. And your ex.' He pursed his lips into a smile and dropped his gaze to the ground. 'Aiden is lucky to have you, it's an amazing thing what you've done. Just remember, you've got people around you who do support you.'

'Thanks Nancy.' He stepped forward and brushed his lips on her cheek and as he did she closed her eyes and took in the sweet smell of his aftershave. Every inch of her body tingled, wanting more. But she felt herself already pulling back. She couldn't get too close. His situation was complicated enough as well as her own – they didn't need to make it more confusing. 'I'll see you tonight in the hall then?'

'Yep, see you there.'

She closed the door and smiled to herself. After such a shitty day yesterday, maybe things were starting to look up.

'Mum, I need a poo!'

And now she was back on mummy duties.

***

Harriet walked back to the pool area having picked up Tommy from the kids' club. 'Only for half an hour though Isla, because we need to go back and see how Nancy and Jack are.'

'Ohhhhh!' Isla did her best pouting performance and threw her arms up.

'Isla, we've been down at the pool pretty much all day sweetheart, poor Jack has been inside.'

'Tell them to come out,' she whined.

'I don't think they want to.'

'But I want to stay here!' She stomped along the pathway,

making her feelings very clear about having to end their pool time today.

'That's enough, Isla, stop being stroppy otherwise you won't get this extra half hour and we can go back up to the room now.' She was really testing her new parenting style. *Stay calm, keep smiling*, she repeated to herself.

'Humph' was the sort of noise she made and Harriet clenched her teeth. She really wanted to check her emails as she'd stayed off them all afternoon and was now starting to feel a little anxious. She also needed to sit down and advertise for a nanny – although advertising was where her expertise lay so it wouldn't be a difficult task. Finding one on the other hand would be. Bethany had texted her after their phone call with a number of the agency her nanny came from so she could take a look. She was still getting used to this newfound friendship from her sister – it felt out of her comfort zone but she knew that in time, she would welcome the support.

They pitched up over to one side by the pool and Harriet managed to grab one of the last sun loungers. 'OK, go,' she said to Isla who was jumping up and down impatiently trying to get into the water. Harriet then looked at Tommy. 'Suppose there's no use trying to put you in the water, hey little man?' He smiled at her and then lifted his hand and slapped her on the nose.

'About right,' she said, placing him on the floor and letting him play with the toys from her bag.

'Hey,' Nancy's voice sounded behind her and she whipped round, surprised to hear it.

'Hey! I wasn't expecting to see you guys down here.' She

looked at Jack. 'Alright Jack?' He half smiled and then sat down on the floor on the other side of Harriet's lounger, pulling out his sketch pad.

'Here, perch on this one, I don't think there are any loungers left. It's well busy down here. We were going to do another half an hour and then come up and see you guys.'

Nancy sat down on the floor. 'Its fine, we needed to get out of the room for a bit anyway – get some fresh air.'

'What are you doing, sit up here you idiot.' Harriet shifted her legs but Nancy held up her hand.

'Honestly it's fine. I'm OK down here.'

'Did Cameron come and see you?' Harriet pulled a face. She wasn't sure if Nancy would have appreciated the little tip off she gave him about the ice cream, but she figured seeing as they were leaving tomorrow, she may as well take the plunge.

'Yes, thanks for that.' She rolled her eyes.

'Oh, was it a car crash? Sorry, I thought it would be nice for you two to chat, he said Aiden was at the club and I found him kind of aimlessly wandering around looking like a lost sheep whilst his sister and that were off playing in the pool. You know, I think he struggles to shut off from work.'

Nancy laughed. 'Coming from you?'

'Hey, I'm getting better!'

'I'm not having a go – just find it funny that you should notice something like that.'

'Well I guess he is similar to me so I notice these things. I get it – it's hard when you have a full on job to just shut off. '

Nancy held her hand up. 'This is a work free zone, no work talk.' Harriet locked her mouth and chucked the key. 'Anyway, it wasn't a car crash. It was quite nice. We sat on the balcony and ate our ice creams and had a nice chat.' Harriet raised her eyebrow. 'What?'

'And what was this nice chat about? Did he declare his love for you – are you going to run away into the sunset and make lots of babies?'

'Hari!'

'What? Let me have my fantasy. It's nearly time to go home and resume the chaotic hecticness that is my life, let me daydream one last time before my brain becomes a mush of meetings and numbers and projects.'

'We had a really nice chat and he kind of opened up to me – he's a lot deeper than we thought...'

Harriet sat up straighter. 'Ooh, that sounds like you have gossip. What's the gossip?' Nancy went to speak but Harriet held up her hand. 'Wait, do we need cocktails for this? Stupid question, we always need cocktails for this. Let me go grab some and you can tell me all about Mr Mysterious.' She jumped up before Nancy could decline the offer and practically ran over to the bar.

'Right here we go, one Tom Collins for you.' She sat back down on the lounger and sipped her drink; it was good! 'So, spill.'

Nancy sipped hers and shook her head. 'I don't want to talk about him and his private business. He's just a deep soul.'

Harriet made a *pfft* sort of noise which caused Nancy to flick her head up and ask what the sound was. 'Nance, you can't tell me he's all deep and then not tell me why. That's just teasing. I'm your best mate, come on, if you can't tell me who can you tell?'

'I get that, I just feel bad. I don't know if I should be telling people his stuff. I wouldn't want him going round talking about what I've said.'

'What did you say?' Harriet questioned.

'No, nothing. I just mean, conversations like that are private aren't they?' She drank more of her drink.

'Yeah I get that, but I'm hardly going to shout it from the rooftops am I? I just want to know a little about the man that you like.' She held her hand up as Nancy began to protest that she didn't like him like that. 'I know I know, you're just having a bit of fun, you don't actually like him like that and blahdy blahdy blah...'

'I just feel bad, like I'm gossiping.'

'Well technically you are – just with me. Come on, I won't say anything. What's that saying ... *hoes before bros?*'

Nancy burst out laughing, spraying some of her Tom Collins over Tommy who was sat in front of her playing with a sunglasses case. He turned round at the sudden moisture shower and Harriet couldn't help but fall about laughing at his little reaction.

'Oh my God, Tommy I'm so sorry!' Nancy picked him up and gave him a cuddle as Harriet rolled back on her lounger, laughing so hard her stomach hurt.

'Hari, I'm so sorry – you watch he'll be rolling around later, half pissed on cocktails.'

'Then I'll be saying "that's my boy."' She sat up and composed herself. 'Right, anyway, you were about to tell me about Cameron. Why is he so mysterious?'

Nancy hesitated but then said, 'OK but you don't tell a soul and you don't tell him that you know.'

'Cross my heart and hope to die.' She crossed over her bikini.

'Aiden is adopted and Cameron's ex left because she didn't want to be a family anymore and he has been single-handedly raising him ever since.' Harriet gasped. 'Wait, I'm not even finished. Last night, he didn't turn up to the dinner date because he found out that his ex is now pregnant with one of his work colleagues.'

'It's like a TV drama!' Harriet's mouth dropped open. 'My God, that is juicy gossip!'

'No! It's not gossip, I'm not gossiping. We are just talking.' She pulled a face. 'Don't make me sound like a gossiping bitch.'

Harriet laughed at her friend's panic; she was so lovely and always trying so hard to please everyone. The fact that this had got her so worked up was kind of sweet. 'Oh relax its fine. Wow, bless him.'

'I know. He's not got it easy.'

'Well good on him for doing it. I tell you what, a doctor, a father who adopted a kid and then raised him on his own and those looks ... you wanna watch your back because if you don't want him, I certainly wouldn't say no.' Nancy threw her towel at Harriet who ducked to avoid it. 'Hey, don't be mad because you have healthy competition.'

'I'm not, you are welcome to him if you want him – he's not my property.'

Harriet decided to test this theory. 'OK, great. So you don't mind if I chat to him later and ask if he wants to go for a drink seeing as you have swanned off twice now?'

'No.' Nancy replied in a clipped tone.

'And if I manage to get a kiss out of him, some holiday romance before we leave ... that would be OK with you?' She tried to hide the smile.

'It's fine.'

Harriet nodded and then stayed quiet. She knew Nancy inside out and knew it would only be a matter of time before...

'But maybe I could just see where things are going with us first...'

'I bloody knew it!' Harriet shook her head. 'You aren't fooling me missy, you are well and truly besotted with the handsome doctor.'

'I'm not, I just find him interesting that's all – intellectually stimulating. We have some good, solid conversations and—'

'And you want to jump on him and ravish his sexy body.'

'Oh my God, Hari,' Nancy said as she stood up. 'Have you no shame?' Harriet poked her tongue out, answering her friend's question. 'And have you seen your son?'

Harriet stopped in her tracks and looked to where Tommy was sitting but noticed he had moved forward slightly and was at the water's edge, on his tummy, patting the water and splashing it, smiling away. The pool was graduated so he was able to enjoy the pool with his top half without getting his legs in. 'Oh my God, Nance, he's playing in the water.' Her eyes were wide in wonder. 'What's happening?'

Nancy laughed. 'He's enjoying playing in the water.'

Harriet sat up and grabbed her phone. 'Oh my God, I have to take a picture of this.' She snapped it and then lowered her phone and watched him. He was having the time of his life, giggling away and splashing his hands down creating sprays of water on his face.

Harriet held out her hand and touched Nancy's. 'Nance, he's doing it. He's in the water.' She stood up and grabbed the little water shoes out of her bag that she'd bought for Isla but that she didn't want to wear. They didn't do any in Tommy's size but she had an idea. She sat down next to him and picked him up, placing him on her lap. 'Hey little man, look at you being a big boy and playing with the water.' She smiled at him and he smiled back. Her heart grew. 'Let's try something.'

She was nervous. But equally she felt a sense of confidence; she was his mummy and she should be there to help him overcome his fears. She took the little shoes and put them on his feet, all the while her heart racing with anticipation. His smile faded but he didn't move. She used the ties on the top to tighten them as much as she could and then she used her hairbands from her wrist to tie them on his feet so they stayed on. 'Mummy is here, let's just try this.' She shuffled forward on her bum, keeping her hands wrapped around his waist. She felt him tense as his feet neared the water's edge, but she kept talking to him, telling him it was OK. Her whole body tensed as she watched his little rubber covered feet enter the water. She did it slowly, bit by bit, waiting for the wail. But it never came. He squirmed a little initially but then when he realised that the water wasn't actually on his feet, he relaxed a little and looked at her.

'There we go! You're so clever! We are in the water, Tommy.' She couldn't dilute the excited face she was pulling and in response, Tommy looked back at her and giggled as the water rolled over his shoes.

The swell of pride that overcame her was immense. This is what parenting was all about. These moments right here. She pulled him closer and squeezed him. They were going to be alright, she just knew it.

Chapter 43

'OK bakers; are you ready to make some masterpieces?' Nancy glanced nervously at Jack who was wide eyed at the amount of people inside the lavishly decorated hall. Streamers of rainbow colours adorned the ceiling alongside what seemed to be hundreds of balloons too. The tables had been rearranged from their usual nightly set up to rows of tables where children could work on their creations. It was surprising how many people had turned up because Nancy imagined a lot of children to be in bed or getting ready to go to bed. It was an activity for the older children but obviously, as it was a holiday, there were quite a few younger ones here too. In the corner of the hall there was a soft play set up for any really small children to chill in whilst the activity was taking place, but generally the younger ones had taken to running aimlessly around the room, high on pudding and sugar. The noise was probably a bit much for Jack, if Nancy was honest with herself, but she had managed to get him here which was progress, even if it was only on the guise that he would see Aiden here and he could then show him his iPad.

'Where's Aiden?' he asked, tugging at her teal green tea

dress which had pink flamingos and foliage on. It was Harriet's dress – a little too *out there* for Nancy – but she had borrowed it to try and look dressier knowing she would see Cameron here tonight.

She glanced around the room, trying to spot either Aiden or Cameron. 'I'm not sure yet, let's go and grab a table over there and that way we will be able to see the doorway when they arrive. How does that sound?' Jack shrugged and followed her silently, looking around. She could see by his expression that he was simply scanning the room, taking it all in, a mental photograph to refer back to at a later date.

They set up at one of the tables which wasn't too close to where all the action was. Nancy wasn't sure that Jack was even going to join in but she figured she had more hope of him doing so if he wasn't right next to all the commotion and drama. Harriet sidled up next to her wearing the most gorgeous black mini dress, which had a bold floral print and long, winged sleeves. The neckline gave a choker effect and she looked absolutely stunning – as per usual. 'I don't know if Isla is going to want to do it. She's having a strop.'

'About what?' Nancy glanced over to Isla who was standing about a metre away from Harriet, a serious pout going on and her arms crossed in defiance. She looked exactly like a mini Harriet. Not that Nancy would say that to her face.

'I told her she had to make the masterpieces first and that she might not be able to eat it afterwards.' Harriet pulled out her compact mirror and touched up her vibrant red lipstick which set off the effect of the dress.

'Oh dear, didn't go down too well then?' Nancy eyed the

red lipstick, wondering if she could ever pull something so daring off.

'What do you think? The poor girl only wants to eat cake and Mummy said no. I think I would cry too, to be fair.' She turned to face her. 'Are you going to join in?' Isla shook her head and stamped her feet. 'There's your answer,' she said back to Nancy.

'What about Tommy?' Nancy looked at him standing up at the table having pulled himself up to grab at the tools laid out for the bakers. 'He looks keen to try it.'

'Yeah, count me and Tommy in, Isla might join in once she sees the others do it, hey?'

'I want some cake!' she said, stamping her foot yet again.

'Well, I want a million pounds darling but I'm afraid we don't always get what we want in life.'

Nancy laughed. 'That is *such* a mum thing to say.' She glanced over Harriet's shoulder and spotted Cameron walking in with Aiden on his shoulders. The two of them were laughing and Nancy found herself smiling as she watched them. Aiden was high on Cameron's shoulders, and his little face lit up as he giggled away at Cameron bouncing him as they walked. His laugh could be heard right across the hall even with the noise level so high and as they reached about halfway, Cameron spotted Nancy and his own face lit up. He walked over – half walking, half bouncing, cue more giggles – and as he reached them jolted Aiden forward and caught him in his arms amidst proper belly laughs.

Nancy's heart jumped as she watched Aiden's little body fly over Cameron's head and land in his arms. Something they clearly did many times but was terrifying to watch. She had her hand on her chest as she said, 'My God, that scared the life out of me!'

'Ah he's alright; he's only ever fallen off twice.' Nancy's eyes opened wide at this revelation. 'I'm kidding,' he laughed. 'It was three times.' Nancy playfully hit him as he laughed it off. 'So you decided to join us today, that's great.' He peered round Nancy at Jack who was standing holding his iPad and staring wide-eyed at Aiden.

'Jack has something he wanted to show Aiden so he insisted we came.' She held out her arm to try and encourage Jack forward.

'What did you wanna show me, Jack?' Aiden bounced forward and Jack noticeably flinched at the sudden movement towards him.

'Remember buddy, nice and calm.' Cameron winked at Aiden and he immediately slowed down his approach.

Nancy looked at Cameron and whispered, 'He is so good.'

'He tries his best,' he replied.

Jack stood for a moment in silence, repeatedly looking from Nancy to Aiden and back. Nancy nodded and tried to silently encourage him and after a moment he said. 'I've got a tablet too. This is my iPad.'

'That's awesome Jack, it's like mine. What games do you have on it?' Aiden moved to be beside Jack but Jack took a step to the side as he replied, moving to keep that little bit of distance between them. He relayed the games he had on there and then started talking about the programmes he liked to watch.

'Isla, no!'

Nancy spun round at Harriet's raised voice and saw Isla standing with a mouthful of cake and biscuits, a look of horror that she hadn't been quick enough to swallow before her mum noticed.

Harriet grabbed her hand and stormed past Nancy. 'I'm taking her to the toilet to clean up, can you watch Tommy?' and she left before Nancy had time to answer.

Tommy tried to follow Harriet so Nancy swiped him up into her arms. 'Hey little man, where do you think you're going?' He wriggled in her arms and tried to get free. 'I'm sorry Mister; you're not following out of here. Stay with me for a minute.' More squirming and now screaming. Full blown tantrum scream. Nancy flinched as the high-pitched noise rang through, right into her ear and she recoiled her head.

'Hey, listen little man, Mummy will be back soon,' Cameron cooed but Nancy shook her head.

'No he's not crying for that, he wants to get down so he can crawl out of the hall door now that it is open.' She nodded to the door that was still wide open from when Harriet stormed through it, Isla in tow.

'WAHHHHHHH!' Tommy continued his tantrum which seemed to have risen up a few decibels again.

Suddenly Jack was at Nancy's side tugging at her dress. 'Too noisy!' he said, grimacing at Tommy's wails.

'I know sweetheart, I'm sorry. Tommy's just a bit upset.'

'I don't like it,' he responded.

Cameron tried to step forward towards Jack but he just recoiled, putting his hands on his ears.

'Shall we go over there boys, where it's not so noisy for you Jack?' Jack shook his head, clearly distressed.

'Do you want me to take Tommy while you sort Jack?'

Nancy tried to hand over Tommy but he just screamed louder, bucking his body and trying to free himself. By this time there were numerous stares from other people in the hall. Some supportive and clearly feeling sorry for Nancy and others with a look of disproval and judgement. Nancy refrained from shouting *oh I'm sorry, has your child never had a tantrum before* and instead opted to try and soothe Tommy again. 'It's fine,' she called over his cries. 'But I tell you what you could do.' Cameron nodded. 'In my bag over there under the table are Jack's headphones, do you want to see if he will let you give them to him?'

Cameron immediately responded and strode over to the bag whilst Nancy continued to try and calm Tommy who was now in full pelt strop, his face a bright crimson colour and hiccupping as he tried to breathe through the screaming. 'Shh, come on Tommy. Just a few more minutes and you can get down. What's this? Do you want to try my sunglasses on?'

He pushed them away.

'How about my necklace, look, you always like playing with my necklace.'

Another squirm and accelerated scream.

She looked up as she heard Jack's shout. A distressed cry as Cameron tried to hand him the headphones. Oh God, she thought, she could see the escalation signs with him. He was getting anxious because of this noise and he was so worked up now that he wasn't able to see anything but the angst.

Cameron looked up to her waiting for guidance as to what to do. 'Here,' she said to him, handing him Tommy. 'He is going to be the easier one of the two.'

Cameron looked at the sweaty, beetroot mess that Tommy was and replied, 'Really?' as he took him.

'Trust me,' she replied, feeling her own anxiety level rise up. She really didn't want Jack to have a full-blown meltdown in here. Not in front of all these people. She felt judged enough as it was, she didn't need that negativity too. Cameron stood with Tommy who was now screaming again at full throttle. Nancy could see Jack starting to rock in the seated position he had put himself on the floor. His face screwed up in turmoil, tears starting to fall down his cheek. She held out his headphones and touched his arm. 'Jack, here, put these on.' His arms flung out and knocked them away. She looked as they slid across the floor.

Deep breath. She retrieved them and tried again. 'Jack, sweetheart, put them on. They will help. It will make it quieter for you.' More rocking and now he was screwed up into a ball. She glanced at Aiden who was standing, wide eyed, next to her. 'It's OK sweetheart,' she said. Bless him, he looked so scared but he put on a brave face.

'I'm OK. Will he be OK?'

'Yes, he will be fine. He's just a bit upset.' Aiden nodded and tried to smile.

Nancy had no idea why Tommy was screaming still – it felt like she had been listening to it for about an hour now. His wails weren't letting up, they only seemed to get stronger and stronger. And then after a minute, there was silence. Nancy felt a glimmer of hope as she heard the cries stop. She took a breath and reached out her hand on Jack's arm when the scream came back tenfold and right next to her ear. Turned out he was only stopping to take a breath so he could continue, the coughing and spluttering causing him to gag. Jack reacted badly to this sudden quietness and then peak of sound again and cried out himself.

Nancy whipped her head round to Cameron and snapped. 'Can you just take him over there please? I can't have him doing that this close to Jack!'

Cameron looked shocked at her sudden outburst at him and retreated further away. Nancy felt bad – she wasn't coping very well with this situation at all. What had happened to all her coping techniques and where the hell was Harriet!

'Come on sweetheart, please, just take your headphones.' He pushed his arm out and knocked the headphones away again. 'Jack, come on! You're not helping yourself.' She sat back on her heels and exhaled. She just didn't know what to do anymore. She had thought he'd made so much progress whilst they were away and yet here they were, back at square one. And all of this in front of Cameron, too. She felt ashamed with herself that she was bothered by that fact.

Chapter 44

'How are you feeling now?' Cameron asked, handing Nancy a drink. She looked up from her seat, smiling weakly at him. She didn't answer his question; she didn't know what to say. 'Don't beat yourself up over it; honestly, he's absolutely fine now, isn't he?'

She looked over to Jack. He was sat on a chair next to Aiden who was busy doing something with the cakes and biscuits on the table. Jack had his back to her so she couldn't see his face, but she could tell he was on his iPad. As usual, always on that damn iPad. Frustration from the whole situation seeped into her mood.

'I know it's easy for me to say and I know no amount of words will change how you feel but please don't beat yourself up – you're doing a great job with Jack. I have only known you a few days but already I can tell this.'

'You're just trying to get in my good books with your compliments again.'

'You mean because you yelled at me.' She looked at him and he smirked, drinking his drink and looking at her over the top of the glass, eyes creased in a smile.

She felt embarrassed as she recalled the moment. 'I'm sorry for shouting at you.'

He held up his hand. 'It's fine – you were stressed.'

'No it's not fine; I shouldn't have taken it out on you. I just...' She hesitated. 'I just feel like I don't know what I'm doing.'

'But you do.'

She shook her head. 'No, I really don't. I start to feel like I am getting a grip on this bloody condition and then he has a moment like that and I feel helpless. I can't do anything and most of the time I seem to make it worse and that absolutely kills me.' She exhaled. 'I really felt I'd made progress over this holiday. He spoke to Aiden, he was doing things socially that he had never done before and especially after our first day when he kicked off at the kids' club – I thought we had cracked it.' She sipped her drink. 'And then this happens and I feel like I'm back to square one.'

'That's not fair, he has made progress. You're focusing on the negatives because of what just happened. You're stressed and so it all looks bleak to you but trust me, he's doing great.'

'Is he? I don't feel like he is.'

'Look at him now – what's he doing?'

She felt the disappointment settle in her stomach. 'He's playing on his iPad – again!' As much as she realised that was his thing – that he found comfort in the things he could do on there and it was his type of escapism – she so desperately wished that he would put more time into interacting socially.

'Yes, he's on his iPad but he's sitting next to Aiden and they are talking – look.'

She glanced over to him again and Cameron was right, he was talking to Aiden. He wasn't looking at him, but he was clearly talking. 'Well, we assume he's talking to Aiden, he could just be talking himself through whatever game he is playing at the moment – neither of them are actually looking at each other, Cameron.'

'That's true, but come on, it's definitely progress, and you can't deny that hey?' She shrugged. 'What are you afraid of?'

She didn't look at him, her gaze fixed on the back of Jack's head. 'That I will fail him as a parent. That I won't be able to make anything better for him and he will suffer when he gets to adulthood because I won't have prepared him adequately for the real world when he doesn't have me behind him every step of the way.'

'That's quite a list.' This time she did look at him and he was smiling at her. 'You are doing the best job that you can.'

'But it's not enough, Cameron. Today just proves that. It's not enough to just try and see what happens. He is struggling and I don't know what to do to help him.'

'Have you got help or support back home? The school? Consultants? Friends?'

She shrugged. 'I have Harriet. The school aren't being very supportive so I think I'm going to have to look into either changing him – which will be horrendous for him to experience – or discussing options with them on a more serious level.'

'Then do that. Arrange the meeting and lay it on the line for them. You are entitled to help.'

'I know but it's not as straightforward as that, there are so many boundaries and challenges and rules when it comes to education and additional needs. I feel lost when I try and decipher it all. All the words sound like a foreign language to me. And I feel like I should know it all and that I'm letting him down by not equipping myself better but it's just so hard to do it alone.' Anger at Pete leaving reared its ugly head again. She was forced to think about what would happen when they got home. Would Pete decide to turn up again? She really hoped not. Up until this holiday she had been desperate for Pete to show up and own up to his responsibilities. Why should she have to deal with it all alone when Jack was his son too? But now her anger had converted to determination to succeed in spite of him walking away. If he showed up now, when they got home, she wasn't 100 per cent sure she would even answer the door to him.

Cameron nodded. 'I don't doubt for a second that it is hard. Being a single parent is no picnic.'

Nancy felt a twinge of guilt. 'I'm sorry, here I am ranting about it all and you've got your own issues to be dealing with. I shouldn't be unloading all of this on you too.' She tried to swallow down the torment that was twisting inside her stomach at the prospect of going home tomorrow and still not being any further along with knowing what to do for Jack.

'Oh, be quiet! I would rather you talk about this than bottle it up and while I can't help with things on the autistic side of things, I can be here as a friend to support you when you're feeling low.'

'You don't have to do that, its fine.'

'Nancy, stop pushing help away.' His voice was firm but friendly.

'I'm not. I'm just saying I don't want to ruin your holiday by being a moaning myrtle.'

'You could never pull off being a myrtle – you're too pretty.' She blushed at his compliment and laughed a little. 'There we go, that's better. It's nice to see that smile back again. I was worried it had disappeared for good.'

She looked over to the table where Jack and Aiden were. 'So what exactly are they doing?'

Cameron shifted in his chair and used his hand to gesture over to the board on the far side. 'Well over on that board is a picture of some structures; a house, a skyscraper, a bridge and a statue. And the children have to use the ingredients they have in front of them to either recreate one of them or design a new one.'

She craned her neck to try and see what was on the tables. 'It looks like they have cake cut offs, biscuits, icing to use as glue, various sweets and chocolates to decorate ... I don't even know what those long things are but I'm guessing they're edible.'

'Maybe you can try one first,' she said and he poked his tongue out at her. She sat up straight and looked over at Aiden's creation and gasped. 'Oh my God have you seen what Aiden's doing? His structure is amazing!'

Cameron peered over, 'so it is. They're doing well – what a team.'

Nancy looked at Jack with his head still in the iPad. 'Well, I think Jack might just be there as moral support but as you say, at least he is sitting next to Aiden and the two of them have exchanged words so what more could I ask for, hey?' She smiled to try and make her comment more relaxed, but she was hiding her disappointment. She so desperately wanted Jack to enjoy tasks like this and to engage with something where he had to work as a team, and she really thought this would be right up his street because it was building, creating structures. It couldn't have been more suited to his interests. But teamwork and social skills were not his thing and maybe that was why he had pulled back. She just had to accept that.

After what felt like hours but was, as they were told by the event leader, just twenty minutes, the children were asked to step away from their sculptures so that the judges could go round and inspect them. It was a brutal process. The guy judging it was a tall man in a suit with a stern face. He looked to be better placed in a Michelin star restaurant giving the chef a mouthful for not providing food worthy enough for the Queen – not judging a children's baking competition at a holiday resort.

As he approached Aiden's table, Nancy noticed that Jack had lowered his iPad and was listening to what the man was saying. 'Aw that's sweet,' she said, leaning over to Cameron. 'Jack's interested in how Aiden is doing – look how intently he's listening to that guy.' She felt a bolt of happiness hit her as she saw his engagement with something his friend had done. Maybe Cameron was right, maybe he had made progress, she was just too close to see it.

Aiden stepped to the side and Nancy and Cameron were able to see the true grandeur of his creation. They stood up and went over to have a closer look as the judge moved on to the next table.

'Wow Aiden, this is awesome.' Nancy took in the structure. She could see immediately what he had chosen to do – it was a bridge. And not just any bridge, it was the Queen Elizabeth bridge. He had all of the different elements covered, each section looking like a scaled down version of the real thing. He had put all the pillars in and some railings and even the wires. 'Matchmakers – that's what those stick things are,' she said, laughing and pointing them out to Cameron. 'Can you believe he did this? And look, the attention to detail is incredible, those dots for the nuts and bolts and that little gate there which I'm assuming is some sort of emergency exit gate thing.'

'Actually, it's there for the workers so they can access it.' Nancy and Cameron both looked over to Jack, surprised at his sudden input.

'Jack is the ideas man.' Their attention went back to Aiden. 'He created the design and I made it – we worked together.'

'Hey that's great – good work boys.' Cameron looked at Nancy. 'Isn't that great?' he prompted, obviously noticing her confused expression.

'Show them, Jack,' Aiden said excitedly.

Jack stood up and gave his iPad to Nancy, swiping the screen to light it up.

Nancy felt a sudden rush of emotion as the screen displayed what could only be described as a to-scale in-depth drawing of the QE2 Bridge. Jack had used an app on there to design it to scale, adding diagrams, labels and various different points of review to work out how they would do it with the materials they had.

'Oh my God,' she breathed, unable to contain the tears that sprung to her eyes. 'Jack'

'Mummy, do you like it?' His little face looking up at her waiting for a reaction. 'Are you sad?'

'No baby, I'm not sad.' She sniffed.

'Mummy is very happy, sometimes people cry when they are happy,' Cameron said, putting his arm around her shoulder and squeezing it gently.

'Jack, show me that other part you did, I want to check that I did it right.' Jack walked over to the table and handed Aiden his iPad.

'Here.' Cameron gave her a tissue. 'You OK?'

'He helped,' she squeaked.

'He more than helped, Nancy, he was the mastermind behind the design. You have a very talented son there.' Cameron's smile was as big as Nancy's.

'I thought he was playing on his iPad because he wasn't interested.' She breathed, unable to believe what had just happened.

'He was working as a team – design and construction. They work well together, don't they?' Nancy nodded and wiped her face with the tissue. Maybe he was making more progress than she gave him credit for. Maybe she needed to accept that he was allowed to have setbacks because he was still moving forward in between them.

Chapter 45

'I can't believe it's time to go home. How fast did that holiday go?' Harriet sat back into her seat on the plane and fastened her seatbelt. She was grateful that Tommy was asleep and would hopefully sleep for the whole plane journey as he had been up most of the night teething and she didn't fancy another tantrum in the confines of the plane cabin. She also didn't think Nancy would appreciate it – she was still recovering from dealing with Tommy's last tantrum. When Harriet had returned yesterday to Tommy's full-blown scream-a-thon, she was shocked to discover that simply taking him into her arms was enough to soothe him. As the holiday had gone on, Harriet had relaxed more. And the more she'd relaxed, the better her time with Tommy had been. Jayne had been right, it seemed he had been feeding off the negativity from her because ever since she had been more smiley and calm with him, the more he'd wanted to be with her. So much so, that yesterday he had wound himself up so much when all he wanted was a mummy cuddle. And Harriet was only too pleased to provide that for him.

'I know, I feel quite sad to go home actually.' Nancy tapped

Jack on the arm and gave him a thumbs up – he returned the signal.

'Me too, although I am excited about some of the changes I'll be putting into place once I get back. Bethany texted me last night and said she would come over and have a cuppa and talk all things nanny-related.' Harriet smiled excitedly. She had told Nancy all about her conversation with Bethany as they'd sat on the balcony for their last night.

'Do you know what, I'm so proud of you. I feel like I am going home with a totally different person.'

'I don't know if I think that's a good thing or a bad thing?' She eyed up her friend who laughed. 'I'm still the same person, I guess I can just see my options a bit clearer, that's all.' That was a lie; she did feel like a different person. And she was positive it was only going to get better once she got home. 'And with Bethany on my side, Mum might actually be a lot more tolerable.' Nancy raised an eyebrow. 'Or maybe I'll just keep avoiding her like the plague,' Harriet added and swiped her phone. 'Twenty-seven emails already and I've only just switched it on – they must know I'm coming home.' As much as she moaned, she did like to feel important to the company and there was no risk of them forgetting about her. 'So, I'm surprised you didn't try to swap seats and sit next to Cameron on the flight home.'

'Oh, be quiet. I'm a grown woman, not some schoolgirl with a crush. I can bear to be away from his company for more than five seconds.'

'Yes, but you don't *want* to be, do you?' She loved teasing Nancy about it because it was so easy. She was clearly besotted with the very lovely Cameron. 'I hope you're not going to get home and be texting Pete.'

'No chance,' Nancy replied. 'He is well and truly out of the picture now. I feel like this holiday has cleansed my body of him and I am ready to go home and start fresh.'

'Nance, I cannot tell you how happy that makes me. It was a long time coming but we got there in the end. I'm proud of you.' She squeezed Nancy's hand and smiled.

'Who are you and what have you done with Hari?'

'What?' she said, offended. 'Can't I tell my friend I am proud of her?'

'Of course you can, but I am not sure I can get on board with the new touchy feely Harriet – next you'll be cleansing my aura.'

Harriet nudged Nancy in embarrassment, and told her to shut up. She was saved by her phone pinging again and as she was about to moan about it, Nancy's pinged too. 'Oh, I've been added to a group on WhatsApp.'

Harriet looked at her phone. 'Me too.' She opened up the group called *Mums Just Wanna Have Fun* and laughed. The profile picture was one of Jayne holding a cocktail – by the looks of it, it was a Sex on the Beach – and she had written in the group:

Great to meet you ladies!
I got home safe – let me know when you're free and
we can have a cocktail night and relive our holidays.
Safe trip xxx

'Aw that's nice of her isn't it?' Nancy said, smiling and putting her phone away but Harriet kept staring at the screen. She'd never really had female friends before; they didn't tend to like her bolshie attitude and no-nonsense approach to life. So this felt weird. There were actually women out there who wanted to be her friend and spend time with her on a social level – and not just because she had been forced to tag along on one of Nancy's night outs. Was this what it was like to have girl-friends?

'You OK?'

Harriet glanced up at Nancy. 'Yeah I'm fine. Just, well, it's nice isn't it?'

'What is?'

'When you make friends like that.' Now she felt stupid. She was aware how silly she sounded. 'I just mean that, well, Jayne is nice, and I like her. That's all.' She shrugged off the comment feeling self-conscious.

Nancy put her hand on Harriet's. 'It's OK you know, you are allowed to admit that it's nice to have friends. I won't tell the people at work that you've gone soft.'

'I haven't gone bloody soft and don't you dare go telling people I have.' She put her hand up to the air hostess who was walking past. 'Excuse me, can I get I drink please?'

'We are just going to get off the ground and then I will be round to take orders, ma'am.'

The hostess walked off and Harriet huffed. 'All I wanted was a Tom Collins.'

Nancy laughed. 'I don't think they do cocktails on here.'

'Are you having a laugh? This is my last bit of relaxation

bliss before everything gets hectic again. Are you telling me I have to land on home ground having had no gin?' Harriet shuffled in her seat and opened the magazine she'd bought at the airport. 'Well, I guess I'll just have to make my own then, wont I!'

***

Landing in England, Nancy was tired and in desperate need of a shower. She weaved through the crowds trying to locate the baggage area with Jack holding tightly onto her jumper. It was noisy, frantic and nobody seemed to have any manners whatsoever today as she was shoved from pillar to post trying to get from A to B.

'Nance, wait up!' Harriet called, pushing through the crowds using Tommy's stroller as a barge to make people move. Random shouts of *hey* and *watch it* were thrown at her as she carelessly kept walking, keeping her gaze forward.

'You just don't give a monkey's, do you?' Nancy laughed.

Harriet shrugged. 'Well if they're not going to move, I'll just have to move them instead!' Isla wailed that she was hungry, tired and bored which was not the best combination for any parent to hear from their child in the middle of an airport.

'Nancy!' She turned around at the sound of her name and saw Cameron and Aiden running towards them. 'How did you find the flight?' He smiled and his big blue eyes lit up. He had chosen to travel in a cream-coloured hoody teamed with denim jeans and trainers. It seemed strange seeing him all covered up seeing as she had spent the last week gawping at his body.

'Yeah it was OK actually. I'm shattered now though. I need a shower and some food and I'll be right as rain.' She glanced at Aiden who looked just as tired and grumpy as Isla. 'How about you two?'

'Well this little guy is knackered, bless him, so I reckon he will pass out on the journey home from here.'

'Is it a long journey?'

'About two hours, providing we don't hit any traffic – which is highly unlikely because we want to get home and whenever anyone wants to get home, every car in the universe decides to come out to play car parks on the motorway.'

Nancy laughed, not taking her eyes away from his face. Although he was smiling, he looked tired. Whilst he had opened up to her on their holiday, she couldn't help but worry if he was going to be OK once he got home. She thought of her own situation. Everyone seemed to be going home with huge lifestyle changes to get used to. She felt sad that she wouldn't get to see Cameron's story and how it played out.

Cameron pulled a package out from his holdall. 'Well, I just wanted to give Jack this present – it's from the both of us.'

Nancy looked at the squared gift wrapped in orange wrapping paper and smiled. 'Nice wrapping.'

He winked at her. 'But there is one rule – you can't open it until you get into your cab.' He looked at Jack. 'Deal?'

Jack nodded, already eyeing up the shiny wrapped parcel.

'Sounds very ominous – why's that then?'

'No reason, just thought it would be something nice for Jack to do on the journey home and then you can rest.'

She smiled at him and said, 'Well, that's very kind of you.' She turned to Jack. 'What do you say to Cameron and Aiden?'

'Thanks.' He took the gift and shoved it into his backpack, zipping it up tight and then placing on his back again.

'You've chosen the right person to keep his word – he won't touch that now until we are in the cab.'

'Well that's why I gave it to you and not Mummy, hey?' The comment made Nancy laugh, mostly because it was true.

'Daddy I'm hungry – I wanna go home.' Aiden sounded exhausted. Nancy was going to miss this little guy too.

'Listen, I'd better get this one back. It was really lovely meeting you guys.' He glanced over to Harriet who was perched on a bench with Isla now lying across her lap asleep. 'And you Harriet!' He saluted and she waved back.

'You too Cameron and...' Nancy hesitated for fear of sounding like a total loser but then added, 'Thank you for making me see that things were, you know, OK.'

He stepped forward and gave her a kiss on the cheek, brushing his soft lips against her skin and lingering a little longer than he really needed to, his aftershave sending her stomach into knots. He whispered in her ear. 'You're doing a great job – don't let anyone tell you otherwise.' His hot breath on her neck made her tingle from head to toe and as he drew away, the two of them shared a moment. It was only fleeting and Nancy wasn't even sure it counted as a moment, but just for a second she felt this immense energy between them and it made her feel like they were the only two people within the hustle and bustle of this airport.

'Oh sorry love!' Nancy was barged backwards as a fellow passenger walked into her shoulder, causing their moment to be well and truly over before it had even got started.

'Bye Nancy.' And he walked off, his arm around Aiden, without so much as a glance back.

***

In the taxi, Nancy shuffled Jack inside before placing their cases and bags in the boot and sliding in herself.

Harriet, Isla and Tommy sat in the row in front of them so Nancy and Jack had been banished to the boot seats in the seven-seater. But she didn't mind. It was nice being back here with just her and Jack.

'I had a good time,' Jack said.

Nancy turned away from the window to face her son. 'Did you?' she asked.

'Yeah.' He shuffled forward and slipped his arms around Nancy, hugging her close and squeezing so tightly. It was contact. Touching contact. And Jack had instigated it. He sure did keep her on her toes, that was for sure. Never one to be consistent. He pulled back and looked at her face. 'Love you, Mummy.'

Nancy smiled. They'd had such a trying year, but this moment was worth it. She felt closer to Jack than she had ever felt. Through all the meltdowns, shouting, rejection and silence, she was never quite sure if Jack had a connection with her. He was always in his own little world and it felt like he'd never let her in. This might have been a one-off moment, and going back to their house might change the dynamics again, but for now, right here, she had that closeness and it felt incredible. 'Love you too, Jack.'

'Can I open this now?' he said, pulling out the orange package and looking at her for approval.

Because of the hassle they'd had at baggage collection and then getting their taxi, Nancy had completely forgotten about the gift. 'Of course sweetheart, well done for waiting like you were asked.'

She watched as he unwrapped the present carefully and meticulously, flap by flap and then opening it up together to reveal a book.

But it wasn't just any old book; it was a book on the rebuilding of the hotel they'd stayed in after it had suffered a fire five years ago. The fire had done so much damage they'd had a complete refurb of the whole resort and this book outlined all the works done, the rebuilding, the infrastructure and tons of before, during and after construction pictures. Jack gasped and said 'wow' as he turned the pages, looking at the structural frames of the hotel he had just spent a week in. Cameron knew what he was doing when he picked this gift. It wasn't just thoughtful, it was special.

'Mummy, I like Cameron – he is cool.' Nancy smiled and nodded. She had to agree with her son. 'What's this?' he asked, holding up an envelope. 'It was in my book.'

She turned it over and saw her name scrawled on the front.

'Oh, this must be for me.'

He shrugged and then resumed looking through his new book, eyes wide in wonderment.

She slid her finger inside the flap and tore it open, pulling out a small white card with a few handwritten words and instantly she knew what she had to do...

Stop thinking about what could go wrong,
and think about what could go right.
X

Epilogue

Twelve months later...

'Jack, come on, are you nearly ready?'

Nancy tidied away her desk of all the orders she had to send out this weekend. Packages and packages lined the window sill in the dining room which had now become the storage space for all her products. The dining table had gone and in its place were two rows of floor to ceiling Ikea storage cubes and a storage chest to hold her delivery supplies. A large poster announcing, Deluxe Designs adorned the wall above a little desk that was set up in the corner by the sofa and reminded Nancy everyday of just how far she had come.

Setting up her own business was never going to be easy, but with Harriet by her side and the support of those around her, she had done it. Now she got to draw and design every day and Jack had even featured on some of the designs that she sold. She was thinking about starting a new range just by him – it could help build his university fund as he said he wanted to go to university to study design. Whether that happened or not, time would tell. But if not, the money from his designs could be for whatever he needed, and it would be something that he himself would have earned

When she started, she designed posters with quotes and simple sketches foiled onto card and framed, but had since developed onto more bespoke pictures and one-off designs for people's houses. It was still a small business but with the wonders of Instagram, she had gone from 78 followers to 18.5k followers in just twelve months and still had, she now realised, huge potential to grow. Her most recent design was a Kindness range which seemed to have taken off on a whole new level, hence the piles of orders stacking up.

'Jack!'

She shuffled some papers and placed them in the to-do pile – she wasn't sure she would have enough time later on to get these orders complete so she would have to allocate some time tomorrow to finish them off so that they were sent out before the weekend. She picked up the empty coffee cups (yes, plural) from her desk and swiped the water bottle up from the coffee table on her way to the kitchen, pulling open the living room door with her foot as she did. As soon as the door opened, Max sauntered in, squeezing past Nancy's foot. With his yellow fur, orange collar and irresistible face, the golden Labrador was the new addition to their family.

'Hey!' she said, walking through to the kitchen as she had her hands full. 'You know you're not allowed in there, Mister!' She placed down the cups and bottle on the side and returned to the living room and just as she expected, Max had already taken up residence underneath her desk. She walked over to him and crouched down, moving her chair out of the way.

His big brown eyes stared back at her, innocently gazing. 'Don't you try and win me over with your puppy dog eyes; you know you aren't allowed in this room when I'm not in here. Too many things for you to chew or swallow.' As she stroked her hand over Max's golden coat, he turned and exposed his belly. 'OK, just one tummy rub, then out.' He definitely knew Nancy's soft spot. She heard footsteps on the stairs and instantly Max's ears were up. 'Who's that?' she teased, taking pleasure in watching him jump up and run to the doorway, greeting Jack as he entered the room.

'Maxy! Here boy.' Jack crouched down and showed Max a treat. Max immediately sat down, not taking his eyes off his master. 'Ready, waiting...' Max waited. 'Paw?' He lifted his left, and then his right paw to touch Jack's hand. 'Good boy. Now leave it...' Jack placed the treat on Max's nose and he stayed frozen to the spot. Not so much as a twitch.

Nancy watched this routine, pride swelling in her heart. Jack had taught Max these tricks pretty much as soon as he'd arrived. It made their bond grow even deeper.

Nancy had done some research after their holiday last year, looking for ways to help Jack with his everyday life. School was out of her hands, but at home she wanted to make sure she was doing all she could to help. She'd stumbled across a website about animal therapy and had found it fascinating. After weeks of research and a visit to a local provider, she found herself volunteering at the centre to learn more. One thing led to another and she was now the proud owner of Max and she regularly took him to other homes and establishments to talk about the benefits of having a therapy dog. She couldn't imagine life without him.

'Good boy, here you go.' Jack gave him the treat. 'Mummy, he's so clever.'

'I know he is, such a special boy.' She stroked Max's head. 'Right, you need to get all your bits ready and make sure anything you want to take to the park, you have with you.' Jack nodded and ran off back upstairs.

Twenty minutes later, Nancy had pulled up outside Harriet's place and beeped the horn.

'Alright, keep your knickers on, I was coming.' Harriet piled into the car after strapping in Tommy and Isla.

'Well, we are going to be late if we don't get a move on.'

'Oh no, we mustn't be late for lover boy,' Harriet teased. 'OK I'm strapped in, let's go.

***

Walking across the field that adjoined the playground, Nancy spotted Cameron first. He didn't see them and was running around playing with Aiden and his niece and nephew. Nancy turned to Jack. 'Did you read your booklets?' He nodded.

'Booklets?' Harriet questioned.

'Yeah, you know the booklet Aiden made last year when we were on holiday, to help Jack get to know him?' Harriet nodded. 'Well, when we arranged to meet up with Cameron and his sister, we didn't know how Jack would react to spending the day around his niece and nephew, so they did another booklet with everyone on Cameron's side of the family.'

'Look at you getting your feet well and truly under the table.'

Nancy whacked her friend on the arm. 'It makes things easier for Jack to have the heads up.'

Harriet smiled. 'I'm really glad you two decided to make things official – I couldn't bear the constant flirting and the *we're just good friends* line you both kept trying to spill to everyone for ages.'

'We *were* just good friends.'

'Hmmm, maybe friends with benefits!'

Nancy tried to hide the smile creeping up on her face. At that moment Cameron turned and spotted them. He raised a hand to wave and when Aiden saw them he came running over, calling Jack's name over and over. He finally reached them and said:

'Jack! I got this new game, you gotta see it. It's awesome. It's a building one – you'll love it! Come on!' He ran off back to Cameron before Jack had a chance to respond.

Jack turned and looked to Nancy. 'It's OK, Jack, go on. You can go. Here, take Max.'

He looked apprehensive but slowly took the lead and walked over to where Aiden was sitting. Cameron reached them and immediately made a beeline for Nancy, pulling her to him and pressing his lips to hers. Nancy heard Harriet groan and walk off towards Cameron's sister, leaving the two of them where they were.

Nancy let the kiss take hold. His lips were so soft as they parted hers, making way for his tongue to playfully slip in and tease hers. He wrapped both arms around her waist and she reciprocated by wrapping hers around his neck, pulling him closer and deepening their kiss. Every inch of her body ached for him when he did this to her. They were still in the early stages of taking their friendship to this next level and so every time she saw him, her whole body screamed for him to take her into his arms and have his wicked way with her.

She pulled away, ending the embrace as he groaned inwardly at her stopping his fun. 'And hello to you too,' she joked.

'Sorry, just can't resist it. I spent far too long trying to hold myself back from you.'

They walked over, hand in hand, to see the others. Harriet had taken up her position on the fold-up camp chair next to the cool box which housed a bottle of wine and she had Tommy on her lap, snuggled in for a cuddle as he had not long woken up. Cameron's sister, Becca, was still running around with her children, trying to kick a ball and carry a baby at the same time.

'So, you managed to peel off each other long enough to breathe, I see,' Harriet remarked.

'You're just jealous, Hari,' Cameron joked.

'Oh, woe is me, I have no man in my life.' She rolled her eyes. 'Please, I don't need a man. I have my beautiful children, my successful job and my Rabbit – what else does a girl need?'

Nancy gasped. 'Hari!'

'What? The kids don't know what a Rabbit is – I could mean a bunny for all they know.'

Nancy shook her head and plonked herself down on the picnic blanket.

'Coo-ee!'

Nancy spun round to see Jayne's bright smile. 'Hey! You made it!' She briefly smiled at Jayne's children as they ran off into the playground.

'Well of course, we didn't agree to monthly get-togethers for no reason.' She sat herself down after giving everyone a hug. 'Have I missed one yet?'

'No, but you literally came home from holiday two days ago – we weren't expecting you to make it.'

'These meet ups are the highlight of my month, I wouldn't miss them for the world.'

Ever since coming back from Ibiza, the girls had made a promise to make sure they made time to see each other, to talk and enjoy having friends around them. And it had been great. Nancy, for one, knew she wouldn't have got to where she was now without having her friends around her.

Becca puffed as she approached the picnic blanket. 'Seriously, these children are determined to kill me. I haven't run that much since I was in the athletics team.'

'Sit down and chill woman.' Nancy held her arm out and the girls hugged and kissed their hellos.

'Oh, who is this gorgeous guy?' Becca squealed as Max ran over to her and began sniffing at her face.

'Oh, you're too kind. I'm Cameron.' He held out his hand and Nancy playfully whacked him in the stomach. 'Ouch!' he laughed.

'You're about as cheesy as they come!' Nancy rolled her eyes. She turned her attention back to Becca. 'This is Max; he's part of our family now.'

'Oh, he's super cute, Cam didn't tell me you got a dog.'

'I didn't realise I had to regularly update you on my girl-friend's life.'

'Oh, be quiet, I just meant that I assumed this would be something you would have brought up, that's all.'

'He's a specialist Autism Assistance dog.' Nancy laughed, interrupting the sibling argument. 'He's trained to help children with autism. He helps with changing routines, reducing certain behaviours, interrupting repetitive behaviours and helping children cope with unfamiliar surroundings. He's there to help with independence but also to keep them safe. Jack finds comfort in sitting with Max when he is particularly stressed or anxious.'

Jayne began to unload her picnic bag, placing the food out in front of them. 'Isn't it incredible? I didn't even know there were dogs specifically trained for things such as autism.'

'I think it's a fairly new thing. I joined this programme so we could get him and sometimes, when Jack doesn't need him, I take him into schools with me to help children who are struggling within the environment and they do things like reading with him and sitting with him in assembly. He is a dog of many qualities.'

She smiled. 'He's also helped me at home when we're having a particularly bad day. After calming Jack, he quite often comes to me and makes sure I'm happy – because reducing my stress means Jack is less anxious too. It's incredible how much having Max helps us.'

Becca unwrapped her sandwiches and took a bite. 'How's the online shop going, Nancy?'

Nancy nodded. 'Yeah, it seems to be growing nice and steadily which is handy. It means I can do that as well as the school stuff with Max. It started as just the prints but now I'm looking at branching out into stationery and notebooks too. They seem to be in demand at the moment, which is great.'

'This is one of her designs,' Harriet said as she pulled her notebook out of her handbag, handing it over to Becca to look at.

'I love it!' She looked at Nancy. 'You designed this?'

'The notebook? Yeah. That's just a prototype one that I was testing out but Hari loved it so I gave it to her. Do you like it?'

'I love it! What else have you got – oh my God, I need to look at your website.'

Nancy laughed and fished out a card from her bag. 'Here – website, number and discount code all on there.'

'Thanks!' Becca pocketed the card. 'Cam, it's my birthday soon, don't forget.'

'How could I forget?' He groaned as he stood up. 'Right, I am going to get the coffees. Nance, give me a hand?'

She nodded and stood, asking everyone for their order and following Cameron over towards the café at the other side of the park. As she sidled up next to him she slipped her hand into his.

'I've missed you,' he said, squeezing her hand in his.

'I saw you the other day,' she laughed.

'Yeah, I know, but a couple of times a week just isn't enough.' He held his other hand up, 'I know, you don't want to rush anything with Jack, I get that and I totally agree and support you wholeheartedly.'

She laughed at his panicked voice.

'I just, well, I miss you when I'm not with you.' He stopped walking and pulled her to face him. 'If I think back to how I was feeling the week before I met you, the days leading up to my holiday last year, I was a mess. I was stressed and miserable and I just didn't have any focus in my life apart from Aiden. And then you swanned into my life like a whirlwind with this awesome little boy who completely captured my heart – and Aiden's!' he added. 'I can't believe how much has changed for me.' He stroked his hand down her cheek. 'I guess I just wanted to say thank you.'

'Why are you thanking me, I haven't done anything.'

'You have! You have done more than you probably realise. I have never been happier and I don't think I have seen Aiden happier either. He adores Jack.'

Nancy nodded. 'Jack loves him too. Cam, you're not the only one who has noticed changes. I would like to take the credit for it all and say that Jack's improvement over the last year has been down to my skill as a parent, but I think a huge part of this has been Aiden. He has so much patience with Jack and their relationship is so special now. If you take away the meltdowns he still has.'

Cameron chuckled. 'You're never going to eradicate them completely.'

'I know.' She reached up and touched his hand which was still on her cheek. 'Thank you for being patient with us – both of us – I promise things will be normal one day and we can have a normal relationship.'

'Nance, there is no such thing as normal. What we have is

special – I couldn't ask for anything more. If it means that we have to wait a little longer before we can be together properly, until Jack is comfortable with us being around more, then that's what we will do. I'm not going anywhere.'

She didn't fight the urge and wrapped her arms around his neck pulling him in for a kiss. She wasn't ready to say it out loud but she knew in her heart, Cameron was *The One*. She was in love with him.

They re-joined the group holding their three coffees, two teas and seven fruit juices and handed them out accordingly. Cameron then walked out in the middle of the field and shouted over. 'Right, everyone up! Kids? Over here!' They did as they were asked. 'Grab a finger,' he said, hand splayed out.

'Oh, I love this!' Jayne said, standing up. Harriet groaned but stood anyway, grabbing Nancy's hand as she did.

'If I have to do this so do you!'

Nancy laughed. 'One in, everyone in!'

They all stood around Cameron, holding on to this hand. 'Are you all ready?'

Nancy looked around the circle. Old friends, new friends and family all here with her. It had been a tough year since her holiday in Ibiza. She still had lots of hurdles to overcome with Jack and lots of barriers to trample down. But they were getting there. She'd found Max, who had changed their life, and she'd taken the plunge and decided to work from home, starting from scratch. None of it would have happened had she not had her friends by her side, cheerleading her and keeping her up when she felt like she was drowning.

And then there was Cameron. He brought a whole new level of special to her world.

He was definitely a keeper.

'OK guys, let's do this ... I went to the shop and I bought some sticky, sticky ... GLUE!'

Acknowledgements

I may write the words on the page but there are so many people involved in writing a book and putting it out there for everyone to read.

Thank you to all at HarperImpulse for supporting me through another book. In particular, there are a few names that deserve a special mention. As always, to Charlotte Ledger for being the first person to take a chance on me as a debut author and cheerleading me along the way. A heartfelt thank you to the incredible Emily Ruston who has really pushed me to get my best work. Emily is an awesome person to work with – this book wouldn't be what it is without her hard work, patience and belief. Thank you to Sahina Bibi for all your work on promoting and getting the book ready to be released – and for always answering my many questions!

Thank you to my agent, Kate Nash, for supporting me and my ideas and for being the calm against my crazy when I need her to be.

Thank you to all the parents who answered my questions and to all those parenting vloggers out there who I binge watch on the regular but would never admit to just how many hours I lose by doing this 'research'.

When I write a book, and because it isn't my only job, I tend to go a bit MIA on my friends and family. So a big thank you to all of my close friends and family for still wanting to talk to me now that it is finished and for understanding when I need to cancel things or work super late to get tasks done. I really do appreciate the support.

My online friends – thanks for always being behind me and for getting as excited as I do when I post book related things. I absolutely love the online writing community and your enthusiasm for the book has been amazing.

As was the case with my last book, I wrote this one alongside completing coursework for my degree. So it feels only fair to say a thank you to the staff at Anglia Ruskin University for understanding that I have additional deadlines alongside university ones and for helping me in every way possible to keep my sanity as I hit those deadlines! Sometimes it was helping me to focus and giving me advice, other times it was simply giving me the encouragement needed to keep going and know that I could do it. I love writing but I equally love being at university and studying early childhood, so by having such an incredible team of people around me, it makes it possible for me to do both.

To my readers – thank you SO much for coming back after my first book and reading this one! Your support and eagerness for this second book has been such a wonderful thing and I am so excited to hear your thoughts.

And finally, thank you to my husband, Craig, and my daughter, Gracie. Both of whom endure, by far, the most stress in this process by being right beside me every step along the way. They see the tears, the laughter, the sadness and the elation that comes with writing a book. They have to put up with me staying up late and getting up early to get edits done and they accept that the house will not be spotless and the dinner will be later, the closer I get to deadline day – but they are still here with me and they always share my pride when publication day finally arrives. Thank you both so much for putting up with it all!